# Greta Gets the Girl

**Also by Melissa Marr**

*Toni and Addie Go Viral*

**A COURSE IN MAGIC**

*Remedial Magic*
*Reluctant Witch*

# Greta Gets the Girl

## Melissa Marr

BRAMBLE

Tor Publishing Group
New York

GRETA GETS THE GIRL



All emojis designed by OpenMoji—the open-source emoji and icon project. License: CC BY-SA 4.0

Designed by Jen Edwards

A Bramble Book
Published by Tom Doherty Associates / Tor Publishing Group
120 Broadway
New York, NY 10271

www.torpublishinggroup.com

Bramble™ is a trademark of Macmillan Publishing Group, LLC.

*EU Representative:* Macmillan Publishers Ireland Ltd, 1st Floor, The Liffey Trust Centre, 117–126 Sheriff Street Upper, Dublin 1, DO1 YC43

The Library of Congress Cataloging-in-Publication Data is available upon request.

ISBN 978-1-250-36486-9 (trade paperback)
ISBN 978-1-250-36487-6 (ebook)



Our books may be purchased in bulk for specialty retail/wholesale, literacy, corporate/premium, educational, and subscription box use. Please contact MacmillanSpecialMarkets@macmillan.com.

First Edition: 2026
Printed in the United States of America

10 9 8 7 6 5 4 3 2 1

To my wife, Amber.

## Trigger warning:

One of the characters in this book is a rape survivor. As a survivor, I do not believe in writing the violence on the page or adding graphic references. The text simply notes that she was assaulted, but sometimes that shakes people, so I am adding a warning.

As a survivor myself, I have been disappointed not to see many authentic representations of the intimacy challenges for survivors. So, I wrote it. Surviving is not the end of joy, but sometimes fiction writes it as if there are no consequences. That's brutally inaccurate for a lot of us. So, too, is the idea that we are forever broken.

# Greta Gets the Girl

# Prologue

## *Kaelee*

Kaelee sat at a café in Dupont Circle with her former boss and current mentor, Toni Darbyshire. She had been Toni's teaching assistant in the fall, but she turned it down this term to finish and hopefully sell a book—the one currently on submission.

No one at the café cared that Kaelee was on sub or that her lunch companion had made the jump from industry news to mainstream news. They were at the café for award-winning sandwiches like the monstrosity in front of Toni. Kaelee marveled at the messy thing, but she was barely able to eat today.

Right now, in Manhattan, strangers were going to be *bidding on* her novel.

"Stop staring at my lunch." Toni grumbled the words, but over the last few months, Kaelee had realized that grumbling was simply Toni's way of talking. She always sounded vaguely agitated—unless she was talking about history or her soon-to-be wife, Adelaine.

"I wasn't looking at your lunch." Kaelee scowled at her.

Toni looked down. "Well, then, stop staring at my chest. That's what's behind my sandwich."

"You're obnoxious." Kaelee smiled, though, grateful for the distraction. "You know damn well I'm not staring at you or your lunch. I don't know why I bother to be your friend."

"Hey, you're the weirdo who wants to be my friend. I'm an

innocent bystander." Toni shrugged and took a huge bite of her sandwich. Toni, who was actually a valued friend, was relaxed here. Sometimes she was like that in her office, and she was definitely like that at A League of Her Own, the local lesbian and queer bar. Overall, though, Toni was prickly. She was *not* sociable.

And finding the right place for lunch was critical. Locals-only spots were the best idea. In DC there were politicians everywhere, so there was a sort of blasé attitude that prevailed toward anyone vaguely important. Visiting dignitary? Politically minded celebrity? The Pope? They all came to DC. Add that to the nonstop stream of tourists and there was always some sort of noise. The locals, however, just wanted to eat their pastrami and relax.

The problem was that Toni and her soon-to-be wife had made a media splash last year because of the television adaptation of Toni's book. So occasionally, tourists would stop if they recognized Toni, and she was as graceful about it as a drunk Southern jock at a tea shop. Currently, though, they were at a tiny table with nary a tourist in sight. And Toni was her smart-assed best self. For that, Kaelee was immeasurably grateful.

*I am not checking email again. I am not. I will not.*

"Did you research any of the editors who have it?" Toni asked after she finished her oversized bite.

"I did not. I took your advice to trust Emily to handle it. No micromanaging." Kaelee frowned. *I could search right now.* The impulse to research the four editors currently bidding on her novel was strong, but she had the combined guidance of Toni, whom she had TAed for the last two terms, and Emily, the agent who now represented both of them.

"If Greta wins, you'll be able to ask me about her, but I don't know any of the others. Who was the editor at Harper that Emily likes?" Toni paused as if she ought to retain all this even though she was secured and settled with Greta Clayborne.

"Is it weird if we end up sharing an editor *and* an agent?" Kaelee asked.

"Different genres." Toni shrugged. "No editor is monogamous. Agents either. So being possessive over them is a waste of energy. And who knows if Greta will even want more books from me?"

Kaelee rolled her eyes. "Book one is a *television show* now, and I bet the sequel will do great."

"Or it could suck." Toni eyed her in the way she typically had only done when dropping academic advice. "Don't think that just because one book succeeds, the next is a sure thing. Publishing is fickle. Enjoy it when you can, but no author is *guaranteed* a successful follow-up."

Kaelee glanced at her smartwatch again. "I'd settle for one success."

"If it's going to auction, there's a good chance you'll have one." Toni gestured. "Check your email. You're squirming like a child who needs to use the toilet. It's irritating." Her expression was friendly despite her harsh words.

An email was there waiting. Kaelee scanned it, feeling like her heart had crawled into her throat and was squatting there, choking her with every too-fast beat. "We sold it. No auction. There was a preempt. Deal memo forthcoming. Emily is going to call."

"Which editor and house?"

"Yours." Kaelee looked at her. "I swear I will try not to drive you spare asking questions."

Toni gave a solitary nod. "Good." Then she smiled. "I'm happy for you, and for Greta, and mostly for Em. This is a good thing for all of you."

Kaelee repressed her snort. *A good thing?* Toni was the queen of calm and understatements.

Yeah, Kaelee selling her book at all was damn good; selling it for a preempt was amazing. She'd pulled it off, sold a book, two books in fact, to a New York editor with a major publishing house. She hadn't used her family name or their connections to do it, either. Her father's voice warning her that she was no one without her family name echoed in her memories. *Watch this, Tripp.* She'd done it on her own as a veritable nobody.

*Fuck you, Tripp,* she amended silently, hoping the horrible homophobic man felt her words like a slap to his face back in North Carolina where he crouched atop his inherited fortune with his intolerant cronies.

After a moment, she added a second "fuck you" to the man her father had pawned her off on as a fiancée when she was barely legal, and her fiancé was old enough to know better. Then she shoved those thoughts away to concentrate on her victory. No use dwelling on the bleak parts of the past when she had a major victory in hand.

*I did it. I really did it.*

Toni nudged her hand, and Kaelee realized she was holding a tissue out. "Your eyes are leaking. You good?"

Kaelee huffed out a laugh. "Yeah, I'm excellent." She swiped at her tears. "I did it, Professor D. I sold an actual novel that I wrote."

"You did." Toni paused. "I won't say this often, but if you want a hug, I'll hug you. I'm proud of you."

Kaelee laughed louder. "I do want a hug, actually. You're the best mentor I could have had through this, and I swear I won't make a habit of hugging you."

Although Toni was only three years older than Kaelee, it sometimes felt like they were years apart in age because Toni had her PhD already, had a bestselling book already, and had an amazing home and life. She had it all figured out. Hell, she was about to have a *wife*. Kaelee, on the other hand, was renting a studio and not even sure she'd finish her PhD.

Toni stood.

"Special occasions only. I have a reputation as being unapproachable." Toni opened her arms, and Kaelee stepped forward as Toni added, "I suppose this means you should start calling me by my actual name if I've hugged you."

After a moment, they separated, and Kaelee teased, "I'd still rather hug your future wife, Toni."

Toni flipped her off. "She's excellent at hugging, but maybe you ought to find a woman of your own. You can afford to date one now."

Kaelee shuddered exaggeratedly. "I might've followed you in terms of agent and editor, but I'm not going to go falling in love or getting married. Hard pass. I don't think I'm built for commitment, and I can't imagine there's a woman out there willing to tolerate my bad habits."

"Probably wise," Toni agreed in a dry voice. "You conquer publishing. I'll teach and write to fill my time when Addie is busy filming."

Kaelee didn't argue. For the first time, she truly understood the tremulous fear that Toni had voiced over her own next book. On one hand, this was it: the dream career was really happening. But what would happen if the next book did not sell or flopped? Finishing one book felt like a once-in-a-lifetime achievement. The sheer will it took to consider doing it over and over felt like a direct road to madness. All books got bad reviews. Most got nothing more than middling ones. And she'd already learned from Toni that sometimes it took the "yes" or "no" of one person to change your whole path. An influential reviewer or book buyer could make or break you. It was all terrifying.

*One book at a time.* That's all any writer could reasonably do. And right now, they had both achieved it. *I just sold two books.*

Adding dating into that mix of emotions? Nope. That was not happening. Kaelee could do a lot of things and do them well, but handing so much power over her life to anyone was not on that list. And being a writer included being intentionally powerless. Often. Repeatedly. She could not fathom adding the emotional upheaval of dating to that already intense roller coaster.

"I am so grateful to know you," Kaelee told her mentor.

"Back at you." Toni gestured at Kaelee's mostly untouched food.

"Now, eat your damn lunch. The nerves ought to be a little settled. Eat your celebratory sandwich."

Kaelee laughed. She'd rather have a drink, and maybe she could call a friend for that later. Lunch with her one and only writer friend was a pretty good start to celebrating.

Six months later

**START OF SEPTEMBER**

# 1

## Greta

On the train down to DC to meet up with Toni, Greta fired off an email to her *other* local author. She hadn't yet met Ms. Carpenter, and as much as Greta felt overdue for a day or two off work, she felt guilt pressuring her to reach out. Establishing a bond with her authors was part of *keeping* them, but this particular writer made Toni look positively social—which was a sentence Greta couldn't quite believe considering the fact that she was spending her afternoon on the Acela just to get Toni to discuss her publishing future. Being more reclusive than Toni had seemed impossible, but Kaelee Carpenter was managing to do just that.

Kaelee,

I will be in town briefly. Would you like to meet up? If I can, I want to catch the Etched by Light: Photogravures, 1840–1940 exhibit. We could chat there or grab lunch.

Your galley pages ought to be hitting the desk soon. The schedule will give you a few days to go over *Revel of Stars and Fire* one more time. Emily also has you on my calendar for a meet and greet with the team, but I am likely to be in town tomorrow so what do you think?

Greta

The reply from Kaelee was a short, terse note.

Ms. Clayborne,

I will check my calendar. However, I am not likely to be free last minute. If that changes in the near future, I will notify you. Thank you.

K. Carpenter

As Greta skimmed the quick, dismissive reply, she sighed. Honestly, she seemed to be collecting brusque authors, first Darbyshire and now this one. Kaelee made Toni Darbyshire seem positively gregarious. The more resistant to connection her authors were, the more Greta felt the urge to add emojis and exclamation points.

Kaelee,

Let's tentatively say 1PM at the Madison entrance steps if you can find the time. If you can't make it, we still have the meet and greet soon. See you then! ☺

Greta

She knew with certainty that Kaelee wasn't going to meet her. For whatever reason, her new author was proving incredibly reclusive. No phone contact. No replies on the request for an author photo. Her bio for the promotional material was as dry as stale crackers.

*Please let her be an introvert!* Most authors were, but there was always a fear that there was a problematic secret, and after photos of Toni and her now-fiancée went viral, Greta was full up on drama. She liked *some* drama. At this point, she was recently promoted with several bestsellers in her stable of authors. Drama of the bestseller list or awards was the sort she preferred. She had goals: eventually to have her own imprint, and along the way to collect more quality books by authors she could build long-term relationships with as they grew together. First step, getting Toni's new book. Second step, bonding with her new author, whose book had what it took to be a hit.

The train pulled into the station with an abrupt end, and Greta slipped her phone into her pocket. She had brought a slightly larger bag than normal, as she was leaning toward taking the day to see a few exhibits. There was something refreshing about Washington, DC, in the early fall. The flood of children was back in school, so although there were still *some* tourists, the city wasn't overrun with them.

The train spilled the standard suit-clad men out of the car. There were a few darker-skinned faces and women, but the business crowd in her car was easily eighty percent middle-aged white men. Whether the other passengers had boarded at Penn Station where she had or been gathered up in Philadelphia or the couple of other stops, this crowd had the look of men who were home for the weekend. Around her was a sea of briefcases, statement ties, and a varying quality of suits. Greta felt her petite stature a little more poignantly in crowds. She was not much over five feet, and she had a chest that announced her presence no matter how she dressed. She mostly wore heels—today it was heeled boots—to appear taller, but they did great things for her legs.

As she noticed several men's gazes, she had a stray thought that a clear label would be nice. Maybe neon. Flashing. Something to be crystal clear that she was not available. Instead, she kept her resting bitch face in place. Greta draped her long lightweight coat over her arm, extended the handle of her bag, and stepped into the fray. A pencil skirt and blazer didn't do enough to hide her pinup-girl curves.

She followed the crowd into the station, resisting the urge to steamroll around a few meandering travelers. Inside, she headed unerringly to the café where she was to meet her author—still vaguely irritated that the *other* local author was not interested in meeting her, too. It was an anomaly to have an author make no effort to meet up.

Editing wasn't necessarily social, but Kaelee Carpenter was an enigma. She had no social media presence, and her persona over email was stiff with only a few exceptions. She'd recommended some music by female-focused artists like Brandi Carlile, Kehlani, and Morgan Wade. They swapped a few book and film recommendations, but aside from those, all conversation was solely on the book. Typically, authors let a few things slip. Kaelee never mentioned anything in her past; in fact, her author questionnaire made it seem as if she had appeared fully formed as an adult. Her only "local connections" were to the college where she was a graduate student.

*And Toni.* She knew Toni because she was her teaching assistant at the college. She had exactly one known connection, and that was to Greta's own author.

Greta responded to mysteries likes cats reacted to closed doors. She didn't necessarily *want* to be on the opposite side of the door, but she also didn't like the door being closed. A part of Greta always wanted to build genuine connections with her authors.

As she walked toward the restaurant where she'd set the meeting, Greta paused briefly to take in the space. The architecture was striking, a high curved ceiling that arched from pillars. The overall feel was of vastness. Between the gilt-trimmed arches and the white and black tile on the floor, it was a marvelous space.

Greta reached the café inside the massive train station, where Toni was already seated. Her author was dressed slightly more professionally than in her initial publishing meetings. Now, she had on a well-tailored suit in a darker blue, a shirt that was more stylish than business, and a smartwatch. The influence of her financial success and her fiancée's Hollywood life had subtle but obvious effects on her attire.

Toni was undoubtedly still acerbic and terse. Most of her private life was closely guarded, but mentioning Addie in a flattering way softened the baseline cantankerousness that Toni exuded like a shield.

*Maybe I just haven't found Kaelee's* thing, *her topic that makes her warm up,* Greta mused.

Toni came to her feet at Greta's approach. She pulled out a seat for Greta and once Greta was seated, she motioned for the server to bring a glass of water.

"Good trip?" Toni asked once they were alone.

"I worked. The Acela is reliable and quiet," Greta allowed. The train ride was like a lot of trains, but this one had a quiet car, which ought to be a requirement on every train. "How are you?"

"We emailed earlier in the week." Toni frowned. "Then I taught. I miss my woman. I miss having a competent TA since you stole Kaelee from me."

Greta repressed a laugh. "I didn't steal Ms. Carpenter. I bought her book."

"Same thing." Toni paused while Greta ordered. Then she added, "Addie sends her best. She's back in LA for the week."

They caught up for a few minutes, discussed the book plans, and then Greta asked, "What's Ms. Carpenter like? She doesn't seem particularly gregarious."

"Greta . . . I'm not great at this sort of thing. Ask her yourself or talk to Addie. I can't spy on her."

"Have I offended her?" Greta fussed with her napkin.

"She's just a private person. It's probably not you. Kae is pretty much a loner. Works out. Writes books in secret. Grades fairly. She's private." Toni took another drink of her coffee. "Talk to Em if you are worried. My guess, since you asked, is that she's overwhelmed. She's reached a pivotal point in her PhD, *and* she has a book launch. Speaking from experience, I can say that juggling two huge things is not easy. Maybe you're intimidating? She was pretty quiet with me the first month she was my TA."

"*Fine.* It helps to hear that she's private in general. I asked her to meet, but she refused."

Toni rolled her eyes. "Kae and I meet for lunch about every three weeks. We chat over coffee in my office sometimes. We're both busy writing books to send *you*, though. Grad school isn't rife with free time, you know, and book deadlines can make everything feel daunting."

"About that . . ." Greta met her gaze. They had *one* big topic to tackle yet, the real reason Greta was here. "You know, I hope, that I am not trying to pressure you to *write* faster. I just want to get the contract started." Greta kept her tone level despite the frustration she was feeling.

"I am well aware." Toni suddenly looked as frustrated as Greta felt. "You and Em have both made that quite clear."

"And?" Greta had taken the Acela to DC in hopes that a face-to-face meeting would help convince Toni to sell two more books—hell, even *one* more book. Typically, she would only meet with Toni if her agent, Emily Haide, were present, but Emily had given her blessing for this meeting.

"I told you already on the phone and in email," Toni grumbled. "I'll let you and Em *both* know when it's written, and *then* you can buy it if it's any good."

Greta swallowed a sigh. "I'm sure it'll be fabulous. I could buy it now, and then—"

"I didn't like the pressure of a deadline." Toni had a look that made Greta completely aware she wasn't liable to budge.

Still, Greta had to try. "But I *agreed* to the extension when you needed it. What if we set a due date longer than we think you'll need and—"

"No." Toni folded her arms and leaned back. "I know Em gave you permission to try to con me into this, but I'm not ready to sign a new contract. The second book comes out next month. Let's focus on that."

"And the early reviews for it are great," Greta assured her. "You've written two fabulous books. Readers will want more. *I* want more."

"I'm working on the third book," Toni said lightly. "I hope to be finished by the new year. Maybe December, but my goal is January. Right before the wedding."

Greta did a little mental math. The first book had released, the show had launched, the new book was about to release, so ideally, she should be editing this one *soon*. She could shift a few things around to keep her desk clear so that when it came in, she could dive in immediately.

"Are you considering selling to other editors? Is that the delay?" Greta hated that she had to ask, but they had a very loose option clause. The clause meant that Greta would get to see the book first, but Toni *could* go elsewhere if they didn't come to terms within thirty days. Any editor in New York would be thrilled to have Toni, despite how difficult she could be personally. Her writing *sold*. The book earned well, and the sequel was already well past earned out on preorders. Greta would fight to keep her, and she had permission to do just that. The figure she was authorized to pay would make news.

When Toni didn't reply, Greta added, "If there is something you felt like we mishandled—"

"No." Toni sighed and sat upright. "*You're* my editor, Greta, and I'm glad you are. I am writing this book without a deadline because that makes it feel less like work. If I get stuck, I can take however long I need to figure it out. Doing it this way has meant that I'm not getting stuck at all. I got stuck with book two because of the pressure."

Greta nodded. Plenty of writers developed their tics and habits. She couldn't fault Toni for her process. That was what mattered.

"I want you to know that I will be ready whenever the book is, and I'm thrilled to continue this journey with you." Greta took a breath before adding, "I thought that perhaps your refusal and Ms. Carpenter's reticence were linked, since you're friends."

"Friendship and business are two different matters for me," Toni clarified. "Kaelee's very private. It's one of the reasons I was glad she signed with you. You're not an asshole."

Greta laughed. "Maybe I'll add that to my signature line in my email—'not an asshole,' says Toni Darbyshire, number one *New York Times* bestselling author."

"I'll deny saying it if you do that." Toni smiled, though. Her shoulders relaxed, and the tense moment was over. "I am not selling my book to anyone else, Greta. When it's done—in a few months at this rate—I'll tell Em, and at that point you'll hear from her or me or both. I'm *glad* you want it, but I'm not ready to sign my name to a paper with a deadline. *Any* deadline. That's it. There's no mystery or machinations on my part or Em's. I just want to write it at my own pace. I'm still glad to be your author, and I really hope you like the book when I finish drafting it."

Greta tossed back her subpar coffee. "Well, I'm glad you're my author, too. When you're ready to sign . . . I'm ready to buy. I thought I was going to lose the auction when Emily was selling the Carpenter book, no mercy in her. Maybe that added to my anxiety about yours." Greta respected the hell out of Emily Haide. She was a great advocate for her authors. That didn't mean she was a pushover, though. "Emily has a take-no-prisoners attitude."

"Em's a baddie. She's always been that way. Honestly, you remind me of her a little. Probably why she knows how to get you to get out the big checkbook."

"Ha. Well, your sales would be a factor this time, Toni." Greta gave her a look, torn between company loyalty and wanting to be fair. "You could demand a lot. I know Em will tell you that, but I want to be clear that we are prepared to offer a generous advance."

Toni held up a hand. "Noted, but . . . no deal talk until the book is ready. You'll know when I'm ready, but until then . . . no deal. No talking about it."

Greta felt a wave of relief at the realization that she had another hit book inbound. "Understood. Thank you for entertaining my anxiety." She smiled. "I suppose I ought to let you head off to wherever bestselling professors go at night."

"Scintillating evening of lesson prep tonight, but I ought to head out before the traffic is *too much* of a disaster." Toni stood and held out a hand to shake, a gesture Greta appreciated a little bit extra. So often people treated her like she was a delicate doll.

Greta smoothed down her sleeves and stood to shake Toni's hand.

Toni added, "Sorry you wasted the trip. A quick chat with me and a 'no' from Kae can't be worth the ride."

"I didn't waste it!" Greta laughed lightly. "We caught up. And I can breathe easier now. I know now that you aren't considering other publishing houses. You don't know how worried I was that you'd . . . found me lacking or someone came along with big incentives. We don't want to lose you. *I* don't want to lose you, so if you are unhappy now or later . . . please, do tell me."

Toni gave her a strange look. "I am not interested in any other editor, Greta. I know publishing is not actually the same as dating, no matter how often people compare it, but I take commitments seriously once I make them. You're the editor for this series. We built this together, you, me, and Em. So as long as I'm writing books about this character, I will be selling them to you *if* you want them."

"I'll want them." Greta smiled at Toni's assurance. Plenty of authors were willing to hop around, even mid-series, and Greta couldn't blame them sometimes. She wanted this series, though, so she'd do whatever she could to make that happen. Fight for publicity? Argue for a higher royalty? Give the author more cover control? She was willing to negotiate.

Toni glanced at the oversized clock on the wall across from them. "What time's your train?"

"I think I'm going to take a day to enjoy the museums since I'm here. DC is nice in the fall. Visiting the museums without quite so many tourists sounds like heaven." Greta had a weakness for museums. It didn't matter whether it was a tiny one-room museum in a small town or the National Museum of something or other, Greta was interested and willing to give it a try.

"I teach tomorrow," Toni started.

"Luckily, you aren't obligated to entertain me, Toni. Teach. Write. I'll book a room and head that way." Greta held up her phone with her booking app. "Go on. I have this."

"Do you want me to drive you to your hotel? Or get you a taxi or . . ." Toni looked at her like she was a vulnerable lamb now.

"I live in New York, Toni. I can handle flagging a cab." Greta didn't want to offend Toni.

At first, Toni gave her a surly look and then after a moment settled on, "Fine. I don't mind driving you, though."

"I appreciate it." Greta smiled, but she didn't back down either. "I'm going to have a cup of herbal tea or something while I book a room."

"Fine. If you have any troubles, call me." Toni looked like she wanted to say more, but she pivoted and left.

There was something both endearing and frustrating about women who were overprotective. Greta often wondered if they'd be so contrary if she were taller. She seemed to evoke a protective vibe in both men and masc lesbians. If not for the fact that Greta was Toni's editor, she would find it utterly charming. She didn't mind it in relationships or in friendships. As a professional, though, she wanted to be treated like an equal, despite her diminutive height.

Once she watched her author exit and knew Toni likely wasn't returning, Greta booked her hotel, and then she opened another app. The app was designated with a stylized S. K. S., nothing anyone would identify if they weren't a member. The Sappho's Kiss Society was a members-only group, vetted and open only to those who completed the requisite interview and background checks, and who were capable of paying the hefty membership fees.

Although she was not closeted, Greta kept her private life private these days. The world was far more tolerant of lesbians than it used to be, but the reality was that she didn't broadcast her life.

She would feel the same regardless of her orientation. The fact that she was the editor for a *New York Times* bestselling historical lesbian novel meant the question had been subtly and not-so-subtly raised more often the last few months. Until such time—in the distant future—as the idea of actual dating was again practical, Greta didn't feel like addressing it. Those who had been around publishing a few years knew that she'd been engaged, but only a few people had met Tasha in person. No one really *knew* her, though.

Greta wasn't even convinced she truly knew her ex, despite Tash's periodic texts to check in on her. They had a wall between them that meant Greta still couldn't say they could be real friends.

*Half the people in my life are reticent about sharing their lives. Or maybe it's because of a flaw in me. . . .*

In her early post-breakup-with-Tash days, Greta had tried several other apps, including the obvious ones like Tinder and Bumble. Those were a little too far outside her current needs, although she could see why they would likely work for a lot of people. Lately, she had started using Sappho's Kiss Society, which catered to her interests more efficiently. SKS was not just a membership group—complete with meetup events—but an app for queer folks seeking other queers and willing to pay for privacy. Greta's profile was pretty sparse. Her profile photo was shadowed, although her full-body photo was clear. She just wasn't going to put her *face* on there too obviously.

Her interests were narrowly drawn: tattooed and athletic lesbians, one night only, no couples, no surprises, no contact afterward. She liked what she liked, especially for one-nighters.

Her profile was under "Marie," rather than Greta. That simplified things if she ever ran into someone in public, too. If they addressed her as Marie, she knew where and why she'd met them. If they said "Greta" or "Ms. Clayborne," that meant she knew them from her professional life. The major upside of the app was the only way to even see paying app users was to buy a rather expensive year's sub-scription. Discretion mattered, and this app catered to those with that need. All the measures weren't perfect, but it did lessen the odds of her work life and her intimate life intersecting.

Greta turned on the setting to update her location in hopes of finding an interesting person in her proximity. Once the app regis-tered that she was in Washington, DC, Greta scrolled through her potential matches until a woman with a lithe swimmer's body stared up at Greta from the screen. "Lee" was the name listed—although at this point Greta assumed that most people's names were as real as the one she gave. Hookup apps were not designed to tell many truths.

Lee's photo highlighted an undercut that looked overdue for a trim, tailored trousers, and a button-up Oxford. In her full-body photo, she had a leather jacket slung over her shoulder, two crooked fingers holding the collar of the jacket. She smirked at the camera like she had done something wicked a moment ago. Angular fea-tures. Arrogant posture. *And active online right now.* That cocky smirk meant it was a safe bet that Greta wouldn't want to spend time with her socially, but for a fling, Lee was perfect.

Greta clicked on the "create connection" button on the wom-an's profile, and then she waited. When her phone buzzed with a notification, she was pleased to see that Lee had reciprocated the connection.

A moment later a message alert buzzed.

**Lee:** Hey. What's up?
**Marie:** In town for the night. Looking
for a coffee connection.
**Lee:** What sort of coffee?

Greta grinned. There was always a chance that someone would misconstrue the message. Words were tricky, even as an editor.

**Marie:** Depends. At Union Station.
Headed to hotel soon. You?
**Lee:** Are you asking me to come meet you?
**Marie:** Yes.
**Lee:** So direct . . .
**Marie:** I know what I like.
**Lee:** Flattery will get me into the taxi.
**Marie:** Should I stay where I am? Or go to my hotel?
**Lee:** Preference?

Greta paused. She didn't want to offend Lee, but she wasn't particularly interested in small talk. Her desire to get to know the women she bedded was typically nonexistent.

**Marie:** How recent is your photo?
**Lee:** Ha! Last month.

The little dots that indicated she was typing appeared then, so Greta waited. After a moment, a jpeg showed up. Greta enlarged it, and a candid selfie of Lee filled her screen. She sat in an office cubicle, dressed in a button-up that was rolled to the elbows. A pair of glasses rested on a stack of papers in front of her. For a moment, Greta wanted to know what was on the papers, where she was, what she did, but that sort of curiosity led to an awkward degree of intimacy. Since her fiancée had cheated on her a couple of years ago, Greta didn't do intimacy. Ever. She was over Tasha, but that wasn't the same as being unscarred.

**Lee:** That's right now.
**Marie:** Let's meet.
**Lee:** About to leave work. Tell me where you want me.

*Between my legs,* Greta thought, but she wasn't ready to be quite *that* overt. In theory the app was secure, but careers had been ruined often enough for lesser things. So until she knew Lee better, she was going to be a little bit cautious. Instead she sent the address of the hotel she'd booked.

**Marie:** I'll be in the lobby. Blue pencil skirt and blazer.
**Lee:** Show me.

After a surreptitious glance around, Greta extended her arm, leaned forward, and aimed her phone camera at her chest. She wasn't adding a clear photo of her face, even now. She added the photo to a message and sent it.

**Lee:** I'll message when I'm there.

With a hopeful bounce in her step, Greta slipped her phone into her bag and went toward the exit. The clatter of her footsteps on the tile made more than a few people glance her way. She had an intentionally sharp staccato walk she'd crafted. Greta had learned to move at the pace of taller people, and she elevated her height three to four inches with heels. The combination meant that her approach was often noticeable—and she liked that. There was something innately satisfying about the interested and hungry gazes on several women's faces, and she could overlook the businessmen. They simply weren't her type. Her type was bold like them, well-dressed like them, but deliciously female.

*Like Lee.*

Impatience filled her as she stepped outside to grab a cab. *Hotel, freshen, meet a gorgeous woman.* It was the best sort of evening Greta could imagine. All the release and none of the entanglements.

**2**

# *Kaelee*

Kaelee hadn't been planning on meeting anyone tonight.

She had just finished reading her *second* book one last time before sending the digital file to Emily. Even though the contract was for two books, Kaelee had developed a humiliating case of cold feet. *What if it's awful?* That second book wasn't anywhere near due yet, but she was afraid it would be so horrible that she would need extra time to start over. Kaelee didn't want to admit to her editor that she had a complete draft already, but she wanted an outside opinion. So she wrote to her agent.

Dear Emily,

I know books don't write this fast! However, this one is
ready, I think. Because it was so fast, can you please
give it a read to let me know if it's okay to send to
Ms. Clayborne? (Reminder: It's due in January.)

K.C.

Her sequel had spilled onto the paper like Kaelee was just an intermediary taking dictation. The thought of slipping and telling her editor that the sequel was written before Emily read it was mortifying. So now Kaelee had to tell her editor to piss off about meeting in person, lie, or try not to blurt it out if she met her. Every option sounded terrible. So far, she'd managed to seem calm and possibly even reserved in exchanges with her editor. To do that, she had refused phone calls and edited her emails to sound direct and focused.

"Control the narrative" had been a bit of business advice that she'd kept as gospel. Right next to it was "keep a written record." The third law, of course, was the hardest for her sometimes. "Only one person can know if you want to keep a secret." Despite all the flaws in the Alden family, the media, financial planning, and business training sessions she'd had to take even in her teen years were still useful.

With that training, she had managed her trust fund, completed two degrees, and was well into a third. *I need to figure out if I want to finish the PhD or see if I can get a master's in lit or an MFA.* Her book deal earlier that year had required both revision of her life plan and facing her actual goals. The general mix of success and feeling like a raging imposter both as an academic and as a writer had left Kaelee a mess of anxiety. She'd considered getting a short-term prescription for anxiety medicine, but instead, she opted to hit the gym harder than she probably should. The only good news was that, luckily, Emily was used to working with Toni, who was a barrel of difficulty. Emily really was the perfect agent for Kaelee.

*And yet I am still thoroughly terrified of fucking it all up.*

The thought of real live people reading her sexy lesbian fantasy romance novel—a genre that was currently called "romantasy" according to Emily—made Kaelee feel anxious, which made her plan to head to the gym for the second time today.

. . . until Marie connected with her.

Now Kaelee had other plans for tackling her excess energy. Sex with the curvy little femme on the app was probably better for her body than another day of overexercising, and it would still ease her stress. Marie was dainty and curvy. That much was obvious in the pictures. Something about delicate women always made Kaelee's logic vanish entirely. Fortunately, though, Marie was just passing through town. One night. No risk of running into her later. Those were the best sorts of women. Temporary connections.

Kaelee grabbed her bag, shoved her stack of scribbled-on pages into it, and slung the bag over her shoulder. It was weightier than the essays she often had to grade for professors, but it wasn't impossibly so. Bag secure, door locked, Kaelee headed to the building exit, pausing to say good night to Stan, one of the cleaning staff.

By the time she'd walked to the far lot where she'd secured a parking pass, Kaelee was feeling almost as confident as she pretended she was. Not quite there, but close.

One of the few benefits of growing up in her dysfunctional family was that she'd learned to pretend. Until she was eighteen, she'd pretended she was a sweet, het, polite girl. It was that or face the wrath of her mother. Over the years, Kaelee and her sister, Betsey, referred to their mom as the "Ice Witch." Julia Alden was a Southern debutante, but under her practiced poise she was akin to any villain. Undoubtedly, Julia had ice in her veins, and blood on her hands.

But Kaelee had escaped the gilded prison where Julia had been her warden.

Now she was living some version of her dream. She'd legally changed her name from Sabrina Alden to Kaelee Carpenter, finished a BA in history and an MA in history, and had done so without drawing much from her accounts. She'd managed to earn scholarships for undergrad, assistantships for the first part of grad school, and so far, she'd had funding for most of her PhD, too. It was only this term that she'd paid out of pocket.

*Because I was busy finishing a novel.*

The money Kaelee had pulled out had then been replaced by the money from the book deal. All told, Kaelee was pretty sure she'd proven her parents wrong—not that she ever would go back home and tell them that.

Kaelee shoved her unexpectedly maudlin thoughts back into the mental box where they lived. That life was not hers. She'd left those people behind, along with their surname.

A quick walk later, Kaelee dropped her manuscript on the seat next to her, briefly debating whether to shove it into the trunk. The truth was, though, that she didn't want to leave it in the car. Her bag—with laptop, toothbrush, and clean clothes for after her planned gym workout—would be on her shoulder. Her book could go in that bag, too.

She let her mind wander to more pleasant topics as she headed toward the heart of the city. Rush hour was well in swing. Tourists who couldn't navigate the streets around the museums darted between cars, and those in their cars blocked the box in a sort of single-minded selfishness that made Kaelee reconsider her hookup. Driving in this part of the city was a bit of a clusterfuck.

*Is the faceless woman worth it?*

Briefly, Kaelee debated heading to the gym instead, but Marie was sexy in a way that hit all of Kaelee's buttons: tiny, curvy, and direct. She might be worth the traffic . . . hopefully. Sex was typically more effective at blunting the edge of Kaelee's anxiety than working out was.

By the time Kaelee reached the overpriced hotel, Kaelee wondered if Marie was a wife who wanted to try something new.

*As long as the husband isn't here, too . . .*

Kaelee had been too mentally exhausted to ask the usual questions on the Sappho's Kiss Society app, so she would need a minute to get that answered before she went to anyone's room. She wasn't interested in any surprise extras in the bed. She'd never been intimate with a man intentionally, and she wasn't going to start now.

After she pulled up to the valet parking, she hopped out of her car and grabbed her bag. She stuffed her manuscript in it and then handed her keys to the valet with the sort of confidence she'd seen her father use time and again and took her claim ticket. So what if her car was not perfect? She was stretching her money for a lifetime, and DC had decent public transportation. Her ten-year-old BMW ran well, despite the odometer's increasingly dire digits.

"Thanks," Kaelee told the valet. "I'm not sure how long I'll be. Meeting a friend for drinks."

As she said it, Kaelee decided that she was, in fact, going to pause for a drink. She was all for clear communication about the goals of the evening, and tonight, she didn't want to go from "hello" to naked with no buildup between. Though BDSM wasn't her usual thing, she had dabbled enough to appreciate the focus on boundaries and consent that was prevalent there—and had expanded that to her life at large. As a woman who had had her own lack of consent ignored in the past, she was extra focused on making sure anyone she was naked with had considered their own lines.

Kaelee strolled into the vast open space of the hotel lobby with the comfort that came from familiarity. She might be wearing faded jeans and well-worn shoes, but every childhood trip in her life had involved five-star hotels. After a while, they all started to blur together, and despite going on a decade of living a simpler life, this was unchanged. This could have been any five-star hotel; they all had the same vibe: polished floors, ostentatious floral bouquets, uniformed staff, and an overall ambiance of privilege.

A part of Kaelee hated that she was comfortable there. Habit was powerful, though, and she knew how to move through these spaces. Alden money insisted she could and would be able to act like she *belonged* to such places, and eleven years of freedom didn't negate eighteen years of training. Her clothes were thrift- or consignment-store buys, and her car was nearing the age of replacement, but she knew how to claim space in bougie places.

A quick glance around the lobby revealed the woman she'd been messaging earlier. The picture Marie had sent had been chest-down, and her profile picture on the app was vaguely discreet. A glance at her made it very obvious that Marie was not hiding her face because she was unattractive in any way. She had a face that wouldn't be out of place on an antique doll or in an old noir movie. A lush mouth, excessively long lashes, and apple cheeks made Marie an almost picture-perfect femme fatale. Her hair, which was a nondescript shade of brown, was twisted up into a low bun. At a guess, Kaelee would put her age as thirty to thirty-five or so. So at most, six years older than Kaelee's twenty-nine years.

She stood, and Kaelee realized that Marie's boots ended in sharp heels that added a good three or four inches to her height. Even so, Kaelee was certain she could lift Marie into her arms with ease. The vision of doing just that was interrupted by the fact that this gorgeous stranger was marching forward with a sway that would charm cobras.

"Marie." The luscious brunette held out her hand to Kaelee as she neared.

"Lee." Kaelee took the woman's hand in hers, pleased at the strength of her grip. "Can I buy you a drink?"

Marie gave her an unreadable look. "If you want one, sure. If not . . ."

"I do. It's been a long day with terrible traffic between there and here, so I could stand a moment to . . . decompress." Kaelee paused. She wasn't sure what precisely she wanted out of that drink and pause, but she wanted to take a beat before going upstairs. Marie's mouth tightened in a pout, though, so Kaelee added, "I'm not having a case of nerves. I can't fathom anyone changing their mind after seeing you."

"Thank you." Marie nodded before gesturing toward the bar. She looked like she felt chastised. "It's fine if you *do* change your mind, of course. I wouldn't want a bed partner who wasn't interested."

"I'm not changing my mind. I simply don't want a beautiful stranger to have to deal with my stressful day," Lee said. "Lead me to the bar, and then to your room if you aren't having cold feet by then."

"No cold feet. No cold *anything*." Marie walked across the lobby with purpose. Whatever she did when she wasn't here, Marie was a woman in charge. Kaelee's interest grew at that realization. She liked an assertive woman more than she wanted to admit, and she liked to be the one to reduce such a woman to quivering.

"Will you be offended if I admit that I like walking behind you?" Kaelee said lightly.

A laugh was her only answer, but Marie's sway grew a little slower, as if she was agreeing to slow things down a touch.

Kaelee followed her to a shadowed corner table. "Would you like me to go to the bar to order?"

"There's table service." Marie lifted a hand to the cocktail waitress, so Kaelee took the seat next to Marie rather than sitting across from her. The petite woman's comfort with control was alluring, and Kaelee had to wonder if she'd stay that way if they went upstairs. Though she only rarely managed it, Kaelee appreciated a woman who could perhaps take control from her.

*It's been so long*, Kaelee mused. Typically, most women saw her masculine haircut and gym-addicted body and assumed that she was only interested in giving. She was often happy to allow that assumption, but she wasn't a true stone top. With the right woman, or enough alcohol, she could sometimes let go.

After they ordered—a vodka tonic for Marie and a cognac for Kaelee—there was a not-unpleasant silence. A good drink, a gorgeous woman, and a nice atmosphere, these were the things that improved any day.

"Are you here alone?" Kaelee asked, glancing toward the lobby.

"Aside from you, yes." Marie flashed an empathetic smile. "Afraid there's a third person?"

"It's happened, and I don't want to end up going upstairs to find an unwelcome surprise."

"I've been there. Not my interest, so no worries." Marie leaned forward, and the motion rather expertly drew Kaelee's eye to the cleavage before her. "What do you do in such situations? I'll admit to being a diva about it. I'm not someone's unicorn to add spice to their marriage."

"I leave. Not big on scenes or dramatics, but men aren't of interest to me." Kaelee thought back to the years she'd been forced to attempt a heteronormative life, to the times that she'd forced herself to try to find a man's awkward fumbling exciting. She added lightly, "I tried years ago. It didn't take."

"I've never tried, but . . ." She paused as the waitress dropped off their drinks. "I'm in room 212. Can you bill them to my room?"

"Flag me down to sign before you go." The waitress smiled. "Or if you need another round."

"No. You can close the tab," Marie said firmly.

The waitress nodded. "I'll grab it now."

"So . . . you're here just tonight?" Kaelee asked when they were alone again.

Marie shrugged. "Maybe tomorrow night or even the weekend. It depends."

"On?"

"My mood, mostly." Marie sipped her drink, and Kaelee appreciated the flirtatious way Marie paused and licked the rim of her glass when she noticed Kaelee's attention. A flirty smile followed, and then Marie added, "There's no one waiting at home—by my choice—so I can stay or go back at my whim. No pets. No work over the weekend. Why not stay here a couple days?"

"Where's home?"

"New York."

"Not bad," Kaelee murmured. "No girlfriend or boyfriend there, then?"

"I wouldn't be planning on taking you to my room if there were. I have never been unfaithful," Marie said mildly, but there was a bite there. Someone in her life had, maybe cheated on her, maybe cheated on a friend, but Marie was hostile over it. Her tone was unflinching, as was her gaze, as she asked, "And you?"

The waitress returned, and Marie signed.

Kaelee was grateful for the interruption. She'd almost laughed at the thought of a relationship. She was terrified of anything even remotely commitment-shaped, personal or career. She'd switched her academic focus from history to lit, and she'd stalled on shopping her book to the point that she already had several *other books* drafted and edited. She'd had *one* relationship in her life, but that was honestly more platonic than relationship. Branson had been one of her best friends, and he knew that she was not into men, but he'd mysteriously ended their faux relationship one day. Without Bran's protection, she'd been forced to come out.

A year later, he watched while Kyle Gray—almost ten years her senior—dropped to a knee and slid a ring on her hand while their families stood around smiling and clapping.

Those thoughts went to bad places, so all Kaelee said was, "I don't do that."

"Serious relationships?"

"Date," Kaelee clarified. "Ever. I have friends, and sometimes I have one-night connections. That's it. Once or twice I had fuck friends. But . . . I'm not relationship inclined."

Marie raised a delicately shaped brow. "I see."

"I was pretty clear on my profile, so if you're looking for something else, I should go before this gets awkward." Kaelee felt regret as she said it, but there would be no confusion here. She couldn't handle getting entangled with a woman who thought a hookup was a prelude to more.

"You should stay." Marie reached out and put a hand on Kaelee's wrist, not gripping it but resting there with purpose. "I don't date either. I have in the past, but it's been years. I don't have the time for that currently, but sometimes I want a bit of affection."

"Same."

"I want exactly what I said: no strings. No nonsense. Just a good night." Marie caught her lip between her teeth briefly. "I'm cautious in writing, but make no mistake, I invited you here for sex and sex only."

Kaelee let her gaze openly run over the curves of the woman in front of her. "Good."

"Tell me something about you. What else do you like?"

Kaelee smirked. "Pretty women with kissable mouths."

"Since you showed up, I'll assume I fit the bill?" Marie reached out again and trailed her fingertips over Kaelee's wrist, lighter now, as if she were feeling the muscles in Kaelee's forearms.

"Yes." Kaelee rested her hand on Marie's leg, high enough that her thumb was almost inappropriate for public. "And you? What do you think?"

"I like a sexy woman who's comfortable on her knees," Marie said, her words even bolder than her appearance.

Kaelee said a silent prayer of thanks to whatever god or being put this woman in her path. "So you enjoy a little worship. . . ."

"Yes." Marie sipped her drink before adding, "I'm happy to reciprocate, of course."

And Kaelee was grateful that they had paused for this drink. Sometimes having a sense of parameters made the evening a lot more enjoyable and a lot less awkward.

"I would rather skip that," Kaelee admitted with a twinge of regret.

Marie's brow rose again. "Orgasms entirely or just oral?"

The level of trust that took was more than Kaelee could offer anyone. She'd tried it once. That was enough. "No *receiving* oral. I'll let you know on the rest. It varies."

"Noted," Marie murmured.

Kaelee had the vague sense that Marie's job involved negotiation. She was very comfortable outlining details—and doing so at a rapid pace. Kaelee wanted her a bit less in control, though, so she said, "At this point, I would be devastated not to have my mouth on you. Anything else on or off the table?"

When Marie drew a sharp breath and smiled, Kaelee prompted, "What else would *you* like?"

"I have been left to my own resources for a few months, so I want sex hard and fast, and then we can reassess." Marie shrugged. "Ideally, I can touch you at some point—"

"Probably. I'll let you know."

"We're fine, then. All my requests are met." Marie motioned toward the lobby. "Shall we?"

"My drink is—"

"Portable." Marie leveled a simmering look at her. "We can talk upstairs if you want, but I'd rather be more comfortable and be able to touch you."

A twinge of discomfort made Kaelee pause. "Are you in the closet?"

Marie slid out of her seat, stepped close enough that Kaelee's field of vision was nothing but breasts, and then said, "Stand, please."

Mutely, Kaelee obeyed, and Marie wrapped her arms around Kaelee's neck and guided her down for a kiss. She barely brushed her lips over Kaelee's, pausing to catch Kaelee's lip between her teeth in gentle nip, and then she whispered, "Kiss me like you want to fuck me."

So Kaelee did just that. Her mouth slanted over Marie's, her tongue demanding entrance. All of her hesitation vanished as Marie was suddenly pressed tightly to her. Kaelee's left hand fell naturally to the small of Marie's back, holding her steady, as the other hand rested at the top of her spine, just under her thick hair bun. Pulling back, Kaelee said, "I want to see this loose and spilling all around your shoulders and chest."

When Marie leaned back, she pulled the pin out of her bun. A mass of wavy hair dropped like a veil around her, and she said, "No closet here. I simply don't want to wait, Lee. It's been months, and you're stunning. Please, come upstairs with me now?"

Kaelee took her hand and left the drink behind.

3

# Greta

Greta followed Lee to the elevator. Often sex with a stranger could be something awkward, but the only other option was relying on nothing but her hand or a toy. *Or dating.* That was off the table, though, and had been since Tasha broke her heart. Two years later, Greta still wasn't looking for love. Hell, she wasn't even looking for an ongoing situationship. She simply wanted the occasional orgasm with another person.

The muscles she'd felt when she'd been pressed against Lee were enough to make her moan in public over a kiss. "I want you naked and against me. Now."

Lee's smile was almost wolfish as she glanced over. They stood side by side in front of the elevator.

"May I pull you closer?" Lee held out an arm in invitation.

Greta folded into her embrace. She didn't *expect* non-sexual affection in a hookup, but she certainly didn't mind the added intimacy. She slid her arm around Lee's back, hand curling around a barely there curve of hip.

"You fit nicely here," Lee said with another damned smirk. She looked a lot like the sort of women Greta found herself drawn toward on the rare occasion that she went to a lesbian bar for anything other than a drink with a friend. Her hair was cut close, but her excess of eyelashes and soft mouth made her undoubtedly female. Her arms, currently around Greta, were solid enough that Greta knew Lee could hold her down.

Lee had an edge that felt dangerous. From her flashes of emotion and defensiveness to her confidence, she seemed a little bit unpredictable. And Greta felt her pulse speed at the thought.

"The elevator is so slow," Greta complained.

Lee flashed her a grin, looked around, and said, "Stairs?"

It was less question than command, but the way she said it made Greta feel like a giggling teenager about to break the rules. Lee looked around as if they were about to pull a prank or something equally ridiculous as they walked over to the door to the stairs. Then she jerked open the heavy door and ushered Greta under her arm.

"I think I ran out of patience after that kiss," Lee murmured.

They were no more than on the other side of the doorway when Greta found herself pinned to the wall with Lee's mouth on hers again. Lee's leg was pressed between Greta's thighs. Her skirt was rucked up, so all that was between them was Lee's trousers and the sliver of Greta's damp panties. She could barely restrain herself from moaning at the welcome pressure. Lee had certainly looked like she was fit under her clothes, and her arm felt like a steel bar, but the leg pressed tightly to Greta was *all* muscle.

Greta whimpered as Lee shifted against her. Lee's mouth moved to Greta's throat and one hand caught a fistful of hair to pull Greta's neck to the side, giving Lee better access.

The *thunk* of the door closing made them pull apart. They exchanged a look, and Greta actually giggled. "Slow elevator. Slow door, too. The architecture is conspiring against us."

Lee stepped back, and as she did, her gaze traveled down Greta's body. "Shit. I forgot about your heels. I'm sorry! We can wait on the elevator." Lee started to turn toward the door.

Greta grabbed her arm. "I walk all over New York in heels. A few stairs are not an issue, especially if I can be naked with you sooner."

The flash of warmth she felt at Lee pausing to worry over her comfort was followed by a trickle of panic. Lee was observant and considerate, had a sense of fun, and was built like she had stepped out of Greta's favorite fantasies. The risk of getting to know a woman who looked exactly like her type was that she might *like* her, not just like having sex with her. They needed to skip past this socializing and get to the part where there were no feelings involved.

Greta held her hand out toward Lee. "Come on."

By the time they climbed the two floors of steps, they'd stopped to kiss often enough that Greta was beyond ready to feel Lee's skin under her hands. They walked through the hall toward the door of the room without another word or touch, but as Greta was unlocking the door, Lee pressed up against her back, pulled back the fabric, and kissed her bare shoulder.

Her teeth grazed Greta's collarbone.

Practically tripping, Greta shoved open the door.

Lee stepped in behind her, lust-blown eyes fixed on Greta.

In a more practiced move than she liked to admit, Greta stripped off her top and skirt. She stood there in a matching panty and bra set. Boots still on, she smiled at Lee and beckoned her forward with a crooked finger. "Come closer."

Lee was momentarily frozen. "Holy mother of God. Look at you."

Greta knew what she looked like, a little curvier in the thigh and belly than society said was perfect, but most women she took to bed liked a woman with curves. A little softness made her feel voluptuous rather than unattractive.

If she had any doubts about Lee's interest, they would've vanished in that moment. "You are the high point of my week, Marie." She stalked forward. "Damn, let me look at you. . . ."

"*Touch* me," Greta insisted.

Lee leaned down and mouthed Greta's nipple through her bra, simultaneously slipping a hand inside the other bra cup. "All my birthday gifts at once, right here."

Greta cupped the back of Lee's head, not holding her still but holding on to her as Lee suckled one breast and pinched the other. When she used her teeth before switching sides, Greta felt a flood of heat between her legs.

Lee's mouth was mapping the contours of Greta's throat and breasts, so Greta let out a surprised sound when Lee's hand slid between her thighs a moment later. She could feel the curve of a pleased smile as Lee discovered how wet she already was.

"Eager."

"Very," Greta agreed. "*Touch* me, please. More."

"Yes, ma'am," Lee said. "Happy to do exactly what you want."

The moan Greta let out was as much from the words as from the feel of Lee's fingers skating over her damp panties. Teasing wasn't usually Greta's preference. She liked a hard, fast fuck, but right now, she simply wanted Lee however she could get her. That was as much as her mind could process.

"Tell me what you want," Lee whispered. "Shall I touch you like this, darlin'?" Her fingers teased over the silky fabric of Greta's panties. "Or like this?" Lee's hand slipped under the fabric, fingers stroking from opening to clitoris. Her touch was slow and gentle, not lingering anywhere or slipping inside.

"I need . . ." Greta trembled.

"*Tell* me, Marie. Do you want a slow, soft touch?" Lee's fingers continued to taunt as they leisurely explored the slick contours of Greta's pussy. "Or do you want me inside you?"

"Yes."

One finger slid into Greta.

"More."

A second finger followed.

Lee's touch stayed slow, tantalizingly casual, as if there was no urgency to her actions. She kissed Greta's throat, her shoulders, her jawline. Not rushing anything.

"Fuck me," Greta ordered or maybe begged. She wasn't sure her voice was steady enough to sound like a demand. "Just . . . *fuck* me like we're . . . in a hurry. *Please.*"

A low chuckle against her throat was the only reply, but Lee's hand sped. Her other hand slid from where it had been caressing Greta's breasts gently, over her stomach and to her hips, where it shoved her panties down.

"These are in the way," Lee reminded her. "Close your legs a minute."

Lee's fingers stayed inside her, seemingly filling her more as her legs closed, and Greta trembled as Lee's thumb pressed against her clitoris.

With one hand Lee lowered the panties, and Greta had to decide between standing there with her panties around her ankles or moving away from Lee's touch to step out of them. She looked at Lee for direction then.

"Arms around my neck. I have you." Lee stared down at Greta as she complied. "Such a good girl. Hard and fast, then?"

"Please."

"Yes, ma'am." Lee guided her legs apart, freeing first one and then the other ankle, and then pressed Greta back against the wall. Lee's fingers went to her clitoris, gently at first.

"*Please.*"

"I like when you say that, darlin'. Keep saying it," Lee ordered, a distinct Southern twang slipping into her voice.

"Pleasepleaseplease."

"Just like that, darlin'. Begging so prettily for me. Such a beautiful sound. So close already, aren't you?" Lee's voice was like honey-coated whisky. One hand thrusting several fingers inside, the other hand working over her clit, both inviting her pleasure higher and higher, until the combination sent Greta spiraling toward her first orgasm with another person in almost six months.

Greta let out a noise that was more scream than moan, and she rested her forehead against Lee's shoulder. When she could speak steadily, she murmured, "Thank you. I needed that more than you know."

Lee smiled at her. "I hope that wasn't *all* you need."

"Six months with no one else, so . . . I'm far from done, if you're still interested."

"Oh, I am." Lee hauled her up so Greta had to wrap her legs around her like a stripper on a pole.

Greta put her arms around Lee's neck, too. "Whoa! You don't need to carry—"

"I *want* to carry you. Why else would I spend hours at the gym other than to be able to hold a gorgeous woman in my arms? You don't want all my work to go to waste, do you?" Lee teased.

"Your shirt is going to be damp," Greta said, feeling awkward for the first time.

"And smell *delicious*," Lee murmured from Greta's cleavage. One breast was no longer in the bra cup, and the other was covered. Lee gently bit the skin that was exposed there. "You're mouthwatering, darlin'. No shame in having that sopping wet pussy on me."

Greta's cheeks flushed. She was blunt, but not all women were okay with being too crass. A part of her loved that Lee was the sort of woman who was. It was freeing. "I like how you talk."

"You like vulgar words, then? A bit of dirty talk for the well-dressed professional?" Lee sat on the edge of the bed, sliding back until her knees were at the edge and her legs hung over. In the process, Greta was now straddling her lap.

"I do." Greta's hands clutched the top of Lee's shoulders at first, but then Lee's hands gripped Greta's back, holding her steady and preventing the feeling of instability that such a position could evoke. "I like everything about your mouth except that it's not on my pussy yet."

"Patience, pretty. I like how you're stretched over me," Lee encouraged before Greta could feel self-conscious about anything. "Wide open like you're about to take a ride."

Lee gazed down at her, eyes simmering with unslaked hunger still.

"I don't want to be the only one who's naked right now." Greta leaned back against the firm arms holding her and started unbuttoning Lee's shirt. "I want to feel more of your skin."

Lee said nothing as Greta divested her of both shirt and bra. She remained silent as Greta reached back and removed her own bra, too, leaving her naked aside from her boots.

There was something intimate about the quiet, and there was something unexpectedly erotic about being naked except for her tall, high-heeled boots. She felt like a naughty model or stripper, curvy and scandalously dressed.

"I like this look." Lee toed off her shoes without moving Greta off her lap. Lee's jeans were still on, but she was now naked from the waist up.

Greta looked over at the mirror above the hotel dresser. Her reflection, especially straddling a woman like Lee, looked sexier than she'd felt in a very long time. "I like it, too."

"Will you stay on top of me?" Lee asked. "If I slide up there to the pillow . . ."

"You want me to stay in your lap?" Greta clarified.

"I want you wide open on top of me. I want you to ride my hand, darlin' . . . or my face if you're willing." Lee stared at her. "What do you want?"

Greta bit her lip.

"What?" Lee slid onto the middle of the bed, tugging Greta with her. "Tell me what you want."

"I want to face the mirror when I ride you," Greta said in a faltering voice.

Lee pivoted, lifting Greta and moving them both so Greta would face her reflection. "Hand or face?"

"Not your hand." Greta looked at Lee's face. "Up there."

"Yes, ma'am." Lee smiled and lifted Greta by the hips. "Bring that deliciousness right up here for me."

"You're just not very patient." Greta's gaze slid over Lee, marveling at the muscles in her arms and the taut stomach. A body like that came from a lot of hard work and discipline.

"Have you seen *you*? Mouthwatering. No rational woman could be patient after seeing you get off, darlin'." Lee rolled her eyes and chuckled again. "Come up here."

Then she guided Greta upward until she was straddling Lee's face.

Greta looked at herself in the hotel mirror. From this angle, she looked like she was alone on a bed, eyes wide in lust, lips parted, hair a mess. Then she looked down to see Lee staring up at her as she licked a long slow stripe on Greta's bare sex. The sound that came out of Lee was more growl than word, and it made Greta want to melt.

Lee's hand gripped Greta's hips hard enough to bruise as she pulled Greta forward and urged her to move so she was riding Lee's mouth. If she'd thought Lee was gifted with her hands, that was nothing compared to what she could do with her mouth.

4

*Kaelee*

Kaelee marveled at how eagerly Marie writhed against her. The petite beauty rode Kaelee's face like a champ at a rodeo, so much so that Kaelee was regretful that they couldn't keep in touch after this. Marie was a dream lover, vocal in all the right ways. She wasn't shy about what she wanted or didn't. She wasn't quiet in her pleasure either. She was demanding—and loud.

Some women were all about the softer things, the way a woman was perfect to hold or only wanted slow and gentle sex. Some women were into the way that femmes made them feel powerful. There was nothing wrong with either of those. Kaelee was happy to break out toys or go to a bar and lead in a two-step if she was going on a date. She was flexible . . . well, as flexible as she could be within the constraints of app sex.

But the thing that Kaelee loved most *physically* was going down on a woman who was at ease with her body. Nothing else compared. The scent, the taste, the feel. Everything about it was a high. And when the woman was as expressive as Marie, it was akin to a sacrament. The sheer bliss that Kaelee was able to give Marie—and a list of women before her—was empowering. There was no shame to wanting to feel that relaxed, that satisfied, and Kaelee felt like she was transported right along with the cries of the woman currently breathing like she'd just run a marathon.

"You're gorgeous, darlin'," Kaelee swore once Marie moved to the side. "Feel a little better?"

"Let me . . ." Marie stretched out in the bed. "Would you strip? I want to touch you."

Kaelee rolled to her feet and shoved her jeans and briefs off. She'd already lost her shirt, bra, and shoes, so she now walked across the room bare-ass naked so she could put her clothes all in one spot. She piled her clothes all together on the desk, and then she tucked her shoes under the desk. When she looked back, Marie had her head propped up in her hand, watching Kaelee.

"I want to ask about the tattoo," Marie said, obviously having read the words that lined Kaelee's spine.

"You can ask me questions, or you can touch me," Kaelee said. "I can't offer you both. Which do you want more?"

"You're cruel, aren't you?" Marie said.

"Sometimes," Kaelee admitted.

"I'm not asking for your hand. I just want to know more about you."

After a moment, Kaelee relented just a little. "It says, 'I am no bird; and no net ensnares me. I am free.'"

Kaelee waited for the obvious reactions people had, remarks on tattoos and attempts to connect, but Marie's was unexpected.

"Paraphrase of *Jane Eyre*." There was no doubt in Marie's voice. That was new in hookups. Apparently, Marie was a bit of a book lover.

"Yes." Kaelee eyed her with increased interest. "No one usually gets that."

"Majored in English."

"History," Kaelee offered with a shrug. "I liked the idea of not being ensnared. Untrapped. Uncaged."

"What thinking woman *doesn't* like freedom?" Marie said with a laugh. "Maybe not always the same way. I almost got married once. It didn't feel like a cage, though."

"To a woman?"

Marie rolled her eyes. "Obviously."

"Not totally obvious. I was engaged to a man." Kaelee flinched internally at the thought. Kyle was an asshole. Older, interested in Daddy's money, and she was just the obstacle he was told to conquer in order for him to access it.

"I find that unexpected." Marie's expression was carefully shuttered.

"It wasn't my idea." Kaelee shrugged. "I'm free now, though. My family arranged the engagement, and I was expected to go along with it like a pawn. Somehow they were *stunned* that I was actually not interested in him or any man." Kaelee laughed, thinking back to her parents' reactions. Sure, she had different clothes and hair when she lived in North Carolina, but how had they not noticed? Kids at school had. Her family never *saw* her, though. Being different was so far outside their conception that they couldn't even imagine it.

"I'm sorry."

"Thinking about this is a mood killer," Kaelee said lightly. "I have a work obligation tomorrow anyhow, and you seem sated. Maybe I should go."

"Where do you w—"

"No," Kaelee cut her off. "You're easy to talk to, Marie, but I don't *do* this part. I am not here to make a friend or date. I came here to fuck. Just that. You got what you wanted, so maybe I ought to head out. I'm not expecting you to get me off. Lots of women don't, and I'm fine with that."

"Whoa. What I *want* includes having my hands on you." Marie sat up. "Let me apologize, Lee. I simply find people interesting, and you're . . ." She lifted one shoulder in a half shrug. "You're gorgeous, mysterious, and I'm a little languid after you . . . took such great care of me."

"I don't want to share life stories," Kaelee stressed. "Sex? I'll stay. Chatting? I'm out."

"Stay a bit. Let me make it up to you. I won't ask any questions about anything but how you want me to touch you." Marie was practically purring. "Let me make you feel good. Please?"

Kaelee nodded, but she wasn't sure she wanted to stay if they were going to uncover old wounds.

Then Marie pulled back the sheet and invited her into the bed. Kaelee was horny as hell; getting a woman off left her on the edge of orgasm every time, and tonight, she wanted to feel Marie's body against her own when she came. The problem with hookups was that Kaelee wasn't able to have enough trust to be on the receiving side of anything other than basics, and often not even that, but there was still something wonderful about letting another person's hands drive her to orgasm when Kaelee could manage to surrender enough control.

"What do you want, Lee?"

Typically, Kaelee lied a little, but for a change she said the truth: "Slow and soft until I can't resist. Make me wait for it, or I won't get off."

"Hands? Toys? I have one in—"

"No. Just your hands." Kaelee had the occasional fuck friend once or twice where she could share more, but she wasn't great at letting go of control at the best of times. She was surprised that she was managing to do so tonight. What Kaelee wanted most was to have someone she trusted enough to surrender control to, but she couldn't do that, not fully, unless she was friends with her lover, and that hadn't happened in years. With this curvy stranger, though, she felt uncommonly at ease already. Kaelee said, "Even when I say I want faster, stay slow until . . . the end."

"So I have permission to tease you until you are begging?" Marie laughed softly. "*Excellent.* If you change your mind for real, I want a safe word."

Kaelee paused. She respected the way Marie *also* focused on consent. "Trollbridge. If I say trollbridge, you need to stop."

"Perfect." Marie's hands were nothing more than butterfly touches at first, caressing Kaelee's chest and arms and stomach.

Fleeting touches dropped lower, but Marie was the opposite of how she'd been when Kaelee was getting her off. She'd been desperate then. Now, as she touched Kaelee, she was careful, slow, as if they had forever to stay this way.

By the time Marie's fingers slid over Kaelee's sex, parting her folds but barely applying any pressure, Kaelee wanted her touches to be faster and harder. She arched into every delicate stroke and tease. Hips lifting like a demand. That was the part about masturbation that was hard. She didn't have the willpower to deny herself a hard, fast release.

"You can go faster," Kaelee breathed. "Just a little."

But Marie just chuckled. "No. I want to see you tremble, Lee. You're nowhere near eager enough yet."

"I feel pretty damn eager," Kaelee whispered as Marie slid her fingers inside so slowly that Kaelee chased them with her hips, forcing them deeper inside.

"I bet you can be *begging* in time," Marie taunted, one hand glancing over Kaelee's clit and the other rhythmically but slowly fucking her. "Can't you?"

"Maybe."

Marie paused, stopping completely as Kaelee approached her orgasm. As Kaelee's hips chased her hand, Marie reached up and stroked Kaelee's breasts so softly it tickled. "Right there at the edge, aren't you?"

"Yessss." Kaelee writhed under her. "More. Please? Just a little harder. *Fuck* me."

Marie resumed stroking, slowly at first and then faster and faster until Kaelee was gasping. "Just a little harder . . . ? A little faster? Is that what you want?"

"Yes. God, yes. Harder. Please, darlin'," Kaelee begged.

Marie stopped. Again. Denying her release instead of going faster.

Three more times they repeated the pattern. Each time, Marie resumed her leisurely touches that sped little by little until eventually

Kaelee was sweating, twisting, thrusting her hips up in search of relief. "Please, darlin'. Don't stop again. *Please*. I need more."

"I have you." Marie covered Kaelee's mouth, slanting over her lips and swallowing her cries as she fucked her deeper, harder, faster.

And when Kaelee felt that spine-straightening orgasm tear through, she thought she might actually have met the perfect lover. *This*, this edge of shattered, was what Kaelee needed, and it was damn near impossible for her to feel comfortable enough to let go this way with strangers.

Afterward, when the only sound was their breathing, Marie brushed the sweat from Kaelee's cheek. "You're stunning, you know? I feel like my holiday weekend has already been the relaxation I needed."

"See you in another six months," Kaelee joked in a scratchy voice.

"I honestly wouldn't be opposed. I'm not looking for dates, but a night with you again?" Marie let out a low moan. "I'd be amenable to more."

Kaelee rolled out of bed and went to the bathroom to freshen up. She couldn't stand to stay still after the writhing, begging, needy state she'd been in. Too real. Too vulnerable.

When she returned from the bathroom, she stood at the end of the bed and composed herself mentally. In a casual voice, she offered, "Message if you're in DC again."

"And if you're in Manhattan . . ."

For a moment, Kaelee debated telling her that she'd be in the city for work, but that could lead to questions, and questions could turn into a connection. In a city of over eight million people, they weren't likely to run into each other again. Not accidentally. If she decided she needed another night, she'd message, but not now. That felt too much like making plans.

Kaelee lifted Marie's hand, turned it over, and kissed the tender skin on the back of her wrist. "Thank you for a great stress reliever."

Marie laughed. "The thanks is all mine." She didn't reach out, but her eyes were soft and inviting. "It's a shame you can't stay."

"Sorry, darlin'." Kaelee stood and walked over to her tidy pile of clothes. She always was careful to keep everything together. Less chance of leaving something important behind that way.

Marie said nothing as Kaelee dressed.

The silence stretched, uncomfortable, until Kaelee suggested, "If you need anything while you're in the city, you can message for that, too. If anything goes wrong or . . ." She felt foolish suggesting it. That was how people ended up in messy situations. "Since you're alone and all . . ."

"What if I need another pressure valve release?" Marie sat halfway upright, so the sheet fell lower and exposed her breasts.

"Two nights in a row?" Kaelee shook her head, both in response to the words and the visual temptation. Marie had perfect breasts, pert, generous, and sensitive. Kaelee forced her gaze away from them and said, "I could like you, unfortunately. Next month? In six months? Maybe. Not tomorrow. There are rules, though, I need to follow so I keep things orderly."

Marie's laughter trilled out. "I think I'm glad we don't share a city."

The fact that Kaelee wasn't the only one tempted to break her own rules made it urgent that she leave. Now. She finished buttoning her shirt, walked over to the bed, and bent down to kiss the beautiful woman still lounging there. Then she dropped a kiss on each breast.

"I might have rules, but I'm not a saint, Marie." Kaelee pulled the sheet up to hide the tempting bounty. "Message if you're in DC again someday."

Then she left the room as quickly as she could without actually running.

# 5

## *Kaelee*

**OCTOBER**

A month later, Kaelee's stress had once again become unbearable. She hadn't used the app, but she had opened it a few times and browsed. Sometimes the problem with a great one-nighter was the knowledge that the next one simply wouldn't compare. Extra gym sessions hadn't been enough to wash away the panic over her meet and greet in New York. So the *next* solution to that anxious ball in her gut was often a good fuck.

*Pick someone new,* her heart urged.

*Message Marie,* her impulsivity demanded.

*Do something,* her libido whispered over and over.

Healthier ways to cope with anxiety did exist. Exercise was her default, but when it wasn't enough, the alternatives were chemical or sex. And right now, exercise wasn't fixing her stress at all. Kaelee had to go to New York for her meet and greet with her editor and the team on the following Monday. New York was where Marie lived, and the temptation to send her a message on the app was a burning need the last few days.

*Sex with her was amazing. Why not?*

The "why not" was the part that was harder to own. Kaelee felt like even though they'd kept conversation minimal, she still was intrigued by Marie. So Kaelee had asked if Toni would tag along—like preplanned cliterference. It was a solid plan; they could hit a bar, meet their agent, and Kaelee could resist meeting up with the deliciousness that was Marie. Kaelee wasn't sure she'd ever craved another person the way she craved Marie. She'd had several sex dreams the likes of which she hadn't had in her entire life. Sometimes people just clicked, and unfortunately, Kaelee had clicked with Marie.

*I'll keep busy. Meet someone at a bar here.*

The night before, Kaelee had spent an hour on the app, looking at profiles and weighing the possibility of connecting with someone new. She had not picked anyone up *or* replied to anyone on the app. She couldn't find anyone who excited her the way Marie had.

Today, though, Kaelee was standing in the doorway of Toni's office and trying to quell a rising wave of panic. "You can't *bail* on me. What if—"

"Nope. Nothing you say will change it." Toni was at her desk swapping files out of her messenger bag. Toni said, "Sorry. I can't go up to the city at all. I sent you and Em both a message."

"It's only Thursday, Toni."

"I know."

"Maybe we could go on Sunday, then? Just for the day." Kaelee wasn't the sort to beg, but right now, her voice came out whiney. "Come on, Toni . . ."

"No. I initially said maybe, not yes. This isn't *bailing* on you." Toni scowled at her, a look that used to be intimidating enough to make Kaelee shut up. Not anymore.

Kaelee glared at her in a way that she couldn't imagine doing a year prior. "You aren't even going to come with me for one day? Seriously? You're . . . just *ditching* me?"

"Sorry. Addie was able to get away for a long weekend, and . . ." Toni looked up from her organized chaos of essays and file folders. "I haven't seen her in five days. I have priorities that don't include you or Emily or trains."

"Ugh. I need friends who aren't perpetually in a honeymoon stage," Kaelee grumbled. She pointed at Toni. "I'm going to replace you with someone single. I'll go to a writers' conference and find a new friend, one *without* a happy relationship."

"I understand you're disappointed," Toni said, not sounding the least bit apologetic. "You're also overreacting, Kae. It was a loose 'maybe' of a plan . . . is that worth ending our acquaintanceship?"

"*Friendship*," Kaelee corrected with a scowl. "Damn you. You're my friend."

"I know." Toni flashed her a grin. "You're tolerable, too. Which is why you'll forgive me for switching a 'maybe' to a 'no.'"

Kaelee sighed.

"Are you actually anxious about the meeting?" Toni asked gently. "Greta's great, and Em has your back. That's what agents do. They are your buffer, confidante, partner in facing any chaos. The publicist I had was pretty fabulous, even though I hate dealing with that sort of stuff. They're all good people. And you know I couldn't come to the actual meeting anyhow."

"I know. They'd be all aflutter over their *star* and forget I was there," Kaelee teased.

Toni shook a finger at her. "Keep mocking me, and when your book explodes into awards and sales and bestseller lists, I'll just prop up my feet and laugh at your karma."

"Oh no, the karma of succeeding . . ." Kaelee rolled her eyes. "You're ridiculous, you know? Thanks for the pep talk."

There really wasn't anyone like Toni. Finding a mentor who understood both academia and the publishing industry was akin to locating a copy of Shakespeare's First Folio.

"I know you're being weird about this, but I'm not sure why," Toni bluntly pointed out. "What's the real issue? If I thought it was about the meeting, I might have tried harder. Is that it?"

Kaelee felt her face flush. "I met this woman on the app I use."

"Your sex app?"

"Can we not call it that where people might overhear? It makes me sound like a perv." Kaelee moved into the office. "But yes, *that* app."

"Hey, if I wasn't about to be happily married, I'd be happy to know that app exists." Toni shrugged. "Trying to meet anyone when my book made me end up on television interviews and all that, plus trying to be sure I didn't accidentally hit on a student. Ugh. The single life is hard."

"How do you accidentally hit on your student?"

"Not mine. Any student." Toni scowled. "You can't do that and expect to be taken seriously as a professor."

"Well, this woman isn't a student." Kaelee thought about Marie's forceful personality. "I think she's in business or something. Very adept at negotiating."

"You don't know?"

"Sex. App," Kaelee said with a shrug. "I wasn't dating her. We met. We fucked. She's on my mind. She was in DC, but she lives in New York."

"And this has what to do with me?" Toni gave her a perplexed look.

"I thought if I was hanging out with you, I might have the self-control to . . . *not* see her." Kaelee felt stupid saying it aloud, but there it was.

"Because great sex is a thing you suddenly want to avoid?" Toni folded her arms and gave Kaelee a stern look. "I like you, but sometimes you're weird as hell."

Kaelee laughed. "I like you, too, but you're being downgraded. Once I find someone to replace you, you're going to be my backup wing woman."

"To help you avoid sex?" Toni shook her head. "I don't get it, but I guess we all have our priorities. My priority is Addie. She's coming home, and I . . . missed her." Toni still looked vaguely constipated when she admitted to missing her soon-to-be wife, but Kaelee wasn't cruel enough to comment. The queen of cynicism had changed into the queen of domesticity since she got engaged.

In a last-ditch attempt at creating a way to have the self-control she lacked with Marie, Kaelee suggested, "Invite her, too. I like Addie.

We can take the train on Sunday, grab dinner, and head to the bar. Then you can go back to DC."

"Nope." Toni flashed a wolfish smile. "She's been on set more often for the extra episodes they added, so I'm not going anywhere this weekend. Watching people fawn over my woman isn't my idea of a good time. Next week, you and me. Bar. Dinner. Whatever."

"*I* put up with people fawning over *both* of you, you realize?" Kaelee grumbled. "I manage."

"It's different when you have to tolerate everyone in the room looking at your future wife covetously." Toni scowled to herself.

"Overreaction much?"

"Tell me that when you find the right wom—"

"Whoa there!" Kaelee held her hand up as if to stop that damning statement, even as her thoughts drifted to Marie. She was rare in that she was still intriguing, but that didn't mean Kaelee was going to start thinking domestic thoughts. "Not now. Not ever. Why would you say that? We've discussed this."

"Says the person who needed to find excuses not to see the woman she seems to desperately want to see." Toni laughed.

"That's different," Kaelee objected. "I don't usually drink at the same pond twice."

"Uh-huh. *That's* the issue." Toni shook her head. "She lives in New York, right?"

"Well, yes."

Toni gave her a look that was both amused and pitying. "Kae, I say this with all seriousness, if you want to see her when you're in town to get your fix, do it. Meet her. Get her naked. Leave. It's not like you do anything different just because it's the second night."

"She's just sexy and smart, and I let her . . ." Kaelee flushed but forced herself to continue, "I let down some walls with her."

This time Toni stared at her kindly. "So see her one last time and then get out if you don't want more."

"I'm not a relationship person."

"Oh, me either. I said that right up to when I was at risk of losing

Addie." Toni's expression shifted into something raw and fierce, and Kaelee could easily see why so many women stared at *her*. Toni was a surly woman socially, but she was charm personified in a classroom or interview. Kaelee suspected she was even more so on a date.

*No wonder Addie is so happy.*

In some ways, Toni was as much role model as friend. She was more masc than Kaelee, and her attire reflected it. Kaelee knew from the past that she *could* wear a skirt comfortably at one point, but these days, she was more at ease wearing trousers than dresses, more comfortable leading than following, and admittedly, she was fond of waking up with a woman who looked like she'd need a stylist to control her morning-after hair if she was feeling reckless enough to stay overnight.

*Someone who looks like Marie.*

"Don't deny yourself joy, Kae." Toni caught her gaze. "See the businesswoman. Enjoy your time, and then if you're afraid you might catch feelings, bail."

"I don't catch feelings," Kaelee stressed. "Settled lesbians are as bad as ex-smokers or ex-drinkers. Just because you fell for someone doesn't mean the rest of us want to start U-Hauling." Kaelee took a small step backward. "I accept you, soon-to-be married and all that, but don't go flinging your get-wifed-up curses at me."

The leftover smile from Toni's laughter made her look uncharacteristically approachable. "Next week. Addie will be gone for work, and we'll grab a drink. I need to ask you a very important question about whether you want to be in my wedding party or Addie's." She paused then and glanced at her watch. "Any news on the book? You know if you *need* to talk, especially about that, I'm here."

"Bound manuscripts are out, so as of this time next week the first group of strangers will be reading it." Kaelee scowled. "Wait. Back up. Wedding party?"

"I need a second person. I wanted to ask you, but Addie says she should get to ask you, too. She might be messing with me because I didn't do it yet." Toni frowned for a moment. "That's good about doing bound manuscripts and ARCs."

"That's what Emily says." Kaelee realized she sounded as anxious as she felt.

"Em is typically right about everything," Toni said lightly. "Don't tell her I admitted that, but . . . she's rarely wrong."

"It's different for me than for you, I think. I *want* this career." Kaelee felt foolish admitting it, but that was the crux of the matter. She wanted to sell this book and dozens more in the future. She wanted the powerful agent. Toni had bumblefucked her way into a writing career, and a TV adaptation of her book. Her goals had been different, and Kaelee had watched her struggle with a surprise second career.

"If the book reaches readers, Em will sell foreign rights and more books. This is just step two or three. You got an agent. You sold two books. Now? You just need readers to find it."

"And if it doesn't work?" Kaelee asked.

Toni shrugged again. "You write a new one. Sell it or self-publish. Finish your PhD. Don't focus so much on *what if x or y goes wrong.* It's a good book or Em wouldn't have signed you. She's practical. She won't make money if it doesn't sell well, and you were going to go to *auction*, Kae. You're fine."

*What if no one likes it once it's on shelves? What if it sucks? What if they read the ARC and then hate it so much that the publisher cancels it? I can't do this and—*

"Whatever thoughts go with that face you're making, stop them," Toni cut in, hand lightly resting on Kaelee's wrist now.

"Does the panic ever get easier?" Kaelee stared at her mentor.

"Not so far," Toni muttered.

"Next week, lunch. Maybe drinks. I will need to vent and tell you I'll be in your wedding."

"Done."

"Give Addie my love," Kaelee said lightly. "Tell her I fully intend to admire her bridesmaids, so she needs to pick a pretty one for me to walk with."

"Just don't be looking at my bride. Everyone does that, and I swear she finds my reactions funny." Toni made a surly noise. She was absurdly possessive of Adelaine, which was occasionally hysterical to watch. Toni's fixation was never in a controlling way, but in a *why does everyone keep trying to talk to my woman* way. Addie, for her part, seemed to think the whole thing was adorable.

If Kaelee were the relationship sort, she'd look at them as a model for what she might want, but she was perfectly happy with her no-strings life. She liked the women she bedded, and she liked that none of them wanted more. She liked that none of them asked about her job or family. Everything was kept on the surface. They could talk casually about music or shows or food. It was a choice, one necessitated by her original surname—which she had changed for privacy years ago—and her family.

"I expect you to keep me posted on news on the book," Toni ask-ordered. "Em won't update me, so text me when you get reviews or anything."

"Yes, Professor D."

"Not *your* professor *or* the professor you're TAing for this term." Toni closed her messenger bag and walked toward the door. "Actually, who are you TAing for?"

Kaelee stepped aside. "Err, no one."

"No one? What about funding? Are you living on *book* money?" Toni gave her an incredulous look. "They took *months* to sort out the contract for me, and I know your D and A was decent, but that's just leaving you the on-print and foreign rights sales, but you don't even know how long it'll take to sell it in the first place and—"

"Toni." Kaelee was touched that Toni cared enough to lecture her. "I don't technically need the book money."

"How is that possible? Loans?" Toni leveled a look at her.

Kaelee repressed a sigh and started walking to the exit adjacent to the lot where Toni parked. "I have a fund."

"A *fund*?"

"A trust fund. From my grandmother." Kaelee squirmed. "She left me money, quite a lot of it . . . so I don't need to get a TA to pay for things, but I like to not count on my fund. I wanted it to last, and professor salaries aren't great."

"I feel like I'm missing a detail about you right about now. A *trust fund?*" Toni didn't stop walking, but she waved at the department head as they passed him. "Harold."

"Miss Carpenter. Dr. Darbyshire." He smiled in his affable uncle way. Kaelee wasn't even a part of the history department, but he seemed extra fond of her because her master of arts was in history.

"Yes. I changed my first and last name years ago, but my family has money. I have a slice of it in a trust fund." Kaelee struggled to keep her voice level. Money was an understatement when it came to the generational wealth the Aldens had. She kept her tone light as she added, "Their money comes with strings, though. The kind women like you or me can't accept, so I decided in college that I'll make my own damn fortune."

"And you chose *academia* to do that?" Toni shot her a look and teased, "Here I was telling people how smart you were, but if you thought teaching was the way to riches . . ."

"Shut up." Kaelee grinned. "Think of my fund as a really nice safety net. I could probably live on it for thirty years. Adding in the book money . . ." Kaelee shrugged. "I'm okay. I live tight. Basic apartment. My car's paid off. I don't have a lot of expenses."

Her only real indulgence was the dating app she used, but her privacy mattered enough that it was a logical expense. She didn't even have streaming channels. No fancy restaurants. No new clothes unless it was essential. Kaelee was the sort of frugal she suspected would horrify her parents.

After a moment, Toni caught her eye. "You'll want to tell Em about your family, and then with her guidance, talk to your publicist."

"Maybe." Kaelee was embarrassed by her family. There was no way around it. The last thing she wanted was to tell anyone that she shared even a drop of DNA with her intolerant father. She'd distanced herself intentionally. "That family isn't the sort of people I want to associate with. I haven't spoken to them in a decade."

"You aren't even using their name talking to me now, Kae." Toni pushed open the door to the outside. Fall had turned the college grounds into a crisp wonderland. Not quite winter, but the fluctuating weather meant there were flowers still, but also the damp decay from a few heavy rains.

"You didn't ask," Kaelee hedged.

"I won't either." Toni shook her head. "Keep your secrets close, but talk to your team. I learned that the hard way. When that blew up . . . all the news stuff with me and Addie . . . it was a *lot*. If you are avoiding saying their name, it means I might recognize it. That means you need to warn the team."

Kaelee said nothing. Things were different with Toni and Addie. Toni's book was a huge breakout hit, and Addie was the lead actor in the adaptation. They were both public personas. Kaelee, very intentionally, was not. She had some relatives with Names, but personally, she was careful to stay under any radar. Just a woman at a university, a person in a crowd, a lesbian with no ties. Nothing about her was remarkable in any way the media should care about.

Telling her agent and publicist would mean there were two more people who knew. One person can keep a secret; two people might not. If she told Emily *and* publicity, too? That was inviting exposure. And as much as folks might call her paranoid, she grew up with publicity people. She knew better than to trust most of them. There were plenty of publicity and marketing people who would do despicable things to get coverage. Kaelee had zero interest in telling them anything that could be buzzworthy. There were great publicists, and there were . . . other sorts.

"I have it under control," Kaelee said finally. *This* part of her life she had figured out. No contact with the fam. No ties to them. She'd worked on creating a separate identity for years; she had invented herself, and nothing was worth risking her privacy. "I'll text you if I get any good book news."

"Or *bad* news. I'm here for listening to either." Toni looked like she had more to say, but when Kaelee simply nodded, Toni slid into her Jeep instead.

*Would she still smile at me if she knew where I come from?*

*If she knew how much money Tripp has donated to politicians trying to strip away our rights, would Toni hate me? Or look at me differently?*

Kaelee's family spilled their money backing the kind of politicians who wanted to limit anything that loosely fell under the umbrella of LGBTQ or women's rights. Book banning, bathroom bills, trans athletes, birth control limits, whatever issue was about taking rights away from people, they were onboard. Coming out in a family like that was one of the single most horrible things Kaelee had experienced. Her father had smacked her when she stood up to him, more than once. No guilt, no hesitation. He simply hit her. When Kaelee came out, her mother wept, dropped to her knees, and started praying loudly. Her sister just looked at her like she'd taken a shit on the rug.

If not for her trust fund from her grandmother, Kaelee would've been unable to live an authentic life.

So, no, Kaelee would absolutely not be naming names. She wasn't one of them, properly disowned unless she "stopped rebelling" and became magically heterosexual and conservative, as if that were even possible.

*They'd rather I live a lie than be happy.*

And Kaelee would rather succeed on her own terms.

6

## *Greta*

Mornings were invented by Satan himself. Greta was certain of that. At least in the summer, publishing closed early on Fridays. October Fridays? Not even the fall flavors at the coffee cart in the lobby could ease her mood at this hour. The worst part was that it was her own damn fault. Being successful in business required trade-offs, and no matter how often the publishing industry was romanticized, it was an *industry*. Climbing the ladder, even in publishing, meant prioritizing. That was the only reason that Greta Clayborne, a dedicated night owl, was trying to become an early-morning person.

"Marketing needs to go over some things with the Darbyshire book later today when they get in," her assistant, Ian, said in lieu of a greeting.

Greta nodded.

Ian was the sort of man who managed to sound kind and wonderful no matter what he said. Objectively, he was attractive. Even though she didn't find men personally appealing, she could still see *why* so many people gave Ian long looks. He had the sort of flop of hair that probably required more hair products than Greta had ever mastered. Under bright lights, the red highlights in his hair turned the shock of overly long brown waves into something unusual.

"You were probably already at the gym today, weren't you?" she accused.

"Yes. Do you need a workout buddy?"

"Piss off." She eyed him the way she looked at anyone trying to sell her anything when she was minding her own business.

"Difficult morning, boss?" Ian asked cheerily. Unlike Greta, Ian was one of those damnable morning people. Aside from that particular character flaw, she liked him more than anyone else in the building. Strangers, colleagues, delivery people, no one was as wonderful as Ian.

Except it was only five in the morning. At this hour of the day, Greta hated everyone equally. Even Ian.

"I'll turn on the kettle," he said, watching her warily. "You seem particularly . . ." He shook his head and repeated, "I'll just turn on the kettle."

Greta sipped her still-warm cup of coffee as she glared at Ian's horrid cheerfulness. "Good. Coffee then tea. Isn't there a rhyme about that?"

"Greta . . . dear, dear Greta, that's liquor and beer." Ian headed toward the counter where the stainless steel electric kettle gleamed like a beacon.

She looked around the blissfully empty office. That part she could get used to if her body ever agreed to mornings. "You know you don't need to come in early just because I do."

"Respectfully, you're an asshole in the morning, and I like this job, so my function is to protect the rest of the company from you until you switch from angry, feral possum to human."

Greta flipped Ian off. "No one else is here."

"Last month. Andrew and Eliza." He smothered a smile. "I believe they said you 'hissed like a one-eared alley cat.'"

"Once. They were loud, and I was reading." Greta had the wherewithal to admit that she was, perhaps, in some situations, not capable of people-ing when it was this hour.

"I picked up pastries," Ian called over his shoulder as he led the way to her office, the one she'd coveted not quite a year ago, the one with an actual door rather than the cubicle maze where she'd been not too long ago.

If she had a younger brother, she thought vaguely that she would've hoped he was just like Ian—and not just because of the pastries. Ian was a good guy. Sweet. Efficient. Painfully intelligent. Someday, she'd be both proud and crushed when he went off to be an editor on his own. For now, though, he was waiting in her office with notes on the last two books she thought were worth a second read. They weren't The One, but not being the book she was chasing didn't mean they weren't wonderful in their own ways.

For every career-building book, there were another half dozen that were simply solid books. They'd earn, or garner awards, or occasionally be surprise hits or flops. They were the backbone of publishing, essential in the same way the big hits were.

"All in order with the Carpenter meeting?" Greta asked. She half expected Kaelee to cancel the meeting or ask to switch it to video. She'd never had an author so unwilling to meet with her or even hop on the phone. So far, Kaelee was strictly email—and terse email at that.

"Kaelee Carpenter and her fabulous agent will be here on Monday." Ian pulled out his tablet. "Meetings with art for the cover concepts—unless you want to email those?"

At Greta's shake of the head, Ian continued, "Marketing wants to go over their plan. Digital, publicity, major accounts, and library will be present. Then lunch with you, Carpenter, and Haide. I made reservations at two places. Menus sent to you and Haide for review. Then I'll cancel the one you don't want, or I'll go myself. Afternoon meetings follow."

Ian had a cheeky smile that made Greta think he could charm the scales off a snake. Greta ignored him, reread her draft to Kaelee, and hit send.


Kaelee,

We are looking forward to meeting you in person. Ian booked two places for lunch. LMK which works.

Emily has your schedule for the meet and greet with

the team, but if you have any questions, call me or email Ian. We will meet with publicity, marketing, a few people from accounts, and art/design.

Greta

She ought not feel so irritable over this, but she was starting to think Darbyshire was about to lose her title for crankiest author.

"What's wrong?" Ian sat in the chair across from her desk. "Sip."

"I'm not a toddler." Greta still took a sip of her lukewarm coffee. "I don't know how we're going to tour Carpenter if she's a recluse. Do we have any pictures? Anything from her socials?"

"Nothing." Ian tapped a foot as he thought. "What if we ask Toni to send us a candid of her? Or are there any on her account?"

Greta looked at him a beat too long before saying, "Toni's fiancée hired someone to do Toni's socials. Can you picture *Toni* promoting her books?"

Ian cracked a smile. "Fair. She's more likely to toss a manuscript on your desk and saunter out than talk about the books. Ever. How can someone with such an exoskeleton write such"—Ian made a noise—"angsty, swoony stuff?"

"Did you just refer to her as having an exoskeleton?" Greta deadpanned.

"Tell me I'm wrong. Seriously. Tell me." Ian folded his arms and glared.

"Ian."

Her assistant made a *hmph* kind of noise. "Maybe she has a ghostwriter! She's secretly a giant beetle like the Kafka book? Or a hedgehog?"

"Seriously?" Greta cracked up at the thought of that. "Toni's a bit prickly, but she's sweet on the inside."

"Just like a hedgehog." He sighed when Greta raised both brows. "*Fine*. She's complicated, so maybe Carpenter is going to surprise us, too. Maybe she's just shy." He folded his hands and glanced at the ceiling. "Lord, don't let her be another hedgehog."

Greta held up her phone so he could see the email she had just received.

Ms. Clayborne,

Noted.

K.C.

Ian chortled. "What's worse than a hedgehog? Those little fish that if you step on them, you get envenomated. What are they called?"

"Do you mean a stonefish?"

"Yes!" Ian nodded. "She's a stonefish. What's with lesbians being so cantankerous?"

Greta scowled. "Did you *seriously* just say that? What's wrong with you, Ian? That's—"

"Please! I love cranky women." Ian smiled. "I work for *you*, boss. Sip. Wait? Are we still un-caffeinated enough that I have to act like you're a sweet little cherub? Sip."

There was no polite answer there. Ian would make his remarks, as if she could become provoked. She certainly couldn't use herself as an example of being *not* prickly either.

She was crankier than usual the past week. *And I know where there's a cure.* An irresponsible part of Greta wanted to pretend she had work in DC and take the train down for a day. She knew it was foolish, but she'd resumed her life of functional celibacy after her one evening with Lee.

*And thought about her incessantly.*

# 7

# Kaelee

Kaelee opened the messages on the dating app several times on Friday and then again on Saturday. Hearing from her editor, hearing from her agent, knowing people would be reading her book, knowing the deal would be announced soon . . . it was a lot. She had a long mental list of all the skeletons that could reach out of the past and ruin her present. Logic was pointless when her anxiety spiraled like this.

*My biological family doesn't care about me.*

*It's not like they're out there looking for me.*

*I changed my name so I won't tarnish their sterling reputation.*

She was ninety percent certain her family had simply washed their hands of her and said *good riddance to bad garbage* or whatever the religious version of that was. They probably claimed to pray for her, but they weren't praying for clarity or even acceptance. They were praying she would repent and change.

*Tripp Alden could never be wrong! Ergo, it must be me.*

*He's such a narcissistic fuckwad.*

Kaelee hated that so many thoughts of her father had crept into her mind lately. She'd removed the name he'd given her at birth, combining her maternal grandparents' names—Katherine and Leland—so as to honor them. Kaelee was a name of her own choosing, *and* she'd removed her father's surname. She wasn't even going to pretend that "Carpenter" was anything but a jab at him, too. She wore a common name, instead of the one he was so proud of, not that she thought her father even knew her current name. He wasn't likely to care enough to track her down.

*I'm just being paranoid.*

What reason would he have to decide to keep tabs on his lesbian daughter who defied and embarrassed him?

But thinking about him led to thoughts of her farce of a fiancé, and thinking about Kyle was a surefire way to give herself insomnia. She'd been a victim, and neither her mother nor her sister had been there for her. No one had. She was alone dealing with the fallout of a rape that had resulted from her father *assigning* her a fiancé—and that fiancé taking what he thought was his.

*Never a-fucking-gain.*

Kaelee didn't exactly share her past with people. She didn't want pity *or* the rubbernecking trauma lovers asking questions. The past was the past, and it needed to stay there.

But thinking about the secrets she'd lived with made her wonder if her publishing dream was foolish. She didn't want to be in the public eye. Ever. She didn't want to be found by her father's associates or Kyle's and have her life wrecked by them and their hateful, narrow-minded lives.

*I need an anchor.*

*I need a . . .*

Without letting herself spiral any more, she opened the dating app and started typing a message.

**Lee:** Last minute trip to NY. You around tomorrow? Monday?

**Marie:** Maybe tomorrow. Work on Monday.

**Lee:** All day and night?

**Marie:** Noooo. Work all day. Free after. What time?

**Lee:** Work meetings all day Monday. Maybe dinner? You?

**Marie:** Are you asking to meet for
dinner or have me for dinner?
**Lee:** I want to have you.
**Marie:** Yes.


Kaelee relaxed. Foolish though it was, just chatting with Marie made her feel better, especially the fact that Marie replied so quickly. Kaelee was insecure about her life plan, her book, her decision about whether to finish her PhD, but she was sure of her body and what she could do with it.

*It's not like I am trying to claim it's a healthy coping plan, but I'm not using anyone either. We are both going into this with eyes open. Just a fling. Just a fuck.*

Typically, she went old-school when she traveled, but more and more, that had led to awkward *I'm not looking to date* conversations, as if *I'm only in town for the weekend* was somehow unclear. So many people were looking for that media-created lie that there was such a thing as forever love or that wanting it was something everyone felt. That was pheromones or some other hormone talking. There was even research that kissing and cuddling created some bonding chemical in people. Love was just a mix of biology and societal training.

Lust . . . was something else, and Kaelee would own having that. That was the only reason she'd been tempted to go to the city early. Lust, plain and simple.

Her phone chimed, and the group chat with the rest of the English grad students was a flurry of conversation. A group of them were headed to a dive bar, Marley's House, for drinks and pool, or maybe drinks and darts, or possibly a band. She honestly couldn't tell. The conversation was happening too quickly.

She grabbed a jacket, wrapped a scarf around her throat, and headed out. She paused to throw all three locks. Maybe it was obsessive or paranoid, but she had the super's permission to add extra locks. There was a fourth lock, but that was one that could only be locked from inside. Technically, she had to keep a duplicate key on file for every lock, but she figured she wasn't violating any terms if she didn't *have* a key for it.

She attached her keys to the carabiner that she'd stitched inside her pocket with a Kevlar thread. There was zero chance anyone was taking those without her noticing.

*I'm not paranoid. I'm just prepared.*

By the time she got to the bar where the department seemed to cluster, Kaelee felt a familiar wave of *fuck you, Tripp* wash over her. Mentally, she could summon up the expression of disgust he felt at the thought of his child in a place like this. *Aldens* did not drink in places where the floor was sticky or there were black light stamps on the backs of everyone's hands.

Kaelee *Carpenter,* however, most certainly did.

About six of the English department grad students were all huddled in the area around the dartboards. A very soulful singer, far too good for this bar, was accompanied by an upright bass and a woman on keyboard. Suddenly the cover charge seemed like a small price to have paid. Music like that would get swept into somewhere with a better budget soon enough.

Marley's House had carefully constructed the dive vibe, though. The drinks were still on the high side for a dive, but on the low side for NoVA. It was cheaper than Georgetown bars, though, so that was a plus.

"There you are!" Cherie flung herself at Kaelee as she joined the crowd.

Everyone else nodded or said hi. Only Cherie was so forward. She didn't mean anything by it. She greeted everyone that way. She was a freckled white beauty with shampoo-commercial hair and a love for the WNBA that rivaled the fiercest fans out there. "Drinks on you?"

"Why would I do that?" Kaelee signaled the bartender all the same and ordered. "One of whatever that is, and a double shot of the Macallan."

"Sherry oak, eighteen, or . . ."

"Sherry oak."

The bartender turned away, and Cherie leveled a look at her. "Oh! Are we having a drink to celebrate?"

"Celebrate what?" Kaelee knew what she meant, but she wasn't ready to deal with it.

"Didn't you see the department newsletter?" Cherie tossed her hair with the kind of gesture that was both unconscious and painfully attractive. If she ever actually came out, hearts would litter the ground at her feet.

"No . . ."

Cherie shoved her shoulder gently. "News like that is something you *share* with your friends, in case you were wondering for the future. The right move would have been calling me and saying 'Guess what?' and then preening."

Kaelee sighed. "It's complicated."

"Well, of *course* it's complicated. Half the department will hate you. Some will think that Dr. D greased some wheels." Cherie held up a hand when Kaelee tried to object. "But some of us are just damn happy for you."

"Yeah?"

"Well, yes." Cherie gave her a strange look, paused, and then said, "Look. I don't know what you've been running from, but I know there's something in your past you don't want to share. Like recognizes like. That doesn't mean that *no one* wants to cheer for you."

Kaelee paid the bartender and turned away from the bar to stare at Cherie. "Right. Well, I sold two books."

Cherie lifted her wineglass and lightly tapped it to Kaelee's glass. "To giving them hell and being better than they thought we were."

After they took a drink, Kaelee said, "I sold them six months ago, and I feel a little odd about the whole thing. I'm going up to Manhattan to meet my editor on Monday."

"Need a friend to come along?"

"Seriously?"

Cherie shrugged like it was no big deal. It was huge, though. "I mean, I would have to spend the whole time grading but if you needed me to . . ."

Kaelee rolled it over in her head. She could cancel on Marie. She could just focus on work. Maybe see a show or something. That was the smart idea.

Evander, one of the grad students who was pursuing a PhD in something that crossed into linguistics and Afrofuturist literature, came over then. "Did you read . . ." She braced to hear him say "the department newsletter," but he mentioned a journal article instead.

Evander looked like he was a stereotypical jock; he had a build like a linebacker that was honed by a lot of hours at the gym. The six-foot, five-inch Black man had to curl forward to talk to them, which he did as he started explaining the article he was going to forward them a citation for that week.

Cherie met her gaze and grinned before saying, "Tell us about it, Ev."

And they stood in pleasant company, talking about the pedagogical inconsistencies of whichever article had rattled Evander. Sometimes, Kaelee thought she'd end up staying and finishing her PhD just because of the people. Here, she felt normal, not stand-out, not strange or off-putting. Academics were her crowd. The bookish people, the nerds, the people who stood in a bar talking about research and books.

Four hours later, Kaelee was on the verge of pleasantly buzzed, talking to a woman who was increasingly flirty, but when she asked if Kaelee wanted to leave with her, Kaelee . . . couldn't. Her mind was full of someone else, so she said, "I have an early trip tomorrow."

"You don't know what you're missing," the woman said.

"Definitely my loss," Kaelee agreed. She wasn't going to say or do anything to make another woman feel bad about herself, even if she had decided not to fuck her.

After she left, Kaelee started to make her round of goodbyes. Only one person remarked on her book deal, so Kaelee was fairly sure most of them hadn't seen the newsletter yet.

"Did you just turn that woman down?" Cherie gave Kaelee a look that she usually reserved for criminally bad fashion choices.

"Don't overthink it."

Cherie swirled her drink and stared at Kaelee. "You sick?"

"No."

"You don't have a thing for *me*, do you?" Cherie's expression was taunting, and her gesture at her voluptuous self was one Kaelee dutifully followed with her gaze. She was a gorgeous woman. Generous curves. Confidence. There was nothing at all unappealing about her. Cherie said, "You know, I might be curious, but you're too . . . not my taste, so there's no reason to turn down"—she waved toward the exit—"her."

"I am not even going to try to unpack that." Kaelee paused. "If you need to talk about that curiosity, I'll listen, but I don't crawl into bed with bi-curious friends."

"Ouch. And also, glad to hear you are actually admitting we're friends." Cherie's gaze traveled over the bar. "I heard that word, you realize. You called me a friend. Now you're stuck with me."

"Oh no. How horrible." Kaelee rolled her eyes. "Fine. Yes, I hereby acknowledge that we are friends."

"Good." Cherie tapped her fingernails on the glass as she watched Kaelee. "Did you *meet someone*?"

"Not really."

"Oh my goodness! You did!" Cherie leaned in. "Tell me everything."

"Just a woman I connected with through the app." Kaelee tried to change the subject. "Casual. Not like it was anything."

"Uh-huh." Cherie put her empty glass on the bar. "You don't look like it was nothing."

"It is. I got the taste of her, and it's clouding things."

Cherie gestured. "Walk with me. My car is across the street." As they made their way through the crowd, she added, "So do I take that as a *literal* taste? Or is this metaphorical taste?"

Kaelee laughed. "Are you asking out of your own curiosity or . . . ?"

"Both maybe?" Cherie looked a little sheepish. "I don't think I could do *that* with a stranger. You always say it so casually, though. Like you just met her and you . . ." She gestured toward the floor.

"Went down on her?"

Cherie nodded.

"Do you go down on men the day you meet them?" Kaelee asked.

"No, but—"

"No different, Cher." Kaelee opened the door for her. "There's not, like, a lesbian rule book. I've known who I am and what I like for a long time. When I first came out, I wasn't all about the pussy as soon as I met someone, but I met Marie through an app designed to let me get laid and get gone afterwards."

"Oh."

Thinking nothing of it, Kaelee put her hand on the small of Cherie's back as they crossed the street. They were always touchy-feely. It was no different to Kaelee from steadying a stranger. Cherie had had a drink or two, and they were friends.

"You do that all the time. You're, like, a gentleman," Cherie blurted. "I like it. You're more chivalrous than any of the guys I've dated. I want that."

"So date a different type of guy."

"I don't want to lately. I want someone who gets me. Someone like you." Cherie folded her arms. "Not *you,* though. Sometimes, I just want a woman to actually *date.* Preferably one with arms like yours. All those hours at the gym. Maybe that's the answer. Go to your gym."

"Okay. Is there a question in there? And can you find it for me?"

Cherie leaned against her car. "I should get a rideshare. I think I'm tipsy."

"You are. Want to crash on my sofa instead?"

"Probably a good idea." Cherie locked her car again and took Kaelee's offered arm. "See? Stuff like this. I want to be treated like I'm special. You treat me like that and don't even want to have sex with me. I want to try dating a woman. Be my lesbi-coach!"

Kaelee couldn't hold back her laughter. There was something delightful about exuberant women. Thoughts of Marie intruded again. Tiny, curvy women were a weakness. "If I met you in a bar and didn't know you, I'd totally make a move. You're beautiful, Cher."

"Ugh. Find me a date then." Cherie scowled. "I have no idea how to approach a woman."

"Same way as you approach a man, I bet. You just say, 'Hi, do you want to get naked?' Totally works for me." Kaelee tried for a straight face, but Cherie wasn't the only tipsy person. "It worked on Marie."

"I can't decide if I want to ask a million questions or not," Cherie whined.

"Later when you're sober, you can make a list, and I'll answer them." Kaelee steered her around a group of drunk men who went from looking at Cherie like she was a snack to glaring at Kaelee, as if her presence had stolen their chances.

"Ugh. It's like they think women can't be friends if they're queer," Cherie blurted loudly. She paused, giggled, and said, "I think I just came out! I mean, to strangers and all, but—"

"And to a friend," Kaelee corrected her.

"Yes!" Cherie caught Kaelee's gaze. "Friend, I think I'm queer, and I want to date women. Like seriously. Not like you do."

Kaelee nodded. "Well, then I can be your wing woman or coach, but not in any naked ways!" She shook her finger at Cherie. "I only fuck women I don't consider friends."

"Kae? You need some serious therapy or a good woman to get rid of whatever baggage you're toting around. You know that, right?" Cherie patted her face. "I want a woman with cheeks like yours, too. I could cut my hand on these."

Kaelee chortled. Even in her tipsy state, she couldn't make herself deny that more therapy was probably a good idea. Sometimes the childhood admonishments not to air dirty laundry were still so limiting. Secrets only empower the guilty, but knowing that didn't quite release her from the pressure to stay silent. She resisted, but that wasn't enough.

*I'm going to make an appointment to hash through this, if for no other reason than knowing Tripp would hate it.*

**8**

## Greta

Greta was nestled in her bed reading when her phone buzzed with a notification. She flipped it over to see a picture of her ex. Tasha smiled in that way that had once made Greta feel like she was safe, like everything was perfect. Shoulder-length, golden hair framed a face that would not be amiss on a celebrity. In the picture, Tash was laughing. They'd had a perfect night at the ballet. *I need to change that contact picture.* Seeing her photo felt like cold water over Greta's mood.

"Are you injured?" Greta answered.

The line was silent a moment too long. "I can't call an old friend?"

"Friend?" Greta echoed. "Did you misdial?"

"That's a no then, Greta?" Tash laughed. "Still not ready to put the past behind us?"

For a moment, Greta wanted to say yes. She'd tried that a handful of times after the breakup, but half of those had ended up in awkward morning-afters. Tasha only called when she was already drinking, when she wanted affection, and although Greta understood . . . it also *hurt*. Whatever Tasha was chasing in her life had meant breaking Greta's heart, and that wasn't something she could keep letting herself forget.

"I'm in bed, Tash. If you're not injured or in some sort of peril, and you don't seem to be, I don't have much to say." Greta closed her eyes against the flicker of a tear that threatened.

"I miss that bed sometimes."

"You chose to leave it."

"And you," Tasha added. "I miss *you* sometimes."

"You left *me*, too," Greta pointed out acerbically.

"Friends without sex, then?" Tasha suggested. "Could we try that? I don't want to be your enemy."

Greta sighed. "You aren't. I can't keep letting you in, though, when you've had a few drinks and want to get off. I deserve more."

"I never meant to hurt you," Tasha whispered.

For a moment, Greta wished she could lie and say that Tasha hadn't hurt her, that they had been in different places, but she wasn't sure that lies were useful when they both already knew the truth. "You want to be my friend? Let's try lunch after the holidays."

"As friends?"

"Yes, Tasha, as friends who used to be something else but will not ever again." Greta grimaced. "You only want more when you drink, and I don't want anything from you. Not now."

"Are you seeing someone?"

An image of Lee flashed into her memory, but all Greta said was "Not really your business."

"Fair."

They said their goodbyes, and Greta dropped her phone to her lap. Tasha was far more together than when they split, but every few months, she called. They hadn't seen each other in months—and hadn't landed in bed in longer. Somehow it felt different, using an app to meet strangers and sex with your ex. One felt like being unable to move forward, and Greta was determined not to do that. Not again. No matter how lonely she felt.

When her phone buzzed again, Greta assumed it was Tasha a drink later. So she ignored it to continue reading. The autumn chill outside wasn't enough to make her crank the heat in her apartment yet, so she had taken to editing in her bed under her thick duvet. She intended to have her edits mostly finished before she met her author on Monday next week, so she had her assistant print the manuscript, and now she was working on it old-school—pen on paper. That was how she'd read the first draft, the one she'd preempted. That made it feel strangely *right* to work on this draft of the book the same way.

The phone buzzed yet again. This time, when Greta looked at the message and saw it was from Lee, Greta couldn't stop the wide smile that took over her face. For someone who insisted she didn't talk, Lee had sent a chatty message.

**Lee:** One of my friends just came out to me.

**Lee:** Are you there?

**Marie:** Was she asking for you to . . .

**Lee:** No. She pointedly said she didn't want to fuck me.

**Marie:** Foolish woman.

**Lee:** Yeah?

**Marie:** Definitely. I want to fuck you.

Greta waited for a reply to her bold statement. Her statement wasn't exactly a surprise. *I'd take the train to DC for just a few hours with her.* She'd almost admitted as much in person when they'd been in DC, but it was almost a minute later when the response from Lee came in.

**Lee:** Favorite sex act?

**Marie:** Depends on my partner. I'm not shy.

**Lee:** Meaning?

**Marie:** What do you want? I'll probably try
it unless it's degrading or dangerous.

**Lee:** We're at a party. Fancy catered
mess. Are you wearing panties?

**Marie:** Did you ask me not to?

**Lee:** Yes.

**Marie:** Bare and in a skirt.

**Lee:** Good girl. Where do you want your reward?

**Marie:** Dealer's choice. Will you fuck me in the
library? Behind the shed when they could hear us? Or
is your hand under the table and between my legs?
**Lee:** Best puzzle game *ever* right here.
**Marie:** Ha! Better if it was in person. Naughty
board games? I could do that too.
**Lee:** Coincidentally I'm catching an early train to
the city tomorrow. Wanna play a game with me?
**Marie:** You'll be in MY city earlier? Name your
place. I'm there. Name your game. I'll consider it.

For a moment, Greta wondered if she'd been too forward. They'd
had an electric connection when they met, and Greta wanted more
of that. That didn't mean she wanted to swap cute nicknames, but
it did mean she was still thinking about Lee—and not just sex. Conversation and sex with Lee both sounded good.

So did naughty puzzle games.

Or public sex.

Or . . . a lot of things. The mysterious woman from DC had filled
Greta's fantasies since they met.

There was something intriguing about the woman with the book
tattoo and obvious fondness for secrecy, the sense that if they actually talked they'd get along with their clothes on. Not everyone
in DC was in politics, but Greta could see Lee working for an ad-
vocacy group, as a progressive lobbyist, or even at a research think
tank. Maybe law? Lee was obviously clever and discreet, and she had
the money to pay the Sappho's Kiss Society membership fees. That
meant she did *something* that paid well.

As much as Greta didn't know if she was ready to try actually
dating, she admitted that she felt a lot closer to ready when she
thought about Lee. Maybe it was time to try again. Maybe she ought
to broach the subject with the sexy woman who was commanding
and secretive.

Greta's notifications chimed again as she put aside the manuscript she was reading, drawing her into the present.

**Lee:** Are you at home?
**Marie:** In bed reading.
**Lee:** Something good?
**Marie:** Hot lesbian romance.
**Lee:** Oh? Where are your hands? Show me.

Greta paused at that. This had taken a sudden turn, and she wasn't sure how much she wanted to risk on an app. *How blunt is safe on here?* Sure, she paid for privacy, but what if Lee ever found out who she was? She didn't seem like she was the sort of person to ruin a woman's reputation, but people could surprise you. Tasha was supposed to be forever, had claimed she needed the security of a ring even though Greta wasn't ready, and then she was the one who panicked and moved out.

**Lee:** (If this isn't a thing for you, that's okay.
I have just been thinking about you, too.)
**Marie:** What were you thinking about?
**Lee:** A make-believe party where
you are riding my face again.
**Marie:** Please.
**Lee:** Send me a picture for now.
**Marie:** Of?
**Lee:** Something to inspire me.

Greta weighed the thought of it. As long as her face wasn't in it—or the book she was editing—a picture was harmless. *Right?* Lee looked almost her same age, and there was nothing improper about two consenting adults exchanging selfies over a secure app designed for sexual connections.

Greta rolled over so her chest was against the mattress, arched her back slightly and tugged her shirt lower. She wanted the camera to capture cleavage but no nipples, and then held her arm out and took several shots. She picked the best one and clicked send. Then she deleted all of them.

**Lee:** Gorgeous. I love your breasts.
**Marie:** Thank you. I grew them myself ;)
**Lee:** Shall I worship them tomorrow?
**Marie:** I do like worship.
**Lee:** Your body is made for it.

For a moment, neither one replied, then Lee messaged, deleted it, messaged again. The thought of sentences *not* sent was maddening for Greta. She wasn't exactly Pandora with a box, but she was immeasurably curious, more so when she knew someone was self-censoring what they said to her.

**Marie:** What are you not sending?
**Lee:** I want you to touch yourself for me. I want to see.
**Marie:** No pictures of that. You have to
come here to see that show. But . . .
**Lee:** What?
**Marie:** I touch myself to thoughts of
you almost every night lately.
**Lee:** Now?
**Marie:** I was reading first.
**Lee:** Put the book aside, Marie. Whatever
you do now, I'll do tomorrow.
**Marie:** To me or to yourself?

Again Lee went silent, and Greta knew she was pushing the other woman's boundaries. Lee, for whatever reasons, had already admitted to having control issues. Some women were like that, and typically Greta was fine with it. She *wanted* to please Lee, though. That one orgasm she was allowed to give Lee was hot, and Greta had liked that Lee had asked to be denied and teased. That was the kind of self-awareness that led to explosive sex.

> **Marie:** I want to see you as many times as
> it takes to be allowed to taste you.
> **Lee:** No promises there.
> **Marie:** Fine. You can distract me some
> other way. Fancy a walk through the
> park with me? Sex in the wild?
> **Lee:** Sex in Central Park? Bit risky.
> **Marie:** Not if no one knows.

Greta sent a picture of a toy she'd bought to use with Tasha *after* the breakup, back when Greta thought they might reunite. The vibe slipped into a pair of panties.

> **Marie:** Unused. My ex wasn't willing. Are you?
> **Lee:** Maybe. Seems more like a third encounter thing.
> **Marie:** Tease. I would agree to a third
> time. Right now, I'll already agree.
> **Lee:** Not like dates, but . . .
> **Marie:** Agreed. Parts of me would
> really like more time with you.
> **Lee:** Are those parts wet right now?
> **Marie:** Yes. Thinking about you does that.
> **Lee:** Send me a picture. Good girls get rewards.
> **Marie:** You first.

The answer was instantaneous. The image was a live picture, the sort that has just a couple of seconds of motion, and that motion was Lee with a bright blue vibrator sliding into her glistening wet pussy. All sense of hesitation in Greta vanished.

**Marie:** Pack that. Please.

Then she shimmied out of her bottoms and snapped a picture with her legs splayed open. She attached it to the message.

**Marie:** Toys. Your hands. Your mouth. I want all of it.
**Lee:** Tomorrow. 1pm. Meet at Penn Station.
**Marie:** Yes.
**Lee:** I need to go now. I need both hands.
Be a good girl and do the same.

Then the little dot that showed she was online vanished, and Greta wasn't sure if it was panic or actual need that made Lee run away suddenly. *She* was the one that brought up a third meetup, though.

*Maybe she just means Monday? Two back-to-back nights?*

Greta wasn't sure. She'd take it, though, whether it was Monday or later, even if it meant that the third visit was the end. She let her mind fill with the memory of the sight of Lee when she was approaching orgasm. Seeing her let down her walls, knowing that Greta's had been the touch to make that happen, felt like a victory to savor.

Ultimately, Greta wanted to make Lee feel as good as Lee had made her feel. She thought about all the ways she could do that while her own fingers stroked faster. The photo of the vibe thrusting into Lee's welcoming pussy looped over and over on the screen, and Greta imagined that it was her hand fucking Lee. That Lee was open and eager for her. That Lee had handed over the control for a moment.

When Greta reached orgasm, she was still staring at the video. She sighed contently. While masturbating was not quite as satisfying as being with someone, this time was better than usual. There was just something hot about knowing that in DC Lee was doing the same thing, about knowing she was just as excited by their encounter.

Greta stretched and closed the app after sending one last text.

**Marie:** Thank you. See you at 1.
Message when you get here.

Maybe after this weekend they could try video sex or phone sex. The app had a way to do that without sharing real phone numbers. She hadn't used it, but she'd break the rules for Lee. Try new things.

The next day, Greta woke far too early and cleaned pretty much everything in her apartment. Fresh linens were the first thing. Her old soft sheets didn't seem like *company* sheets.

Her phone notifications buzzed.

**Lee:** Still on?
**Marie:** Yes.
**Lee:** On schedule here. Do you live
in the city? Or in Jersey?
**Marie:** City. Do you live in the District
or outside the Beltway?
**Lee:** Inside. Are we playing Q&A?
**Marie:** Can we?
**Lee:** NY or Chicago pizza?
**Marie:** NY obviously. You? And pie or cake?
**Lee:** All pizza is good. Dessert is different. Tart.
Then cream pies, chocolate, banana, lemon. I
have a whole pie rating system. Cake last.
**Marie:** Pie is serious stuff, huh? Key lime here. Then
banoffee, then chocolate cream, then mixed berry.
**Lee:** Are you trying to trick me into confessions?
**Marie:** I'm intrigued. What if we were friends?
**Lee:** Would friends still have sex?
**Marie:** YES.

As she waited for a reply, Greta opened her closet and put everything connected to her job inside it. There were ARCs, advanced review copies, and a manuscript from Ms. Carpenter, the author Greta was meeting Monday—the one she'd been reading when Lee messaged.

She glanced at the pages now, feeling awkward. The author wrote sex bluntly, and though it wasn't the *point* of the book, only a nitwit would think that sex didn't advance the plot. Learning to trust someone required emotional vulnerability for most people, so a romance that showed that vulnerability was not *failing*. Closed-door sex was fine, too, and Greta almost wished she could ask Ms. Carpenter to do that instead—not because the sex scenes were bad but because Greta was so keyed up already that she couldn't edit this weekend when the sex on the page was that raw.

**Lee:** I will consider this.
**Marie:** I'm a good friend.
**Lee:** . . .
**Marie:** What?
**Lee:** I'm better at sex than friendship.
**Marie:** Luckily, I want both.
**Lee:** Thinking. Be patient.

Having a conversation about sex in the real world after she'd been reading a sexy manuscript added a weird association to the book, one she hoped never to admit to anyone. Greta sighed at the thought. Her author, Ms. Carpenter, already seemed about as approachable as day-old warm fish at the market.

*Maybe Ian will be able to charm her on Monday.* Greta sighed. *I certainly can't.*

Greta's job was an odd mix of personal and removed. She loved what she did, but there was a definite awkwardness to writing notes to a stranger about their detailed sex scenes or about the emotional breakdown of fictional characters. Finding the line between helpful and harsh took practice.

*No more reading* that *book in bed, though.*

She couldn't associate an author's book with her own intimate life. She'd only been editing in bed because she worked there at home sometimes—although she knew it was a terrible habit. Last night, though, getting sexts from Lee made her associate that bed, that moment, that manuscript she'd set aside with a memory of the video clip from Lee.

*I will only work on that book at the office,* Greta resolved.

Keeping her work and home separate would certainly make her current prowl through the apartment easier. For a moment, Greta was grateful that she didn't have to tell Lee what she did for a living. Greta was proud of her career, but she thought back to when Tasha would introduce her and how she laughed off Greta's work.

*What would Tash think if she saw the book I am editing now?*

Admittedly, Tasha had her own baggage about sex, and after a lot of thinking, some therapy, and a not insignificant number of nights with strangers, Greta realized that part of the reason they fell apart was their attitudes toward sex. Tasha still had some shame attached to being a lesbian. The result was that she could only have sex if *Greta* asked for it. Half the time, it also felt like Tasha couldn't get off unless she had a drink or three. The rest of the time, there was a lot of cajoling involved. Even their post-breakup hookups had only happened after drinking.

*Maybe I have a type. Beautiful women with complicated boundaries.*

Greta wanted Lee to be *not* her type. Her baggage was already visible. Control issues of varying degrees warred with any kind of letting go. That ought to be a red flag, but if it was, Greta's libido had decided to be a bull and charge right at it.

"I'm not looking for someone to fix," Greta announced to her empty living room as she scanned every surface for hints of where she worked.

A flickering memory rose up of a drunk bar connection and a woman who was embarrassingly interested once she heard Greta was in publishing. That was one of the few times she'd ever lied outright about her job. She claimed to be a courier for editors. Even that wasn't enough to dissuade the aspiring writer—who honestly could have been a fabulously talented writer, but Greta had worked too hard to build a reputation. She wasn't going to ruin it by fucking someone who wanted to sell her a book.

After one last walk-through to verify that any incriminating evidence was tucked away, Greta was sure her apartment was tidy enough and all identifying things were hidden. It was time to shower and dress.

*What do I wear for a not-date with a woman I want to fuck?*

She weighed the options while she showered and shaved everywhere that needed tidying. She wasn't a jeans person. They were fine, but she'd yet to find a pair that didn't make her curves look overly emphasized. Short with great legs turned into something that made her look *too* inviting when she dressed that casually, at least that's what Tasha had always said.

*And despite two years apart, I still think about her criticisms . . . Even though I know she still wants me, she didn't want to stay with me.*

Greta made a mental note to buy jeans that made her feel confident and work on wearing them in public.

*I apparently have more body positivity issues when I'm dressed than when I'm naked!*

Then, she pulled out a simple wrap dress. Dark blue with tiny little sprigs of flowers, it highlighted her trim waist, and the top dived deep between her breasts, and when she walked, flashes of leg were evident. This wasn't a dress she'd ever wear to work because she felt like a bit of a sexpot in it, but it was perfect for meeting Lee.

She slipped on one of her various pairs of tall black boots and added a black leather jacket she only wore outside of work. Idly she wondered if Kaelee rode a motorcycle. She certainly had the attitude for it.

Back before Tasha, when Greta was in college, she had briefly dated a woman with a motorcycle and a basketball scholarship. Her ex was dedicated and genuinely good at her sport, but Greta was not the right match. On the other hand, the payoff for going to all the home games, though, was that her ex was the kind of strong that made Greta's knees weak and her panties drop. She'd realized that athletes might not have been her match, but strong women were.

Women like Lee.

Greta kept her thoughts as mild as she could as she made her way to Penn Station. She wasn't looking to date, but . . . maybe soon. Maybe it was time to start reconsidering the options. Something about meeting Lee had opened up a crack in Greta's heart and let the fear out. Greta had known logically that she couldn't judge all women by Tasha and her hang-ups. Unlike Tash, Greta's sports-loving ex had definitely been looking for forever, even back then.

*Lee isn't, though. And she's the one I want right now.*

Seeing Lee a second time might've stirred up thoughts of a future, but not *with* her. Lee was crystal clear on that front, and Greta was going to respect that boundary. Maybe they could end up friends with the occasional night together. That wasn't a relationship. Right?

Her phone buzzed as she walked to the meeting place they'd set earlier.

**Lee:** Early. Lunch together? Or should I
grab something before you get here?
**Marie:** Here already.
**Lee:** Willing to share a meal?
**Marie:** Yes

For someone adamant that she wasn't interested in a date, Lee was certainly the one to blur lines so far. Grab a drink. Text socially. Grab lunch. Those were date adjacent. Or maybe they were headed toward being friends.

*Friends do all of that . . . which is why Tash isn't actually my friend. Those aren't things I want with her. With Lee, though? Yes. Definite yes.*

As Greta approached the crowd, she had a moment to take Lee in before she turned. She had on a pair of jeans, name label but well-worn, ankle-high hiking boots that looked like they'd seen some miles, and a plain blazer. As she turned, Greta saw that Lee had a slogan T-shirt under her jacket proclaiming "A well-read woman is a dangerous creature."

Instead of putting her backpack on the roller bag, Lee had it on her shoulder.

"Hey." Lee smiled, but she didn't reach out. She shifted the bag on her shoulder, hand clenched on the strap. "Looks like there are a couple options for a place to grab a bite that might be cheaper than hotel lobby food."

"Can I take one of those?" Greta offered. "Or do you want to put the shoulder bag on the roller bag?"

"No." Lee's smile was tight. "Meeting files. I'm paranoid, I guess." She gave an awkward laugh.

"Big meeting?"

"Maybe? I don't know. I'm starting a new job—no, I don't want to talk about it—but I'm afraid I'll fuck it all up." Lee shook her head. "Sorry. You probably don't want to hear any of that."

"I do, actually. I want to hear it." Greta took a deep breath. "So, what if we tried that whole maybe being sort of friends thing?"

Lee gave her a look. "Define 'friends' for you."

"I guess just people who sometimes talk but are *not* dating?" Greta was about to share her actual name, but Lee looked like she had just swallowed a bug.

"Give me a day to think?" Lee shook her head. "What I need right now is a sandwich and an orgasm. Care to join me for that?"

"Let's grab a cab. That's faster to get both of what you want."

"To where?" Lee asked.

"My apartment if you want. Your hotel if you prefer." Greta shrugged like it was no big deal. To some degree, it wasn't. She was willing to go to a hotel as they had in DC or to go to a restaurant first. What she wanted, what she'd craved since Lee had walked out of the hotel room door a few weeks ago, was another night with her.

Gently, Greta added, "Unless you have early check-in? Or had your heart set on a restaurant? I can be flexible."

Lee grinned. "I remember how flexible you are."

"Name your terms, Lee. You know what I want. . . ."

# 9
## *Kaelee*

The thought of going back to someone's place was somehow less awkward than inviting anyone into the space where she slept. Even if she was in a hotel like she was tonight, Kaelee had a thing about space. She suspected it was a result of having been violated in a space where she ought to have been safe. Since Kyle, she always had a pit in her gut at inviting anyone into her apartment unless they were truly close. Back in DC, she'd invited exactly two people to her apartment: Toni and Cherie. She thought she'd be okay with Toni's future wife, Addie, or with Evander, but she hadn't felt the need to test that theory.

Realizing that Marie could easily be on her trusted-people list after such a short time unsettled Kaelee, but she was an expert at compartmentalization. So she shoved that thought down deep to ponder later.

With a quick peck on Marie's cheek, Kaelee said, "That's perfect. I can order the takeout later tonight if you have sandwich supplies or something at your place."

"Done." Marie pivoted and marched away, glancing over her shoulder. "Let's go. The sooner we grab a cab, the sooner I can get you naked. You should know, though: I'm a step ahead of you."

"Oh?"

A man walking by gave them a second look, but right then, Kaelee couldn't find it in her to care. She smiled, looked Marie over from head to toe, and asked, "Are you not wearing panties under that?"

"If you're subtle, you can find out yourself in the taxi."

"Excuse me?" Kaelee's brows shot up.

Marie laughed. "Lee, I'm not as sedate as you seem to expect. One of my exes had quite the exhibitionist streak." She shrugged. "I realized I liked it, too."

And Kaelee followed after her with a silent prayer of thanks. Becoming friends with this woman might be a dangerous prospect, but Kaelee felt sure she could resist catching feelings. Sex *and* friendship could complicate things, so she needed a minute to weigh it. Realizing it could work didn't mean she was ready to commit to that decision, but Kaelee could admit that it was tempting. *Marie* was tempting.

On the street, Marie gestured to the taxi stand.

"Love the shirt," Marie said lightly.

"I can't spend all my hours working or at the gym." Kaelee shrugged. "I read a lot."

"Same." Marie put a hand on Kaelee's arm. "I like the results of the gym hours, though. In case I didn't mention that last time."

Kaelee smirked. "Which results? The muscles? The strength? The improved lung capacity and energy so I can fuck you longer?"

"Yes. That." Marie squeezed her arm. "*All* of that."

They stood in a silence that ought to be awkward, but somehow felt comfortable instead. After a moment, Marie pivoted to face her. "Dietary restrictions?"

"Food that's not expired?" Kaelee offered with a shrug. "I have no known allergies. Not celiac either. I'm not a huge meat eater, but . . . I grew up in a steak and potatoes household."

"What's your stance on salads?" Marie cocked a hip, stared at her, and asked the question like it was the most serious topic ever.

"Versatile. Cheap. Happy if they have tofu, chicken, or steak on them." Kaelee frowned. "I don't think fish and salad really works, though. I like salmon, but not on salad. Salmon is for sushi or maybe as a main entrée. Not on my lettuce."

"Chinese takeout?"

"I'm a fan." Kaelee grinned. "I spend an hour or two most days at the gym, so I eat like there are no rules."

Marie gave a nod. "I walk every day, but I'm not really a gym person. Far too many offers to 'help' me." She made air quotes. "Typically by men. Not my scene."

Kaelee rolled her bag forward and paused as it was their turn, but she had no address to give. She looked at Marie and said, "That's you. Address?"

Marie rattled something off, and Kaelee pointedly tried not to listen. It was a little foolish, perhaps, because she'd need to get a taxi out later. Trying not to memorize addresses was on the list of rules to prevent relationships.

She opened the door for Marie and then put her own bag in the trunk before going around to the other door.

Once the taxi driver slid into traffic, Marie looked at her. "So your friend needs dating help?"

"Cherie." Kaelee paused, realizing that she had used a real name. "She wants someone who treats her like she matters, *and* she wants that someone to be a person who gets her where she needs to go."

Marie made no move to reach out, so Kaelee put a hand on her knee. It wasn't hand-holding or anything. It was just a way to touch her. Perfectly normal. Nothing weird about wanting to have contact with the woman she intended to have moaning in the next hour.

"It speaks well of you that she asked you about that." Marie parted her knees slightly, an invitation that Kaelee wasn't sure she should take.

"How long to get there?"

"Usually not very," Marie said with a laugh in her voice.

Kaelee gave her a stern look. "Be good."

"Yes, ma'am." Marie practically purred the word, and Kaelee couldn't help but laugh as Marie scooted a little closer.

"Patience is a virtue." Kaelee kept her hand right where it was, not accepting the invitation—although she considered it for a brief moment. They had all night, though, and a quick touch in the back of a New York cab wasn't exactly the thrill she was seeking.

After a moment, Marie said, "You know, when I was a kid, I thought the expression was 'Patience is a virgin.' I spent a lot of time wondering what a virgin was, and then when I found out when I was in middle school, I had a lot of questions about who *Patience* was. It was incredibly awkward when I transferred schools to St. Lucia's and met not one but *two* girls named Patience."

"Tell me you didn't!" Kaelee said.

"Sister Theresa was not amused when I asked *which* Patience was the virgin in the expression, and if it meant she would have an immaculate conception like the Virgin Mary." Marie smiled widely at the memory. "I was so grateful that my nonna had a sense of humor when Sister Theresa called her."

The cabbie laughed from the front seat, obviously listening to their conversation. "My abuela would not have laughed at that."

Marie met his eyes in the rearview mirror and nodded. "Patience wasn't laughing either." Then she glanced at Kaelee. "I got sent home the next day for announcing 'Maybe Patience is *not* a virgin!'"

Kaelee laughed. "Tell me you didn't say that loudly. . . ."

"At lunch," Marie confirmed. "She shoved me and left."

"Poor Patience." Kaelee squeezed Marie's knee. "So Catholic school?"

"All twelve years," Marie confirmed.

"Are you . . . close with your family?"

"Now? Yes. There were years when I think they wished I was more like Patience, though." Marie stared at the window then, drifting into thoughts that Kaelee both wanted to ask about and didn't.

*Not a date. I do not date. This is not a date. Friends chat.*

The cab dropped them off in front of a nice building that had a very late 1800s architecture vibe with arches at the top of tall windows that were evenly spaced on a grayish stone front. A tall iron fence with spiked tops encircled the property.

Despite knowing that personal details weren't the way to keep a distance between them, Kaelee felt like a jerk for not saying any-thing personal. "I have no contact with my family," she blurted out. "Changed my name. Left. My grandmother was cool, but she's gone now. My parents are hardcore evangelicals of the 'hate the sin *and* the sinner' sort."

"They're missing out. Even without knowing you *that* well, I'm sure of that much," Marie said lightly, directing her to the front of the building and keying in a five-digit code on a box. "I have a few cousins who don't stay in touch because of their closed-mindedness. My parents are great, though, and Nonna is amazing."

Once they were through the gate, Marie gestured toward the front of the building and walked up the steps to the main door, where she waved a pass at another box. "You don't need to tell me things if you don't want, Lee. I would like to be your friend . . . maybe friend with extras if that works for you, but I'm not trying to pry out se-crets. I'm just a talker."

Marie shrugged, and her tone was light. She held the unlocked building door open and nodded toward the stairs. "Fourth floor. Do you want to take the elevator?"

She gestured to the side, where a cage-style elevator waited. The car was open and looked ancient. The metal cage had been painted a bright teal at some point, but there were faded patches now.

"Does it work?"

"Most of the time. It's as slow as walking up the stairs, though." Marie looked down at Kaelee's bag. "Your call."

"Stairs." Kaelee said nothing more as she followed her up the first flight and the second. Then she added lightly, "This was the better plan."

Marie glanced over her shoulder. "Why's that?"

"You have an amazing ass. I half thought I'd imagined how per-fect it was because I was desperate at the hotel, but it's just right, a Goldilocks-level ass."

The answering trill of laughter made up for Kaelee's feeling of awkwardness. "Goldilocks ass?"

"Not too flat, not too big. Just right."

"Oh, Lee, I could like you," Marie said quietly. "You're irreverent and gorgeous and . . ." Her words faded into a sigh, but Kaelee understood. They had a strong physical spark, but she *liked* Marie, too. She liked making her laugh, liked her joyous personality, and found her sense of adventure tantalizing.

*I don't date. I need to get out of here.* Kaelee's panic flared at the comfort she felt around Marie. They very obviously had the potential to be friends, but how was that even possible when they were likely both lying about their names and everything else?

By the third floor, Kaelee suggested, "Can we agree to saying something like 'can't answer' rather than lie?"

"Are you lying about things?" Marie asked. "Other than your name, of course."

"Not your real name either, then?"

"My middle name. Catholic school." Marie glanced back again. "At least I landed with Marie rather than Mary. The Devon family named all seven of the girls Mary, so the last six went by nicknames or middle names. I'm a middle-name Marie. My brother is a middle-name Joseph."

Kaelee offered, "Lee was my grandfather's name. So what were the other six Marys called?"

"Matrice for Mary Therese, Mary Ann was just Mary Ann, Elizabeth for her middle name, Celeste for her middle name . . . and I can't think of the other two." Marie stopped at the landing. "This floor is mine."

"The whole floor?"

"Each floor is an apartment." Marie keyed in a code, and then she turned two locks. "Oh! Kate! The other two sisters, twins, were Kate and Frankie, short for Mary Catherine and Mary Frances."

She opened the door and stepped aside, sweeping one arm out in a gesture of welcome. "Welcome to my home. Would you like a sandwich, salad, or sex?"

Kaelee stepped over the threshold and pushed her bag to the side as Marie closed the door and locked it. "Would it be rude to ask for all three?"

"As long as you don't want them at the same time, that's fine." Marie stepped up to her and tilted her chin upward, seeking a kiss, which Kaelee happily bestowed.

*Kissing her feels right.*

The intrusive thought made Kaelee decide to skip over the softness they were drifting toward. She slid both hands along Marie's spine and over the curves of the gorgeous woman in front of her, stopping when she had two handfuls of firm ass in her palms.

Marie pushed her hips forward and straddled Kaelee's thigh. Her dress parted in the process, and Kaelee pulled back.

"I have one spare pair of trousers, and as much as I want to have you up against me, I can't walk around with that kind of perfume on my jeans, darlin'. So tell me, are you really not wearing knickers under there?"

With a laugh Marie flipped her skirt up. "No."

"Lord have mercy. Keep that dress right like that." Kaelee stepped past her and walked over to the kitchen. She washed her hands and looked back at Marie. "I'm not touching something that pretty until any germs from the train and taxi are off my hands."

"Oh."

Kaelee gestured at the kitchen table. "How sturdy is this?"

"Sturdy," Marie said with a breathier voice.

That decided everything that mattered just then. Kaelee crooked her finger and pointed at the table. "There. Now." When Marie didn't move instantly, Kaelee pulled the chair out. "Come join me. I'm not so sure about *real* exhibition, but . . . I'm happy to put you on display right here. Does that work for you?"

Marie nodded. "Yes, please."

"Such a polite girl, aren't you?" Kaelee watched as Marie swallowed. "And you like praise."

"Yes." Her cheeks pinked slightly at the admission.

"And punishment?"

"I don't know," Marie confessed as she stepped up onto her dining room chair like it was a ladder. Kaelee kept her there, standing on a chair in the midday sun with her skirt hiked up and her pussy exposed.

"What if someone can see in your windows?" Kaelee glanced over. There were thin shutters, so it was unlikely. "Do you think they are looking at you? Watching you?"

"I'd be fine with it," Marie admitted. She paused before adding, "I'd like it. You can open the blinds."

Kaelee did so. "What else do you like?"

"I liked the orgasm denial thing you let me do with you last time. Watching you like that was sexy," Marie admitted. "And you talking to me the way you do. I like that."

"So praise, exhibition, and one of us not being entirely in control," Kaelee surmised as she stroked a hand along Marie's bare legs. "That's what the remote control was about."

Marie nodded, already trembling.

"And you like this, don't you? Me staring at you? Making you wait?" Kaelee thought about all the things that weren't as possible in one-night-only encounters. Maybe friends with benefits was exactly what she needed. She already instinctively trusted Marie. With time, Kaelee was sure she could lower a few boundaries with her. The thought of that sent a flash of heat throughout her body. "If we're going to do this semi-regularly, we can explore some things."

"If you want." Marie stared down at her.

Kaelee chuckled. "Have you seen yourself, Marie? I definitely want. Sit down here on the table like the delicious treat you are."

Marie's breath caught, but she obeyed.

"What a good girl. Why don't you wait right there while I hang up my jacket."

"Okay." Marie watched her as Kaelee folded her jacket and put it over the back of a different dining room chair.

"Such a good, patient girl, aren't you?" she murmured approvingly.

"For the right reward," Marie countered.

"If you want a reward, you need to stretch out for me." Kaelee helped her recline back. She stood over Marie as she spread her legs as far as they could comfortably go and gently pulled her bottom toward the very edge of the table. The whole time, Marie watched her attentively, keeping her body pliant in Kaelee's hands.

"I wish you could see yourself right now, darlin'. Trembling and exposed. Your chest is heaving. Did you notice that? I can't decide if I want those pretty titties covered or bare."

Hurriedly, Marie reached up and pulled at the dress, tugging the cleavage so that her bra-clad breasts were partly exposed.

"More," Kaelee ordered.

Marie loosened a tie at the waist. In a moment, her dress gaped open. She was dressed in nothing more than a bra and boots now.

"There you are. Perfection." Kaelee caught Marie's hand and directed first one and then the other to the juncture of her thighs. "Hold yourself right there, darlin'. Show me where you want me."

Marie widened her legs more.

"I wish I could paint, Marie. You are a glorious vision." Then Kaelee slid her fingers over the warm wet lips that were exposed for her. "I want you to think about how ready you are *right now* and remember that you got here without me hardly laying a hand on you. That's what I want when we have our eventual video call, Marie. You just like this. Are you going to do that?"

"Maybe."

"Maybe?" Kaelee echoed.

"You can try to convince me," Marie taunted.

"That's why I ask about punishment," Kaelee said as she loudly dragged the chair forward. "That sassy attitude."

"Maybe." Marie's voice quivered. "We could negotiate."

Kaelee wasn't sure about that, but she was sure of what she'd been craving. She lowered her mouth to her waiting feast.

# 10

## Greta

An hour later as she stood in her kitchen making sandwiches for them, Greta admitted, "I feel like all my norms are a little muddled right now." She was naked still, aside from her boots, which was not how she usually walked around her home.

"Why's that, darlin'?" Lee leaned against the counter, hands in her pockets, shoulders loose and slouchy like she didn't have a care in the world. "And do you want help?"

"No." Greta gave her a look before resuming slicing a tomato. "Because I'm not sure I can sit at the table and eat a sandwich like it's no big deal when you just . . ." She gestured with her knife. She wasn't sure of the words, a rare event for her. Finally, she decided on, "Ravished me? Devoured me? *Right there.*"

Lee smirked. "I was promised lunch. So I pulled up a chair and—"

"Hush." Greta laughed at the ridiculousness of it all. They weren't even sharing their real names. For all she knew Lee could be lying about *everything,* but the app vetted everyone. Membership required submitting backgrounds, financials, criminal history checks, and annual medical reports. It was thorough, specifically to look for safety issues and weed out any red flags.

"So . . . friends talk. Tell me three things about you that are true."

Lee sighed. "Are we sure about this part? Trying to be friends, I mean."

"I enjoy your company so far. Maybe you'll tell me something horrible, but right now, I like talking to you." Greta took the drying heart of romaine and switched to her lettuce knife. She wasn't entirely sure that bruising the lettuce really mattered, but she had resolved to treat Lee to her best hospitality. Really it was only reasonable after the way Lee had treated Greta's body.

"Fine. I was born in the South," Lee said.

Greta's laughter came out like a bark. "Caught that when you started letting your accent free. How about something I *don't* know?"

"I'm a grad student."

Greta pointed her bright blue lettuce knife at her. "Really? How old are you?"

"Twenty-nine. You?"

"Thirty-three." Greta frowned. "How in the world can you afford the app membership if you're a *student*?"

"Is that one of your questions?" Lee asked. When Greta nodded, Lee added, "My grandparents were wealthy. They left me a fund that makes student life affordable. I live *mostly* like a student, but the app is my indulgence. Plus, there's the new job. I can afford it, Marie. I'm not here as a con woman."

"Well, obviously. If you were, I suspect we'd be at a restaurant rather than in my kitchen." Greta held up an onion. "Yes or no onion?"

"No onion." Lee stared at her. "So you know I'm a student, that I don't like onion, that I lived in the South, and that I live in DC now."

Greta rolled her eyes. "The stuff I figure out doesn't count on the list."

"Fine. I have my master's in history, and I'm working on a PhD in another field. That's why I read *Jane Eyre*. I like both lit and history." Lee pushed off the counter and walked over so she was standing behind Greta. Without actually touching her, she stood close enough that Greta could feel the heat of her body. "I also like naked women making me sandwiches. Does that one count?"

"Nope." Greta looked over her shoulder and grinned. "Observational notes, Lee. I can tell you like that because you put your hands in your pockets, so you don't touch me. Your eyes tell me a lot."

Lee chuckled. "Guilty as charged. So tell me something about Marie, thirty-three, lives in a one-floor apartment, no pets, decent job to afford this place. Wears dresses. Has an exhibition streak. Likes books."

"Books was going to be my big reveal," Greta teased. "However can you tell?"

"Just a few overstacked bookshelves in here. Big clue."

"Ham, roast beef, chicken, or turkey?" Greta asked.

"As one of the three things I am to tell you?" Lee asked lightly.

"Absolutely not." Greta slid to the side. "I will observe which you use. All the sandwich things are here." She pointed at the bowl of tomato, the tidy stack of chopped lettuce, carrot shreds, sprouts, two kinds of cheese, several meats, as well as assorted spreads. "Steadily gathering information, so you have to reveal something juicy."

Lee gave her a dirty look and licked her lips. "Oh, I like your juicy—"

Greta slapped a hand over Lee's mouth. "That's not what I mean. I know you like *that*. Observational skills."

Without missing a beat, Lee licked the palm of Greta's hand.

Greta giggled and pulled her hand away.

"I must have not been doing a good enough job if you could still observe things."

Greta stepped back again. "Make your sandwich."

She thought Lee was going to resume her closed-book stance. Maybe being friends wasn't possible. They were still lying about their real names, avoiding sharing jobs, and maybe that was enough of a clue.

Then Lee said, "I saw the first Darbyshire book on your shelf. Have you seen the show?"

For a moment, Greta froze. She considered admitting that she saw it *before* it was public, that she had read the sequel, that she had edited both of those books. But Lee was staying so close-lipped that Greta couldn't do it. She couldn't tell her what her job was. Yet.

Instead she said, "Not a fan of the book or show?"

"History major. So yeah, I was definitely a fan. I even went to one of her signings. She lives in DC, you know."

"Which do you like more, the book or the show?" Greta asked.

"The book is better, although the show is good, too. That lead actor . . ." Lee had an odd smile. "She's something."

The urge to defend Addie flared in Greta. She *was* something. She was a sweet, loyal, incredible woman, and she kept Toni happy in a way that made her easier to deal with. Greta felt like she was going to have to spill everything.

Then Lee said, "The author is a lucky woman. I've seen them around the city a few times. They seem perfect together."

And Greta relaxed and said only, "They really are. I've seen them in Manhattan. We have associates in common, actually." That wasn't a lie, but it really wasn't the whole truth either.

*What am I to say? That I know them? That I edited the book?*

Lee hip-bumped her. "Make your sandwich. Want to watch an episode of the show while we eat?"

"Are you trying to avoid chatting with me?" Greta asked, tone as nonthreatening as possible.

"Nope. I have it on good authority that friends watch shows together." Lee smiled disarmingly. "In fact, I have watched the entire first season at least twice because so many of my friends are invested in it."

"Same." Greta fixed her sandwich. "Water? Wine? Juice? Soda?"

"You don't need to wait on me," Lee said a little sternly. "How about you point out the cupboard, and I'll get us both a drink."

Greta pointed. "Wineglass for me. In the fridge is a bottle of white I opened last night. Pour me a glass?"

Lee nodded and got them both a glass of wine. Greta tried not to think how nice it was to have someone at ease in her space the way Lee seemed to be. She wasn't as crude as she tried to seem either; she knew exactly which glasses to use. Lee pulled out white wine glasses, smaller bowls like a champagne flute, but shorter overall than either red wine glasses or champagne flutes. Greta had all three, as well as martini, margarita, cocktail, and highball options, and, of course, water tumblers. She hadn't been able to throw them out when she and Tasha split, although the last time Greta had anyone over in a group had been several years ago—with Tasha.

Thoughts of the life she thought she would have put a damper on Greta's mood. Tasha's decision to upend their lives shouldn't mean that memories of her could intrude as often as they were lately. At least now they were not tinged with rage or betrayal, merely a sense of letting go, but Greta was ready to skip over this whole process of healing.

*But not so much that I can be friends with Tash. Not now. Hopefully someday . . .*

Being around Lee and the emotions she evoked triggered something for Greta, some urge to move on, and she wasn't ready to face what that meant.

*I need to get my head together.*

Greta walked past Lee and went to the bathroom to grab a robe. She washed her face and stared into the bathroom mirror. "I am overreacting. Lee is nothing like Tasha. I am not dating her. Everything is okay."

She'd never felt so emotionally unsettled by a hookup, but she'd also not made a habit of inviting people to her home.

When she came back, Lee looked at her, expression open and worried. "Are you okay?"

"I was just realizing you're the first woman who's been in my kitchen since my ex." Greta shook her head.

"How long ago?"

"Two years." Greta cinched the robe belt tighter.

"Do you want me to go?"

"Not at all."

"You got dressed. . . ."

Greta shook her head. "No, I put on a robe. I didn't want to sit there and shiver while we watched a show. Plus, I am not going to sit on my sofa naked while you're still fully dressed."

Lee removed her shirt, leaving her in a sports bra and jeans. "Better?"

"Some." Greta walked to the sofa and sat on one end and looked back at Lee.

Lee followed with the drinks and her own sandwich, and Greta took in her ease at carrying everything else and asked, "How long did you wait tables?"

"You're good at this game." Lee sat and gave her an appraising look. "About three years during college. Flexible hours, no taxes on tips meant more in my pocket. I was on my own by then, and every dollar mattered." She took a bite of her sandwich, and after she finished it, she added, "I pay *all* my taxes now."

They ended up chatting rather than watching the show, and afterward, Lee took away the dishes and went to the bathroom while Greta wondered if this was the end of their night.

When Lee came back, she was no longer wearing her jeans. She smirked as she stood there in a bra and briefs. "I took off *two* things, Marie. It's only fair that you remove at least one. . . ."

"I'm only wearing one."

"Fine. I'll agree to you removing just one thing." Lee sighed like it was a huge concession. "Do you want to stay out here? Go to your bed? Am I to leave?"

"Stay here." Greta stood, dropped her robe, and spread it out on her sofa. "May I touch you?"

"You don't have to, you know. I don't keep score." Lee stood staring at her. "Just pleasing you is a joy to me."

"That's not a reveal either. *Observation*," Greta said softly. "I knew *that* already. I pay attention to you, and I bet you know me better than you think. Things you've observed. You know I want you to feel good. You know I want you naked against me. What else? You know I like books, lesbian historical television, and you know where I live, how I like my sandwich. . . ."

"True," Lee admitted. "I know how you taste, how you laugh, that you probably would've had onions on that sandwich if I wasn't here."

Greta laughed softly.

"*You* know how to seduce me," Lee whispered.

"See? We aren't *just* strangers." Greta was staring at Lee.

When Lee nodded, Greta asked, "Do you have the toy from the picture?"

"I do. No bag searches at the train station; it makes for easier packing when you take a train. Carry-on luggage can be awkward in airports." Lee stood there, chatting as if that was why she'd asked.

"Will you get it?" Greta turned the television onto a channel she'd occasionally streamed since Tash left. A lot of the listings were cringe, but she had a "rewatch" option on a film listed that she had liked. "How about this? Women directed. Women owned."

Silently, Lee walked away and went to her luggage. She made another trip to the bathroom, and when she came back, the dildo was still damp. "I washed it so—"

"Not for me. *You*." Greta put her back against the end of the sofa and opened her legs. "You sit right here. Back to me. Throw your legs over mine. If the mood strikes you, do something about it. If not, no pressure . . ."

As Lee stared at her, Greta shoved the coffee table back from the sofa and turned on the video, jumping forward so it was already past the awkward setup scenes. On the screen, two women had arrived at a rental house only to realize that the homeowner was still there.

Lee pushed down her briefs and sat between Greta's legs. She took Greta's hand and put it firmly on her stomach, so Greta was half holding Lee.

"No promises," Lee whispered, but she put the dildo on the robe in front of her wide-open legs.

"No demands." Greta kissed her neck. "I like this, too. Just holding you, feeling your skin against me as I watch the movie."

"She's going to watch them fuck, isn't she?" Lee asked.

"And *we're* going to watch them." Greta draped her other hand over Lee's parted legs, casual but not actively touching Lee intimately. "If you want me to touch you, let me know. I'm yours to command."

"Not right now."

They were silent as they watched. The couple on the screen went from talking in whispered voices to opening the bedroom door partway, allowing the older woman to look in if she happened to walk by or hear them.

The "older" woman was probably only four or five years older than the couple, but she was dressed as if she were older. Dowdy glasses, a high buttoned blouse, and a long skirt were supposed proof that she was older than the couple. As she stood in the hallway, she unbuttoned her blouse and played with her nipples. The couple paused their make-out at the sound of the homeowner moaning.

"I like imagining her watching us right now, admiring your body as you watch her," Greta whispered. "I bet she'd be touching herself already if she could see you."

A few minutes later, Lee moaned softly as she shifted against Greta, but she still didn't touch herself. So Greta kissed her neck again and whispered, "I love this film. It just works for me."

"Yeah? Why's that?"

"Beautiful women who like to be watched." Greta made a small approving noise. "She's the director, too. Owning her body. It's powerful to do that. To take what you want. I like when you take what you want, too."

"I'm not like this with people I don't know," Lee confessed as her fingers parted her folds. "Not . . . so free."

"Can I touch you, too?"

"Please." Lee stared at the screen like she was transfixed. "Truth number two, I like to *watch* more than I like to *be* watched, but under the right circumstances, like right now, it's good to be watched. . . ."

Greta traced Lee's already wet pussy, slowly and gently, keeping the pace Lee had set already.

"I feel guilty not touching you right now," Lee confessed a while later. Her hand was on the dildo now.

"What if you pretend you're fucking me when you use that on yourself," Greta suggested.

Lee nodded, but she didn't move yet. "Can we shift a bit? This isn't the right position for me."

"Put me where you need me."

So Lee turned them, so she was sitting facing forward, ass almost on the very edge of the sofa, legs still parted over Greta's lap. The position felt more precarious, but Greta kept one arm wrapped firmly around Lee's waist.

For a moment, Lee shivered. "Cold air on very hot skin." She stared at the screen where the owner of the house had just asked to film the two renters. "Rub my clit, Marie, like she is on the screen."

Greta obeyed, matching her pace to the film.

A few moments later, Greta looked down as Lee slid the dildo home, fucking herself in time with the action of the couple on the screen.

"So beautiful," Greta whispered. "You are so stunning like this, you know."

"You make me *feel* beautiful," Lee said, voice barely audible over the sounds of the moans on the screen. "Safe. Wanted. Powerful."

"Same." Greta stared at the now glistening dildo thrust into Lee's body and hoped upon hope that this was the start of something that could continue.

For a few moments, the only sounds were hard breathing, moans, and begging from the screen—and from Lee. When she reached her orgasm, Greta's arm tightened around her as her back arched.

They stayed that way for several moments until Lee stood on shaking legs. She stared down at Greta. "Your turn." She tugged Greta to her feet and lifted one leg, so a moment later, Greta's foot was resting on the sofa. "I'm parched after all that."

"There's wine—"

"Not *quite* the nectar I want." Lee shoved the coffee table back, sloshing the rest of their wine, spilling it onto the table.

And Greta decided she wasn't about to complain, not when Lee was retaking control. Lee's need for control was the price of time with an amazing person. She was worth it.

## 11

## *Greta*

The next morning, as she walked into the office building in Midtown, Greta was grateful for the sunglasses that shaded her tired eyes. She'd added anti-redness drops and used her "emergency moisturizer," a bee venom–based cream that tightened the weary skin around her eyes. Typically she put work above everything. She knew better than to try to pull all-nighters, for whatever reason, at this point in life. She wasn't *that* old, but she didn't have the ability to go without sleep the way she had in her early twenties.

*Lee was worth the lost sleep.*

They'd been up until well after midnight, and then dozed briefly only to wake and have sex again before Lee washed up and left with a promise to message after her big meeting.

Greta wished there was another option for them, one that wasn't only the choices of friends who fucked or never seeing her again. What they'd done already was enough that Greta couldn't guarantee that she could remain emotionally detached. They clicked. They laughed. They had orgasms.

*Oh my God, the orgasms . . .* If they had been dating, Greta was fairly sure that finding time to do anything but have sex would be a challenge, but they lived in different cities. They weren't going to date.

Want to go to a show or something tonight? As friends?

she quickly texted.

**Lee:** Sure. Do you want me to grab tickets?
**Marie:** No, I have a pair I was going to toss to
hang out and have orgasms with you later.
**Lee:** Want to do both? With me?
**Marie:** Yes please. I may need a nap first.
**Lee:** Same. Message you after meeting and
naps. Wait. Broadway is dark on Mondays.
**Marie:** Not on Broadway. Explain
later. Elevator here. Must run.

She surrendered her sunglasses, wincing at the harsh lights as the elevator was about to stop on her floor. She was rarely this late, even though it was barely eight o'clock, but Ian was waiting in her office. He had a stack of pages in his lap, which he set aside as she walked in.

"Triple-shot latte. Coconut milk. Mint." Ian walked over and handed her the cup of coffee. Today was not a tea day.

"Remind me to never fire you." Greta gratefully took the coffee. It was just this side of too hot, but today it was fine. If all went well, she was hoping to take a sick day or a work-from-home day tomorrow. Generally, she was not keen on coming into work this tired, but this was why God made subways—so dead-on-their-feet New Yorkers could get to work without being a danger to themselves or others. Walking felt complicated.

"So much better. I don't want to scream suddenly." Greta took another long drink.

"Hangover?"

"No. Just up too late. A friend was in town unexpectedly." Greta tried to keep the memories of Lee out of her mind. Her burning cheeks let her know she'd failed.

"Mmmhmm." Ian gave her a look that said he heard what she hadn't said aloud. "I figured that out when I saw on the tracking app that you were at the train station and then didn't leave your apartment."

"The *what*?"

"Tracking app. I told you I was sharing your location with me. How am I to look after you if I don't know when you'll be here?" Ian gestured for her coat.

"You track me?"

"Yes, and you can track me." Ian had his back to her as he hung her coat on the coatrack that had come with the office. "We talked about this, Greta. If you're going places you don't want me to know, switch it to off."

She stared at him, mouth slightly agape.

He glanced back. "Just because you aren't showy about it doesn't mean I'm not aware that you're . . . one of us."

"I'm not closeted, Ian. I just don't have a person in my life. If I did, I'd bring her to *some* functions." Greta couldn't stop the mental image of showing up with Lee at a few events. In reality, most of the things she attended were still business. Agents worked the room. Editors always wanted the next hit. Her social lunches or cocktail parties for this or that book event were still work. They looked like a social life to outsiders, but they were work. "I like my private life private."

"Obviously. You don't owe *anyone* any explanations." Ian settled back into the chair beside her desk.

Greta realized that his stack of pages was on a lap desk. "What's that?"

"Gay literary mystery."

"I haven't acquired one of those. . . ."

"Yet." He gave her a wide smile. "I was thinking of acquiring it if I can get my boss to agree."

Greta laughed, grateful for the topic change. "You know your 'boss' trusts you, right? You have great taste, a strong editorial eye. . . ."

"I don't want to abandon you, and I still want your guidance."

"My advice wouldn't end if you were working on books without me," Greta stressed. "I ask others—including you—for opinions. Even if you were to take a job elsewhere—"

"Not the plan!" He met her gaze. "We can't change the industry if we don't have more queer editors in the larger publishing houses. I want to be one of them, but I'm not ready. Not entirely. But if you co-acquire this book with me . . ."

"I need to read it first."

Ian nodded. "I don't want to leave you and become a full-time editor. Not anytime soon. I want *this* book, though." Ian put his hand on the pages almost affectionately. "Middle-aged gay author, activist, and it has the kind of authenticity I want as a reader. Not the *othering* of gay men that I run into when I'm looking for a book *for me*. I get that those books have a readership, which is fine, but . . . they're not written by or for gay men."

Greta took another drink. "I hear you. I'll prioritize it this weekend."

"That's all I need." Ian beamed in a familiar sort of joy. She'd felt that, the hopeful feeling before acquiring a book, the gleam of excitement.

They settled into their individual work stacks, and there was a part of Greta that was grateful they'd developed this friendship, as well as their work relationship. After roughly an hour, she looked over at him. "I like that you work in here some days."

"I started because it makes people leave you alone when you're in a less charming mood," he said mildly. Then he shrugged. "I stay because you're my friend. I like being around you."

"We ought to grab coffee sometime outside work."

"Your treat. I can't expense the coffee if it's not work." Ian's words were a challenge or maybe just a question.

"I'd like that." Greta didn't really have much of a social life the last two years. She worked. She worked some more. She had flings with strangers. Aside from visiting her sister every so often, she was isolated.

*Intentionally so.*

Maybe it was time to rediscover that part of her life, too. Her breakup with Tasha had led to a lot of withdrawing when she realized that all her friends were *their* friends. Tasha wasn't ready for their life together, even though she had pressed for marriage to the point that Greta felt like she had to ask her to move in, had to put a ring on her hand.

Then six months later, Tasha moved out and took all their friends with her.

*And I crawled into my shell.*

Lee was the first person since the breakup who had made her ponder if she was ready to try dating again. Not *just* because of the sex, either. They'd had fun talking yesterday.

*Maybe it was the idea of having a friend to spend time with. . . .*

But Ian was her friend, too, and maybe Emily Haide could be. There were other editors and agents she was friendly with. Maybe she had the possibilities of social outings and just hadn't admitted that.

*Maybe I need to find a book club or something. . . .*

Almost two hours later, her phone buzzed, and Ian grabbed it. She was inordinately glad that he wasn't ready to move on to another publisher. He could. Plenty of places had been trying to lure him away the last year, maybe thinking that he was the reason Toni Darbyshire was with her. Ian was decidedly out, and a lot of people were new enough not to realize that Greta herself was also out. Being privacy focused meant that a fair number of people were oblivious; they hadn't met Tash because it was so long ago in publishing time. Turnover in the industry was frequent.

*Or maybe it's because I don't match their stereotypes.*

"I'm glad you haven't left for greener pastures," Greta blurted out. She wasn't usually so blunt or emotional, but she would be lost if Ian did leave. Training a new assistant always had a learning curve that wasn't ever as easy as she expected.

"I have no intention of leaving. I do think I ought to get a better raise this year." Ian grinned as he stood. "That was the front desk. Your author and the delightful Ms. Haide are on their way up."

Greta nodded. "See them to the conference room for me. Art needs to talk to them now before we do anything else."

"*You* aren't meeting them at the elevator . . . ?"

"So far, Carpenter is as approachable as an old hound with a sore tooth. I want to have something for her to focus on when we meet, and you're a bundle of happiness so . . ." Greta made a shooing motion. "Go be charming. I'll be in with the art."

Ian laughed. "I am *always* charming."

"I am not."

"Obviously," he teased.

Once he was gone, Greta called the art department. "Our author's here."

"On the way," Shay said in her perpetually cheerful voice. "I'll grab Charlie. It's the only way to separate her from her work."

"The problem with a good publicist," Greta agreed with a laugh.

She had a great team. Charlotte was the kind of publicist other publishing houses would love to steal, and Shay headed up a group of designers who were either creating the trends or finding ways to keep their spin on existing cover trends fresh. Ian, of course, made Greta's part of the book process run smoothly. Marketing was still in flux. They had good people, but they weren't as gelled as the other departments.

*They'll still charm even a shy author like Kaelee Carpenter.*

With that thought in mind, Greta walked toward the conference room, expecting to have all of five minutes there without the distraction of art and publicity. *This will be fine. We'll get the author over her reserve.* Greta saw Emily, the agent for this book and Darbyshire's books, through the glass walls as she stepped in. She saw the back of another person, short dark hair that looked a lot like Lee's.

"Hi, I'm Greta. How lovely to meet y—" Her words faltered as the author turned around.

The look on her author's face was as stunned as the feelings churning in Greta's stomach.

*My author couldn't be . . . She wasn't . . .*

But then *Lee* walked over and took Greta's still outstretched hand. "Hi. I'm Kaelee Carpenter. How nice to finally meet you in person."

# 12

# Kaelee

In the list of ways today could go tragically wrong, not even a hint existed that "fucked my editor" could be a possibility. She'd known that Marie was a fake name obviously, as was Kaelee's own shortened version of her name. They'd admitted as much yesterday, and no one was completely honest on apps, and on an app designed to help people maintain their privacy, Kaelee assumed lies were far more common. It was why she didn't want to talk about jobs or real life with women she met through Sappho's Kiss.

*I was in her apartment.*

*Of course Marie had read Toni's book and seen the show, she's Toni's editor. She's my editor. Marie is Greta.*

*This can't be happening.*

"I'm sorry," Kaelee blurted out, trying to sound less panicked than she was and hoping everyone thought she was just an anxious author. That part was certainly true until *this* moment. *It's hard to find my editor intimidating when she rode my face and begged me to fuck her.* Kaelee glanced at Greta, making eye contact in what she hoped was a *come with me now* and *we need to talk* way.

Kaelee tried to sound calm and asked, "Can I run to the ladies' first? I should've stopped on the way in, but before we get started . . ."

"Of course!" Greta, who was her actual book editor and somehow also the woman she was knuckle-deep inside last night, sounded strained.

*Do they all know something is wrong right now? Can they hear it?*

"Let me show you the way," Greta said, gesturing to the hallway in the same way she had navigated Kaelee through her apartment building last night.

Emily gave Kaelee a tense look and whispered, "Are you okay?"

"Totally. Can you take a look at the covers while I'm gone? I'd love your thoughts. I just . . . need a moment to pull my nerves together."

"Do you want me to come with you?"

"I'm fine. Ma— *My editor* can direct me," Kaelee choked out. She affixed her plastic smile, the one she'd perfected in the Alden household. Her face felt too tight, as if she could crack and something precious would spill out. It had been so long since she needed to pretend a dumpster fire was okay.

"Right this way," Greta said, standing in the doorway of the conference room and gesturing toward the hall again. "Ms. Carpenter."

*Do not touch her. Do not even brush against her.*

Greta's heels made no noise on the low-pile, industrial-grade carpet. Voices rose and fell from cubicles; machines hummed softly in the background. The two of them, however, were silent as they walked toward the restroom. They couldn't talk freely out here as they walked passed cubicles of people, guaranteeing a lack of even the semblance of confidentiality.

A few tense moments later they arrived at a restroom, which was currently empty. Greta jerked open the door with considerably less grace than she normally had. "Here we are." Greta sounded louder than normal as she added, "I'll just pop in and check my makeup while we're here if that's okay. There are multiple stalls."

"Sure . . . ?" Kaelee stared at her editor, trying to wrap her mind around how impossibly awkward this was. They were inside a corporate bathroom and smiling tensely.

*I had her bent over the sofa last night. Both of us moaning. Watching porn.*

Kaelee felt like she was breathing too fast. Panic threatened to rise and carry last night's meal with it. She was going to puke in the bathroom at her publisher's office. Kaelee wished she had an anxiety pill just then. In terms of most awkward possible reveal, this was it.

*I fucked my editor.*

Greta click-clacked her way inside the bathroom. She pushed open all three stalls and verified that they were totally alone. Then she stared at Kaelee. "Oh. My. God. I cannot believe that you . . . that we . . ." She was wide-eyed with what looked like the edge of a full-blown panic attack. "I can't believe that you're *Kaelee Carpenter*."

At least Kaelee wasn't the only one shaken by the fact that they knew each other. There was small comfort in that fact. They were both overwhelmed by the mess they'd found themselves in.

"I am so sorry," Greta blurted out. "I had no idea. I mean, Lee, Kaelee, I guess I should've said, 'Hi, are you by any chance an author?' But do you know *how many Lees* I've met?"

"No . . . ?"

"Exactly. A lot. There were a lot." Greta leaned against the wall, closed her eyes, and took several deep breaths. She opened her eyes and added, "It's such a nongendered name and—"

"Hey." Kaelee stepped in front of her, too close to be casual, and asked, "Are you going to freak out for a while yet? Because I bet we don't have *that* long until someone checks on us. Both your assistant and my agent could tell something was off."

"You're right. Of course you're right. Fuck." Greta took a loud breath, her head tilted back like she was staring at something on the ceiling.

*Lies. Everything was lies.*

"Fuck." Kaelee counted her breaths, forcing herself toward a calm that she didn't feel.

"You're my *author*."

"I am aware." Kaelee folded her arms over her chest. "It certainly creates an awkward thing. I mean, I was liking our power balance the way it was, but you're in charge of my book's fate so . . . I guess that changes things."

Greta gaped at her like she was unstable. "I can't ever see you like *that* again, Ms. Carpenter. We will pretend it never happened and—"

"Guess that 'being friends' plan was a wash, then," Kaelee sniped, feeling immeasurably insulted. She hadn't done anything wrong, but she felt like she was paying a price.

*Like I'm losing her.*

As much as Kaelee understood the logic in Greta's words, understood that she had to let this go, let *Marie* or Greta go, and she couldn't even argue, it stung to be tossed aside so easily. That was why she didn't let feelings get involved, why she didn't let her walls down. People always disappointed her. Greta was no different, apparently.

"Lee . . ."

"I don't use that name professionally, *Greta.*" Kaelee went into a stall, mostly to buy herself a moment to push back the sense of heartbreak that was churning in her stomach. She closed the stall door and took a moment to just think. She had started to let Marie in. She knew better, but she had still done it. Now she needed to pretend that the woman she's been growing closer to was a different person entirely. She'd finish her meeting and head home. She wasn't going to have dinner—or sex—with Marie again. What they'd shared was functionally dead with no warning at all.

*Don't be so weak*, her insecurities ordered. She had spent a lifetime so far hiding her vulnerable parts, and this was the woman who could influence her career succeeding or failing. *She can crush my dream.*

When Kaelee walked out and stepped around Greta to wash her hands, she could almost feel Greta staring at her. And unlike last night, this stare didn't make her feel warm and safe.

*How could I have been so stupid?*

"Can we talk tonight?" Greta asked quietly. "This was obviously not your fault or mine, but it happened, and now we need a plan."

"Do I tell Emily?" Kaelee met Greta's gaze in the mirror.

"I don't know. If you decide to do that, can it wait until you and I talk?" Greta pressed on her eyelids as if to hold them still or push back pain. "I have no right to ask you that. As your editor I would never ask you to keep book-related things from your agent. I hope you know that. However, this is personal. We need to talk and decide what, if anything, we need to share with her or with the company."

"You're still the person I was starting to trust." Kaelee realized she sounded irritated in a way that did neither of them any favors, so she tried to soften her tone. "All I need to know is if you're going to cancel my book deal. The ARCs and the announcement are about to go out, and . . . it's a good book, right?"

"No! I'm not going to cancel it. Why would I do that?" Greta looked at her like she was speaking in tongues. "I don't know if I can edit your second book in good conscience. This won't mean canceling anything, or *you* losing anything. I'll make sure you are protected. You did *nothing* wrong."

"Neither did you." Kaelee frowned at her. "And you aren't as observant as you claimed if you think I'm not losing something."

Greta shook her head. "The priority is protecting you, the book, the house. I'm in a position of power over your career. This could . . . ruin me. If people found out that I . . . that we . . . I'd be done. Maybe I should be."

"Absolutely not! You had no idea I was your author. I'm not going to lie, and you're not going to lie. We met as strangers, Greta. That was it. What we do next is the concern. So let's get back to the meeting. I heard my editor was a real powerhouse, and I want to hear what the marketing plans are," Kaelee said lightly. She couldn't stop the urge to look after Greta, who seemed to have the same reaction. "I don't know how to tell my editor that I'm terrified of a tour, and I really, really would like to stay as reclusive as possible. I'm hoping that will be something my agent can address."

They stood in the small bathroom a moment.

Then Greta visibly straightened. She pulled her shoulders back and met Kaelee's eyes. "I feel like something beautiful was just torn out of my reach. I want you to know that. You are an amazing woman, Lee. That could have been more than sex for me. I think it already was becoming . . . It doesn't matter now, does it?" She opened the door and in a professional-sounding voice said, "If you want a more leisurely tour of the offices, I'm sure either my assistant, Ian, or any of your team would be happy to show you around and load you up on copies of our upcoming books."

Kaelee *had* to get her control back so she could manage this meeting. Following Greta's lead to talk about books seemed like a wise plan. "Any luck on getting Toni to sell you a new book yet?"

"She'll send it when she's ready." Greta nodded her head once, as if emphasizing her own declaration. After an extended minute, she said, "Speaking of, how are you progressing on your sequel?"

"Finished it before I sold book one. Revised it." Kaelee shrugged like it was no big deal. "Emily's been reading it. I think she's almost ready to send it to you."

"Really?" Greta paused mid-step and glanced over at her.

"I had it in my backpack yesterday." Kaelee shook her head, as if the gesture could stop the flood of images that were roiling in her mind. Her voice came out wobbly as she added, "Sent a partial of a *new* book to Emily already, too. I *want* this career. Toni may still waffle on it, but I have no doubts. I want to write, preferably commercial, popular fiction."

Greta met her gaze. "I won't let what happened derail that, Kaelee. I promise."

They reached the conference room again. Greta opened the door and motioned her inside.

With a resolve she hated to call up, Kaelee smiled and stepped forward.

Now instead of a stack of glossy cardstock, the pile of oversized cover mock-ups were spread out in a row along the table. Six concepts. Each one had her name and her title. Seeing the row of covers with her name on them made her forget everything else for a moment.

"I'd buy this one if I saw it." Kaelee tapped the corner of the fourth cover. The blue background jumped out in a way that made her think of books in the genre that were on her shelf. "I don't love that font, though."

Emily's smug smile was unmissable as she looked around the room at the assembled group.

Kaelee asked, "What?"

"That was my *exact* opinion. It's always refreshing when an author thinks marketing-wise, not just 'Oh! Pretty!'" Emily gestured expansively. "Look at the others, too. Obviously, something about that cover resonates. Are there others that jump out at you?"

It felt like a quiz, one she really wanted to ace as Greta watched and waited. The desire to impress her was awkward, but it was undeniable.

Kaelee paused and looked at each cover, thinking of the hot books in the genre. She didn't want hers to look like a riff on any of them, but she wanted to match them tonally. As she went through the row, commenting on what did and did not do those things, she caught Greta's approving smile.

That expression ought not warm her the way it did, but she couldn't ignore the flush of happiness she felt. The worst part of this was that she realized that she and Greta *really* clicked in their interests. *Greta liked my book.* They shared an interest in fiction, not just in a love of reading, but in books and publishing. Greta had edited the best book Kaelee had read in historical fiction, and she'd edited Kaelee's own book. More and more, Greta was revealing herself to be exactly what Kaelee craved in a friend, as well as still being her ideal lover.

*And I can't have her in that way ever again.*

By the time the morning meetings had ended, they were behind the planned schedule. The publicist, Charlie, looked at her with an assessing gaze. She was a tall woman with the sort of debutante beauty that would make Kaelee's mother ask about her "beauty regimen," but she also had an understated way about her. With more attention to style, Charlie could force every eye to her. Instead, she wore no noticeable makeup—including the sort necessary for a natural look. Her blazer was boxy rather than slim cut, and both her trousers and shoes were basic black.

Like recognizes like, and Kaelee knew without asking that Charlie had secrets. If anything, it made Kaelee relax as she realized that Charlie was probably intentionally downplaying her beauty. There was little chance she didn't know what she looked like, not with that kind of confidence.

"It can be a lot," Charlie said. "We're pros at this, but you have to be willing to trust that."

"I'm certain you're all great at your jobs," Kaelee said.

"Ha! Spoken like a woman used to handling dissent." Charlie eyed her, handed over a business card. "We really are on your team."

"Unless the book fails," Kaelee muttered.

Charlie reached out, not quite putting her hand on Kaelee's wrist. "Our job is to make sure it doesn't."

"You can't guarantee that. Any of you. Ever." Kaelee sounded confrontational, which was the wrong tactic here, but she couldn't stop her fears from burbling from her mouth. "What if something awful happens? Or worse . . . what if *nothing* happens?"

"Then we reassess for the paperback release." Charlie shrugged. "Go to lunch. Relax."

"Why don't we just get carryout? Or delivery or whatever?"

Kaelee tilted back in her chair after noticing Greta look at the clock and then at Emily. "I don't need to go to a restaurant. At home, I'd be making a sandwich or grabbing takeaway to eat at my desk."

"We can wrap this up and still more or less make the reservation," Greta started. "Ian?"

"On it!" Ian was already on his feet.

"*Or,*" Kaelee said firmly, drawing a curious look from both agent and publicist. "We focus and get this finished. I don't need wined and dined. I need marketed and promoted, and getting finished sooner means I can take the train home sooner."

Charlie gave her a beaming smile, and Ian eyed her curiously. Greta looked away, but not before Kaelee saw a disappointed look wash over her face. *She couldn't possibly think I'm staying now?* Of course Kaelee couldn't ask that.

"What if we agree to a *celebratory* meal later, Kaelee?" Charlie eyed her again, and Kaelee made a mental note that the publicist was a little too observant.

"I have a train back to—"

"Not tonight. On the event of your first big victory. That way no one feels like we are neglecting you." Charlie had an expression that said she threw down a challenge, a dare of sorts.

"You are more optimistic than I am," Kaelee pointed out.

"I know." Charlie met her attention head-on. "However, my job requires me to think big, and *Revel* makes my job easy. I read the book, Kaelee. This isn't just a case of getting the cover copy and talking points. That happens, too, but I read your entire book. I *know* how to get publicity for a book like this."

Kaelee laughed. "That confidence you're flashing around probably makes your job easier, too."

"Confidence and bravery, those are the tools that publicists need." Charlie shrugged like it was no big deal, but she looked a little smug, too.

Kaelee eyed her with more curiosity. "What exactly do you see as your job?"

"Easy. Stay in the background. Insist people notice the star I am pointing out to them." Charlie tapped her pen against the table. "I can work with you as is. A little media training wouldn't hurt but—"

"I worked with Rossi and Aubert years ago."

"Oh my."

Kaelee's opinion of Charlie went up as she peered at Kaelee. The media management company her father had used was hella expensive, but they were good. The old man might be a misogynist and a vile homophobe, but he knew where to spend his money in order to hire the best. Kaelee hadn't fallen prey to the lie that people with evil views were all stupid. Tripp had built his financial holdings, ruthlessly and well. He was a smart man, and he hired smart people.

"May I ask why you had media training?" Charlie asked politely.

This was the time, the logical opening to tell them who she really was . . . well, who she *used* to be. The only thing Kaelee had to do was open her mouth and say it, tell them her father was a generous donor to the far right, admit that she had been raised in a hyper-religious household. She could omit the trust fund part.

*And the predatory ex.*

*And the money he funneled to book banning.*

*And the fact that he's dangerous.*

Instead she shrugged. "My father's company had them on retainer. He got me a few sessions before I went and embarrassed the family. You know how parents can be." Kaelee braced for more questions, hoping to counter them without confessing her familial history. "I can handle interviews. I don't love them, and I'd prefer to avoid any visual media."

Greta's gaze darted to Emily, who was watching the back-and-forth between Kaelee and Charlie with an increasingly blank expression.

*So no avoiding tour . . . or interviews.* Kaelee winced internally.

Charlie leaned forward slightly, not smiling now. "So let's talk about the tour. We're liking six cities, but once we get early reads and account numbers, we may want to increase that."

"Or decrease it," Kaelee suggested hopefully. Tour was not appealing in any way. Neither was any TV exposure. She'd felt sure that those things weren't in her future. Most authors were lucky to get an assigned publicist or a publisher throwing money at promotion. *How do I express gratitude without seeming contrary?* At such moments, it would be genuinely great to have Toni there to offer tips.

*Although those tips hadn't saved Toni from travel. . . .*

*But my book is so much smaller!*

"I sincerely doubt that tour will decrease," Greta spoke firmly. "The team will get your book in the right hands. Toni's endorsement carries weight, too. And of course, the book is simply delicious."

Kaelee studied her expression and posture in search of a lie or deceit. Pulling on every media training lesson she had to keep her expression closed, Kaelee asked, "You mean that?"

"I preempted," Greta stressed. "I had never met you, have no loyalty to Emily—"

"Gee, thanks," Emily drawled.

"The point, Ms. Carpenter, is that this team can see what I saw at first read: a successful book that with the right backing could be a season standout." Greta looked down then, lifting the meeting schedule as she did so in an obvious statement of changing topics in some way. After a pause, she carried on. "Right. Well, accounts and marketing and the demographic for books like yours have us ending in California or starting there. Chicago, obviously. Seattle?"

Charlie picked back up from there. "We could do both Seattle and Portland, but I wonder if we ought to look at a few of the cities where Toni's book stood out. The numbers out of Houston look incredibly strong. What do we think about starting there?"

"In Texas? With my *sapphic* fantasy?" Kaelee frowned. Her only experience with the state had been via her father.

"In Houston, Austin, and San Antonio, there are a lot of our target readers, and the major cities skew blue." Charlie's smile was brighter somehow, even as her voice took on a cajoling note. "Trust me, Kaelee. There are so very many amazing booksellers in *every* state. I won't steer you wrong."

"Charlie is a master at this," Greta interjected.

"Right. Texas. California. Pacific Northwest." Kaelee shook her head, marveling at the thought that there were already four cities, possibly five, she'd be visiting as an actual author. "Not North Carolina."

"Why?" Charlie and Greta both said at once.

"I don't want to see my family." Kaelee cut her gaze toward Greta.

"Sounds fine." Charlie made a note before tapping her fingers on the table pensively. "Richmond has an excellent morning news program. . . ."

She looked so harmless, but it was quickly apparent that Charlie was the queen of fast-fired topics that made it hard to refuse *everything* on her plan. The epiphany made Kaelee hopeful for her book but also cautious about her secrets.

Ultimately, the afternoon part of the meetings stretched until almost three o'clock. It would've been longer, but they hadn't taken the long gap for lunch that had been on the schedule. Various people from different accounts, marketing, library, and design filtered into the room. Kaelee felt more than a little overwhelmed by the number of people dedicating their days to making her book able to reach readers. There was a weight to it that she hadn't expected.

*I won't let them down. Any of them.*

# 13

## Greta

At the end of the meeting, Greta casually opened the app on her phone to message Kaelee. Emily side-eyed her for looking at her phone during a meeting, and there was no way to say, *Oh, hi, I'm not ignoring her. I'm messaging her to say I need to talk, in person, tonight, because we have been having incredible sex that must now end.* There really was no *polite* answer she could say in public, so Greta simply ignored Emily's disapproving look and opened the app quickly. She made eye contact with Kaelee and then sent the message.

**Marie:** Please talk after work?

After everything that had happened, how much Greta had hoped that they could be friends at the least, she felt like a weight was filling her stomach and something acidic was trying to escape her throat. In the next few minutes, everyone else was milling around the conference room, talking socially to Kaelee and trying to make her smile. They all knew she'd been reticent to come to the meeting, aloof in her email, and their charm was on high effort now. It had been the whole meeting, and Charlie, especially, had been adept at managing Kaelee while Ian had been reserved. A few times, Greta glimpsed the strong-willed woman she knew, but in sum, Kaelee seemed to continue to be standoffish.

*How was that shy-seeming author the same woman as the one in my apartment last night?*

Greta clutched her phone briefly as Kaelee glanced over at her. Then she placed her phone face down on the conference table and turned to smile at Emily. The willowy agent had pulled her hair back in a slightly too-tight chignon. Her eyes had the telltale shadow of frequent long nights with not enough of a recovery between them.

"Are you okay?" Greta asked Emily quietly. They weren't close friends, but they'd shared enough celebratory and commiserating conversations in the roller coaster of the last year of the Darbyshire book that they weren't just colleagues anymore. "Work? Life?"

"Work's good." Emily's smile was as tense as her expression. In this industry, long hours were the norm, and they all knew it.

"And outside of work?" Greta pressed.

"There's an outside of work?" Emily countered, looking slightly more genuine in the moment.

"Fair, but . . . you're okay? Toni's okay?" Greta pressed. She hadn't known initially that her star author and the typically shrewd agent in front of her had grown up together, but after buying Toni's book, Greta understood that Emily was protective of her in the way a fierce older sister was. Greta had been grateful for—and occasionally envious of—their friendship. Most of her relationships with close friends had been worn and battered by Tasha's dramatics.

*I need more friends,* Greta admitted. *Real friends, not fairweather ones.*

Emily glanced over to make sure no one was listening, and then said, "Toni's fine, and I will be. Had a lump. Then a breast biopsy. It has had me worried, and typically I'd talk to my bestie but . . ." Emily shrugged. "Toni has a lot on her plate, and she doesn't need me adding—"

"Bullshit. That woman would chew glass for you. She has no deadline, and her fiancée is doting and happy." Greta shook her head before piercing Emily with a look. "Last I heard, her mother was doing as well as she ever is, too. Talk to her. That's what friends do."

Emily sighed. "I know I ought to. Toni is so *much* when she worries. It might not be obvious by her prickly exterior, but Toni is the sweetest woman I've ever known. If she knows I'm worrying, she'll end up camped out on my sofa and making chicken noodle soup." Emily's lips quirked in a small smile. "She's sure soup cures everything."

"We should all be so lucky to have loyal friends like her." Greta glanced over at Kaelee, who was now cornered by her increasingly enthusiastic publicist. Charlie would shepherd the release like a mother pit bull guarding a newborn pup; she was a glory to behold when she was allowing her charisma to run free.

"Charlie took a liking to her," Greta remarked. "Maybe Kaelee will warm up to her."

Emily followed Greta's gaze, which couldn't stay off of Kaelee despite efforts. "What do you think about Kaelee?"

*I think she's stunning, and funny, and needs someone to love her . . . and in more than a few brief moments I wanted to be that person,* Greta thought. Aloud, she said, "She's talented. More commercial than Darbyshire, too. The sex in the second draft is sizzling, but not gratuitous. Well, maybe a *little* gratuitous in the second act, but readers will love it."

"She has the sequel ready to submit."

Greta nodded, pretending not to know as much. "Do you think she'd be amenable to having Ian as her primary editor?"

"I thought you loved the first book?" Emily prompted.

"I do."

"Yet you want to pass it over?" Emily frowned. "Ian's great, of course, but . . . why?"

*Because last night, she was spread open like a gift while I touched her,* Greta thought, cheeks burning at the mental image.

"With Toni's new book coming in, you know I'll be busy there and—"

"Toni's not going to be done for a couple months. Kaelee's new book can be in your inbox by Friday." Emily nodded like she had solved a potential problem. "She's driven."

"I can see that. Two books already?" Greta aimed to keep her voice completely level. "I just don't know that we are the best fit. She seems not to like me, which is fine, so if she wants to shift, I will understand. That's all. Sometimes people just don't connect. Maybe she'd be happier with Ian. Just ask her. I want to publish her, but Ian has an easy way about him that I lack."

"Did she say something?" Emily pressed.

"Nothing like that. She's fabulous. She's done nothing amiss. I just want her to be happy. Ask her for me. That's all." Greta resisted a dozen other things she could have and likely should have said to Emily about Kaelee. The words were there on the tip of her tongue, but she wasn't sure she could violate Kaelee's privacy that way. Instead, Greta asked, "Do you feel like she'll do okay with the marketing plan? She seemed pretty resistant to any touring or events. I don't want to start waving around contract clauses. . . ."

"I'll talk to her. She knows there's a tour clause." Emily shot a smile at Kaelee, who was now watching them intently. "Like Toni, but . . . more so."

Greta sighed. "I figured that out. For *Toni*, I can bend on that point, you know, for book two. Whatever terms we set for Toni's next contract are not precedent for *all* your clients, though, and that includes a tour clause. Toni has the power to negotiate there, but Kaelee will likely need to tolerate a four- to six-city tour at minimum."

"I can manage both of them." Emily looked around the room. "It's easier when we all want the same thing: the books to sell."

*I suspect I want a few other things, too,* Greta thought, but that certainly wasn't a conversation she intended to have—at least not until she talked to Kaelee. *What if Toni knows, too?* Greta wasn't a prude. She wouldn't have acquired Kaelee's extra spicy book if so, but she wasn't the sort of person who made her intimate life public.

Discretion was a habit she'd adopted because Tasha was an attorney, but Greta *liked* her privacy now.

"You'll tell me when you get biopsy results?" Greta asked quietly. "I don't want to pry, but if you need a friend . . . you can reach out."

"It's probably nothing. I had been thinking about doing the gene testing already, but . . ." Emily shrugged. "I'll tell you, though, when I know, and you're right. I'll talk to Toni. I'm sure it's fine, but it's hard not to worry—and I didn't want her to bundle me off to her guest room either."

"I get it. Every woman deals with the worry at some point," Greta murmured. "If it's not a pap, it's a biopsy. I think we'll all have some reproductive drama . . . even those of us who aren't at risk for things like pregnancy."

*I said it. If I have to tell Emily, I've prepped the field.*

*Or Kaelee could just accept Ian as her editor.* That was a nice, tidy solution. No admissions, but the book and its lovely author were protected. *And Ian is ready.*

"Ah. I wasn't sure how out you were." Emily eyed her. "You acquire lesbian-focused books, have a gay assistant, and have built an incredibly strong female team. . . ."

"I'm not actively dating, but I don't hide my identity either." Greta shrugged, wincing internally over the fact that she really wasn't actively dating. She'd thought about it, wanted to try it again, and now that the end was here, she could admit to herself that the thought was entirely because of Kaelee.

"Same," Emily said. "Although I'm more bi or pan, not strictly lesbian." Emily glanced around the room, looking at the assembled group and undoubtedly realizing that they had a *very* queer team for a very queer book.

Emily glanced at Greta. "After Toni's and Kaelee's deals, though, you and I are going to have a reputation for queer-only authors."

"Good!" Greta laughed. "I'm glad we can have that reputation and a job these days. It wasn't too long ago that books like theirs weren't picked up by bigger houses. As a young reader, I didn't see myself in books very often." Greta heaved a deep breath and added, "Anyhow . . . I'd like to know when you get the biopsy results. Toni ought to know, too."

"Fine." Emily pointed at her and smiled. "You and I are going to have a luncheon socially at some point, too. We spend far too much time on work things to not socialize."

Greta tensed, feeling guilty, and said only, "The wedding is only a few months away. I assume you're in the party. Best woman?"

"Toni agreed to a tuxedo dress." Emily laughed. "I think she's going to ask Kaelee, too, or maybe Addie claimed her. It's a small wedding party. I haven't asked Kaelee just in case they didn't say anything to her, but I assume we'll all be there."

Greta's mind filled with the possibility of dancing with Kaelee, of talking to her in a social setting as a friend or editor, and she couldn't stop the smile that came over her. Maybe the upside of their affair ending was that Greta would get to know her as a casual friend.

Then Kaelee was headed their way, and Emily's professional expression returned. Before Emily could say anything that involved whisking Kaelee away, Greta spoke. "I promised Kaelee the ten-cent tour of the office, and since I was going to work from home today until our meeting was scheduled, I could walk her to the subway or put her in a cab after that."

"You're not coming to the cocktails at the thriller conference?"

"Ian is." Greta waved to him, beckoning him closer.

His cheerful smile was like medicine to her mood, and she knew he could tell that there were things under the surface today. Charlie likely could, too. Greta hoped they'd assume it was just because everyone was handling Kaelee with kid gloves.

"You summoned?" Ian teased.

"Emily is headed over to the Killer Cocktails event." Greta waited for a moment since Ian's megawatt smile made it clear that he understood what the next part of her statement might be. "There's a pass for one of us to go, and that headache from earlier is threatening to flare up. So unless Ms. Carpenter would rather you do the tour, I was thinking you could take my place.”

“You’re lucky I plan ahead for your dastardly schedule shifts,” Ian mock grumbled. Then he turned to Emily. “Walk with me. I know I have an emergency jacket in the closet in our—in *Greta’s* office.”

“‘Our office’ is more appropriate, especially since you’re about to start acquiring a few projects,” Greta pointed out with a smile.

Emily raised her brows in interest, as Greta had hoped, but she was talking to Kaelee: “Do you mind? I could go late and—”

“I’m sure M—*my* editor, *Greta,* can be trusted, and if not, I can hail a cab just fine. You realize I have visited the city dozens of times.” Kaelee had a fake smile on as she looked at Greta and then back at Emily, and Greta felt sick that she’d lost the real version of Kaelee, the one she’d known as Lee.

“If you’re sure, I’ll call you tomorrow then to discuss any follow-ups?” Emily half asked, half declared.

“Sounds good,” Kaelee said cheerily.

They all said their goodbyes then. Once Emily and Ian left, and the rest of the team had cleared out, Greta turned to Kaelee. “What do you want to do?”

“Am I talking to Greta the editor or Marie the . . .” Kaelee swallowed. “I don’t know what to call you.”

“I’m the same person.”

Kaelee gave her a look. “I’m guessing that most of your authors don’t have you beg—”

“Kaelee!” Greta looked through the glass walls. “Obviously our incredibly *recent* past makes things a little awkward. Do you want me to pass your book over to Ian or another editor? I suggested it as an option to Emily in case you want to switch editors.”

“Why?”

“If you’re uncomfortable.” Greta tried not to let a quaver into her voice. She’d just lost her friend Lee, and she might be losing a book that she was very optimistic and excited to launch. She wanted to do right by both the book and the woman, though.

Kaelee sighed. "I guess being friends with your editor is weird?"

"Not at all! I'd love to stay your friend and your editor, but . . . this is your decision." Greta folded her arms over her chest. "At least I know you don't hate me. When I emailed, you were so formal. I started thinking you were either extremely introverted or maybe . . ."

"Bitchy?"

"Well, *yes*." Greta paused, eyes going wide as she realized that her author refused to meet her in DC so she could have sex. "You said you couldn't meet up when I was in DC."

"I had plans."

"You did not. You met me for . . . you met me at the hotel," Greta countered, voice dropping to a whisper at the last word.

"Meeting an editor for schmoozing? Pass. Meeting a sexy woman for a stress reliever? Yes." Kaelee smiled in a way that tightened Greta's body in anticipation of something that could never again happen. "I have priorities."

"You're terrible." Greta laughed.

"You'll get used to it since we're going to be friends," Kaelee countered. "Dinner and a show?"

"No office tour?"

"Honestly, I have no interest in that." Kaelee paused and tilted her head. "Maybe that's a silver lining. I'm not nervous around you now. When you were the big-shot editor who could make or break me, I was terrified."

Greta shook her head. "I don't know how to be your friend and your editor."

"Too bad." Kaelee stared her down. "Your edits were good, and I know you didn't buy my book because I give excellent oral."

"Stop."

For a brief moment, Kaelee seemed to drop all her walls. "Look. I just lost something that I was willing to move outside my comfort zone to have, so I'm probably going to make smart-assed comments when there are no witnesses. It's that or find a bottle and a woman, and as much as it pains me to say it, I don't want anyone but the woman I just lost."

"Oh."

"Maybe this is just my bad luck. Maybe it's a good thing, and now that we fucked it out of our system, we can be friends." Kaelee's fists were tightly curled, and her voice was drawn taut. "It's not like we could've had an actual relationship, and sex with the same person always eventually gets old, so this could be for the best, right?"

"That's definitely one way to look at it." Greta kept her voice light, but the truth was that she didn't think that sex with the same person *always* became stale. And even if that were true, she couldn't imagine that they were anywhere near that point.

"Would you like to get ice cream and go for a walk in Central Park?" Kaelee blurted out.

Greta smiled. "I would. Let me get my bag and switch into walking shoes. Come to my office . . . ?"

Somehow every sentence felt potentially dangerous right now. She didn't know Kaelee Carpenter, author, and what she knew of Lee was sexual and flirtatious. Navigating a new dynamic felt fraught.

Kaelee trailed behind her, silent and tense.

"Everyone here thought you were incredibly shy," Greta offered as she opened the door to her office.

"I'm not. I was nervous, though." Kaelee walked over to the window, staring down at the city.

"I remember you mentioning that about your meeting."

Kaelee glanced over at her. "You're kind of a dream editor, and I was intimidated."

"No need. Seriously, I bought the book because it's good. As an editor, the success of a book reflects on me, so I want you to succeed beyond your dreams." Greta pulled off her boots and slipped on tennis shoes. Business women in skirts and sneakers was a common enough sight here that she no longer felt awkward about the pairing. She certainly could walk all over in heels, but right now, this felt like a better choice. Not sexy. Not anything but casual. "And honestly, I *like* you as a person. Charlie did, too. So do Ian and Emily. You make people want to invest in supporting you, Kaelee."

"Thank you," Kaelee said, sounding a little shy. "I really do want this, the career, the book to flourish. That's all true. I know you hear a lot from Toni about how she wants to teach—"

"She likes the writing life, too," Greta said firmly.

"I think so, too, but this? This whole career? It's a dream I was afraid to own. I don't want to fuck it up." Kaelee looked so vulnerable in that instant that Greta wanted nothing more than to hug her.

"I believe you'll have it," Greta offered. "There are no guarantees in this business, but you wrote a damn good book. That's where the rest starts."

Kaelee nodded and then she gestured for Greta to walk in front of her. It was familiar and new all at once, and Greta's heart tightened a bit over both parts. She reminded herself that it was not atypical to walk out of the building with an author. Hell, they were supposed to go to lunch together. There was nothing here to raise brows or spark whispers, but as they left the office, Greta was careful to keep an exaggerated amount of space between them.

The reality was that it was less about appearances and more about Greta's overwhelming urge to touch Kaelee.

## 14

*Kaelee*

Now that they were alone again, Kaelee was struggling to remember that Greta was her editor, not the gorgeous woman she'd exhausted the night before. She'd managed fine during the meeting, but being alone with Greta complicated things. They made it to Central Park in comfortable-ish silence, but Kaelee had to resist the urge to put her arm around *Greta*. It wasn't as if they had walked around all couple-y in the past, but being aware that she couldn't touch Greta was doing something to Kaelee's impulsivity.

"I wish we'd had a chance to use your remote control toy before we discovered this," Kaelee said as they walked along a path inside the park.

"Damn it, Lee. You can't *say* things like that. Not now." Greta's cheeks were bright red.

"*Kaelee*. Not Lee."

"Right. Using your correct name ought to help, right?" Greta smiled tightly. "As I said, I suggested to Emily that your next book be with Ian. Perhaps that would be for the best."

"So you don't love the book as much as you said?"

"Now who has a praise kink," Greta muttered.

Before Kaelee could reply, Greta shook her finger at Kaelee and added, "As I've said several times, I *love* the book. I offered a preempt. I'm putting my name, my currently very well regarded reputation for finding hits because of Toni's book, on the line by saying that I wanted it enough to pay high and fast so I could have the privilege of editing it."

"You don't need to say—"

"I wasn't finished. The characters are raw and damaged, and the setting is rich in history. I can *tell* you have advanced studies there, Kaelee." Greta walked faster and faster as she spoke, as if her agitation powered her feet in some way. "Your prose is polished without reading as pretentious."

"Then why would you give it to someone else to edit?" Kaelee stared at her, frowning. That was a lot of praise to support tossing her away to another editor, even though Ian had seemed like a great guy.

"Because even as good as it is, I like *you* more. I don't see how I'm to *do* this right now. Fuck. I was planning on finally getting my mouth on you. Third night, Kaelee. And now . . ." Greta flung up her hand as if she had just tossed something in the air.

"You're really fucking hot when you're pissed off."

"No. That's the problem." Greta rubbed her eyes with a thumb and index finger like she was pinching her stress away. "I cannot be hot *and* be your editor, Kaelee. One or the other, not both."

Kaelee winced at the edge in Greta's voice. "Sorry."

"This is my career. You can go to another editor, but if people thought I fucked you to get your book . . . If they thought this was some #MeToo thing . . ." Greta paused and took a deep breath. "I worked my ass off for this career. I can't screw it up. I sacrificed *everything* for this."

Kaelee felt guilty. "We were both blindsided."

"Yes," Greta grumbled. "And I have to figure out how to be sure you're taken care of—which switching to Ian would do—and that my reputation is safe."

"I have no intention of telling anyone." Kaelee caught her hand. "I can keep secrets."

"I hate this." Greta pulled her hand free. She weaved and shoved her way through a small crowd.

Kaelee stayed close enough to be in the wake of her charge. When they managed to get farther away from the small swarm of people, Kaelee pulled Greta into the grass and away from the path. A few people were enjoying the unseasonably warm fall air on a blanket with what appeared to be an actual picnic basket at their side.

"I'm not going to ruin your career," Kaelee promised in a low voice even though no one was near enough to hear them. "I give you my word. You did *nothing* wrong. Lots of people use apps to hook up, and you had no idea—"

"I have an email exchange asking you for an author photo." Greta rubbed her eyes again. "This would be so awf—"

"You *do* have that exchange, and I didn't send one yet. You didn't know what I looked like. You had no idea I was your author when we connected." Kaelee reached out as if to take Greta's hands, but she stopped so her hands were outstretched but not touching Greta. "I give you my word, as your new friend, that I will not let the two nights we spent become public or damage your reputation. You can trust me; I swear it."

Greta nodded. "In case it's not blazingly obvious, I have a few trust issues."

Kaelee smiled. "Same."

"My fiancée, Tasha, hated my job," Greta continued. "She hated that it had occasional evening or weekend requirements. She hated how often I checked my messages or when I stayed up reading so I could find the hot new book. It wasn't like she couldn't watch a game or movie *next* to me while I read, but she felt rejected."

"And?" Kaelee wanted to know. Honestly, she wanted to know everything about Greta.

Greta sighed. "And Tash started fucking around with both men and women. She was never really sure what she wanted, and that's okay. Not knowing is fine, but she *claimed* she knew. She claimed I was what she wanted, that we were forever, that we ought to have already been married, that I was the problem. She wanted me to find a new career. I said no." Greta let out a pained laugh. "Then she started fucking people, all while she accused me of cheating. My late nights at the office or lunches with agents made her angry. Normal editor things were an issue for her. She started suggesting I was sleeping around. I wasn't; I swear it. Even after I realized she was out with other people, I was still faithful. I was a fool. So I joined the Sappho's Kiss Society, and I decided that was *enough*."

"Was it?"

"Until I met you." Greta stared at her. "You make me want to try dating again, Kaelee. I want days like yesterday. Lunch half naked, talking about shows or books, afternoon sex. I want to laugh and feel like we are working together. I *like* being able to get you comfortable enough to give me a little of your tightly held control."

"I like all of that, too." Kaelee felt like she might start crying. "We can have all of it but the sex, though. Friends do a lot of that. Maybe it's even better that—"

"Liar. The sex is still part of what I want, and you can't tell me you don't feel the same."

"I liked the 'friends with benefits' idea," Kaelee said levelly.

"You're the whole damn package." Greta sniffled.

"I would like to hug you," Kaelee whispered. "Friends hug, right?" She opened her arms in invitation. "That's not a big deal."

Greta shook her head. "I don't hug. I barely even talk to anyone socially. I feel like I fucked everything up. My trust issues led to the app, led to fucking my author. How?"

"The app is designed for people with trust issues."

"Fair." Greta looked more and more like she was about to cry, and Kaelee couldn't deal with that kind of vulnerability.

*This feels too real already.*

Kaelee's panic twisted up inside her until she blurted out, "My father announced my engagement in the society page, although I hadn't been dating my supposed fiancé. I thought—I *think* he's a raging hemorrhoid." Kaelee caught Greta's gaze, grateful that no one seemed to be paying any attention to them as they stood having a far too emotional conversation. "I never agreed to marry him or . . . do anything with him."

Kaelee didn't typically say the words to define what had happened. They were too heavy. Too dark. Too likely to result in her being called a victim. Today, she made an exception.

"My father handed me over to him like it was the Middle fucking Ages, and his rising star in the company had paid a sheep and a few chickens for the right to my body." Kaelee heard the rage she rarely admitted to still having. "We all have skeletons, Greta. We don't need to dance with them."

Greta stared at her, swiped at her now-wet cheeks, and said, "Fucking writers knowing the right words. How am I not to like you?"

"*Your* fucking writer, Greta. It's okay to like me a little. We're friends now, right?"

"This was not the plan I had for tonight."

"Same." Kaelee weighed the impossibility of suggesting one last night. "So what if we—"

"No. Damn it. I cannot. You cannot." Greta made a frustrated sound. "Please don't finish that thought. I can see the way your body shifts when you're . . . thinking about sex."

"Really?"

"I'm observant, Kaelee," Greta said dryly. "But you need to work with me to keep the innuendo and bad ideas to yourself. I can't be the only one trying to figure this thing out. We are banned from even talking about it, or I need to stay completely away from you. Okay?"

Guilt rose up like a hand choking Kaelee, and she nodded. "I'll do better. I swear it. We can be friends, and that's more than I usually offer people." Kaelee motioned her forward. "Let's take a walk in Central Park, and then I'm going to get my bag and catch the Acela back home."

"You're leaving tonight? That's not going to leave time for a very long walk or dinner. The last train is eight or nine at night," Greta started.

Kaelee motioned her forward. "It'll take a little time for me to be around you without testing your boundaries, Greta. An hour-long walk might be the longest we *should* do this. We can figure out how to be friends. I'm sure of that, but I can't turn myself into someone casual with you quite that quickly."

"Why?"

"Don't ask me questions like that. I'm trying to follow your rules." Kaelee swerved around a couple taking pictures of pretty much everything.

"I'm asking." Greta caught her arm. "Say it. Admit that it's not *just* sex we were sharing."

"Fine! I could've continued what we were doing, and it felt like it could be . . . more. You're an incredible woman. Not like I thought we'd end up forever or something ridiculous like that, but friends with benefits with *you* is the most I've wanted from anyone in my entire life." Kaelee glanced at a mime who was seemingly arguing with a businessman, who may or may not have been in on the act.

"We already agreed that the 'friends' part still can exist. . . ."

"I know, but I really, *really* fucking loved the other part, too," Kaelee reminded her. "So if we're doing this new 'friends *without* benefits' thing, I'm going to need a minute to learn how to keep from wanting to fuck you."

"Are you saying you'd still want to have sex, knowing who I really am?" Greta asked.

"Yes."

"Oh." Greta gave her a perplexed look.

They walked through Central Park with distance and stilted conversation between them. Every so often, that awkwardness was interrupted by passionate exchanges on books, movies, and artists. And Kaelee did her level best to remind herself over and over that having so much in common did not mean they were ever going to have been more than friends and former fuck buddies.

*This is better. This is the real person. She's not lying about things.*

"Okay, so . . . Patience? True story?" Kaelee prompted eventually as they were headed out of Central Park. Kids were playing some odd version of soccer meets American football that looked like they had a set of rules, even if no one outside the game knew what they were.

"Completely true. Patience was a monster at first, and honestly I couldn't blame her. Luckily, we made up. By the time we were in high school, Patience was very much not a virgin, and I was the lucky girl who made that happen."

"You deflowered Patience?" Kaelee exclaimed.

"And two of the Marys." Greta shrugged. "Catholic school. Best place ever for a budding lesbian. So many girls only thought of penetration by penis as sex, and they were curious . . . or unsatisfied by fumbling boys who had no idea that sex could be good for a girl."

Kaelee laughed before admitting, "I could've appreciated a young Greta. I was a late bloomer. I think I was almost eighteen when I figured out that I looked at girls the way I did because I was a lesbian, not because I was judging their hair or clothes like people thought."

"I can't picture you like that!"

"Hair to my mid-back, tight skirts, plenty of makeup." Kaelee thought back to the image she'd adopted then. "That was what ladies were to look like, dress like, sound like, and for a lot of years, I followed their rules. I had a boyfriend, gay as can be, and I didn't mind even though I hadn't figured out how to explain why I was okay with his complete disinterest in kissing or anything. We let people think we 'went all the way' at junior prom, as my friends all did, but in truth, we watched old movies, ate pizza, and danced around the hotel room. Both our reputations were secure, though, because we lied, and that was all that mattered at the time."

"Do you keep in touch?"

"Sometimes. He does some sort of surgery in California. Loves his job, his husband, and their toddler." Kaelee thought about Branson. His family had come to terms with his bombshell about being gay pretty quickly; not without drama, but not with the sort of violent reaction that Kaelee had. They'd been a lot less happy about Bran moving to California. The men in their family went to Duke, tradition blah blah, but they still got over it.

"This whole 'editor who asks all the questions' is a side I wasn't expecting to meet," Kaelee pointed out after a few silent moments walking. "I could get used to it."

"Same on the not-a-locked-door part of you." Greta smiled. "I like this being honest and getting to know you."

Kaelee wasn't going to admit that this openness was unique to Greta, not when that led to taboo thoughts. Instead she simply said, "I should grab coffee so I can be awake for the ride home."

As she was turning away, Greta said, "Ian is a great editor, you know. If he takes on your book and—"

"Could we have sex if I was his author?" Kaelee asked.

"We shouldn't." Greta crossed her arms over her chest, like she was trying to shield herself. "I'm still the acquiring editor and . . ."

"Then what would I gain by switching?" Kaelee stared at her. "If I could still be with you, I'd consider it."

For a moment, she thought the answer would change. She thought maybe Greta was really as into her as she seemed, but she shook her head.

"The deal announcement goes out this week," Greta said. "I will still be listed as the acquiring editor in it. Not Ian."

"That's the plan," Kaelee said flatly. "Lots of people become friends with their editors. We just are starting there. No big deal."

They exchanged a look, but neither of them pointed out that they started out as a lot more than friends. Neither of them pointed out that they were both mourning their loss. This was it, then. The end of what could have been.

Kaelee fixed a smile on her lips and gestured for Greta to walk with her.

*Friends. We're good.*

She told herself that it was enough even though she knew it was a fucking lie. She wanted it all: friends, fucking, maybe forever. Being with Greta had been the closest to content that Kaelee had ever been, but she wasn't enough for Greta to be willing to find a way to make something work between them.

*Maybe I will never be enough for anyone.*

# 15

## Kaelee



Even though they were no longer having sex, Kaelee still woke up with Greta on her mind most days. Before she even rolled out of bed, before coffee, before the gym, she thought about Greta. Sometimes it was Greta Her Editor, who was asking about cover copy—the words on the book flap—or opinions on a bunch of fonts for her name on the book, but mostly it was Greta Her Friend.

> **Greta:** If you had one superpower?
> **Kaelee:** Teleportation.
> **Greta:** Really? You could have anything.
> Breathing underwater, flying, telepathy.
> **Kaelee:** Nope. Don't want to read minds.
> I can get a ticket for a plane. I want to
> pop from one place to another.
> **Greta:** I want an eidetic memory.
> **Kaelee:** Nerd. Smartphone. Take a picture
> of the file. Boom, perfect recall.
> **Greta:** Nerd? Ha! How many degrees do you have?

Kaelee smiled at that. Their exchanges were always light, and one part of their conversation was a long-running Q and A about everything. On some level, Greta Her Friend, Greta Her Editor, and

Marie Her Lover were three distinct sides of Greta, and the horrible truth was that Kaelee realized that she actually liked all three of them.

*She's everything I could want in a woman. . . .*

At least when they were several hours apart, Kaelee found it a lot easier to avoid the temptation to drop to her knees and worship Greta. There were a few too many nights—and mornings—when *Marie* in all of her writhing, moaning beauty was the memory Kaelee thought about. A few times, Kaelee had debated asking if phone sex was off the table, but she knew that answer.

And it was the right answer.

She knew that, too. So she put in a few more gym hours than she used to. More weights. More cardio. More sweating out her stress. Kaelee debated finding someone to fuck, but she didn't want anyone else. She didn't want someone she couldn't let walls down with. Kaelee wanted her friend.

Unfortunately, she'd learned years ago that the surest way to destroy a friendship was to fuck. She wasn't going to deny that she looked at her newest friend and weighed the thought far too often. Even when she was at the gym, campus, or at the bar with friends, as she was tonight, Greta was on her mind.

*No sex with Greta. She said so.*

"What are you scowling at?" Cherie threw a dart with laser precision. "I have another date coming in thirty minutes, so talk fast before you wander off to sulk in the corner."

Maybe it was odd, but Kaelee had started going on a few of Cherie's date meetups. Not on the actual date, but just to the location as a backup to be sure Cherie was safe. Cherie had one couple show up seeking their unicorn, and one creepy man who had posed as a woman on an app because he wanted to "convert" a lesbian, so Kaelee had taken to going out to wherever Cherie was meeting her date to make sure the person or situation wasn't something problematic.

*I can edit in a bar as easily as my office,* Kaelee told herself.

"Are your edit notes awful? You keep scowling that hard, you'll wrinkle." Cherie pouted as if the thought of wrinkling was sad.

"No. Edits are actually done. I'm tinkering at this point," Kaelee confessed.

"Is it your celibacy problem?" Cherie's next dart was tight enough to the one in the bull's-eye that the first dart that was there wobbled and fell. "Don't think I don't know the *my girl isn't getting any* look."

"Maybe? I'm not used to wanting things but not going after them." Kaelee scanned the bar, mostly out of habit. "I wanted Marie, but that ship sailed. And no one else . . ." She shrugged. "And I'm feeling paranoid this week, I guess. My door was unlocked the other day. I'm probably just forgetful and left it that way, but . . ."

"Anything missing?"

"No. I could have forgotten, or maybe the super was up, or . . ."

Cherie plopped into the chair opposite her. "Trust your gut. You know that. Whatever the secret you don't tell me is, it's enough that you have four locks. That speaks. *Trust your gut.*"

Kaelee nodded. "I am getting it rekeyed."

"Good." Cherie eyed her and said, "You need to figure out how to get that smile back, too. You have the career, the TA, the first of two degrees. So, what are you missing? What would make you smile? New car? Wasn't your book deal . . . *significant?*"

Kaelee flipped her off. "My car still runs fine. I'm not going to replace her just because I got a check."

Her book deal wasn't the sort of money Toni had made, but she had been paid one hundred twenty-five thousand a book. Signing for two books meant she had been paid sixty thousand, less her agent's fifteen percent, already. That left her with fifty grand in her account, which replaced almost all her living expenses during the years she finished college and her master's degree. Then there would be a check when the book was accepted. That covered the rest and gave a slight cushion. Her teaching assistantship had already kept her withdrawals low, but the first publishing checks replaced all that she had withdrawn.

The on-print check would put her balance *above* the original figure.

"Okay, your car runs, and your clothes aren't that tattered." Cherie gave her a once-over. "And even if they were, you are so cheap you squeak."

"What does that even mean?"

"I don't know. Cheap shoes? Ass clenched so tight it's rubbing?" Cherie waved her hand. "How am I to know? Do I look like a linguist to you?"

"Don't knock linguists. They're often good with their tongues." Kaelee kept a straight face as she made this declaration. "Worth looking for if you're dating . . ."

"Perv." Cherie rolled her eyes. "You talk like this when you're defensive, you know."

"Ouch." Kaelee put a hand over her heart. "You're brutal, Cher."

"Call a locksmith." Cherie poked at her phone. "Now. Leave a message. I can stay there tonight, and we'll move something in front of the door. Do you have pepper spray?"

"You have a date."

"I also have a friend who is anxious and opening up. Do you know how often that happens?" Cherie marched over to an empty table. "You sit here until my date ends. Then we go home. Research locksmiths while I'm busy."

Kaelee followed her gaze to the doorway, where a very femme young woman was pushing up her glasses as she fumbled for a wallet, obviously being carded. As Cherie walked away, Kaelee cringed. This was not the chivalrous woman Cherie was seeking. She certainly wasn't the *throw her down and ravish her* sort either. At least she seemed like she was actually in the right age group for Cherie. There had been one man who showed up with a girl young enough to be his kid, and the pedo vibes were intense. They'd separated the man from her long enough to check that the young woman wasn't being sex trafficked. It was all sorts of ick.

Tonight, at least, there was nothing creepy or potentially illegal.

And hey, maybe Cherie would click with the awkward woman and reassess what she wanted.

*Like I did with Greta.*

That was the other thought that was worrying Kaelee. She wasn't sure who she could talk to about that. Certainly not Toni! *Oh hey, I've been naked with our editor, and I can't stop missing her.* That sounded like a horrible conversation. And she thought maybe she could talk to Addie, but since Toni and Addie had zero secrets, telling Addie was telling Toni.

Cherie was new to dating women, but not new to *dating.*

*Maybe I ought to talk to her.*

First, though, Kaelee opened her browser and searched for lock-smiths.

An hour later, Cherie stood at the barstool beside her. "Any luck on locksmiths?"

"I have one scheduled for tomorrow," Kaelee admitted. She glanced toward the table where Cherie had been meeting her latest date. "No love match?"

"She was sweet." Cherie frowned. "Maybe I'm asking for too much. Maybe I just need to try going on a few dates with one person."

"I'm not the right person to give dating advice. You want sex tips? I have you covered. If you want heart stuff, I'm not her." Kaelee had settled her tab earlier and was nursing a glass of water. Getting drunk when she was already on edge seemed unwise. "Ready to head out? If you changed your mind about crashing at mine, I can drop—"

"Don't be a dumbass." Cherie waited patiently for her to stand. "If you feel more at ease, we could go to my place. My roommates are quiet."

"I'm okay at mine. There's a lock that's only secured from the inside, so really . . ." Kaelee shrugged. She wasn't about to inconvenience people because she was anxious.

"Come on. Pajama party time. We could get ice cream and watch a movie." Cherie widened her eyes in a way that would not be amiss on manga art or a cartoon deer.

They were almost to her car when the phone chimed with a North Carolina exchange. She ignored it. The same number dialed back. Again she declined the call. A different North Carolina number dialed, and this time she answered. Typically, she didn't answer any numbers with that prefix, but she felt awkward with the insistence of it.

"Hello?"

"Sabrina?" Her father's voice rolled across the line, thunderous and terrifying as he once had been to her face.

Kaelee started shaking. How did he get this number? Why? Her skeletons weren't things she liked to ponder, and he was the puppet master behind most of them. Controlling. Hateful. Vengeful.

"We heard this nonsense about your *book*, Sabrina. Aldens don't make spectacles of themselves. They don't embarrass the family name. Put a stop to it, or I will." His voice was thick with the drawl of home, but it was, as ever with him, laced with the imperiousness that had no place in her life.

She shook so much that she closed her eyes against the fear crawling up her throat. Once, he'd been her daddy, her haven against nightmares and bullies; once, he'd been the man she trusted to keep her safe. When she stopped being the child he wanted, he morphed into someone heinous.

"You have the wrong number," she managed to say somewhat steadily.

"You listen to me—"

"No." She opened her eyes, swallowing back enough of the fear to stop from sounding so weak and breathy. "I will not listen to you. My name isn't that. I don't know you or want to, and you have no business issuing me orders."

He was deathly quiet for a moment. "No one embarrasses my family, Sabrina. If you think your stunt is going to be tolerated, you're gravely mistaken."

"I am no part of *your* family, so my life doesn't concern you." Kaelee disconnected the call and promptly blocked his number. Her hands were shaking, and tears of frustration and terror raced over her cheeks.

Cherie wrapped both arms around her and squeezed.

"I don't know how he found me," Kaelee breathed.

*Maybe the locks were a clue.*

*My God. Does he know where I live? Do I need to move?*

For several moments, she stood there. Cherie rubbed small circles on her back, soothing her like she was a startled child after a nightmare, and murmuring, "You're okay. You're safe. I'm right here with you."

"Would you think I was insane if I asked if we could crash in a hotel? My treat?" Kaelee straightened, swatting at the tears still on her face.

"Do we need to call the police?"

"No. No threats were made, not really. They can't do anything anyhow." Kaelee started walking. "I have my gym bag in the car, and we could stop at your place, and you get things or . . . hell, I'll buy you pajamas and whatever makeup things you need or . . . I mean, you could stay at your own place, and I—"

"Hush. We'll go have us a posh PJ party. Room service and high thread counts. I'm bringing a cooler, though. Ice cream—which I can grab at my apartment, too—and a bottle of wine. I have you, Kaelee. Friends don't panic alone." She offered Kaelee her elbow. "Let me be your knight for a change. You always look after me."

Kaelee gave a watery laugh and blurted out, "My family disowned me. That was him. My father. He wants me not to publish my book because it would embarrass him."

"Well, fuck him and anyone else trying to put their egos in your way." Cherie made a noise somewhere between a growl and a huff. "And your book is fantasy, right?"

"It is."

"Well, how in the name of all that's rational is that anything to do with him? I can see him being upset if it was a memoir telling the world he's an ass waffle, but—"

"Ass waffle?" Kaelee echoed.

"Are you publishing it under *his* name?"

"No." Kaelee paused. "We don't have the same surname either. Kaelee Carpenter didn't exist until a few years ago."

"Well, of course you did. You just didn't have your real name yet." Cherie held out a hand. "I'm driving. I know you have your control issues, but tonight, you need to let a friend handle some stuff, okay?"

Mutely, Kaelee handed over her keys. The last time she had to figure out how to escape her past, she did it on her own. Tonight, she was grateful to have a friend at her side, especially one willing to take the reins while she had a small meltdown.

16

## *Greta*

Midnight came and went, and Greta was still awake. Insomnia happened. It wasn't a regular issue, but tonight, her mind was running too fast. She couldn't sit at her table or her sofa without memories of Kaelee flooding her mind. Not just the sex, either. The thought of Kaelee leaning against the counter, flirtatious and shy in alternating moments. The thought of snuggling up to watch a regular show together. The sight of Kaelee shelf-reading and commenting on titles she'd read. Greta wanted that. She wanted a woman in her life and in her home. She didn't want just anyone, unfortunately.

*I want* that *woman.*

Greta hadn't even realized that she had been missing the possibility of something new and exciting until Kaelee had brought it into her life. The constant possibility of a message or a bold request was exciting—like dating. Even though they had initially agreed that it was just sex, within two face-to-face meetings they had already revised that to friends with benefits. Shifting to just friends instead of toward dating meant that Greta was forced to confront her own desire for a real relationship.

Tasha had moved on before they'd even separated, yet it had taken Greta over two years to reach this point. Her scattered one-nighters with Tash hadn't helped, but that hadn't seemed to be an issue at first. Greta hadn't even realized she was ready until she met "Lee."

*Maybe it's time to date for real.*

A twinge in her chest made Greta pause. The app she usually used was for casual encounters. Sappho's Kiss definitely had the implied option of more, but they had a setting users could select from to state interests. Greta knew the option was in there. The choice boxes a user selected were for one night, something casual, online fun, or "more." Her profile as Marie was set to casual and one night. Changing that to "more" seemed like saying she was done using the app for one-night-only connections.

*Am I?*

She considered switching her settings, but in the long term that meant not using the app to meet another one-nighter. Her gut said that Sappho's Kiss Society wasn't the place to go for dating. So Greta looked up a few articles on what sites were good for genuine queer connections, and then she downloaded Her, Zoe, Taimi, Bumble, and a couple of others. Most had monthly fees, but they were low. The hard part was adding her profile photos. On the Sappho's Kiss Society app, no one seemed to care that she was wary about showing her face. They knew members were vetted—and that the app fees restricted who could join—so by default if a person had an account, she was a *real* person. Every user had their real identity, credit reports, and medical checks on file with the company.

What if people mistook her unwillingness to show her face on these other apps as indicative that she was using a fake identity, married, or cheating? What if she did show her face and then she was approached by someone in the industry? An agent or editor? An author?

Greta was spiraling with panic when she got a notification of a message from Lee on the SKS chat. She flipped over instantly.

**Lee:** What are you doing?
**Marie:** Why are you messaging HERE?
**Lee:** . . .

She stared at the little dots that started and stopped several times before deciding she was too impatient.

**Marie:** Are you ok?
**Lee:** Sure.
**Marie:** Do you need to call?
**Lee:** I'm fine.
**Marie:** So . . . ?
**Lee:** I miss your pussy.

Greta gasped at the blunt statement, not sure how to reply. This wasn't how they spoke, not now. In addition to their text thread, they had spoken a couple of times a week since New York. She stared at the phone.

**Lee:** Sext me.
**Marie:** We can't. You know that.
**Lee:** Cancel the damn book.

At that Greta closed the app and called Kaelee. "What's happening right now?"

"Nothin'." Kaelee slurred the word. "I'm a fucking imposter, Marie. Can't do anything right. Can't please anyone. 'Cept you. I pleased you, didn't I? Let me do it again. I'll be good to you."

"Sweetie, you sound drunk. Where are you?" Greta didn't hear any chatter or music. Instead everything was echoing vaguely, like Kaelee was in a small empty room. "Are you safe?"

Kaelee burst out laughing, a bark of noise. "That's a really great question. Am I? Do they know where I am? I mean, not tonight. I'm mostly sure they don't know where I am tonight. Didn't go home just in case. Can they be tracking my telly-phone, though? These are good smart questions. You're smart."

Greta felt panic rising at the things Kaelee was dancing around.

"Are you alone? Do you *know* where you are? Did you meet someone and—"

"Can't meet anyone. They're not you. I just want your sweet, juicy pussy, Marie. You took it away, though. Left me." Kaelee let out a burp. "Don't drink the wine. I'm telling you. Wine's bad."

"Are you at a bar?"

"Nope." She laughed. "Can't get drunk in public. 'S not safe."

"Okay. So are you at your apartment?" Greta's mind spun. She couldn't get to Kaelee to help her. She was hours away. Maybe she needed to call Toni. She was local *and* friends with Kaelee. It wasn't the worst idea Greta had ever had. Sure, it might invite questions from Toni, but if Kaelee was in danger, Greta was willing to answer them.

"Can't go to my place tonight. Doors unlocked themselves. Either the super's not super, or I'm sleepwalking, or"—her voice dropped to a raspy whisper—"maybe they found me."

"Who? Who are they?"

"Can't tell you." Kaelee had sounded matter-of-fact until she mentioned being found. Her voice wobbled as she continued, "Maybe I ought to just vanish again, so maybe the book needs canc'ling. I wouldn't be your author then, so I thought you might sext me. *Sext me,* Greta. You know, like tex' sex."

"Kaelee, you need to tell me where you are."

"Are you coming here for sex?" Kaelee sounded far more excited by that. "I can prob'ly crawl into the tub and clean up." Crashing noises followed that. "Got to get my jeans off, though."

"Do not get in the tub. Do you hear me?" Greta panicked at the thought of Kaelee drowning herself, passed out in a running tub.

"Okay. You like tellin' me what to do? If I'm drunk enough, we could try that."

Greta's heart felt like it had cracked at the tone in Kaelee's voice, raw and fragile. Carefully, she said, "If you need to get drunk to do something, I don't want you to do it. I want you to take care of yourself."

"What am I to do, then? I don't know what I'm to do, Greta." Kaelee sounded like she was weighing a much larger question about life.

"First, open your phone and put it on speaker."

"Okay. Done." Kaelee sounded far away. "Now what?"

"Now you send me your location. Right now." Greta knew this was incredibly outside the norm of an editor-author friendship, but they weren't just that, even if it's what they were trying to be.

When Kaelee sent it, Greta could see that she was in a hotel. "What room number?"

"Eighteen-oh-six," Kaelee answered. "Are you really coming to see me?"

"No, sweetie, I'm not. I just need to know you're okay. You don't sound okay right now." Greta's mind filled with visions of overdoses, being roofied, alcohol poisoning.

"I don't drink like this. Not in lots of years," Kaelee whispered. "I'm not a great drunk."

"It's okay. Did someone make you?"

"He can't make me do anything. Not ever again." Kaelee's voice was stronger now, thick with anger. "Calling and threatening me."

"Who?"

"Fucking Tripp."

"Tripp?"

"My father," Kaelee whispered.

"I need you to promise me that no matter what, we will discuss this tomorrow." While she was waiting for a reply, Greta pulled out her laptop and sent a text to Toni Darbyshire asking, You awake?

Kaelee's sleepy, drunken voice sounded less alert as she said, "Why do you care? You don't even know all my names. You were going to give my book away to some other editor, toss me out. That's it. Too bad, too sad, go away, 'Brina."

*Brina? Who the hell is Brina? Another app name?*

"I care because we're friends. I like you whether you are Kaelee or Lee or Brina or any other name you want. I care about *you*."

Greta sighed. "And I wasn't tossing you away. I was trying to take care of you *and* your book."

"I want you to take care of me," Kaelee whispered. "And my book."

"Okay."

For a moment there was only silence, then Kaelee said, "He scared me when he called. He's a bad man."

"Then we'll figure it out together," Greta promised. Her phone buzzed. Toni was calling her. She looked down and realized that there were three texts from Toni.

**Toni:** Did you mean to text me?
**Toni:** Greta? Hello.
**Toni:** Damn it. Now I can't focus. Calling you.

At that, Greta made a quick decision. "Kaelee, I want you to drink a glass of water. I'll be right back."

Then she flipped over to Toni's call. "I know it's late, but I need you to check on Kaelee. I'm texting you her address and room number."

"Kaelee. My TA Kaelee?" Toni sounded off. "I need a little info here, Greta."

"She needs a friend, Toni. I'm in Manhattan, and you're both in DC so I just need you to make sure she's okay. She's drunk or drugged or I don't know. She called, and . . ." Greta huffed out a breath. "There's something that happened. I'm not even sure what, but she's a mess."

"About the book?"

"No. In her personal life." Greta weighed the incredible awkwardness of what she was about to do. "Just so you know before she says anything in her drunken state, I met her before. I had no idea who she was then. Just a . . . hookup. Tonight isn't about that, but she's drunk right now and sounds like she's in a bad way and called me. So in case she says anything, I just thought I should tell you."

Toni sighed. "You know she doesn't date, right?"

Greta snorted. "Neither do I. It was a hookup, but now things are odd. When I bought her book, I had no idea that the author I was emailing was the woman I—"

"Don't finish that sentence." Toni sounded like she was flinching. "You better tell Em, though. Seriously. I don't want to be the person caught in the middle."

"Just go check on Kaelee. Please?" Greta asked.

Toni disconnected, and Greta flipped back to her call with Kaelee only to be met with silence. She had no idea what had happened. "Kaelee? Are you there? Kaelee?"

All she heard in return was silence. Not a ringtone. Not a reply.

# 17

## *Kaelee*

Kaelee woke in an unfamiliar room. Not the hotel she'd been in with Cherie. Not her apartment. Panic started to bubble in her stomach, along with the remnants of too much wine. Her head was thudding as she stumbled out of the bed and fumbled for a light. A note on the nightstand next to her was propped up next to a tall travel mug and a bottle of acetaminophen.

> *Kae,*
> *Don't think about leaving before we talk. Water. Pain relief.*
> *Use it.*
>
> *Toni*
> *P.S. You smell like booze and vomit. Shower. Clean clothes.*
> *Come upstairs.*

*Shit!* She was at Toni and Addie's townhouse. An oversized Vienna College sweatshirt was haphazardly folded next to a pair of sweatpants. Next to them was a plastic bag that had a stickie on it saying "gross clothes in here." Kaelee washed down a couple of acetaminophen with half the water there and went to shower.

While she was standing under the hot water, she remembered Greta calling after Kaelee had messaged her.

Kaelee rested her head on the wall of the shower, trying to remember how much of an ass she'd been. The parts she remembered were mortifying enough that after her shower she went out and grabbed her phone, which someone had kindly put on a charger. She scanned the text conversation as well as the app before sending a new message.

> **Lee:** I am so sorry about last night.
> **Marie:** T said you were alive and at her place.
> **Lee:** I am. I shouldn't have reached out. Rough night.
> **Marie:** You are my friend. Calling friends is fine.
> **Lee:** I can see our messages. How bad was the call?
> **Marie:** Doesn't matter. Still my friend. Still worried
> when you were hurting. Sorry/not sorry about calling T.
> **Lee:** It's ok. Does she know?
> **Marie:** Enough. Talk to her as much as you need.
> I'm ok with it. We will need to talk to E too.

Kaelee flinched at the thought of telling her agent she had crawled into a bottle last night. She wasn't embarrassed about having sex with Greta, but being drunk was another thing. Kaelee wasn't the sort of person to get drunk or stupid like that. She had, however, maybe snapped a little under pressure.

> **Lee:** I am so sorry about all of it. I don't do that. I swear.
> **Marie:** Are you safe? That's all I care about.
> **Lee:** I'll let them know that none of what happened
> with us was after you knew me as me.
> **Marie:** I trust you. Call me later. Please.
> **Lee:** Will do.

Right now, Kaelee wished she could call Greta right this minute, but she wasn't going to have that conversation in Toni and Addie's home, not when there was a risk that they could hear her. Feeling like a disobedient child, Kaelee got dressed and went to find Toni or Addie, not sure which woman was home. When she was a teen, she hadn't ever gotten drunk or made an ass of herself. Doing it at almost thirty stung her pride.

Failing to eat, drinking on an empty stomach . . . there were a number of stupid-assed things she'd done the night before. Explaining how it had happened didn't undo her mortification that it *had* happened in the first place.

Toni looked up at Kaelee as she walked into the living room. She was seated in a rather Victorian sofa with fringe under it. A stack of books sat next to her, along with a notebook. When she set aside the book she was actively reading, a fluffy cat looked up and hissed from her lap.

At the sound, Toni ruffled the cat's fur and said, "Take no offense at his drama. Oscar Wilde is a grump. I'm not even sure he likes *me*." She stared down at the massive cat, a Maine coon or something similar, with a fond look. "He likes Addie. Sometimes Em. He accepts my love grudgingly when they aren't here."

The cat looked perfectly content in Toni's lap, so Kaelee had her doubts about the other woman's interpretation of his opinions. It certainly seemed like the cat's objection was simply about having cuddle time interrupted.

Kaelee stood there awkwardly, not sure what she was to be doing right now. What she *wanted* was to call a ride and get out of here without chatting. "Addie's not home?"

"She is. She went to read in our room when she heard the shower turn off." Toni motioned toward the kitchen. "She made you a cup of tea before she left. She says coffee will be too harsh for your stomach as drunk as you were. I asked for a little privacy to talk to you, so you didn't feel like we were ganging up on you."

Mutely Kaelee went and grabbed the cup of tea, added milk, and came to sit in the living room to face her former boss, now friend.

Finally, she said, "Thank you both. You didn't need to bring me here, but I appreciate it."

"Oh, that's not what our *editor* said when she texted me in the middle of the night in a panic." Toni stared at Kaelee, looking a little too much like a surly mother for Kaelee's comfort.

"Right, well . . . I had a thing happen. Bad decisions were made and—"

"Cut the bullshit." Toni sat forward on the sofa, spilling the irate cat out of her lap in the process. As the cat headed out of the room, Toni ordered, "Talk."

"You know I don't talk about my past—"

"I do, but I *also know* that I had to crawl out of my cozy bed with my naked woman in it, and go out into the cold weather to fetch your drunk ass. Then I had to watch Addie fuss and bother over you instead of crawling back into my bed."

"Was she still naked?" Kaelee joked.

Toni leveled a look that would once have been intimidating—okay, it was still a little intimidating—before replying, "No, she was not naked then. I'm not a fool. She was all wrapped up in a fluffy little jacket and pink sweatpants and . . . that's not the damn point. Don't try to distract me, Kaelee. *You* don't drink like that. I'd know if you did. My father was a founding member of the drunk assholes club. You, Kaelee, are not. So what happened?"

Toni crossed her arms and waited until Kaelee relented.

"My father heard about my book deal, and he called me. I didn't cope." Kaelee sipped her tea, trying to decide just how much to share. At least this was slightly easier than the other part of the conversation, the part about why Greta was the one Kaelee called. "He doesn't approve."

"You never mention your family. Did you talk to Em about them yet? Did you tell Greta?"

"No. I told you I haven't spoken to any of them since I left roughly a decade ago. I didn't think he even knew *how* to reach me." Kaelee wrapped her hands around the mug and hoped upon hope that she wasn't going to fall apart in front of Toni. She probably had done so last night, but at least the memories of it were hazy. "He's not a fan of women who love women."

"Are you in danger?" Toni asked, cutting to the chase.

"No . . . ? I don't think so. Probably not?"

"Did he threaten you?"

That was a much harder question. Kaelee rolled over the things she could retain from that call. She was sober, but fear could be just as circuit frying as wine. "He told me to put a stop to the book. He's . . . embarrassed by it."

Toni looked contemplative. "We're going to keep in touch about this. I think you need to talk to Em and to Charlie. She's your publicist, right?" Kaelee nodded and Toni continued, "Do you understand? You need to *talk to them*. You will do so. Probably Greta or Em first. But you also need to keep me in the loop. You're in my wedding. That is, like, legitimate friendship, so it means I get to fucking worry over you. Clear?"

"You don't need to—"

"I said no bullshit." Toni scowled at her. "If this wasn't a big deal, you wouldn't have gotten skunk drunk, and I wouldn't have had to go peel you off a hotel bathroom floor."

"Fine." Kaelee felt tears threaten again. "I don't want you to think I'm a fuckup."

"Dealing with other people's drama is *not* how we define ourselves. Do you think I'm a fuckup?" Toni stared at her now, as if weighing things Kaelee couldn't see.

"Obviously not."

"I sold my books because my dad took another mortgage on my mother's house, ran up debt, and died. I got lucky and *The Whitechapel Widow* did well, but it was a Hail Mary pass for me." Toni held her gaze as she told her this. "So I'm not going to judge you because your father hates queers. I will point out right now that I hate him by default. I have no time for homophobes or bad fathers."

Kaelee nodded. "Thank you."

Just as she relaxed, though, Kaelee caught a look on Toni's face, and her throat tightened. The other shoe was about to hit the floor—or maybe kick Kaelee's ass. Either way, she tensed in anticipation.

"Finding out that you fucked our editor, on the other hand, I'm feeling a bit judgmental about," Toni said, sounding far surlier than Kaelee liked.

She flinched. "Do I get to plead the Fifth or something?"

"No." Toni sighed. "What in the hell were you thinking, Kae? You can't . . . you shouldn't . . . Seriously. That's not cool. What were you thinking?"

"That she's gorgeous," Kaelee said sheepishly, ducking her head at the confession. When Toni said nothing else, Kaelee looked at her. "I swear to God, Toni, that I had no idea she was my editor."

"*My* editor, too."

"Right. Yours or my editor. She was in town and there's an app—"

"You slept with Greta when she was here? When?" Toni gave her a strange look. "September? Don't say September."

"September."

"Damn it. She came here because I refused the contract. If I'd have just sold her the books, she wouldn't have come to DC, and then this"—Toni waved a hand at Kaelee—"clusterfuck could've been avoided." Toni slouched back in her seat. "Kaelee, you cannot hurt Greta. You need to understand that. She's a good person, good heart. You can't just treat her like the women you fuck."

"I know."

"I don't think you do. She called me in the middle of the night and told me you needed me. She risked her *career* to do that. She put herself on the line because she was worried about *your* safety." Toni looked like the proverbial disappointed teacher in that moment. "You can't—"

"Toni," Addie's voice cut in. "I don't think Kaelee intends to hurt Greta. Do you?"

Kaelee had never in her life been so grateful to see the vivacious actor who had padded barefoot into the room. She was cradling the fluffy Oscar Wilde like a large infant in her arms. The cat was purring so loudly that Kaelee could hear him like he was beside her.

*Maybe he does like her more.*

Kaelee held up a hand like she was making a vow or swearing in court. "I have no intention of hurting her. I met a sexy woman on an app, one who reached out to me first by the way, and she asked me to meet her. I did. Then I saw her in New York *before* I knew she was my editor. If I'd known she was my editor—"

"And *my* editor, Kaelee. *My. Editor,*" Toni interrupted. "Greta is the woman who bought my books, changed my stress level to manageable, published a book that led to seeing Addie again and—"

"Shush." Addie curled into Toni's side, looking for all the world like she was unaware that Toni was increasingly agitated. "What Toni means to say is that she is worried about Greta, a woman she's grateful to, and what she would say eventually is that she's worried about you, too, and this could get sticky."

"Yes." Toni smiled at Addie before turning her very focused glare back at Kaelee. "Worried. That's the word. Just that."

Addie pinched Toni's leg, and Toni caught her hand and held it in hers.

Kaelee straightened her shoulders, sipped her tea, and smiled at them as best she could with her increasingly present headache. "Greta and I are friends now. I called her to, umm, cancel my books, and she overreacted. To be clear, though, I wasn't the only one on the app or in the hotel b—"

"Do not talk about her in that way." Toni pressed her lips together. "My editor does not have a sex life. She exists at her desk at the publisher's office. Just there. She is always at the office, not on sex apps."

Addie giggled and patted Toni's lap consolingly. "I think Toni is worried about both of you, or she's just sleep deprived and cranky."

"And why am I sleep deprived?" Toni muttered, looking at Kaelee pointedly.

"Look. Greta and I are friends who fucked a few times," Kaelee said, feeling guilty for the words even as they left her lips. "There is nothing to worry about here. I'm sorry she overreacted, and I'm sorry I got falling-down sloshed because of my panic attack."

"And you are not canceling the book," Toni added. "You kept saying that last night. Canceling the book and leaving. You will not be doing that. If you did, my wedding would be short a person, and you don't want that, do you? That would upset Addie and—"

"It would upset you, too," Addie said softly.

"Correct. That's exactly why I won't run. I won't ruin your wedding party." Kaelee, calmer today already, smiled at them both. The reality was that Kaelee wasn't going to let that man ruin her life any more than he already had. He was several states away, and there was nothing he could do legally.

"Don't be difficult. I'm tired." Toni frowned then. "Greta. Greta is the woman you went to meet in New York when you asked me to stop you from calling her. You met her because she was here to see me, and I stayed here and *told you* to meet the app woman. I told you to go have carnal relations with my editor."

"Toni . . ." Kaelee looked at her mentor. "I would have seen her again anyhow. She's been like an addiction. She's sexy and funny and—"

"No. She lives in her office and does not *ever* have sex with you." Toni folded her arms and glared. "And you're going to talk to Em about your mistake with Greta and about your family, so I don't have to lie to my oldest friend who also happens to be our *agent*," Toni pressed.

"Yes, Mother." Kaelee nodded.

"And you will never, ever again talk to me about having sex *with. My. Editor*," Toni grumbled.

"What if I call her by a different name to talk about her? I'm actually freaking out a little about this," Kaelee finally admitted, grateful that she could talk about the knot of confusion inside her.

Toni made a pained noise and said, "I need more coffee if I have to hear this. My editor exists in a perfect state of suspended, untouchable bookish space. No rakish women debauch her. No one can upset her. And when the office lights go out, she sleeps, to be woken only when the workday resumes again."

"Oh, honey . . ." Addie patted Toni's knee. "Greta's human with a normal appetite, and interests, and Kaelee is gorgeous. It makes perfect sense."

"Nope." Toni gently untangled herself from Addie and went to the kitchen to start another pot of coffee.

Once she was gone, Addie crossed her legs so she was folded up like a child at a preschool class and propped her elbows on her knees, leaned forward, and said, "Tell me all about it."

Kaelee lowered her voice and confessed, "I *like* her. Greta, I mean." Louder she said, "I like *Marie*, this woman I met who is not an editor at all." Then at a normal volume she continued, "We text every day, and when I was first seeing her . . . the sex was everything I want. She's fucking perfect. I feel safe with her."

Addie gave her a sympathetic look. "That's huge."

"It is." Kaelee looked away. "I have trust issues that make some parts of casual sex harder, but . . . I know I'm not relationship material. We were going to try friends with benefits, which would be perfect, but then I found out she's my editor. So we're doing this friends thing, but I like her. I really *like* her."

"Oh, Kae, I'm sorry." Addie shook her head. "Could you turn your next book in early and once it's edited . . ."

"Already submitted it," Kaelee said.

"You thought people accusing you of getting ahead with my help was mortifying, what if this gets out? Ha!" Toni called from the kitchen. "Casual sex is not worth burning your career *or my editor's career.*"

Addie rolled her eyes. "Ignore her. True love overcomes. Look at us!"

"It's not love," Kaelee said quickly. "We're just really compatible."

As much as Kaelee wanted to believe that there was a solution, the court of public opinion could be rough. She'd already seen cruel remarks on social media that her book was overhyped because she used to be Toni's TA.

"Sure, look at us." Toni brought over a tray with a cup and a pot of tea for Addie. "Let that steep another moment," she murmured before speaking louder and adding, "Having our lives dissected in the tabloids was awesome. Highly recommend."

"Worth it, though." Addie stared up at Toni with the same joyous smile that captivated millions on the screen. "Love is worth all the slings and arrows."

"Not exactly how the quote goes," both Toni and Kaelee said at once.

Addie picked up a sugar cube and sucked on it before dropping it into her cup. "Academics." She poured tea over the cube in her cup. "Writers." She frowned briefly. "Wonderful, grumpy women with all their walls."

Addie watched them both as she stirred the tea with a dainty spoon from the tray. "So unwilling to take risks until you are on the edge of losing the most important thing in the world."

"Which is?"

"Love," Toni supplied.

"Greta can't *love* me," Kaelee protested. "She's become a great friend, and I want more. I miss the tas—"

"No!" Toni glared at her. "My editor does not have sex, especially with you."

"Would you grab me one of those little biscuits? The shortbread fingers? The ones I like?" Addie fluttered her eyes at Toni, who went to grab whatever it was she had just requested.

Then Addie looked at Kaelee and bluntly said, "Of course she could love you. You're perfectly lovable, and Greta is a smart, wonderful woman. I'm sure she sees that beautiful heart of yours. You're smart, talented, and loyal. What's not to love?"

Kaelee shook her head. "I don't want what you and Toni have.

I just want to have sex with the woman I chat with every day. Just casual. Nothing emotional. Friendship and orgasms."

"You're deluded," Addie said with a singular nod. "Greta put her reputation on the line to make sure you were okay when you were drunk and alone. She clearly *likes* you, too. What we need to sort out is how to get you to look beyond your baggage and fears. It's hard sometimes if you are refusing to admit your own wonderfulness. We could start with affirmations."

And Kaelee couldn't even try to argue with Addie. There was something irrepressible about her energy. The best Kaelee had to refute Addie's optimism was "My past has some things in it. She doesn't deserve having to risk herself because of that."

"I regret to inform you that you are not in charge of what risks she decides to take." Addie primly accepted the cookie that Toni brought her and dipped it into her tea. "What your partner sees in you is outside your control. What she does with her heart is, too."

Neither Toni nor Kaelee replied to that.

Addie continued, "Would either of you try to tell a woman what to do with her own body?"

"No." Toni frowned.

"Of course not!" Kaelee added.

"Then what makes either of you think that you can tell her what to do with her own heart." Addie crossed her arms. "Poor Greta. I know just what she must be feeling. I had to put up with this one's self-doubts, so I am something of an expert on women like you now." She pointed at Kaelee. "You need to stop refuting her feelings and know that she has valid reasons for them. If she feels emotions for you, that's up to *her*. You don't get to control her heart!"

If *Addie's right, I can never let Greta find out how I already feel about her.* The thought of Tripp Alden's long reach, his deep pockets, his hateful words spilling into Greta's life was enough to make Kaelee debate running, upending her life.

*One phone call from him is not reason to burn it all down,* her logic argued.

*Do we really think that's all it'll be?* her fears whispered.

"That helps make sense of things, Addie," Kaelee said. "Thank you."

Addie frowned. "Why do I think you took exactly the wrong conclusion from this?"

Whatever happened, Kaelee would do her best to shield all her friends—*including* Greta—from it. Maybe it was time to reconsider her life. Maybe it was time to move on. There were too many wonderful people who could be at risk, including the couple talking to her, the friend who drank with her, and the woman who sent Toni to rescue her. She had good friends, and Tripp would hurt any or all of them to get to her.

## 18

## Greta



At first Greta thought the simple texts from Toni that Kaelee was safe and fine might be the end of it, but Toni—who was not a fan of phone calls at the best of times—called the office the following Monday. Before she took the call, Greta walked over and closed her door.

"How is the book going?" she tried.

"That's not why I'm calling," Toni countered bluntly and quickly. "And you know that."

Greta sighed. "I know. I am in the office right now, and I can't really t—"

"You don't need to say anything that anyone will overhear." Toni cleared her throat. "I honestly can't decide which of you to lecture more. I already spoke to Kae since she was in my house after you sent me to fetch her."

"I do appreciate that, you know. I realize it was probably awkward, but the *situation* was unplanned. It was a surprise to both of us," Greta stressed, watching the world through the glass of her office windows. "When I found out who she was, that was the end of the rest."

"*Was* it the end, Greta? I thought you both texted all the time, or was Kae lying to me about that? I sure as hell don't get daily 'good morning' texts from my editor. And no one I've met in the business so far gets them." Toni sighed, paused, and Greta could tell she was reining in her temper. "This thing between you is very clearly *not* over, Greta. You and I can both see that." Toni already sounded strained, like she would literally prefer any other topic. "Kae's a lot more fragile than she admits."

"I know."

"She has feelings for you, and I heard the panic in your voice the other night. You have feelings, too. This could get messy. Trust me when I say you don't want to get stuck in some media storm like Addie and I did."

"I *know*," Greta said again.

"Get in front of it, then." Toni paused. "Tell Em. And then can we please never discuss it again? Both of you need to stop this. You cannot text all the time and then tell me you're not getting all *enmeshed*. You should stop this before one of you gets hurt."

"I'm meeting Emily for lunch today, just so you know." Greta sounded small to herself, but she still added, "If you want to sell the new book to someone else—"

"I'm not stupid, Greta. I don't think you suddenly stopped knowing how to edit because you . . . because you both . . . you know. You didn't take advantage of her. I know that, and I know she didn't take advantage of you either. She has feelings. You *both* do."

"We agreed that was not the case," Greta said tightly. "No feelings."

"Right. That's exactly how feelings work, isn't it? You just say, 'No feelings here.' You're smarter than this. I'm not an expert, but I *know* I made a lot of stupid mistakes running from how I felt about Addie." Toni made a grumbling noise. "You get that I'm not a fan of all this gooey talk, right?" Instead of letting Greta answer, Toni carried on without pause, "What I'm trying to say is don't fuck with my friend if you aren't willing to be all in. You both have too much on the line."

"I'm very much aware of the risks to her career and mine," Greta countered in a low voice. "I offered her a new editor."

"I'm not worried about your *careers*. Seriously, Greta? You're both smart and talented, and you did nothing wrong because you weren't aware of the business part." Toni sighed loudly. "I'm *worried* about two people I like who will get hurt if they don't get their heads out of their asses."

"She is my friend. The other thing is over." Greta didn't add that she wanted more, but she wasn't sure that was a secret right now.

"Sure. *Friends*. You both keep saying that, but I heard your feelings the other night, and Addie plucked Kae's feelings right out of her while I sat there trying not to hear it. I had to hear things about you that I would like to bleach from my memory. Just . . . be careful. Be smarter than I was when I was falling in love and in denial," Toni said, and then in her usual abrupt way, she added, "That's it. Goodbye."

Toni disconnected without waiting for a reply.

For several moments, Greta sat there rolling over the things that Toni was intimating. Was Kaelee *in* this emotionally, too? That seemed to be the opinion Toni held. Greta had also felt like Kaelee wasn't as casual as she claimed to be, but *Kaelee* had repeatedly insisted that she didn't date, that she didn't want that. Even if she did have feelings, Kaelee had made herself clear on the topic of relationships, and Greta had to respect that. She couldn't fathom risking everything with another woman who wasn't ready for love. It had taken her two years since Tasha to even want a friend with benefits. Now, though, Greta was thinking about more.

*I just want a home with a woman who loves me. I want to laugh and make love and share each other's life.*

The dream sounded so simple: true companionship, intimate connections, and lasting love. The fantasy of finding that—or losing it—was the heart of an entire industry of music, film, books, advertisements, and journalism. That hope of finding someone who made the load lighter and the miles shorter, the nights safer and the days brighter, drove billions of people to consume media telling them the impossible could happen. Sometimes, Greta would admit, it seemed so statistically unlikely that finding and keeping love could happen.

Finding love was hard enough, but making it last? That was beyond impossible.

*But it's what I want.*

That was what she'd wanted before Tasha, with Tasha, and now that she was healing, Greta's desire for true love had returned. She'd let Tasha's cheating make her forget her own dreams and hopes, but now that her heart was recovering, she could move on. Despite how it ended, there had been good times with Tasha. The possibility of forever had not turned into reality for them, but maybe this time, maybe this woman could be different.

*I could love Kaelee.*

That was the truth that terrified Greta more than anything else. The industry obstacles could be manageable for both of them if this were real, but Greta couldn't stand the public humiliation of putting herself out there, letting her colleagues see that she was in this place emotionally, if Kaelee didn't even want the same thing—and she had said repeatedly that she didn't. Her actions said otherwise, but her words mattered, too.

Being the only one trying to move forward wasn't the path to making a relationship work. Greta had already learned that lesson. She'd had her heart broken as much by hope as by Tasha's actions.

*Kaelee is a friend. We are friends who text and don't get naked. That's all this can be.*

That was the only option, no matter how much Greta wished they could be more. She couldn't move forward with her own life or in being a good friend to Kaelee without cutting this hope of *more* out of her heart. First, she'd need to tell Emily about the mistakes with her author, explain it to Kaelee, and then . . . try to date again, try to find someone who was emotionally available.

Resolved, and reeling from her far too raw conversation with Toni, Greta was vaguely mortified that she was in this situation. Toni wasn't her *friend*, not really. If anything she was Kaelee's friend, and Greta had violated Toni's trust by putting her in the awkward situation of keeping a secret from her agent. Aside from how ragingly unprofessional it all was, Greta had failed at being a friend to Kaelee—or maybe she had just been an overbearing friend. She wasn't entirely sure if her choice to call Toni that night was an overreaction or not. People died of alcohol poisoning, not to mention Kaelee's absurd idea of crawling into the bathtub when she was barely awake.

Of course, none of that made today's luncheon any less dreadful.

"Are we acquiring something new?" Ian asked, looking at the last-minute meeting with Emily on the schedule.

"We will be when Toni finishes her book," Greta said, not lying but not really capable of admitting why she was meeting with Emily. "This isn't about Toni."

"Hmmm. Well, I like the second Carpenter book. I know your taste well enough to know you do, too." Ian tapped his pen on his cheek absently as he pondered. "Are we talking numbers on one or both? I can get th—"

"Ian." She met his gaze and smiled. "Emily and I are just having lunch. She's delivered not one but two excellent books to me. With the early reviews, store buy-ins, and general buzz, I'm expecting Kaelee to be the second bestselling author whose books Emily has sold to me. So we're having lunch."

Ian gave her a look before saying, "I can tell when you're nervous, boss. Wait." He lowered his voice. "Is this a lunch date or a lunch *date*?"

"No!" Greta's face burned with awkward embarrassment, which probably didn't make her denial sound very convincing.

"I wouldn't have clocked her as your type, but . . ." Ian shrugged. "Whatever. Go be social. I'll see you at two for the note swap on the batch of pitches I flagged."

Greta plucked her oversized sunglasses off the corner of her desk, wound a fuchsia scarf around her neck, and grabbed her coat. Then she set out to meet the agent for two of her most promising authors to make a confession that could cause more drama in her life than anything since her breakup with Tasha. At least that was semiprivate. Anything Emily decided here would be far from that.

Greta opted not to bring up the call from Toni, but she paused in the lobby and sent a text to Kaelee.

**Greta:** Talking to E today.
**Kaelee:** You don't have to.
**Greta:** I do. She needs to know. Also Toni
will tell her. Better to come from me.
**Kaelee:** I can call her . . .

Greta smiled. She wasn't sure which "her" Kaelee had meant, but it could have been both or either. Kaelee was as protective a friend as Greta had ever had.

**Greta:** If you want to for YOU, fine. I will
still talk to Emily, and I talked to Toni.

There was not much to say now. She and Kaelee had a past, a recent past but still, that was all over. They were friends now. The fact that Greta treasured each text—even silly memes and links to articles—was just friendly fondness. It *had* to be, for both their careers.

*And the frequency needs to decrease. A lot.*

*I can't try dating anyone else if my heart is tied up with Kaelee.*

Greta ducked her head against the sharp November wind and set out to meet her judge and jury. Emily was loyal, reasonable, and savvy. That gave Greta a reason to hope that they could figure out the best plan of action together. The priority was making sure that Kaelee, who was at the start of a promising career, would be looked after, protected, and feel secure.

First, though, Greta would throw herself on Emily's mercy.

## 19

# *Kaelee*

## THE DAY BEFORE THANKSGIVING

Her family could torch everything Kaelee had built. Her friends. Her career. Her future. *And whatever is happening with Greta.* The smartest move was to break her lease and get out of DC, start over somewhere new.

*Maybe I could get a fake identity.*

But Kaelee had good friends and the start of a dream career, and she almost had a third academic degree. She didn't *want* to run.

Today she had gone to the gym for two hours. Free weights and cardio usually helped Kaelee feel in control, kept the anxiety at bay, and even decreased her libido. Today, all it had done was take the edge off. Somehow even grocery shopping made her think of Greta. *Naked on her table. Making lunch naked.* Kaelee needed to find a casual connection. *Less time thinking of Greta. Less time texting Greta.* They weren't going to end up finding a way to be . . . anything, really.

*I need to move on.*

*I can't be what she needs.*

*I won't put her at risk.*

Kaelee grabbed ten yams, brown sugar, too many apples, and some candied pecans to make her contribution to tomorrow's group Thanksgiving meal. Cherie was making potatoes and some sort of casserole. Evander was on turkey duty. Another grad student,

Malachi, and his two partners were doing pies. Someone else had rolls or bread. The holiday was too short for a lot of broke-ass grad students to go home, and others, like her, had no home to go to. So they all made a group meal. This was her second one, but it was apparently an ongoing tradition. *Most* of the group called it Friends-giving or Carbs-giving, although Evander had declared it Cal-Free Day with a group text that any food items consumed that day with friends were calorie-free, a claim Kaelee countered with an offer to organize a group run for anyone not gullible enough to believe his magical declaration.

This part of life, friends unconnected to publishing or her past, was the most stable part of Kaelee's life. That was why she was still pursuing a PhD, not because she necessarily wanted a future in academia but because she liked having her ragtag family of students just a little while longer. She had enough credits—and two full novels she could submit as her thesis. The MFA only included one, so she could submit that, check what classes she needed—if any—and finish her degree. That would free her.

*In case I really do need to run.*

Absently, as she waited in the grocery store checkout line, she texted Cherie a note that said, My life is better because I know you.

Cherie called a minute later. "Are you dying?"

"*What?*" Kaelee opened her bags and started to scan her groceries one-handed.

"That was a goodbye-flavored text if I ever saw one," Cherie pointed out. "You dying? Leaving town? What's happening?"

Kaelee forced a laugh. "You're so much sometimes. I was emotional. Friendsgiving meal. My book coming out. Realizing my classwork for the degree is done." Kaelee balanced her mobile on her shoulder as she weighed the yams and continued to check out. "I'm glad to know you, so I thought I'd say it."

"Well, friends stay in touch even after degrees. You hear me? You aren't leaving me." Cherie didn't have to be in front of her for Kaelee to know her right hand was in the air shaking and pointing as if they were face-to-face. Kaelee recognized the tone well enough to visualize the gestures that went with it.

"Not leaving you right now, Cher." Kaelee finished ringing up, paid, and carried her bags to the car. A large manila envelope waited under her wipers. Her old name was scrawled across it.

"Are you still there?" Cherie's voice felt like an anchor, something to clutch as panic threatened to rise and choke Kaelee.

Trying to sound calm, Kaelee said, "Hey, since I have you now . . . I hate to do this, but I can't make it to dinner tomorrow. I need to go out of town for the weekend. Please don't be mad at me!"

"Seriously?"

"Uh-huh. A work thing."

"On *Thanksgiving*?"

After scanning the parking lot for anyone suspicious and seeing no one, Kaelee looked back at the envelope. Her old name, Sabrina, was scrawled there in familiar handwriting. Kaelee hadn't seen her mother's elegant, swooping script in years, but she knew it instantly.

*Is someone in a car watching me?* Kaelee's gaze swept over the parking lot, looking for anyone standing near enough to grab her.

"Kaelee?" Cherie's voice tugged her attention for a moment. "You still there? Are you okay?"

"Yeah. Sorry. Got to go. I need to go . . . away. I'm leaving for the weekend. I'll let you know when I'm back, sorry about the yams." As she spoke, Kaelee pivoted, looking at the nearest cars and feeling grateful that it was broad daylight. She couldn't decide if she was more at risk opening her car door or standing there. She walked to the trunk, put the groceries in, and then looked around again. She looked inside the car—front and back seats.

Nothing. Just that thick envelope pinned under her wipers. Kaelee grabbed it as if it were hiding a copperhead about to bite her. She wished she could toss it away just as quickly as a snake's strike. Nothing *they* sent could be good.

*How did they find me?*

*Why are they doing this?*

*What's in it? What do I need to know? Do I?*

With the envelope still in hand, Kaelee got into her car, heart pounding in her ears. Even though all the car doors were locked, she started to shake. Small trembles turned into larger ones as she looked around. The desire to open the envelope warred with the fear of what horrible things it hid. Feeling it through the envelope made clear it was papers; she could feel binder clips and staples inside.

She tossed it on the passenger seat and connected her phone to the car. Kaelee wasn't sure where she wanted to go or what she should do. Leaving an envelope on a car wasn't likely to be considered harassment or any other legally actionable thing, and the truth was that even if it were actionable, she didn't want to get into a legal battle with that man or with his fleet of slick liars. She wanted to use her trust and her book money to live her life, not fight her ghosts.

"Why? Why are you fuckers contacting me?" Kaelee shifted into gear and drove, pulling into the already heavy traffic.

The nation's capital and a holiday weekend made for a bad mix. Even if she had somewhere she wanted to be, Kaelee wasn't sure she'd want to face the flight backups in Dulles or Reagan National; she certainly wouldn't want to be on the I-95 or the Beltway in a few hours. The surface streets were already busy, but not yet stop and roll.

As she drove, Kaelee turned randomly, watching her rearview mirror and wondering if she was being tailed. She couldn't keep eyes on her mirrors and drive safely. There were always so many nondescript black sedans in the District that she couldn't say if they were the same or different cars. All she knew for certain was she didn't want to go home in case she was being followed.

*If they can find my car in a grocery store parking lot, they already know where I live,* logic insisted.

*Which means they can show up at my door,* fear added.

The thought of finding her parents at her door made Kaelee's chest hurt.

She steered away from her address. The image of barricading

herself inside threatened to overwhelm her tenuous grasp on control. She wasn't going to make it easy for them to talk to her face-to-face.

She couldn't crash Toni and Addie's holiday, or even say for sure if they were home. Addie's family lived in California, where the show filmed, too, so the couple crossed back and forth across the nation. *Not with them. Not on a holiday.* She couldn't let the Alden selfishness ruin her friends' holidays either. Hotels were safer than houses in many ways. Room service, anonymity, crowds of witnesses; a hotel would fix this weekend's crisis. For the big picture, she didn't know yet.

Without thinking it through, she hit Greta's number.

Kaelee didn't want to think about why she felt her tension decrease at the sound of Greta's voice a moment later. "Hey! How are your holiday cooking plans going?"

"Decided to bail on this city and drive north," Kaelee said. "I'm thinking either hotel and takeout or . . . I don't even know. I'm not staying here, though."

"Oh . . . Are you okay?"

"Honestly? Not really." Kaelee turned again on a random road, steered into a parking lot, and parked in a vast open space where she could see if any cars or people on foot approached her. She was reasonably sure no one was currently following her. Thoughts of trackers on her car made her debate whether she ought to take the train or even fly to wherever she was going, but right then being without a car sounded a lot like being trapped.

*Rental car. That's the best plan.*

"Talk to me?" Greta asked softly after a long, quiet moment.

"There was an envelope on my car from my family." Kaelee glanced at it in the passenger seat. She didn't feel ready to open it. She needed to see what bullshit it held, but the thought of doing that filled her with dread. She told Greta as much and then added, "I want to run. I know it's just an envelope, but I haven't heard from them in years and now this is twice."

"Running is better than getting drunk. That's progress," Greta said. "Do you need to stop at your apartment before you head out for the weekend?"

Kaelee felt embarrassed that she had been driving around the last week with a packed suitcase in her trunk, but right now it felt like she had been prepared, not foolish. She said, "I have a pair of suitcases and a few boxes in my car. After he called . . . I don't know. I just wanted to be ready in case I had to go."

"Makes sense." Greta let out a long breath. "I don't have plans for the long weekend. If you wanted company . . . I mean, you could come here, or I could meet you somewhere."

"What are you saying right now?" Kaelee watched several cars in the parking lot. Nothing about them seemed alarming, but nothing had seemed amiss before she went into the grocery store either.

"I miss you."

Despite the fear thrumming in her skin, Greta's admission made Kaelee smile. "Yeah?"

"I do. I miss *Lee,* too." Greta's voice was as raw as Kaelee often felt when she admitted that she was well beyond feeling casual here.

"I'm a trainwreck, you know?" Kaelee pointed out. "I would like nothing more than to run away with you, but I am still who I am. Hell, Kaelee Carpenter might not even exist if I have to run."

"You don't have to run."

"You don't know them." Kaelee watched another of the ubiquitous black sedans drive into the lot where she was sitting. "Deep pockets, Greta. Deep hatred."

"Meet me and tell me all about it."

"Are you sure?" Kaelee wanted to.

She wanted to spend several days lost with the woman who was now one of her dearest friends, but she also didn't want to push the boundaries that Greta had demanded. Endangering Greta's career was not acceptable. She wasn't like her father; she respected the boundaries people drew in their lives. She had to.

Carefully, Kaelee said, "I don't want to reject you, but I don't want to pressure you or guilt you into anything."

"I appreciate that, but that's not what's happening here. I miss you, and publishing is closed for the holiday. I . . . want to take a break from everything here. I want to see you. If you want—"

"I do. Whatever you're offering, I'll take it and be grateful for the crumbs." Kaelee relaxed a little more as the car across from hers pulled out. "I'll meet you wherever you want."

"Where were you thinking? Tell me where to go. I can catch a train."

"I'll rent a place and send you an address," Kaelee offered. "I need to drop my car somewhere and get a rental. I don't know if they're tracking my car, so if they are, running in it is pointless."

"*Really?* Your car?"

"When I was a teen, he had a tracker on the car. He always had one on my mother's car. He said it was for our safety, but . . . I don't think that's why. I didn't think so then either." Kaelee thought back to life in the Alden household. Tripp tracked cars, phone calls, spending. Everything in her life was controlled. How her mother lived that way still confused Kaelee.

"What if I rent a place instead? You rent the car, and I'll find a place. Philly is halfway between us. I can take a train there, and you can meet me at the station or hotel." Greta sounded completely matter-of-fact, as if last-minute weekend getaways were normal for them. "I can swing by my place, grab a weekend bag, and be at the train in an hour. Will that work?"

"Yes. God, yes." Kaelee smiled, even though no one could see it.

"House or hotel? I don't know what's left last minute, but if there is a house outside Philly, is that better? Or do you want to stay inside the city in a hotel?"

"If I'm seeing Marie, all I need is a bed and room service," Kaelee said. "If I'm *only* seeing Greta, I'd like to sightsee a bit. If I get both? Whatever you want is good by me."

Greta laughed. "I want my friend and sex. Hotel it is."

"What changed?" Kaelee asked.

"I calmed down a little. You aren't going to expose me, and

really, I don't have the power here. We both do." Greta let out a sigh. "All I could think about were Tash's accusations, and how it might look, and . . . I panicked."

"So what does that mean?"

"Agree to let Ian be your editor and be my . . . friend with benefits? I want to be sure your career is protected, and I want to be with you." Greta's voice wavered a bit. "Unless you need me not to offer sex. I can be there as your friend only. Rent a house with two bedrooms—"

"I wasn't the one who said no more sex," Kaelee reminded her. Then she added, "I'll look forward to getting to know my new editor for the sequel."

"So you're saying maybe we could try again? You'll let me be there for you . . . ?"

"Yes. I fucking love y—*your plan*." Kaelee closed her eyes, realizing that she almost said that she loved Greta. She pressed her lips together. That would've been a disaster. She couldn't love her. They were just friends. That was all they could be. Maybe they could be friends who were compatible naked.

"You too." Greta sounded all soft and inviting in that moment, but a second later, she was all business again, saying only, "I'll text you or call you with the address. Go get the rental car. I'll see you tonight."

# 20

## *Greta*

When Greta disconnected, she found a possibly *too* posh hotel in Center City and reserved a room with a king bed for Wednesday, Thursday, Friday, and Saturday night. It had a modern version of a claw-foot tub, pillow-top beds, and a view of the city. Plus, the hotel had twenty-four-hour room service, two restaurants, and a spa on site. Maybe Kaelee would be offended by the fact that Greta was fond of luxury hotels; some people were turned off by that. Maybe spending several days together would let them discover they were actually incompatible. Maybe it would ease the tension between them.

*I doubt that.*

"Headed out early for the weekend," she told Ian as she closed down everything. He was at his desk outside her office. Few people were still here, but when she worked, he worked.

"At *noon*? Did you decide what to do? Are you going to visit family? Friends? Stay in the city?" Ian was seemingly checking if she needed somewhere to go, and she appreciated it. They weren't outright trying to declare themselves bosom buds, but there had been a definite turn toward friendship.

"None of that. I'm going away with someone I went . . . that I saw on a couple . . . nights out," Greta blurted out. "I'll have tracking off on my phone."

"Oh? Do tell." He followed her into the office and shut the door, so whatever they discussed wouldn't be overheard. "What's she like?"

"She gorgeous, very my type, smart but works out a lot." Greta sighed before she could stop herself. "Just . . . everything I want in a woman."

"And you're going away for the long weekend," Ian clarified.

"She lives in DC." Greta stared at him as if she could somehow transfer the information into his brain without saying it. "It's complicated."

"Oh?" He raised both brows. "How complicated, Greta?"

"*Complicated*," she repeated. "We met before . . . before we knew we had any connection. She's a writer, actually."

"I see. That could be awkward if you were to run into her at work or something and it was a surprise." He shook his head. His tone was half questioning as he said, "Like 'people awkwardly running to the bathroom to figure it out' awkward?"

"*Exactly* like that." Greta felt like her face was on fire. *In for one detail, in for all of them.* She blurted out, "The lunch with Emily was to discuss this. She deserved to hear it from me."

Ian made a sympathetic noise.

"I'll have a handle on it by next week." She shook her head. "I thought I was done with relationships or even situationships, but I want this to work. Maybe it'll turn out to be nothing, but I need to go find out. Either way, I will need you to step up as her editor."

Ian nodded. "Oh, on unrelated notes, I *do* have an editorial letter and line notes on K.C.'s second book ready to go."

Greta laughed at his wide-eyed, faux-innocent expression. "I didn't even realize I was ready to move on, but I am. I want . . . I want the big romance, the person who is my automatic holiday party date, and all of it. I also want *her* to be that person. I mean, maybe we won't click if we are together for four days, though."

"Go get your mystery date," Ian encouraged. "She's a lucky woman to catch your eye. I hope she knows it."

"Maybe it'll be nothing, but . . ." Greta smiled at him, letting her hope leak out more. "I rarely click with people so quickly. I have to see what that means. If I don't, I'll kick myself later."

After she left, Greta headed home and packed lightly, taking no work at all with her. This weekend she was not an editor, especially not Kaelee's editor. She was a woman who just wanted to be loved, to be held, to matter because of who she was.

A few hours later, she was standing in a hotel lobby, thinking back to another hotel where she sat and waited for Kaelee. This time, Greta checked in and sent the room number to Kaelee over text with a message to come up when she arrived.

**Kaelee:** About twenty minutes out.
**Greta:** Dinner out or room service?
**Kaelee:** Room.

So Greta gave in to her impulses, ordered a few options on room service, and asked for it to be delivered in forty minutes. Then she unpacked. Once that was all settled, she still had ten minutes left, so she drew a nice bath and flipped through the hotel television options. Her nerves were less settled than when she'd met Kaelee as a stranger, less even than when she'd met her at the train station. Now, everything was different. They'd chatted, talked about mundane and important things. This was real, though, for both of them.

*We both have the power to wreck the other's career.*

*Neither of us would. I believe that.*

But it was a leap of faith, trusting each other, hoping that trust was not misplaced. Greta mulled it over as she debated the far less weighty topic of pulling on one of the plush robes. She decided she'd keep on her dress instead. She'd peeled off her tights and boots so she had on only a dress and underthings. Once room service had come and gone, she'd be able to take off her dress and get more comfortable.

Fifteen minutes later, a light tap on the door announced Kaelee's arrival. Greta looked through the peephole and then opened the door. Foolish or not, Greta drank in the sight of her. She had a gym bag, a garment bag, and a backpack, but no actual suitcase. Her eyes were weary, and she looked even more muscular, as if she'd been taking her stress out at the gym.

"Hey." Greta leaned in and brushed her lips over Kaelee's in a brief kiss. The mere touch of lips ought not make her heart or body sing, but she'd thought they'd never kiss again. Her heart tightened in joy.

Kaelee's smile came over her face like she was dropping worries aside. "Hey yourself."

Greta didn't offer to take her bag, remembering her tension over that last time. "Long drive?"

"Not as bad as I expected for the night before Thanksgiving. I guess I left early enough in the day to miss the post-work chaos." Kaelee's expression belied the casual words.

Greta opened the closet for Kaelee to deposit everything. "I ordered a mini buffet for dinner. Should be here in about ten."

Kaelee smiled widely. "You're perfect. Have I told you that today?"

"There's a bath ready, too. Should be cool enough by now," Greta continued.

The smile on Kaelee's face morphed into something less affectionate and more ravenous. "Is it big enough for us both?"

"It is." Greta stepped back, slightly out of reach now. "I suspect answering the door naked is not a great idea, though, so I need to wait on room service before I can join you."

"Do you mind if . . ." Kaelee glanced at the bathroom door.

"Not at all. I can bring you something to eat when it gets here."

"You are a *goddess*. Do you hear me?" Kaelee stepped forward, grabbed her by the hips, and pulled her close. "Is this okay? I mean, you kissed me, but . . . tell me your rules."

"No rules." Greta tilted her head upward. "This weekend I am just a woman who went away with someone she hopes will seduce her."

Kaelee stared at her for a second. "So this is just a weekend reprieve?"

Greta shrugged. "I don't know yet. I hope it's more, but can we see how we get along? Maybe we aren't as compatible as we thought."

The look Kaelee gave her was somewhere between amused and sympathetic. "Because weeks of texting about everything didn't clarify that?"

"I like you, Kaelee Carpenter. I like talking to you and texting, and I like that I was the person you called today. And if you're willing to have Ian as your editor—"

"I am," Kaelee interrupted.

"Then we can start with the weekend," Greta finished.

Not breaking eye contact, Kaelee said, "I'll take it. I already want more than a few days. You get that, right?"

"Even though neither of us *do* that?" Greta whispered. "I have spent so many hours trying to make sense of us. . . ."

Kaelee tightened her hold on her hips as she slanted her mouth over Greta's and kissed her. The feel of her body clutching Greta like she was a life raft in a storm was enough to erase any lingering hesitation. Physically, they were aligned. That was a truth unchanged.

Greta's hands found themselves on Kaelee's shoulders, and then one hand snaked upward to hold Kaelee in place, making their kiss last just a moment longer. When she pulled back, Greta admitted, "I have been so worried about you. I don't know why they're back in your life or what will happen, but after your binge drink—"

"I am right here," Kaelee said. Her voice was rough as she added, "Not drinking. Not running far away from you. Right here with you for the next few days. I need to hide for a few days and think, too, and I'm grateful you're here with me while I do that."

"Then get naked and relax in the tub while I get you dinner," Greta suggested. Once Kaelee nodded, Greta added, "Let me take care of you tonight. We can talk or you can share whatever you had in that envelope, or—"

"Or you'll let me have tonight just to have you?" Kaelee interrupted. "I want to have control over my life, clear my head, and sex does that for me."

"If that's what you need."

"I need *you,* Greta. Can I have you?"

Greta nodded. "First, soak away the aches from driving in holiday traffic. Then, I'm all yours."

"Gladly."

Once Kaelee went into the bathroom and shut the door, Greta leaned against the wall with a huge smile on her face. *She wants more, too. I'm not in this alone.* Her feelings bubbled up like a well of happiness, and she stayed that way for several moments. Kaelee had called her, sought her out, and she was here.

When the knock at the door and call of "Room service" came, Greta looked out the peephole again and then cracked the door. She held out her hand for the slip, but she kept her body half in the doorway, so she was standing with one foot behind the door. "I have it from here."

The man said, "Of course. If you prefer, I could wheel it in to—"

"No need. Just leave it right there." Greta signed the slip, keeping the door barely opened still. She didn't expect Kaelee to step out of the bathroom, but just in case, Greta was being careful.

Once the man left and was several doorways away, Greta pulled the cart into the room. "Food's here," she called out. Then she tossed the locks on the door. She poured two glasses of water and grabbed a bowl of fresh berries. Tapping on the door to the bathroom, she asked, "Can I join you? Or do you need—"

"You can come in," Kaelee called out.

Greta paused just inside the door of the massive bathroom. The vision before her made her need to pause and take it all in. Kaelee was naked in the oversized tub. Her head was tilted back, resting on the side of the tub. Her eyes were half closed in relaxation, and the swell of her breasts was visible above the water.

"You're trying to kill me, aren't you?" Greta met Kaelee's amused gaze.

Kaelee laughed. "Not at all. I have plans for you." She sat up, water sluicing over her breasts as she lifted herself partway out of the water. "What's that?"

"Berries. Water. I thought you might want a nibble before you got out."

Kaelee smirked. "Happy to nibble on you. You ought to get naked first. . . ."

"Be good." Greta laughed and held out a raspberry.

Watching Greta the whole time, Kaelee came to the opposite side of the tub, so she was kneeling in front of Greta, and parted her lips. She sucked the berry into her mouth and then said, "I need you closer than this."

"I'm trying to take care of you," Greta protested. "Hot bath. Healthy meal."

"Not what I *need*, darlin'." She reached up with a dripping wet hand and cupped Greta's breast. "Not what you need either, is it?"

Greta's breath hitched.

Kaelee slid her other hand under the skirt of Greta's dress and upward until her hand was over Greta's panties. "Here I am all naked and wet, and you're out there fully dressed. Something's wrong with this situation, don't you think?"

"You're terrible," Greta breathed.

"No, I'm not. Let me remind you how good I am. Take off the dress, darlin'. These things hiding all that lusciousness away from me are already wet. No sense keeping them on now."

Greta peeled her dress off and tossed it behind her.

"Look at that." Kaelee smiled. "My fingerprints are right there. Do you see that?" She leaned forward and pressed her lips to Greta's underwear. "Right there. What was the expression?" She paused like she was thinking. Then she put a hand on Greta's hip. "I licked it; now it's mine."

"Kaelee . . ."

Then Kaelee leaned forward and licked Greta over her panties. "I licked that, Greta. It's mine now."

# 21

## *Kaelee*

Kaelee watched as Greta slid her panties off and stepped out of them. There were so many things she needed to figure out after that damn envelope on her car. She felt weak and out of control of her own life, bailing on her friends, running away from her city, leaving her apartment. But *this* part of life made sense, more than anything else. She knew this. She understood sex with a gorgeous woman.

Right now, Greta looked down at her like she was special, like she was amazing, and that feeling was better than any liquor or even the rush from being at the gym. Kaelee considered telling her how much it meant that she had decided to spend this weekend with her, admitting how afraid and lost she was, confessing how much steadier she felt just knowing she wasn't alone with her fears.

Instead, Kaelee came to her knees and held out a hand to steady Greta as she stepped into the water. "Right there, darlin'. Can you sit right there for me?"

"On the edge of the tub?"

"Yes." Kaelee directed Greta's hands so they were on either side of her luscious hips. "Just hold yourself right here for me. Can you stay like this?" She stared up at her, leaning upward to suck on a nipple before adding, "I need one of these lovely legs up on my shoulder, darlin'."

She bit Greta's other nipple lightly, noting that Greta arched into that more than she did a gentle suckle. So she repeated that action on the other side.

When Kaelee crouched back down, she bit and suckled Greta's inner thigh, leaving a hickey there, before directing that leg onto her shoulder. She met Greta's gaze. "Teeth, huh?"

"Sometimes," Greta acknowledged.

Kaelee bit her again, sucking and nipping and leaving tiny bruises in her wake. "Are you okay like this? Steady?"

"Yes." Greta stared at her like she was transfixed.

"I like having you on display for me, darlin'. Do you know that?" Kaelee leaned in and dragged the flat of her tongue over Greta's already wet sex, and then continued tasting and teasing her until Greta's hand came up to cup Kaelee's head.

Kaelee stopped. "Hand back where I put it, darlin'. You aren't the one in charge right now."

Greta's breathing hitched. "Will I be at all?"

"If you're really, *really* good, maybe later." Kaelee wanted that, more than she had with any other person, but she wanted control right now. *Needed it.* Her life was fractured, and she really had to take control of something, someone, or she was afraid she'd spiral. "Trust me."

"I do," Greta swore, putting her hand back on the tub.

Kaelee rose to her knees again. "Let's try a little game, Greta. You do whatever I say, and if you listen really well, I'll let you tell me what to do later tonight."

"Sober? I only want that if you can stay sober to do it." Greta held her gaze. "I'll do what you say all weekend if you need, Kaelee. If that will make you feel better, I'm here for you, however you need. There's no payment for it, no need to offer me control. I *want* to be whatever you need. That's it."

Kaelee felt like her chest was constricted. She surged forward and kissed Greta, sliding her tongue into her mouth and licking her way inside. She had to kiss Greta in order to keep her own words from escaping. Greta was exactly right for her. She understood the things Kaelee didn't want to admit. She made it feel like Kaelee was normal to have issues.

When Kaelee pulled back, she said, "Games can wait."

She kissed Greta again, and this time she angled her hand so her palm was pressing on Greta's clit and her fingers were stroking her. Greta whimpered into the kiss.

And when they pulled apart, Greta said, "What do you need?"

"You. Naked in my arms."

"May I get up?" Greta asked. "Tell me exactly what to do, Kaelee."

Kaelee stood and held out a hand. "Come dry me off." She held out a towel. "Hard."

Without a word, Greta took the towel and rubbed Kaelee's arms, legs, and torso. She looked at Kaelee as she held the towel in front of her chest. "Here?"

"Yes." Kaelee swallowed. "You should check if I'm wet anywhere else, Greta." Then Kaelee took Greta's hand and directed it down.

"Right here," Greta said, stroking Kaelee's pussy. "This feels pretty damp. Shall I check?"

At first Kaelee thought that sounded exactly right, but as Greta slipped her fingers along Kaelee's skin, she couldn't bear it. The wave of pleasure that threatened to roll over her felt too much like falling. She grabbed Greta's wrist. "Enough. I need . . ."

Without a word, Greta understood. "Tell me. You're in control, Kaelee. Just you."

Kaelee could have wept at both the fact that she *knew* she could eventually hand control over to this woman and the fact that Greta didn't pressure her to do that. She didn't try to make demands. She respected whatever fucked-up boundaries Kaelee had.

She swept Greta into her arms, cradling her, and said only, "Thank you." The words were a thin version of all the things Kaelee could say but talking about all of that wasn't what she needed. Not right now.

Without letting all those words spill out, Kaelee carried Greta to the hotel bed and lowered her carefully. "Touch yourself for me."

Greta stared at her for a minute. "Touch myself in front of you?"

Kaelee paused at the hesitation in her voice. She wanted this, but if Greta was uncomfortable with it, they could certainly do something else. "You like to be on display, darlin'. I like to look at you."

"I do like both of those." Greta glanced at the window. The blinds were drawn, even though they were on the eighteenth floor. "Not on the bed, though . . . unless you need me here."

"What about over there? You keep looking at the window." She held a hand out to Greta. "You want to have strangers watch you, too?"

"Yes." Greta slid off the bed and walked to the window. Beside it was a wooden desk. She stood there as Kaelee pulled open the blinds, illuminating her in the falling light of sunset.

"Turn around. Face the window," Kaelee ordered. She stepped up close behind her, pulling Greta flush against her and keeping her arm around her like a belt. "I have you."

Greta nodded. "You do. I know I'm safe because you're here."

"Same," Kaelee admitted around the sudden knot in her throat.

In the next moments, the only sounds were their breathing as Kaelee used her free hand to pluck Greta's nipples so they stood in sharp points. "Do you think someone out there could be looking out their window to see your naked beauty all on display right now?"

"Maybe. I want them to see what it's like to be touched by you."

"Ah, but they won't see me, darlin'. I'm just the hand touching you." Kaelee whispered the words against her neck, kissing her damp skin between words. "It's you on display."

"I feel reckless with you," Greta whispered.

"I have you. I'll keep you safe." Kaelee would keep Greta safe from all threats. She had to. That was the problem. Greta made everything feel bearable, but Kaelee couldn't risk Greta's safety, or her career. *She deserves better than me.* Kaelee's voice was thick as she swore, "Tonight, I'll take care of all these needs we had to ignore lately. Can I do that?"

"Yes, please."

"Can you do *only* what you're told?"

"For you. Yes." Greta was trembling already.

"Your pretty pussy is hidden away with your legs all closed together like that." Kaelee trailed her hand between Greta's breasts and over her stomach. "Such a bad girl. Hiding yourself. Don't you want to show anyone watching what they can't touch?"

"Yes."

Kaelee pinched her inner thigh. "Open up. Foot on the desk." She steadied Greta as she shifted, propping one foot on the side railing of the desk. "There's my good girl. What should we do, darlin'? You're right here, on display like a treat in a window."

"Kaelee . . ." Greta whined. "Tell me what you want."

"Show everyone out there watching what you do when you think of me," Kaelee suggested. "Show *me*."

Greta's right hand slipped between her legs. Her whole body shivered as she circled her clit slowly. "Pinch me again, please."

Kaelee pinched Greta's nipples again, staring at their reflection in the window as night fell. She was nothing but hands on Greta; most of Kaelee's body was hidden behind her lover.

She whispered, "Do you think that strangers can see you like this? That they have their hands on their lovers' bodies as they watch you?"

Greta moaned and grabbed Kaelee's wrist and directed it lower. "Here."

Kaelee complied, gently, though.

"I wish . . ."

"What?" Kaelee asked.

But Greta shook her head. "No. You're in control."

"Tell me."

Greta met her eyes in the reflection in the window. "I want you to take *more* control."

The words were magical for Kaelee. She grabbed the desk chair and dragged it forward. "Hold this. Bend over. Eyes watching your reflection."

Greta's expression was too blissed out for words. She complied, staring at them in the reflection as Kaelee placed Greta's hands on top of the back of the chair. For a moment, Greta didn't respond when Kaelee nudged her legs apart. Kaelee's hand came down on Greta's ass in a light smack.

The next time when Greta didn't move without Kaelee applying pressure, Kaelee knew it was intentional disobedience. Her hand came down harder. Greta's breath caught, and she met Kaelee's eyes in the reflection.

"Look at you." Kaelee's voice shook. "Hiding your pussy again. Bent over so no one can see."

"But you put me—"

"And now you argue with me?" Kaelee sighed exaggeratedly and swatted Greta's cheeks again. "I thought you could be good, darlin'?"

"I can." Greta widened her legs more as Kaelee plunged two fingers into Greta's dripping body. "More fingers. Faster."

"Good girls help, darlin'. Touch yourself." Kaelee added a third finger, watching as Greta rubbed her clit while Kaelee drove her fingers in harder and faster. Her own body tightened in a way that giving pleasure created. Sometimes she thought she'd get off just from the joy of giving.

The sound of Greta's whimpering and moaning felt loud in the silent hotel room. "Such a good girl, Greta. Are you going to show everyone how beautiful you are when you get off?"

"Yes. Please, yes."

Kaelee leaned forward, her body tight against Greta's, and bit the side of Greta's throat gently. Her free arm wrapped around Greta so that it was like a bandolier over Greta's chest.

When Greta's orgasm hit, her knees buckled, but Kaelee tightened the hold of the arm around her to keep her from falling. Then

Kaelee scooped her up and carried her back to the bed. Greta curled against her like a boneless creature.

"Thank you," Kaelee whispered as she kissed the top of Greta's head. "Are you okay with everything?"

"*Very* okay. I'm the one who's sated, and *you're* saying thank you to *me*?" Greta sighed. "You spoil me, Kaelee. I was afraid we'd never get to do anything again, and . . . I want this. I want *you*. I don't know what that means long term, but I want this."

The feel of her hot wet center against Kaelee's hip was almost as distracting as the pulse between her own legs. Kaelee kept Greta pinned tightly to her side and said, "You were very good. Tell me what to do, Greta."

Briefly, Kaelee hoped that Greta didn't notice that she had used her actual name instead of a pet name, but all Greta said was "Rules?"

"Hold me. Help me. Fuck me. Please?" Kaelee whispered, half embarrassed at how badly she needed this tonight, how badly she had needed Greta ever since they met.

But then Greta asked, "Hard or soft?"

Kaelee struggled to get the words out, but she managed to say, "I want to give you control. I want . . . you to decide. No mouth. No toys. Just you."

"Even when you give me control, it's still yours," Greta promised her as she slid her hand lower. "Take my wrist in your hand. You can squeeze it, if you need me to be faster . . . or you can tell me what you want. Now, later, whatever works. All I want is to make you feel good. You have the control even now, Kaelee. I am still at your mercy."

Kaelee was glad that Greta couldn't see the tears of relief in her eyes. No one had ever made her feel so safe and treasured. And the result was that no one had ever led her toward orgasm as frequently and surely as Greta.

*Whatever it takes, I can't endanger you, Greta,* Kaelee thought as

Greta played her body like she knew Kaelee's every secret already. *I have never felt so sure of my own joy as I do with you.*

Out loud, she said none of that. She'd accepted that her trauma and issues with sex were permanent, but with Greta she felt safer, and her boundaries sometimes faded. Honestly, Kaelee hadn't thought such a thing was possible.

*I'll treasure it while it lasts, but it's not forever. It can't be. I can't endanger Greta by staying in her life.*

## 22

# Greta

Late that night, Greta woke to see Kaelee sitting at the desk illuminated by moonlight and a small desk lamp. Newsprint cuttings and photos were scattered over the surface. Greta wrapped one of the hotel robes around her and went over to stand behind Kaelee.

In Kaelee's hand was a laminated clipping. The only reason it wasn't crumpled unrecognizably was the laminate covering that was cutting into Kaelee's hand. A tiny bead of blood welled up from her palm where the edge had sliced the skin.

*Mr. Arthur Leopold ("Tripp") Alden III of Raleigh announces the engagement of his daughter, Sabrina Alden, to Kyle Gray, a newly promoted senior vice president of marketing at Alden Enterprises. Gray is the son of Eustace and Irene Gray of Charlotte. A fall wedding is planned.*

Under the text of the announcement were two pictures, one of a much younger Kaelee and one of a polished-looking man who was visibly older by at least a decade. In the photo, Kaelee's currently short-cropped hair was a waterfall of waves that flowed over her shoulders. Her salmon-toned blouse had small sprigs of flowers, and there were no tattoos anywhere. Tiny hoops—one set only—were visible in her ears. Her smile looked strained, and her eyes looked sad.

Greta looked down at the desk. Another clipping on top of the mess seemed to be announcing Kaelee's departure. It was mostly about her father, his donations, and how difficult the situation was for the family.

*(Raleigh) Mr. Arthur Leopold ("Tripp") Alden III of Raleigh reported his daughter Sabrina Alden missing on Tuesday. Police have spoken to Miss Alden's fiancé, as well as her sister and cheerleading squad. Alden was to be a freshman at Duke University in the upcoming term, but she'd fallen in with bad elements in recent months. "We want Sabrina to come home where she belongs. We are willing to pay for any leads in her whereabouts," Mr. Alden told reporters. There have been no ransom demands, and Mrs. Alden tearfully expressed her fear that her daughter was unable to contact her family.*

*Several prominent political figures and religious figures, along with Miss Alden's fiancé, were present at the Alden residence. "Tripp Alden, a long-time contributor to the Right Way fund, has supported vetting and training personnel who could bring back family values," said local congressman Mitchell Edward Jones. "He needs our help now. Join us in prayer for his lost daughter."*

Greta looked at the clippings scattered on the desk. "This was what was in the envelope?"

"Yes." Kaelee stared at the assorted mess of articles. "Short version? I was declared missing, and then my parents had a memorial. I'm not *dead*, legally, but they apparently were seeking that. If I died, they could seize my trust fund." She tapped the corner of an announcement that the family was having a memorial so they could grieve and move on. "Last year, I guess, they let the community know that I was 'presumed dead' . . . except he had my mobile number. He obviously knows I'm not dead."

She sounded more rage-filled than sorrowful, and for that Greta was grateful. She kept her voice gentle and low in the dark room and asked only, "What do you need?"

Kaelee looked back at her. "I don't even know. I don't *want* to cancel my book deals or destroy my newly established career. I know that."

"Good." Greta put a hand on Kaelee's shoulder. "Is that what they're asking? Is there anything else?"

Kaelee handed her a folded letter. "She has demands. This is her doing as much as his, I guess."

Dear Brina,

I know you think you can leave your family and life behind. I'm sorry you and Kyle had a fight, but that's no reason to turn your back on all of us. Your father is very frustrated at how your belligerence will reflect on him if you are discovered living your sinful life.

I was not pleased with the idea of having a memorial service, but he thought a memorial would help everyone move on. The event was well attended, and many people said nice things about you.

When his people delivered the news on your book deal, he was livid. You look so much like me. If people were to see the photo of you or pick up that book, they'll think we lied. You have to understand that we simply wanted to stop all the questions. We have tried to be patient while you have your little adventure, but your father says you were already finishing that last degree. We can tell everyone you wanted to be independent and earn your way. Your father spoke to the public relations team. We have a good plan. You will ruin everything with this book and story about being a homosexual.

Sabrina, what were you thinking! You know how he gets, and his reputation will be tarnished if your indiscretions are revealed. Kyle has mended his heart, and of late, your father has suggested that your cousin has been an aid in that. We had hoped your sister would fulfill this duty, but she made other choices for her marriage. Cousin Jordan is such a good girl, and Kyle is willing to honor his commitment to your father by marrying Jordan. He would still marry you, or we can have that wedding for him and Jordan all in order before you return. Then we will pick a younger boy for you.

Nothing will work out if you insist on claiming to be one of those women, though. Good Christian ladies follow their father, then their husband, and God forbid, if he passes, you have a son to look after you. Without firm guidance, well, look at your own situation!

You must stop this nonsense and come home, Brina. Your father's candidate this year is campaigning on a platform of strict morality, and your rebellion must end before it embarrasses everyone. Come home. We'll have a party to celebrate your return, like you're Lazarus returned to the living or the prodigal son come home. It's time to set things right. You owe it to your father.

Julia (Mom) Alden


Greta finished reading and winced. "Does she always sign letters to you that way?"

"I guess when you fail so badly at motherhood you need to find some way to pretend you are a mother," Kaelee said. Her shoulders were tight with anxiety or rage or some combination.

"Is your cousin in danger?" Greta asked.

"You mean, has anyone told Jordan that Kyle raped me? I have no idea. I thought about calling her, but maybe he'll be different with her. I don't know. I'll still probably call her. He was awful. I gagged the first time he kissed me, and I think it hurt his feelings." Kaelee had a faraway look in her eyes. "I told them that night, said that I preferred women, that I couldn't marry him."

"Oh, honey," Greta murmured, stroking a comforting hand down Kaelee's arm and back. "How old were you when that happened?"

"Eighteen. I was planning to start college in the fall, and . . . honestly, I was too young to marry anyone, but Tripp was sick of my disobedience. He told me that if I was going to act like a spoiled brat he was going to make the decision for me. Marry Kyle or no tuition, no Duke, no anything."

"Bastard."

"Yes. Both of them." Kaelee made a noise that was probably intended to be a laugh. "Kyle was Daddy's clone. He did whatever he was told. Honestly, he didn't want a wife, but I came with a promotion to VP in the company at only twenty-eight. A raise? More influence? He agreed to take me."

"And no one thought how young you were was disturbing?" Greta gaped at the thought.

"Darlin', in his version of morals, if a woman can bleed, she can breed. The candidates he backs are the ones who see no issue with *child* brides. I was practically on the shelf for that sort of conservative man." She looked over her shoulder again, met Greta's gaze, and said, "Kyle said my father told him that a lot of women say no at first, but that *he* was saying yes for me."

Tears trickled down her cheeks.

"You will not have to deal with him. Not Tripp Alden and not Kyle Gray." Greta glared at the pages. "I'm so sorry that no one protected you before, but you are not alone."

"They had a memorial, even though they knew I wasn't dead," Kaelee whispered. "They would rather I be dead than a lesbian. I don't even know what to do with that."

"You don't have to do anything with it." Greta took her hands and pulled her to her feet. "We'll talk to legal, and we'll make sure you're safe and secure at any events. I know a few lawyers through my ex's firm, too. Good ones. And when you do events, either Charlie will travel with you, or Toni will. She's already agreed to do a four-city tour with you. And if neither of them can be with you, I will be. I swear to you that you will not be left alone."

"You can't be with me everywhere. Not on campus or at the gym or the grocery—"

"We can figure this out. I swear we can." Greta wrapped her arms around Kaelee. "Whatever it takes. As your friend, your editor, and whatever else I am, I will have your back, Kaelee Carpenter. Whatever they said about Sabrina Alden being gone, *you* are not. You are a phoenix that rose from the ashes of their mistakes."

"I'm scared," Kaelee admitted.

"I know, but we can figure it out. We won't let them near you." Greta cupped her face in both hands. "I care about you. Let me help with this, okay? You're not a teenager facing them all on your own this time. You have friends, money, and a life we will not let them interfere with. Plus, you still have the courage you had to leave their cage. We'll keep you away from them. I swear it."

Kaelee nodded.

"We will need to talk to Toni before the events, and we'll talk to publicity and to legal, but trust me, Kaelee, these people will *not* hurt you. Never again." Greta scooped all the papers up and put them in the envelope. "Next week, we'll talk to legal, okay? Like I said, I know a great firm with great attorneys for the not-publishing parts. We'll make sure your trust is secure."

Kaelee nodded again. "I don't look *that* much like her. Not now. They had a memorial; they want everyone to think I'm dead. I'm not going to say I'm their daughter. Why not just let it go?"

"Fear of facing who you are? That's *their* baggage, though. Not yours. I'm here with you while we figure it out. And you know Toni and Addie and Emily would have your back, too." Greta stared at her. "And Cherie? That was your friend's name, right? Her, too. You are not alone."

Kaelee let herself be led back to bed, and in an uncharacteristic move, she curled her body against Greta, pillowing her head on Greta's shoulder and chest. "I don't understand how they hate me so much that they want to fuck up my life when they aren't even in it. No one will guess that Kaelee Carpenter used to be an Alden. Why try to drag me back? They don't want me, but they don't want me to move on either."

"Some people can't see beyond their own hate. I'm sorry that they are missing out on knowing you, but right now, it certainly doesn't sound like *you* are missing out by not seeing them." Greta stroked her hand over Kaelee's hair and down her neck. "Plenty of people care about you, Kaelee, and I hope you remember that if these asswipes attempt contact again."

They fell asleep that way, with Greta holding Kaelee in her arms, and the following morning, they woke up still entangled.

Kaelee stared at her and said, "You know I don't break down as often as it seems. Yesterday and then the drunk thing . . . before that I don't think I'd been drunk in almost nine years. I'm not fragile like this."

"I don't think you're fragile." Greta trailed her fingers over Kaelee's bare arm. "Even without the family intrusion, I think you're having a lot of upheaval in your life. The book deal is *good* stress, but that doesn't mean it's not unsettling. The stuff between us has been unexpected, and in some ways emotional."

"True. I know you realize I don't let people as close as you are, not in my life and my bed." Kaelee looked uncomfortably vulnerable. "Thank you for . . . everything, really. I was freaking out yesterday, and then I was here with you, and I felt like you were putting my pieces back together and that you didn't mind. I always feel like that with you, like you don't mind the ways I'm fucked up."

"We all have scars. Like physical ones, yours are sometimes obvious when we're naked, but they aren't a reason to overlook all the beauty." Greta kissed her softly. "Your heart is beautiful, and your mind is irresistible. You're smart and smart-assed, and you make me relax. None of that goes away just because you have some trauma."

"Trauma that means I have hangups with sex," Kaelee amended.

"Yes, but yours aren't hangups that make me change how I see you."

"You actually mean that, don't you?" Kaelee frowned slightly. "I usually just keep my limits in place, and a lot of women are fine with it, being a princess and letting me touch without being touched."

"I *like* touching you, but if you genuinely don't want my hands on you, don't want me to get you off, I can learn to adapt." Greta pulled her hand away. "I want you to be comfortable, and I feel like it's a gift when you let me closer."

"I do like you touching me. I feel . . . safe with you." Kaelee lifted Greta's hand in hers and pulled it back to her side. It was a non-sexual touch, but Greta felt like it was also an admission that these sorts of touches, affectionate and casual, were welcome, too.

"We can order room service and spend the day here. Read, watch a show, and have sex if you want." Greta smiled at the fact that they were here at all. "Or we can go down to the restaurant for breakfast and walk around the city. There's a tour of the City Hall Tower that takes you up to see the city. It used to be the tallest building at one point, built early 1900s, right at the turn of the century, I think."

"History nerd," Kaelee teased with a laugh. "I swear sometimes that you are everything I could want if I ever wanted to get serious."

Greta felt like something squeezed her heart, a too real reminder that she already felt something serious. "I'll be here if that happens. Right now, I'm happy to be friends who have a weekend away together, but if that changes . . . I wouldn't object to trying it, trying us with intentions."

"I thought you didn't want that," Kaelee said with a look of confusion plain on her face.

Greta kissed her quickly. "Some rules can be broken for the right person. I'm not *asking* for that, but if you wanted to . . . date with a plan for the future, I'd say yes. You feel like a once-in-a-lifetime person, Kaelee. I decided I won't refuse the possibility if it happens. If it doesn't, I'll still be grateful for what we *do* have."

Then Greta slipped out of bed with a murmured "Dibs on the bathroom!" and gathered up her toiletry bag.

# 23

## *Kaelee*

Kaelee kept replaying Greta's words over the next couple of days as they spent their long weekend in Philly. *Could we date without an endgame? Could it be this easy?* The only marriages she'd seen were ones like her parents' that were about one person surrendering all their power. At least that was all she'd seen until Toni and Addie . . . but they weren't even married yet. *Dating leads to marriage, and marriage is a cage.* Kaelee didn't want that, not for herself or for Greta.

The truth, however, was that Greta and Kaelee fit together in a way she hadn't ever imagined fitting with another person. Whatever was growing between them was more than sexual compatibility. Casual dating already seemed too light for what she felt.

*And that terrifies me.*

*Greta says we can stay casual. . . .*

The problem was that Kaelee felt too much. Already.

Tonight, they were at a restaurant and afterward, Kaelee had possibly the cheesiest surprise in the world planned. She'd told Greta to wear a dress she could move in, and Greta had not disappointed. Even though it was the end of November in Philadelphia, Greta had packed a calf-length red wrap dress with a wide ruffle at the hem that crept up the front of the dress to where it tied at her waist. The sleeves were long and tight, and the neckline plunged so that it almost met the knot at the waist that held the whole thing in place.

"You're quiet tonight," Greta pointed out gently. Her bracelets and earrings sparkled in the low light of the restaurant's faux oil lamps.

"I realized that I'll miss you when we separate at the end of the trip." Kaelee sipped her after-dinner coffee. Her sleep had been erratic the last few nights between nightmares and the middle-of-the-night sex that Greta happily agreed to when Kaelee woke her. "I don't remember the last time I missed someone. I mean, my grandparents. I missed them when they died."

"Luckily there's phone service where I'll be." Greta smiled in that *everything will be alright* way she had, and it was almost enough for Kaelee to believe her. "Whatever happens between us, I want our friendship to be permanent. That means calls, texts, emails, and visits."

Kaelee frowned. "So what makes a friendship a relationship?"

"Intentions. Dating means you *intend* to have a future together. Dating and relationships are building on the hope of marriage and forever, creating a life together." Greta sounded so sure of herself. "I went into my last relationship hoping for forever."

"But?"

"Tasha panicked and cheated."

"What did you do?" Kaelee had watched her mother ignore her father's nonstop affairs like they were simply inevitable. She ignored his demeaning remarks the same way and eventually became his instrument—passing that derisive rhetoric on to others.

Greta glanced down at the table briefly. "I told her I forgave her and suggested therapy." She looked up. "And she moved out instead. She wasn't ready for sharing a place or marriage or even sure she was queer at all even afterwards, except at one AM when she called and we hooked up. For the record, I stopped doing that before I met you."

"I trust you, but . . . ouch on how she treated you. Why not say she wasn't ready when you proposed?"

Greta's tone turned wry. "*She* asked to move in. Her lease was up, and I had bought a great apartment. *She* suggested marriage. That was all her idea, but when things didn't work, she had to believe that *I* was the one who was wrong. She needed to blame someone. I understand that now. For a long time, I thought I misunderstood, but I think it was more a case of neither of us being ready. And sometimes when people are in pain, they hurt others. Maybe your mother is hurting, too, and that's why she wrote to you."

"Maybe." Kaelee looked away, watching for the server to bring the check. "But that doesn't change what happened to me because she let him hand me over to Kyle."

"It doesn't." Greta sighed. "That's the part of dating that messes me up. We all come with baggage of some sort. Who wants to unpack it in front of someone you're trying to impress?"

Kaelee gave her a slow, lingering once-over. "You impress me. That baggage you have doesn't get in my way."

"Same." Greta smiled. "I like the way we have been here on the trip. I feel . . . connected with you."

With an abrupt gesture, Kaelee finally caught the eye of one of the waitstaff and handed him a credit card. "We are running late. Can we get the bill?"

The man left to retrieve the slip, and Greta said, "Late for what?"

"My plan." Kaelee debated canceling. She'd already prepaid, but her date plans really felt foolishly romantic. *We are friends who are casually dating.* Kaelee summoned a ride on one of her apps and then looked at Greta. "I made an appointment for us. You can cancel if you want."

"I trust you."

"I was looking at things to do that weren't bars, meals, and movies," Kaelee started. "Something you might like."

"I liked the walking tour yesterday. The museums. All of it."

"Sure, but . . . this weekend has meant a lot. I was panicking, and you were right here with me. You made me relax and have time to think of plans. I want you to know I appreciate it." Kaelee took Greta's hand in hers. "I want you to know that I appreciate *you*."

"I do know that."

"Okay, so—" Kaelee paused and signed the bill.

She pocketed her card and stood. She might not have liked most of what she had learned in her childhood, but because of it, she knew how a person was to treat a lady. The difference, of course, was that her grandfather did that when no one was watching *and* in public. Kaelee stepped up to Greta's chair and held a hand out as she stood, steadying her on the dagger points of her high-heeled shoes.

She helped her into her coat, and then she led her to the now-waiting car and opened the door.

"This is all very mysterious," Greta murmured.

Kaelee got in and took her hand. "We can leave if you hate it."

"Is it scandalous?"

A laugh burst out. "Not tonight. If you want me to book us something scandalous another night, I can. This is more . . . romantic, I think."

Greta nestled closer in the back of the car. "I like that, too. Honestly, I'd try anything with you. Indoor skydiving, horseback rides, strip clubs, couple's pottery classes, paint and sip, experimental theatre productions, festivals . . . You name it, I'll consider it."

Kaelee squeezed Greta's knee fondly. With Greta, any and all of that and more things on top of it sounded good. For now, she'd focus on tonight's plan. "Pick one for our next weekend getaway."

"Really?"

"I chose for tonight," Kaelee said, ignoring the flare of panic at making plans beyond this trip. She wasn't sure how much time they had before her life imploded—and hoping for weekends away with Greta made her hope that maybe they wouldn't end at all. Maybe Greta was right, and there was a way to stop her father's bullshit before it ruined everything.

*What could he really even do?*

When the driver pulled up at the little dance studio, Greta looked at Kaelee in surprise. "Really?"

"I thought it was different. Memorable and—" Her words were lost under a kiss as Greta grabbed her face and pulled her in closer.

The gleeful look on Greta's face when she released Kaelee was enough to sweep away any lingering doubts. They got out, and for a moment, they stood in the cold parking lot. Then Greta looked at her with such raw affection that Kaelee couldn't deny that they were already deep into the land of actual feelings.

"I've always wanted to do something like this!"

"Have second dinner?" Kaelee nodded at the Chinese restaurant a few doors away. "Your wish is my command."

"Observation, Miss Carpenter. You took me for a private dance." Greta pointed at the dance studio.

"I did." Kaelee held out a hand and Greta took it.

Inside, the studio was warm. The lights were low, and the music was soft. A woman in a flared dress greeted them. "Kaelee and Greta? How lovely to meet you! I'm Inez."

"We spoke on the phone," Kaelee said.

"Yes. Kaelee. Come in. I have water here for you." Inez motioned to a glass pitcher of ice water. "Or tea if you like." Two mugs sat waiting.

"How about we just get started?" Kaelee said. Sitting around would make her self-conscious.

The teacher smiled widely and then nodded once. "Have either of you taken any dance?"

"Ballet," they both said.

Kaelee braced herself against the next admission. "Cheer-related dance, so . . . I don't know if that counts. Nothing since I was a teen."

"Did you look over the options?" Inez directed the question to both of them.

"Rumba," Kaelee said.

"Good!" Inez took Greta's hand and led her to the center of the floor. "You stand like this." She motioned Kaelee over. "Come."

Kaelee felt foolish standing there as Inez positioned her hands on Greta. "I work better with words."

"No touching?" Inez frowned. "I can dance with your lady to show you if you prefer."

The thought of Inez dancing with Greta made an unfamiliar possessiveness surface in Kaelee. "No. Touching is fine, I guess."

Inez smirked, but she said nothing as she positioned their arms in a basic frame. She paused, squeezing Kaelee's biceps. "She is strong, Greta. Her arm is strong, and yours rests there on hers as she leads you. Yes?"

"Yes."

"You hold this hand here in her other hand, lightly, as if you will escape." Inez smiled. "She will pull you back when you pull away. This is how we dance. She will lead you, and when you flee, she chases. You push, pull, and the seduction will continue this way.

"Now we are in the frame, and we sidestep." Inez stood beside Kaelee and demonstrated a sidestep. "We build to the box step."

Then she moved to Greta's side and demonstrated the same move from her position. "Start with the weight here. Then sidestep to the right, then bring the left foot in."

Greta stared at her intently, her lip caught in her teeth as she watched and studied the moves.

Then Inez moved again, saying as she did, "We do this as *slow, quick, quick*, slow, quick, quick."

They tried to do as she instructed while Inez repeated, "Slow, quick, quick, slow, quick, quick." Twice they repeated this before Inez frowned at Kaelee. "Hips. Your hips are stuck. We must move these."

"My hips are *what*?"

"Stiff. Stuck. Not *moving*." Inez demonstrated the moves again. "See how my hips *move*. It's not just the feet. Hips move. Again."

Kaelee tried again.

"Better. Think when you step, you bend this knee. See how my hips swish when I bend the knee like this?" Inez paused. "You hold

Greta's hips now. Greta will move hers, and you will feel how you must move. The lead and the follow both sway, like a cobra charmer."

Inez made a twirl gesture with her finger, and Greta pivoted to put her back to Kaelee. "Grab her there," Inez ordered. "Hold on."

Greta looked over her shoulder. "Come on. Grab me, *darlin'*."

Kaelee gave her a stern look at her attempt at a drawl. "Sassy."

"Sassy is good," Inez pronounced. "Sassy. Fun. Sexy. Miss Greta, sway and seduce this woman."

"With pleasure." Greta flashed a wicked smile at Kaelee. "You like to grab me, don't you? Grab me. Lead me. I'll follow you."

Kaelee was sure she could do better at this without Inez there, but without a teacher, she couldn't follow the moves of the dance. She pushed the self-doubt out of her mind as best she could. "Let's do it again."

"You have the dance frame with your arms exactly, Kaelee." Inez smiled encouragingly. "You hold her well, but you must also relax in the hips more."

Then Inez took Kaelee's position leading the dance and Kaelee stood behind Greta with her hands splayed on Greta's curves.

As Inez led Greta through the same steps several times, Kaelee felt the way Greta was rolling her hips. It felt like the sort of girlish femininity she had rejected when she left her old name and old life behind—but Inez was in the position traditionally filled by a man leading his woman in a sexy, seductive rumba.

*My body knows this sway,* Kaelee admitted to herself. *It doesn't make me less strong.*

"You feel how she moves?" Inez said. "This seduction of the hips is the base as much as the box step. You know these two things, and you can learn the rest easily. You must move like you want her to stare only at you. Seduce her with the way you move your body."

Kaelee nodded. "I can seduce her."

"I am sure." Inez smirked again. "*Lead* her. Hips, Kaelee. Move hips and feet both."

A few moments later, Inez said, "I will make the music louder." She walked away, purposefully leaving them.

Without another person there, Kaelee felt her body relax into the rhythm almost instantly. "I heard what you were trying to do there, darlin'." Kaelee met Greta's eyes. "Flirting with me . . ."

"And reminding you that you are in control," Greta murmured in barely a whisper. "I like this. You leading me."

Kaelee relaxed into the moves for several beats and said just as quietly, "I like *you*."

"Good." Greta stared at her. "We can avoid calling this thing we're doing anything in particular if it means we keep doing it."

"And your job? My family?"

"Fuck it all, Kaelee. We can figure it out. I want this. I want *you*. Dancing. Weekends. Texts. Dinners. All that you are willing to give me."

Kaelee swallowed her reflexive refusal. She wanted the same thing, even if she couldn't say those words right now. "And if I ruin it? If I can't be what you need?"

"I trust you. You lead me, and I'll follow at whatever tempo you need." Greta leaned in like she was going to kiss her.

"No!" Inez interrupted as she walked toward them. "Rumba is tension, not the kiss. You may kiss her after you dance. Build the tension now. Make her wait for you. Tease her. *Seduce* her."

"So rumba is a big tease?"

"Sounds like," Greta whispered. "Shall I tease you?"

"Yes. Seduce me, darlin'."

# 24

## Kaelee



Returning to her apartment after spending several days with Greta was the first time it had occurred to Kaelee how far away from a mere situationship she really was. She had never woken up with the same person in her bed more than twice. The idea of *missing* waking up with someone baffled her.

*We are dating. For real dating.*

Until Greta, Kaelee's sleepover-after-sex policy was almost always akin to last call at the bar: "You don't have to go home, but you can't stay here." She'd used that exact line on a lot of women when she first started having sex. When a few of them were offended, Kaelee then instituted her current "I'll go to their place" policy, which meant *she* could leave. Greta was different.

*I miss her.*

**Kaelee:** I wish we lived in the same place.

**Greta:** I can visit you.

**Kaelee:** You have a day job.

**Greta:** True, but weekends exist. Work
on the train. Spend the weekend.

**Kaelee:** Maybe

**Greta:** May I officially assign Ian as your editor,
Kaelee? I'd also like you to talk to Emily.

Talk to legal. I can get that started. Can I do
what I can to protect you and me both?
**Kaelee:** Ian's great. I read his notes. You can tell who
trained him to edit. ;) Talk to whomever you need. I
want to see more of you without risking either career.
**Greta:** See you next weekend?
**Kaelee:** Maybe? Probably.

Despite how much Kaelee guarded her privacy, the idea of letting Greta into her tiny apartment didn't fill her with the usual fears. Instead, she thought about it with a smile she couldn't erase.

A while later, Cherie popped into her shared office. No one else was in the office but her and a TA who was grading with earbuds in. Honestly, Kaelee ought to, by rights, no longer have an office since she wasn't teaching or grading this term, but since she had every other term, no one had pulled her name or access from the office.

"You owe me answers, Cupcake," Cherie said from just inside the door. She glanced at the other TA and kept her voice low.

"Cupcake?" Kaelee echoed.

"We *need* nicknames. It's an upgrade on our friendship." Cherie sat in one of the empty chairs and spun in circles, tucking her feet up like a small child. She finger waved at the other TA, who pulled her earbuds out and greeted, "Cher. Carpenter."

"Hi," Kaelee said because she had no idea of the woman's name.

Once the other TA left the room, Cherie said, "Nicknames are a sign of increased closeness. You need one."

"*We* aren't dating, Cher." Kaelee put her pen aside and gave her a bemused look. "I don't need a pet name."

"You call me *Cher*. Nickname. However, I have nothing good to call you when I want to whine. I lack a nearby sibling or cousin, and I missed you. It's like not-quite blood sisters." Cherie folded her arms. "Oh! I could start calling you Sissy."

"I wouldn't recommend it." Kaelee stood up, glanced at the other

TA's grading stack. "She's in here working, so we probably need to leave since I'm not going to get any peace unless I talk to you."

"I was sad about the lack of yams, Sissy. Evander's friend brought those soggy-bottomed ones with fluff on them. I couldn't even eat them. I like your yam and apple dish." Cherie pouted as she spun in another circle. "*Yam*-less. You left me yam-less, and we both know that means that something happened."

Cherie plopped her boots onto the floor with a *thunk* and stared at Kaelee expectantly. "Sissy!"

Kaelee rolled her eyes. "Coffee shop, brother?"

"Low blow." Cherie jutted her chest out to accentuate her breasts. "*Not* a brother. Look at these!"

A laugh escaped Kaelee, and she felt lighter because Cherie was at her side. "Those are lovely, but I am not going to answer to *Sissy*."

"Cupcake it is." Cherie hopped up. "Whatcha going to call me?"

"Menace."

"I like it. Cupcake and Menace, BFFs forever." Cherie had the sort of chirpy joy that was either infectious or obnoxious. Luckily, Kaelee found it spirit-lifting.

As calmly as she could, Kaelee filled her in on the envelope and its contents, as well as the letter and Julia's requests. While she spoke, they crossed campus.

By the time they were standing in line at the little coffee and pastry shop on campus, Cherie was vibrating with rage. "A fucking memorial? What coldhearted brand of monstrosity are these people?"

Kaelee shrugged. "I guess they find my lesbianosity too much to face. They are shamed by my existence, appalled by my literary successes, and generally being sourpusses, *but* they kindly suggested that we can all move on if I just return to the fold and marry a nice conservative man they will find for me."

Cherie gaped at her. "You aren't joking? They seriously said that?"

"Indeed. They lack *any* sense of humor, Cher." Kaelee turned to the undergraduate now waiting to take their order. She hadn't been any older than this guy when she was on her own, counting the days to access her trust, and trying to figure out how to adult with no training or realistic preparation. Her mother's lessons on adulthood were more about charm, etiquette, and style.

Kaelee's questions on practical matters when she started thinking about running had led nowhere.

*Because girls don't need to understand money, Brina. Your husband will manage that.*

*Insurance? I don't know. Your father manages that.*

*Oil change? I think your father's assistant has a nice young man pick up the car for things like that.*

Kaelee ordered both drinks, paid, and looked at Cherie.

"Best sister I could want, Cupcake," Cherie murmured. "Honestly. If we need new families, why not just . . . pick them?"

"But you already get on well with yours," Kaelee pointed out.

"Exactly. So I'm an expert on this. I think you should be my honorary sibling. I bet my mom would totally adopt you, too." Cherie flashed a wide smile at the barista and took her far too sugary drink.

"I swear you're half hummingbird. Why not just drink sugar water?"

"I like caffeine in my sugar water, too." Cherie grinned and led them to a table in the corner. She never remarked on Kaelee's need to see the door and windows or explained her own. They both had their own reasons for a little hypervigilance.

The first few days after Philly, Kaelee was even more on high alert. No more half-unlocked doors, no envelopes or anything else, but every car that slowed when she was walking made Kaelee flinch. Every time someone got too close to her, she tensed.

And each time there was a phone notification, she hoped it was Greta. Seeing her had done the opposite of getting her out of Kaelee's mind. The urge to be with her was more intense.

"Soooo . . . where did you go for the weekend?" Cherie slurped her sugar-and-coffee concoction.

"Saw Marie," Kaelee confessed.

"For a date or . . . ?"

"The whole time. I panicked when I got that envelope. Called. Told her. She met me." Kaelee tried to downplay it, but from the wide-eyed look Cherie had, Kaelee was completely unsuccessful.

"So you went to the sexy woman from New York to lick your *wounds* by licking her . . . ?" Cherie cackled, making a half shriek in the process.

"Cher."

"Did you kiss everything and that made it better? Or did she?"

"Seriously? How old are you?" Kaelee cracked a smile, though, ruining her attempt at chastising Cherie.

They sat in comfortable silence for several moments. Then Kaelee blurted out, "I think I might be able to let her, though. I trust her. I don't usually have that kind of ease, you know, being a *lickee*. I mean, I take care of my needs, and that's enough."

Cherie gave her an assessing look. "Is it, though?"

"It can be. Honestly. I know that might not make sense, but for me, it often is. I just . . . I think I want more with her. I feel safe enough with her to . . . try intimate things I don't usually do." Kaelee sipped her too-hot-still coffee. "I *like* her, Cher. I like her too much."

Slowly, as she always did when reaching out to Kaelee, Cherie put a hand on Kaelee's wrist. "She's a lucky woman, then, but you need to know that if she hurts you, I will gut her with a fish knife."

Kaelee blinked at her before erupting in laughter. "If you could handle even gutting a fish, I might find that more convincing. Do you remember that restaurant with the fish that still had a head? I thought you were going to puke every time you mentioned it."

"Fine." Cherie shook a finger at her. "If she hurts you, I'll embarrass her, yell at her, whatever it takes. I want you to be happy, Cupcake. You deserve it."

Kaelee shook her head. "I think I could be happy with her. It's complicated, but I never even thought about *trying* dating until her. I'll suck at it, probably, but she makes me think about things . . . stupid things, relationshippy things, when really I ought to be thinking about my career and what I'm going to do if my parents try to ruin it."

"Who says you can't have it all?" Cherie caught and held her gaze. "I'm going to find love and great sex even if I have to date everyone on all the apps. I'll find my person. I *believe* it, and I can believe it for you, too, if you want." She paused and gave Kaelee a silly look. "All you have to do to enlist my optimism on your behalf is let me call you Cupcake or Sissy. Deal?"

"Fine. You have a deal." Kaelee held out a hand to shake. "Hi, I'm Cupcake."

"Yes!" Cherie pumped her fist in the air. "That was what I wanted to name this little Pekingese pug—is that a Peki-pug?—but my mom said I couldn't get one because I'm allergic."

"So I just agreed to you calling me by the name you picked for a dog?"

"I suggested it for my next sibling, too, when she was born, but apparently, they think Cupcake isn't a 'person name.' Ha!" Cherie pulled out her phone. "I'm going to tell them I just had someone introduce herself as Cupcake."

"You're impossible. You do realize that, don't you?" Kaelee stared at her, smiling more than she had since leaving Philly. Cherie was a spot of joy she didn't want to lose, much like her career and her thing with Greta. Kaelee *liked* her life. It was worth trying to keep. "I'm really glad you're my friend."

"Glad enough to make me yams and apples this weekend?"

Kaelee pushed the possibility of Greta visiting out of her mind and said, "Definitely."

## 25

# *Greta*

Greta spent the next weekend being ignored by Kaelee, and her valiant choice to decide she was going to wait until Kaelee was ready was already going horribly. By Monday, she was in her office holding a beautiful copy of Kaelee's book. The book wouldn't be on shelves for almost a month yet, and publicity would be doing a limited mailing of the final copies to key influencers and accounts.

Greta put the book on her desk, cleared everything from around it, and took a picture. She emailed it to both Kaelee and Emily with a "Look what arrived!" note.

While she waited for a reply, Greta opened her email, checking for emergencies. There was one from Toni that said, "Want to buy a new book?" She'd attached a document and cc'd Emily.

Greta laughed and replied to both: "Offer letter in my draft folder already."

"No! Read the damn book first, or I won't sell it. There will be a quiz," Toni replied, cc'ing Emily again.

Again, Greta barked a laugh. "Of course there will."

Ian popped his head into the doorway. "What are you chortling over?"

"Toni sent her book."

Ian frowned at her. "Did we buy it already? I didn't see a deal m—"

"No. She sent the manuscript, cc'd Emily, and said I have to read it before offering." Greta shook her head. Toni Darbyshire was grouchy at the best of times. She'd earned enough on her first two novels and the show that she could actually *continue* to not sell the book. She certainly didn't need to sell one with having both a job and royalties. Greta shook her head, but she was still smiling as she said, "She says she'll quiz me before selling."

"You know she'll sell it to you eventually," Ian pointed out. "No one else would be as devoted to her or her series."

Greta nodded. "I don't mind reading first, but yes, I know she'll sell it to me. I worried in the spring, but . . . I've realized that Toni sees the selling as a formality at this point. She already submitted the book."

Then Greta's phone chimed. She and Ian both saw Kaelee's name on the screen. "I need to get this."

"So you're officially seeing her?" Ian wasn't judgmental; he sounded curious.

"I am." Greta couldn't say what "seeing" Kaelee meant, but whatever it was or would evolve into was better than *not* seeing her. That much was clear. As Ian left, Greta looked at the message.

**Kaelee:** Come here this weekend.
**Greta:** Where? To DC?
**Kaelee:** yes
**Greta:** Let me see what I can do.
**Kaelee:** I needed to think. Sorry I was silent.
**Greta:** And? Any conclusion?
**Kaelee:** My apartment is not much more
than a closet. I want you here though.
**Greta:** I can book a hotel.
**Kaelee:** No. Come HERE.
**Greta:** To stay this weekend?
**Kaelee:** Or sooner.
**Greta:** Sounds like a date.

And in her typical, thinking-too-hard, panic response, Kaelee went silent for several minutes. Greta felt like she had a vise squeezing her chest every time Kaelee went silent. The trio of dots that indicated she was typing appeared and vanished several times. Then a message appeared.

**Kaelee:** Check your email.

Greta refreshed and saw a link to a cloud file called "Alden Notes," and then it was followed by another text message.

**Kaelee:** Read this before any decision about dating.
**Greta:** Your family?
**Kaelee:** Yes. There's a lot more where that
came from. Read it, and then you can
let me know if you're still visiting.
**Greta:** You aren't responsible for their actions.
**Kaelee:** They can hurt you. Embarrass you. Out you.
**Greta:** Nothing here is embarrassing. Being involved
with a smart, talented, beautiful woman? How awful.
**Kaelee:** Read it. Decide. Let me know.

Greta sighed and opened the file. There were articles on a conservative political group, a Southern religious group, articles in which Tripp Alden voiced his various hatreds in coded words. Book banning, anti-choice legislation, bathroom bills, a lot of conservative causes, and Kaelee's father was repeatedly on the extreme side of it. At this point, it wasn't surprising. People who tossed around the word "freedom" a lot rarely meant freedom for *everyone*. They meant freedom for them with a side order of the right to control and limit other people's freedoms. Sober people never walked up and announced that they were sober; only drunks said that. Likewise only those who were trying to *limit* other freedoms said they were pro-freedom. It was mind-boggling.

And that hateful family had raised the kindhearted woman Greta was falling for. The truth was that liberals didn't "convert" people as effectively and consistently as restrictive families did. Developing empathy for fellow humans was often all it took to turn away from a lot of those narrow ideas—which ultimately were rooted in fears that had festered into hate.

An hour or so later, Greta picked her phone back up.

**Greta:** Reading these things affirms that
you are amazing. You were surrounded by
hate but developed a beautiful heart.
**Kaelee:** He'll find a way to hurt your career.
**Greta:** Thank you for the warning.
How's Wednesday or Thursday?
**Kaelee:** Really?
**Greta:** No doubts on my side. At all.

Then Greta walked out to find Ian. He needed to call Kaelee and start the introduction phase of being her editor—and they needed to get in front of the potential issues with Tripp Alden.

She found Ian in Charlie's office.

"If you want to take me as your concert date, I'm in, but if you wanted to check your date pool first—"

"I'm exhausted." Ian shook his head, grinning wildly. "You're the only one who will go with me and not expect orgasms afterwards."

Charlie laughed either at the words or the expression on his face.

"I don't expect orgasms from you either, Ian. Coffee? Patience with my schedule? Sure. That's all, though," Greta said as she approached them.

As he looked back at her, Ian blushed. "Well, I just meant—"

"Fun people?"

"I'm sure you're fun, boss. We just don't like the same things."

Ian shook his head. "I'm sure museums are exciting for you, but I like . . . more music and chaos."

Greta gave Charlie an appraising look, taking in her sensible trousers, blouse, and blazer. "And *you* go with him?"

"Sometimes."

"Huh." Greta realized she knew little about their social lives, and impulsively, she added, "Tell me next time. Maybe my date and I can join you."

"Your date?"

Greta shot a look at Ian before pulling her shoulders back. "I'm seeing an author. Romantically. I met her before she was my author . . . under an assumed name . . . and now we are dating."

"Good for you, boss." Ian nodded. "So I assume I have my first official author?"

"Second. I think you ought to offer on the gay mystery you had me read," Greta said. "You're right. It's a solid book. I will, of course, be here to advise you on both as needed."

Ian's small smile blossomed into a wide beaming one. "I'm going to go make some calls. I have a couple agents and an auth—"

"In a minute."

Once they were in the room with the door closed, she said, "Kaelee started life under another name." Greta took a breath. She had Kaelee's permission, but that didn't make this easy. "Her father has reached out in a threatening way. He'd like the book canceled. He's extremely right-wing, and having his daughter in the media as a lesbian has upset him even though they have not had contact in a decade."

"So damage control," Charlie surmised.

"One of us ought to be present at each tour stop," Greta suggested.

"I'll talk to the stores, too, as we schedule to check safety and security." Charlie was already in problem-solving mode.

"I'll get the notes on the next novel prioritized to distract her," Ian added.

Greta nodded at both of them. "I told her she has the best team, but . . . I'm anxious for her, too. I think we want to have legal brought up to speed."

"As her editor, I'll handle that," Ian offered. "Charlie? Want to come with?" Then he looked at Greta. "We'll keep you in the loop, boss, but don't you worry. We'll keep our author safe as houses."

"I know." Greta impulsively hugged Ian. "Thank you. In related notes . . . I'll be headed to DC and working remotely the rest of the week." Her cheeks burned in embarrassment, even though she was not sure why. Maybe it was simply admitting she had a life outside the office.

Charlie caught her gaze. "She seems lovely. I hope this works out for both of you. You deserve it after the way things went with Tasha."

"Sometimes, things just aren't the right time or place," Greta said quietly. "Tasha isn't a bad person. She just wasn't *my* person. Maybe Kaelee won't be either, but I want to find out."

Afterward, as she was walking back to her office, Greta realized that she might have more friends than she realized. She'd closed herself off so much that she failed to notice the great people right in front of her. Opening her heart to Kaelee was having the side effect of opening her heart in general.

By Wednesday evening, Greta sat on the train thinking about the last time she took the Acela from Manhattan down to Union Station. That was only a couple of months ago, but that trip had changed everything. Meeting Kaelee was the single best thing that had happened to her in an already victory-filled year. But now Greta had to decide if she was going to see her one remaining author from DC—as opposed to the last trip, when Toni met her at the station and Kaelee refused to meet her.

*Kaelee's not my author anymore, not really. Ian is her editor. I am . . . I don't even know what the right label is now.*

Greta gathered her weekend bag and her work bag, which held

her laptop, and walked out of the train car and into the station. Unexpectedly, Kaelee was waiting at the seating area. She looked more relaxed than Greta expected, a long winter coat folded over her arm and a scarf wrapped around her neck. Without a word, she held a hand out for Greta's shoulder bag.

"You don't have to carry my things," Greta protested briefly.

"True, but I want to." Kaelee still had her hand extended. "Please?"

Greta kept her roller bag, but she handed over her work bag, which Kaelee promptly shouldered. Then Kaelee held her arm open, inviting an embrace.

"Can I kiss you yet?" Greta whispered as Kaelee wrapped a strong arm around Greta's back and held her close for a moment.

"Please." Kaelee shifted so they were face-to-face. Her smile was a little embarrassed as she said, "I don't know if I can manage much more than kisses tonight. I slept horribly last night. If I wasn't picking you up, I'd already be asleep."

Greta pressed her lips to hers in a brief, chaste kiss. "Just like Philly—and actually just like in Manhattan before I knew your name—I'm not here just for sex, Kaelee. I want to see you, talk to you, and be around you. Plus, since I have work to do while I'm here, and I grabbed dinner before I caught the train, an early night sounds perfect. Work during the day, and after work . . ." She gave a sort of shrug, limited by the fact that Kaelee still held her close.

"After work tomorrow, we have dinner plans." Kaelee swallowed visibly. "To go out."

"Oh?"

"I made reservations, and then a show." Kaelee nudged her forward, taking her hand now, and then led her through the station. "There's a ballet I wanted to see at the Eisenhower Theater at the Kennedy Center. I wasn't going to spend a night alone there, and I don't really think going as a third wheel with my friend and her fiancée is a great plan."

"I wondered why you said to bring a nice dress." Greta flashed her a warm smile as they dodged a man scurrying toward the departure area. "Are you taking me *out*?"

"On a *date*," Kaelee said, pausing before weaving through an oncoming crowd.

"Is that so? Are we . . . *dating* now?" Greta was trying to keep up on Kaelee's acceptance or categorization of what was happening between them.

"We are going on a date, and I'm hoping to seduce you after that date." Kaelee sounded less pained each time she said the word "date." She motioned toward the parking garage sign. "This way."

Greta followed along, her bag clacking behind her. "Well, I have it on good authority that your date is very attracted to you, especially if there's great conversation and you're dressed up."

"I'm not wearing a dress."

Greta smiled. "Excellent. I will be, and I'm hoping that my date will be wearing something with buttons I can slowly open after we are back at her place. I'll have you know I am exactly the sort of woman to round all the bases on the first date if things go well."

Kaelee led her to a worn BMW and opened the trunk. "I have to tell you something, darlin'."

"Yes?"

"I think this isn't our *first* date." Kaelee put the bags in and slammed the lid. She turned from the trunk to face Greta. "I mean, 'a rose by any other name,' right?"

"So we're doing this?" Greta rested both palms on Kaelee's chest and leaned up to kiss her chin.

"If it quacks like a date, walks like a date, has sex like a date . . . Am I wrong?"

"No. I thought the same thing." Greta reached out and cupped her face. "Are you okay with that?"

"I think I actually am." Kaelee turned her head and kissed Greta's palm. "I can't give you a dating-toward-a-commitment promise right now, but I can date casually. Is that okay?"

"Of course it is."

Kaelee walked to the passenger door and opened it. "I thought about it last weekend. About what I'm feeling. About what we're doing. We're *dating*, and I like it."

"It certainly looks like that." Greta slid into the car. It was pristine, despite age. "You take good care of your car."

"I take good care of anything that's mine," Kaelee said before closing the door and walking around to the driver's side. When she got in, she turned on the car and then reached out and took Greta's hand.

Greta didn't resist or comment. What was happening between them seemed to move along at its own pace, and realizing they had both admitted that they were dating after the weekend in Philly basically just meant they were on the same page—even though they had both initially sworn they had zero interest in dating.

They were both quiet as Kaelee drove toward a building that looked more like a house than apartment. The harsh streetlights didn't do it any favors, but it was surprisingly large. Greta asked, "You have a house?"

"No. I have a studio on the third floor." Kaelee pulled into a parking spot and came around to open Greta's door. Kaelee extended a hand to her to steady her while she stood.

"You don't have to do that. I'm stable on my heels. I told you that when we met." Greta followed her to the trunk.

Kaelee held her gaze and said, "I told you, Greta: I take care of anything that's mine, and I want you to be mine." Then she pulled out Greta's two bags as if she hadn't just said something momentous and continued, "My place is small. It's not fancy."

"Will you be in it?" Greta paused and when Kaelee nodded, Greta added, "Then it's perfect. I'm here to be with you."

Kaelee's nod was brief, and her expression tightened as she looked at the building.

"If this is not comfortable for you, I can stay in a hotel," Greta offered. "Honestly, it's—"

"I've never brought anyone date-ish here. That's all." Kaelee straightened her shoulders, pulling them back resolutely. "I do want you here, but it's still . . . a lot to make sense of. I'm planning dates and having you stay with me. I didn't plan to catch feelings and . . . it's just that I might need a minute or weekend or whatever to let my panic pass here and there."

"Understood." Greta's heart felt too full as she followed Kaelee inside the building. "I feel incredibly lucky right now to be welcomed here. Are you good with going inside?"

"If you are . . . It's a tiny place. Cramped." Kaelee started toward the building even as they spoke and carried Greta's bags up the stairs, toting both bags with ease.

"I'm not here for the apartment," Greta reminded her, trailing behind her up the narrow steps.

At the door of the apartment, Kaelee used three more keys on a series of locks. Inside, she relocked all of those *and* a fourth one that had no external key. She looked down like she was expecting judgment, but if the extra security on the door made her feel safe, why judge? Some people had alarm systems, video monitoring, handguns, and dogs. Others lived in gated communities. From what Greta had read about Kaelee's family and what she knew about Kaelee's assault, Greta couldn't fault her for having a few extra locks.

"I won't be going out without you, so I don't expect to need a key ring. I was hoping either I could edit here, or I could come onto campus and work in a library or coffee shop." Greta kept her tone mild, hoping it would clarify that she was not judging or reacting in any critical way.

Kaelee flashed her a warm smile. "Ten-cent tour. This is the living, bedroom, dining room, and kitchen." She pointed to a door. "That's the bathroom, and behind you is the exit."

Greta took in the small space as she removed her coat and scarf. Kaelee had constructed a room partition of sorts with three very tall bookshelves that divided a sleeping area. The table was a three-seater, as the fourth side was against the wall. "It's a bit bigger than my first New York apartment. I had a futon that was also my bed."

"I have a futon for the living area, but I splurged on the bed when I sold the books." Kaelee motioned again to the bed. "It's one of those foam mattresses that enlarges as it is freed from the packaging. I'm not entirely sure how it'll come out of here when I move. Same with the bookshelves. I brought them in unassembled."

"I brought you a gift for your shelf." Greta reached in her shoulder bag, which was still on Kaelee's shoulder, and pulled out the red-and-silver-wrapped package.

Kaelee took it. "I do like books. Can I open it now? I didn't get you anything. Christmas is a few weeks away yet."

"Open it. It's one of the most riveting books I've read this year. I wanted you to have a copy." Greta leaned down and unzipped her boots, leaving them at the door next to Kaelee.

After Kaelee put their coats on a row of coat hooks, she carried the wrapped book to the futon, sat, and carefully unwrapped each seam. When she reached the book inside, she met Greta's eyes. "That's mine. Greta . . . that's *my* book."

"It is." Greta watched Kaelee trail her fingertips over the cover. "It's a phenomenal book. I feel so grateful to have been the editor." She sat next to Kaelee. "The night you messaged when I said I was reading, that was your book. I had it in my closet when you were in my apartment."

"If you'd have said the book's name or the author or anything . . ." Kaelee shook her head. "I'd have figured it out."

"And I would have lost that night in New York. I'm *glad* I didn't know who you were when we met or when you messaged that weekend," Greta confessed, staring at her with her heart in her throat. "I'm sorry I hesitated when you asked if letting Ian edit the sequel could mean we . . ." Her words trailed off. "I wanted *more* already then, and I wasn't as worried about my career as my heart. You even said no to talking, and I was already interested in more after we texted and then . . . I just thought that since you weren't interested, I could use the book to keep my distance."

Kaelee took her hand. "Not seeking feelings and ignoring them when they sneak in seem like different things. I wasn't looking for this either, you know? I'm terrified of how much I already like you."

"I get that. I have a terrible history with dating," Greta admitted.

"Well, I have none." Kaelee pulled Greta closer. "I am not ready to think beyond *now*. I don't want to hurt you, but I'm not looking for forever or marriage." Kaelee stared at her like she was expecting anger. "I want to try *dating*, but I don't have long-term goals. Marriage is a trap to control women, typically. I don't want that for either of us."

"It's not *always* a trap." Greta snuggled in closer and rested her head against Kaelee's, so they were forehead to forehead. "I'm not looking for a ring. I just want to be around you and have you naked. Are those things both on offer?"

"For you? Yes."

"Then we're fine," Greta promised. "That's enough. *You* are enough for me."

Kaelee pulled her into a tender kiss that felt like it was filled with words she wasn't saying, and Greta melted deeper into her embrace. Knowing the future was uncertain seemed perfectly fine because right now, the present was exactly what Greta wanted. A woman she was falling for had her arms around her, had planned a date for tomorrow, and was kissing her thoroughly.

*What else is there?*

Kaelee leaned back slightly, her words warm against Greta's lips, and asked, "What are your opinions on quickies?"

"With you?"

"Yes, with me," Kaelee said. "If I'm dating, it's going to be exclusive."

"Thank God. I wanted to ask, but . . ."

"Ask for what you need. Always. In bed and out." Kaelee sounded incredibly serious for a moment. "So many of us are trained not to ask for what we need from the world. I don't want that for us or anyone, really."

Greta nodded. "I want you to do with me what you will. I'm always interested in sex with you . . . but what happened to 'not tonight'?"

"I might not be able to stay up all night like in Philly, but I was a fool to think I could have you in my apartment and not touch you," Kaelee confessed sheepishly.

"Then *touch* me. I'm yours now." Greta reached down to untie her wrap dress, but Kaelee caught her wrist.

"I prefer unwrapping this present myself."

26

# *Kaelee*

Waking up and not being alone in her bed seemed like something that would unsettle her, but as Kaelee opened her eyes to stare at a naked, sleeping woman nestled against her, that wasn't the emotion that filled her. Kaelee's arm and leg were tossed over Greta like she was a body pillow, holding her close. Instead of feeling panicked, Kaelee felt languid and comfortable, ready to cancel everything and stay in bed. Kaelee shifted the leg that was pinning her.

"Morning," Greta said in a sleep-raspy voice.

Kaelee kissed the side of Greta's neck just under her ear and whispered, "Good morning. I need to shower and get ready, or I'm not going to want to get out of bed at all."

"Can I use your bathroom first?" Greta asked, looking over her shoulder. The braid she'd put her hair in before bed had started to unravel, so her hair was a chaotic mix of contained and wild. "Then I'll shower after you."

"Tea or coffee? I'll start something so we can have a cup before we leave." Kaelee balled her hand to keep from undoing the remains of the braid. There was something addictive about grabbing hold of that mass of waves. "I picked up a few types of tea, coffee beans, and a couple types of juice. I could make breakfast if—"

"Just juice. I'd feel guilty working in a café and not buying coffee and a pastry." Greta scooted out of Kaelee's arms. "Be right back."

The apartment rarely felt too big. It was a cramped studio, although Kaelee had a guest room of sorts—the futon—for when Cherie stayed over. This morning, though, it felt too big. Greta walking away for even a few minutes made Kaelee tense. She darted a look at the bathroom door a few times as she made coffee. Generally, she was low-key agitated when Cherie was here, and she was the only regular guest. With Greta, however, agitation was not the emotion rolling through Kaelee.

Kaelee loved that even her cheap coffeepot had an auto-brew function. She concentrated on her routine, pouring a cup of coffee, stopping the machine mid-perc to do so. Fix coffee. Grab shower. Drink now cool coffee. Routines were grounding, and the temptation to ignore her responsibility to stay with Greta made Kaelee well aware that she needed to be grounded just then.

Greta came out of the bathroom, her hair slightly less chaotic now that the braid had been released. "All yours."

"Thank fuck." Kaelee walked away from the coffee machine and pulled Greta into her arms.

Greta laughed. "I meant the bathroom."

"If I had planned ahead, I wouldn't be busy today, but I told a professor I'd grade for her." Kaelee pointedly did not name which prof. "I can walk you to the coffee shop nearest when we get to campus and then . . ."

"Do I know the professor?"

"Yes." Kaelee kissed Greta quickly and darted away. "I'm not thinking about that," she called before going into the bathroom. "I'm really not ready to listen to Toni's thoughts on us."

After a quick shower, Kaelee downed her now temperate coffee. Greta was sitting at the table looking at her email as if everything were casual and normal. Maybe to her this wasn't a big deal.

"How often do you spend the night with people you meet at bars or on the app?" Kaelee blurted out.

"Over the last year?"

"Yes."

"Counting Philly and last night?" Greta stood up and stepped closer.

"Yes." Kaelee braced herself for the proof that she wasn't special, that this wasn't a big deal.

Greta held up one hand. "Four nights in Philly. Plus last night. That's . . . five."

"So only me?"

"Do you want me to include the year before?" Greta asked softly. She paused, holding the same number of fingers up. "Only you. Before that I was with a fiancée, so that was every night."

"Am I a rebound, then?"

Greta gave her a strange look. "A rebound? Two years and change later? No, not at all. You're someone I like, someone I care about, someone who woke my heart up after I thought it was irreparably shattered."

"Oh."

"Don't panic on me, please." Greta stepped closer and put her hands flat on Kaelee's chest.

"Okay." Kaelee stared at her. "I don't want to fuck up and hurt you."

"Same." Greta rested her cheek against Kaelee's chest, and she wrapped her arms around Greta to hold her there.

"I've *never* dated," Kaelee whispered. "Are there rules?"

"Treat me *exactly* as you already are," Greta suggested. "Don't overthink this."

Kaelee nodded, but the panic still filled her. The only examples of relationships she'd had growing up were ones she now considered toxic. More recent, she'd seen Toni and Addie, who functioned a lot like friends who couldn't stand not to touch. Was their relationship an oddity or was it more normal than ones like her parents' marriage?

She hadn't seen her father hit her mother often, but she'd seen the handprints on her arms often enough to know that he squeezed too tight in anger. Her mother typically wore long sleeves year-round.

Kaelee remembered the flinches when he raised his voice. Her aunt and uncle were much the same. Kyle had expected the same. Plenty of women she'd seen reacted with that haunted deer look.

*Not Granny Kay, though.*

*Not Toni and Addie.*

*Not any of the girls that Evander brings around.*

Kaelee countered her own gut fears with a steady stream of facts. She'd done so for years. Logic didn't erase panic, but it made it crawl back into its box typically.

27

## *Greta*

By early afternoon, Greta was so lost in the new manuscript she was reading that she called Emily. Admittedly, Greta felt vaguely tempted to walk over to Toni's office and ask for her quiz, but the snow was falling faster than before and the thought of sliding through it seemed less than appealing. And, of course, Greta thought she'd better handle the business part first. Emily had already emailed in response to the offer Greta had sent that morning.

"I've read more than enough to know I'm buying Toni's book," Greta said in lieu of a proper greeting.

"One or two pages?" Emily teased.

Greta was relieved that they were able to talk as if the awkward conversations about her personal life had not happened. "I've read the first two hundred so far."

"Well then. You really *did* prioritize it."

"I took two days out of office to read." Greta stared out the coffee shop window at the light fall of snow on the campus grounds. "What are Toni's counterdemands?"

"I haven't told her you offered yet. She is genuinely serious about you reading it first." Emily sounded somehow both amused and exasperated. It was a mix of emotions Greta thought of as the "Toni reaction" at this point.

"Okay, so what are *your* demands?"

"Better escalation clause on paperbacks. Higher royalty overall on paperback and flat fifteen percent on hardcover." Emily paused before adding, "Less of a tour clause."

"Emily."

"She'll ask. You know she will, so I'm putting it on the table."

Greta smiled. She'd already told the contracts team that this would be a sticking point, so she had authorization to decrease the requirements. She wasn't going to admit that yet in case she needed it later. "I'll see."

"She will want either only a one-book deal or the second book to have more flexibility." Emily sounded less sure of herself now. "She's considering a spin-off stand-alone."

"This book ends unfinished," Greta objected.

"I thought you were only at two hundred?"

"I read the end already," Greta admitted.

Emily laughed. "Three books, then."

"Sold. Seven fifty each." Greta had the leeway to go higher on the advance, but she'd save that if she couldn't get all the other clauses. Having something in her pocket to bargain with was standard tactics if she needed to counter any other objections.

"Let me run the offer by her and get back to you by end of day," Emily said. Then she paused and awkwardly added, "She's serious about the quiz, though. She wrote an actual quiz. I told her she was being ridiculous, but she's afraid you'll just buy it without loving it because the first book sold so well."

Greta laughed out loud. "Send it. I'll fill it out."

"Done . . . and the Kaelee situation?"

"Ian is the editor of record now," Greta said. "I could be objective, you know, and I adore her book, but this clears the way for . . . seeing her socially."

Emily was silent for several heartbeats. "Ian's a great editor. Nothing else changes?"

"We are consulting legal to make sure they are aware of the situation with her parents reaching out aggressively." Greta realized she sounded stiff, but she was worried—not about losing the book, but about Kaelee's anxiety and the possibility of threats to her. All she added was "They're powerful and homophobic."

"So I hear," Emily murmured. "Do you have a personal attorney you can recommend? I think just having the publisher's attorney is insufficient."

"Agreed, but I'll need to talk to Kaelee first. I won't overstep. I'm not her editor now, Emily. I'm just a woman who cares about her," Greta pointed out.

They exchanged other updates, on both Toni's and Kaelee's upcoming releases, and then Greta said, "Do you mind if we add another date and start the tour in Houston? There's a mystery bookstore there that does on- and off-site events. The events coordinator is amazing."

"Murder By The Book?" Emily clarified.

"Yes." Greta noticed that the snow was getting heavier and heavier outside and wondered if Kaelee's office had a window.

*Does she know about the weather?*

"I have no objection to launching there. Why not DC, though, since both authors live there?" Emily prompted. "Or New York?"

"I wanted a mystery store, and that one *also* does a great job with fantasy, so . . ." Greta started packing up while she watched the snowflakes outside. "Think about both topics. Get back to me. This snow is getting thick and—"

"Snow? Where are you?" Emily asked. "I don't see a single flurry outside."

"I'm not in the city," Greta said with a wince. "I need to run, but I'll expect your email."

Emily sighed. "No one warned me that cat herding would be an easier career path than agenting. High-rise window washer? Goat shearer? So many options, Greta. So very many."

Greta laughed in relief that Emily sounded resigned rather than angry. "You'd be bored doing anything else. Talk later."

Once Greta ended the call, she texted Kaelee. The snow is heavy out there. How much later do you think you'll be?

Kaelee didn't reply, so Greta called. If she'd thought she might be in class, she wouldn't have, but she was in an office grading. Only it wasn't Kaelee who answered.

"Imagine my surprise," Toni said. "I look over to see my friend's phone and your name is there."

"Hi." Greta smothered a sigh. "She was to be grading, and I wanted to see if she was aware of the snow."

"So you check the weather forecast for all your authors now? I guess you must do these calls alphabetically because *I* live where it's snowing, too. Was I going to be the next call, Greta?" Toni's voice was muffled then, obviously talking to someone in the room with her. "Your phone rang, and I thought I'd answer it since it's *my editor* calling."

"Well, maybe she was calling about my book," Kaelee said in the background.

"Seems suspicious, Kae, since *our agent* said she got Greta's out-of-office mess—" Toni interrupted herself and said, "Greta, where *are* you right now?"

"Give me the phone," Kaelee said in the background.

Then the phone was obviously snatched away. Kaelee's voice was no longer in the background. "Hey."

"I'm sorry." Greta braced herself for reprimands. Tasha was always quick to criticize when Greta embarrassed her.

Instead, though, Kaelee said, "I think we're going to have to tell Toni we're dating sooner than expected."

There was a commotion in the background, and then Kaelee said, "I'm almost done here. Are you done with . . . the thing you were doing?"

"I am. Do you want me to walk to you?"

"Of course not, it's snowing out there!" Kaelee sounded outraged, but at least there was no noise in the background. "Let me grab my stuff and come get you."

A short while later, Toni and Kaelee trudged into the coffee shop. Greta's eyes widened in surprise when she saw Toni, but she composed herself quickly as the two approached and stomped off the snow on their legs.

"My car was plowed in," Kaelee said grumpily. "And *someone* thought it was better to drive me instead of help me shovel it free."

"We can take the subway to your apartment a few blocks from here. I pulled up an app," Greta said, determined to stay calm. She wasn't doing anything wrong by dating Kaelee, so Toni could take that glare of hers and turn it somewhere else.

"I'll get you home safely." Toni nodded. "I'll drive you and leave you there, *or* you could come to my place and use the guest room. Addie's home, and we'll all be snowed in within the next forty-eight hours. Might as well have a house party. Board games and reading?"

Greta smiled. She knew Toni well enough to see her offer as fond overprotectiveness. She *also* knew this wasn't really her decision. She might be Toni's editor, but Kaelee was Toni's friend.

*And I'm here as Kaelee's date.*

"I'm sure Greta and I are fine on our own, but thanks." Kaelee looked like she had been chewing glass. Her teeth were gritted, and her lips were pressed together.

"Everything's closing. Do you have a generator?" Toni scowled. "You know that super of yours will not clear the sidewalk, and you'll be out there shoveling and then inside in wet clothes with no heat and—"

"You're, like, the overbearing older sibling no one really wants," Kaelee muttered.

"You and Greta will be trapped together in a storm, no power, no water." Toni shook her head. "That's one way to see if you're compatible. It's like the road-trip test: if you survive it with feelings intact, maybe it's real."

Kaelee looked at Greta, a question clear in her eyes.

"As long as I'm with you I'm fine. Whatever *you* want works for me." Then Greta looked at Toni. "We can be noisy, though, so is your guest room on the same floor?"

Kaelee and Toni both looked mortified.

"Kae can sleep on the sofa," Toni countered. "Problem solved."

"I don't think we ought to have sex on your sofa," Greta said lightly. "Best she stays in the guest room with me."

"Greta . . . my editor doesn't . . . you shouldn't . . . this is not right," Toni managed.

"I'm not Kaelee's editor." Greta stared at Toni. "I'm your editor. Just yours, but Toni . . . seriously? I'm not a monk."

"Fine. Be human." Toni threw her hand up. "Just leave me out of the drama if you split up."

"Fine," Kaelee said quickly.

Greta took Kaelee's hand and squeezed. "No drama."

"Kae used my guest room when you sent me to fetch her. It's ground floor, private bathroom." Toni let out a slow breath. "Look. I'm not trying to be overbearing. I would offer my guest room to Kae if you *weren't* here, Greta. They're slow to clear the roads, and last year, Kaelee got trapped without heat for three days. I worried. I just added a generator at my place that automatically kicks in or something. I don't know, but it's supposed to mean that I have heat and lights . . . and I planned to just force her to stay at my place next storm. You can ask Addie if you doubt me. She knows."

Kaelee shot Toni a fond look. "That's sweet of you."

Toni flipped her off and added, "Staying with me might not give as much privacy for you *or* for me, but we'd be on separate floors. Basically, if you come now, I know I wouldn't have to go out to drag you back if your power is out by tonight."

Kaelee gave a nod. "Fine. I can stay in your guest room. Greta, do you want to join me or take the Acela back home? Hell, I can take the Acela and come to your place."

"I've never negotiated a book deal with the author sleeping in the same building," Greta murmured. "On the other hand, I *have* had sex where other people might overhear, so that—"

"Will not be an issue. I have a stereo on the main floor. It'll be on twenty-four hours a day." Toni looked vaguely embarrassed.

"You see? That awkward feeling? That's how it'll go if you try to offer an opinion on Kaelee's sex life again," Greta said with a pointed smile. "I'm not her editor anymore, so there is nothing at all untoward here. Take your attitude, fold it up, and tuck it somewhere dark. Clear?"

"Yes."

"Still invited for the storm?" Greta asked in a friendly voice.

"Yes." Toni gave her an appraising look.

"Perfect, then." She held out a hand to Toni. "Hi, I'm Greta. I'm here visiting Kaelee for the weekend. We're dating, long distance because I work in New York. And you are?"

"Toni. Friend to Kaelee. I guess I don't . . . know you?" Toni looked like she might laugh or scowl. It could go either way. "Pleased to meet you."

"You don't know me this weekend. Shall we stop by your place for our things, Kaelee?" Greta asked, smiling at Kaelee now.

Kaelee pulled her in closer to her side. "You're fucking amazing, you know."

"Sorry about missing the ballet," Greta murmured quietly.

Kaelee swept her up in a cradle carry to move her to the sidewalk, which was already plowed or shoveled. Quietly she asked, "Seriously, though, would you rather catch the train? Stay at my place and gamble on the heat? Get a hotel room?"

"I honestly just want to be with you. Wherever you are." Greta caught her gaze. "Do you think your power will go out?"

"Probably within the next few hours," Kaelee said. "It goes out constantly. I suspect that's part of why the rent is so low."

"Are you okay with staying at their place?"

"I am. I just feel like I'm failing you. My apartment is too small, and I can't keep it heated well enough—"

"The heat is because of a storm. Also your apartment is *not* too small."

"And the date I planned isn't happening." Kaelee opened the front door of the Jeep. "And another woman is driving us."

"So you provided a chauffeur, and we'll *still* be together. Please relax, it's not a test, and if it were, you're not failing it." Greta closed the front door and opened the back door. "All I see is that you are able to sit next to me, and we might get snowed in together."

"You're both giving me a pain behind the eyes," Toni said, staring at them in the rearview mirror with a fond expression now. "You may be perfect for each other."

Greta squeezed Kaelee's hand. "I guess tonight is our first double date."

"I'm not rearranging the wedding party for you, though." Toni scowled. "Addie has it all figured out. There will be no changes to the bridal parties. You hear me?"

**28**

## *Kaelee*

Toni was idling downstairs while Greta and Kaelee gathered a few things. In addition to clothes and toiletries, Kaelee picked up a few bottles of wine and the cheesecake she'd bought yesterday. She added a book she was reading, a board game, and a few fluffy things for Greta to wear.

"I don't imagine you packed sweatshirts or flannels."

Greta took a flannel from her hands and said, "I have one."

"I was grabbing it for you." Kaelee snatched it back. "This one is my favorite, though, so it does not get carried off to Manhattan. You can *borrow* it when you're in DC."

Greta kissed her cheek. "Sounds perfect. You are an excellent date." When Kaelee tensed, Greta noticed and added, "To be crystal clear, I mean that. I'm having fun."

Kaelee nodded. "Wait up here." She took her bags down to the Jeep and then ran back upstairs for Greta's things.

The drive to Toni and Addie's townhouse was a little dicey. The salt trucks and plows were trying, but it was always harder to keep up with snow in progress than it was to clear it once the skies were no longer pouring it down.

"I'm a safe driver," Toni promised when Greta gasped the second time. "I wouldn't let anything happen to either of you."

"I know," Greta murmured. "It's not you I worry about." The car that had made her gasp and Kaelee flinch was driven by someone who failed to know that brakes on slick surfaces would lead to skidding and donuts. A few feet to the left and they'd have been spinning from impact. Instead there was a symphony and horns and the driver somehow regained control to continue on down the road to terrorize others.

"Are you okay?" Kaelee asked Toni in her calmest voice.

"Ready to be off the roads. Why in the hell can no one here drive worth a damn?" Toni's wipers and defrost were running full out, but the snow fell faster and faster.

Kaelee watched the thick, wet globs of snow gather on the windshield. These were the sort that accumulated and took down power lines. "You were right about the power," she muttered.

"I know." Toni's hands were tighter than normal on the wheel.

Snow built up on the sides of the road and trees as they crawled toward the outskirts of the city where Toni lived. Kaelee added, "I give it until evening at best."

"I'll see if we need to do anything about the generator. I feel like it just starts if the power goes out." Toni finally exited the Beltway onto side roads, steering them from steadily moving but slow traffic to what looked like a hockey game played by cars. Not everyone was sliding, but the side roads had not been treated yet, so the intersections were an adventure.

By the time they reached Toni's place—where the entire community lot was as cleared of snow as possible with it still falling—all three of them let out sounds of relief.

"So this is where we *stay*," Toni announced. "I'm not driving anywhere else until the roads are salted, plowed, and ready."

Addie stood at the open door of the townhouse. Even though she wasn't stepping into the actual snow, she was practically engulfed by an oversized cardigan, fluffy sweatpants, and knee-high snow boots. "Good thing I ordered groceries earlier before the roads were a mess."

"You didn't drive, did you?" Toni glanced at a tiny car heaped with snow.

Addie laughed and tapped her chest. "California girl. No snow driving skills. Don't want any either." Then she motioned them all toward her. "Inside. It's too cold out here. I started a thick vegetarian soup that ought to be ready soon. Tomato, onion, leeks, and some assorted things that tasted good with it. The bread is bakery, not homemade, but it's yummy. Are either of you gluten-free?"

"No restrictions for either of us," Kaelee said, glancing at Greta and hoping that answering for her was okay. Was it too couple-y? "Go on in. I'll grab our bags."

"I'll take this one." Greta snuggled closer to her briefly, before heading to the door with her bag of laptop and chargers and the manuscript.

"You brought snacks." Toni nodded approvingly at a couple of the bags she was pulling out of the Jeep. "The best guests bring snacks, not the weird ones either. Addie's parents brought some sort of jalapeño jelly and dried wild game and something that I think had drugs in it. There's no graceful way to ask your future in-laws if the baked goods are supposed to make you need a nap, is there?"

"Are we okay?" Kaelee asked, pulling out the two bags of clothing and essentials that she and Greta had in the Jeep.

Toni sighed. "So Ian's editing your next book?"

"He is." Kaelee nodded and put her messenger bag over her shoulder. "Emily knows I'm seeing Greta, too."

"Just don't break Greta's heart, okay?" Toni paused and held Kaelee's gaze. "Maybe I shouldn't sell her *three* books in case she breaks your heart, and I need to find a new editor. That would suck, by the way. I like her."

"You don't have to do that! Greta's amazing. Sell her all the books!" Kaelee shivered and followed Toni to the townhouse. "My romantic life shouldn't matter in your career."

Toni scoffed. "You're my friend, Kae. I'll sell her the new book. It's done. I think I'm not selling whatever comes next yet, though. Not until you two either commit or quit. I can write without a contract."

A tangle of guilt and affection filled Kaelee at that. "You'd do that?"

"Dumbass. Of course I would." Toni grinned. "I'd also refuse to sell more just because it's good to have no deadlines, so don't be weird about it. Come on. We need to check the generator."

Dinner was hearty, both the soup and the bread, but Kaelee secretly wished she could pour a pile of meat into it. Bacon or ham, maybe. They sat around the living room with their wine and a few candles. The generator was, in fact, an automatic start—which had been their hypothesis. That was proven true when the lights flickered and died, only to pop back on a few seconds later.

The sound of the central heating turning back on was a huge relief.

Outside, the snow had already accumulated a good eight to ten inches, and Kaelee was glad they were tucked in somewhere more spacious than her little studio. Greta was just as cuddly around Toni and Addie as she was when they were alone in a hotel or at Kaelee's apartment.

"I set the heater to cool down a bit, but not as much as usual just in case the generator stops or fails or whatever generators do." Addie pulled her cardigan around her like a cozy blanket. "So I'm taking this one to bed. Your room has clean linens on the bed and fresh towels. Oh, and I put a heavy spare quilt down there just in case. We'll see you for breakfast, hopefully with heat still by then."

Addie took her wineglass in one hand and Toni's hand in the other and called, "Rest well."

"Shall we?" Greta asked.

Somehow going to the guest room felt more intimate romantically. Kaelee nodded, but she wasn't sure what the rules were. *Do I lead her by the hand like Toni was led by Addie? Is that a year-two thing? Do I need to do anything?* Kaelee stared at Greta briefly, but she wasn't offering any cues on what was expected.

"Less panic," Greta said after a moment. "Overthinking is the enemy. You're still you, and I'm still me. Nothing has changed except we're in the fifth new bed we've shared."

The pressure in Kaelee's chest let up as she caught Greta's smile. "You're good at knowing what to say."

"How about this one? *Come to bed with me, Kaelee.*" Greta walked toward the steps. "I've had enough of not touching you today."

# 29

# Greta

On the second day without the ability to leave, Kaelee had grown visibly agitated. By midday, Greta watched her pace the house like a caged animal.

"She's worse than me," Toni said in a low voice. They were standing in the kitchen waiting for coffee while Addie was off somewhere, and Kaelee was walking around from window to window as if she'd spy something in the thick snow outside. "Is this because of hearing from her family?"

"You know her family was threatening her?" Greta matched her volume to Toni's, although there was no chance of being overheard.

"They aren't going to show up at my door." Toni looked out at the unmarked snow all the same. "Right?"

"The man has deep pockets, lawyers, politicians, and likely a few police who seem willing to do as he wants. I'm not sure what he can do." Greta had been weighing the possibilities. If Tripp Alden wanted to avoid publicity, he couldn't send the media after her. Was physical violence the real threat? Kaelee had experienced gaslighting, physical, verbal, and sexual violence because of that man. Her fear was logical—even if *what* they should fear was still nebulous.

"Kae lives at the gym. I suspect the lack of exercise is adding to her agitation." Toni stared at the coffeepot like it was insulting her by not being instantaneous. "Addie's feet look about your size. I'm sure there's boots you could borrow since you only brought those high-heeled things. Utterly impractical of you."

"Maybe I should invite Kaelee to the room to try to wear her out." Greta bit back a smile at Toni's expression. "But honestly, even when we have sex all night, she never runs out of en—"

"Stop." Toni's back was to her now as she fixed her coffee. "No joking about that. My editor doesn't have sex."

Greta chortled. "Lies. At least I'm not in the news like you and Addie were."

Toni sighed loudly. "True. So . . . you're dating? Put her in front of your career?"

"Yes. She's an incredible person." Greta squirmed slightly. "I have other authors, you know. One of them is going to have another best-seller soon."

"Hmph." Toni stepped to the side and gestured at the coffee machine and assorted creams and sweeteners. "By the way, I graded your quiz on the book. You passed. You can buy the book."

This time Greta's laughter was loud enough to draw Kaelee's attention. She popped into the kitchen. "What's so funny in here?"

"I'm allowed to buy Toni's book." Greta held out her free hand, and Kaelee stepped closer.

Once Kaelee had Greta snuggled in against her side, she asked, "Do you think the author or editor might allow me to read the book if I take a quiz?"

"It's not edited yet." Toni scowled. "Probably filled with typos, insufficient plot points, and maybe it's a terrible—"

"It's absolutely *not* terrible," Greta interjected before taking another drink of the coffee she now clutched in the hand not curled around Kaelee.

"—book that will fail," Toni continued, ignoring Greta entirely. "And honestly, Kae, sitting down right now doesn't seem like an option with the way you pace around like a convict awaiting escape."

Kaelee flipped her off but said nothing. Even nestled into Greta's side, Kaelee was squirming.

"Do you want to go for a walk? I don't run, but maybe getting outside would be helpful," Greta asked.

"Yes!" Kaelee squeezed her like she'd offered something incredible. "Two days of being away from the gym has me a little stir-crazy."

"We hadn't noticed," Toni muttered. "If you got up earlier you could've gone for a run with me."

Kaelee shook her head. "Naked woman in bed. Couldn't move."

Toni walked away without an audible word. So Greta looked at Kaelee. "Are you regretting staying here?"

"I'd have ended up here with or without you. Toni started thinking she's my older sibling or something. Honestly, it's a weird problem. My friend Cher claimed me as an honorary sister recently. What I lack in blood family, I collect in declared family." Kaelee kissed Greta's temple.

"Rest assured, I have no familial feelings toward you. My thoughts are one hundred percent grounded in sex, dating, and friendship," Greta declared.

"The same." Kaelee took the coffee cup from Greta's hand. "I can go out by myself again today if you want to stay in where it's warm. I bet you can find a book on the shelves or—"

"I just need warm boots, and I'm good."

"They cleared the lot and at least one of the side roads," Kaelee said. "I watched when I was—"

"Pacing," Greta supplied.

"Addie says these are between a size six and a half and eight. Something there ought to fit you." Toni dropped several pairs of boots off. "I don't know why we have so many sizes. Something about her mom leaving a pair here." She gestured toward the downstairs. "Coat closet has hats, scarves, and coats. Borrow whatever."

"Can we go into the backyard?" Kaelee asked as they were wrapping themselves up in layers. "I have never seen snow quite this deep and undisturbed. My building has no yard and, well, I grew up in the middle of North Carolina . . . not exactly a winter wonderland."

Greta took her hand, slightly awkwardly with the bulky mittens she wore. "So no snow angels?"

"Do sand angels at the beach count?"

"Absolutely not." Greta shook her head. "Sand castles don't count in lieu of snowmen either, you know."

"I suspect we're a little old for doing all that." Kaelee laughed. "I just want to see the snow up close."

By the time they were standing outside in the tiny yard behind Toni's townhouse, Kaelee was bouncing on the balls of her feet like an antsy athlete, and Greta wasn't sure that a walk was going to be enough to take the edge off her energy—at least that was her excuse if her next move went poorly.

She scooped up a few handfuls of wet sticky snow when Kaelee wasn't looking and tossed the first snowball at the back of her head.

"Hey!" Kaelee pivoted just as Greta launched the second snowball. It smacked her high on the chest, and a puff of flurries lifted into her face on impact. The result was that Kaelee had a brief snow cloud obscuring her vision.

Greta ducked behind a tree in the far side of Toni's yard.

Kaelee was laughing as she lifted a handful of snow and stared at Greta. "I played softball, Greta."

"Field hockey," Greta countered, spying a garden rake in the small yard. She made a dash for it, but the first snowball smacked her just above the knee.

They volleyed several rounds, both hitting their target every time as they chased each other around the yard. Then Greta had an idea. She grinned at Kaelee, and then she charged her as best she could in the knee-high snow. Her run was a bit slower than planned, but she still toppled Kaelee into a snowbank.

"Gotcha." Greta was sprawled out on top of Kaelee, both of them half sunken in the deep drift.

"You are ridiculous." Kaelee stared up at her. Her cheeks were pink, and snowflakes glittered on her eyelashes.

"And you are the most beautiful woman I've ever seen." Greta kissed the tip of her nose, the edge of her eye, and then pressed her lips to Kaelee's in a brief kiss. "Snow angels?"

"We're going to be too cold to walk," Kaelee said.

"One snow angel, and then . . . we walk." Greta plucked at the ski pants she wore. "I feel pretty toasty and dry still."

"Fine. So do I." Kaelee lifted Greta off her and pushed to her feet. "Teach me."

Greta stood and walked several steps away, looked behind her, and flopped back into the unmarked snow. "You find a good place, no rocks or things to hurt yourself."

She lifted her arms to the sides and made sweeping motions. "You make wings like this." Then she swept her legs open and closed. "And then the foot of the robe."

Kaelee stared down at her with a bemused smile. "You should look ridiculous right now."

"Are you saying I don't?"

"I'm saying you look beautiful." Kaelee shook her head, as if clearing it. "I don't feel casual, Greta. Not when I look at you. Not when I hold you. Not when we talk. What am I supposed to do about that?"

"Try not to panic? That's what I'm doing. I put *you* in front of my career, Kaelee. You're not the only one in this place," Greta said softly. "I told my assistant, my head of publicity, my biggest author, *and* her agent that I am seeing you."

"I'm afraid." Kaelee reached down and grabbed Greta's outstretched hands, pulling her to her feet and sliding her arms around her. "I'm falling, and it's *terrifying*."

Greta hugged her. "It's okay to fall. I am, too. I am not trying to trap or control you, Kaelee. I just want to be with you."

"Same," Kaelee whispered. She caught Greta's mouth in a tender kiss, and then said, "Okay. Fall backwards? Flap my arms and legs, and then what?"

"Then take my hands. I'll help you stay steady," Greta said. "Just like you did for me."

Kaelee's voice sounded tight as she said, "I think I'm not used to having anyone do that. Be patient with me?"

"I have and will," Greta promised, knowing full well they weren't talking about just this moment. "I promise I'll be here."

## 30

# Greta



After their walk, they ended up coming back to the house to find themselves ambushed by what turned into a team snowball fight. Inside, they warmed up with some homemade cocoa and then they all nestled under blankets to read.

The next day was watching a few holiday movies—including *Die Hard*, which Toni and Greta *both* argued was the epitome of a Christmas movie. After a couple of years without a friend group, Greta was enchanted that the four of them managed to both enjoy time together and apart. This was what, Greta realized, she wanted: a partner, friends, and laughter. She was starting to think impossible thoughts of plans to work around the rest of the holiday season.

*Could we just alternate weekends?*

Together but not in the same city was possible with a train connecting their two cities. First, however, they had Christmas, New Year's, and Kaelee's book launch. There would be plenty of nights together the next six weeks.

*Not as many as I want.*

Greta felt increasingly unhappy to be apart, although that urge felt like it was too much, too fast.

*I'm not that sort of person—and neither is she.*

Finally, it was time to talk about the future, plans that needed to be made, conversations that needed to happen. The roads were cleared, and Greta had to return to New York for in-person meetings and practicalities.

"So I talked to Emily," Greta said as they were sitting on the guest bed, just the two of them. She leaned back on the mountain of pillows with her legs extended in front of her on the still unmade bed. "And I talked to Ian last week, too."

"I know. I told you it was fine, and I heard from both of them, and Charlie." Kaelee sat on the foot of the bed, not touching Greta at all. "I heard from legal at the publishing house, too."

"Good. I won't be cc'd unless you ask them to do so, since Ian's your editor now. You ought to talk to Emily about *who* your family is. She's your agent. She'll be at your side and—"

"Will *you*?"

"Yes. Even if we weren't anything but casual friends, I'd be here," Greta swore.

"I have you, Toni and Addie, Emily, Ian, my friend Cherie. . . ." Kaelee shook her head. "It's strange to realize I'm not on my own facing him this time."

Greta crossed her ankles primly; wearing her uncharacteristically long plaid skirt and oversized cardigan made her feel *almost* modest. "Even with all of us, I think you need to retain counsel outside of the house, though. I'm advising you that as your . . ." She floundered over the word.

"Person?" Kaelee suggested tentatively.

"Right. Your *person*." Greta smiled at her. "I like that. Your person."

"The firm I used for the name change stuff was just . . . someone cheap I found, but I don't think that's the caliber I want if I really do have to deal with Tripp's lawyers." Kaelee made a frustrated noise. "I hate spending my money on this. I mean, I have it . . . but lawyers are so fucking expensive, and he's like a bloated tick. I don't even know how to tell if a firm can manage to stand against—"

"I know a firm." Greta caught and held Kaelee's gaze. "A great one."

"Your ex?"

"Not *her*, but her firm. I met a lot of great lawyers there, and some of them are vicious in the best ways."

"Is that weird for you?" Kaelee asked.

"No. I'm not asking you to work with Tasha," Greta stressed. "May I call the firm, though? Someone else there? Set up a consultation?"

"Do it." Kaelee put one hand on Greta's crossed ankles. "Thank you for being here this weekend, and Thanksgiving, and dealing with this. I worried that I'd lose out by losing you as an editor, but . . . I like having you in my life this way."

"I have fun with you," Greta said. "Maybe that doesn't seem like a huge thing, but I was so focused on work that . . . well, I think I was hiding until I met you. So don't think for a second that we aren't both getting something more from this."

"Good." Kaelee stalked toward her. "We have forty minutes till we have to leave. Any thoughts on something fun to do?"

Greta giggled. "Board games?"

Kaelee growled as she pushed up Greta's skirt to her knees and wrapped her hand around her ankle to uncross Greta's legs. "No. Although you look innocent enough to prefer that sort of fun in this skirt."

"Snow angels?"

"Closer. Show me again how that snow angel pose works?" Kaelee kept hold of Greta's ankle, gently gliding it across the sheet. "Something like this?"

"Yes." Greta moved her other leg so Kaelee could crawl between the wide vee of her legs.

She looked up at Greta. "I love you like this. Wide open and ready even in your sweet skirt and cardigan."

"I was cold."

"Oh?"

"Probably because I forgot a few layers," Greta said with the most innocent look she could muster, unbuttoning the blouse she had under the cardigan and pushing it open. She started to pull it off.

"Leave it at your wrists."

Greta complied.

"Snow angel," Kaelee said. "Where are your arms for that?"

"Wide out to make wings." Greta opened her arms, and the shirt and sweater that she'd shrugged off and pinned under her made her feel like her arms were restrained in that position.

"Can you keep them there?" Kaelee asked. "I feel like you'd like restraints, darlin'. Maybe next time I visit we can try that. . . ."

Greta's lips parted on a gasp at the thought. "Yes, please."

"Darlin', you forget more than your bra today." Kaelee pushed her skirt the rest of the way up and stared at her naked sex. "Were you hoping for a goodbye kiss?"

"Maybe."

Kaelee got up and walked over to the bedroom door to double-check it was locked. Then she came back and stood beside the bed. With the barest glance of fingertips, she traced Greta's sternum and bared breasts. She trailed her fingers to Greta's stomach until she met the waistband of her skirt. "Someday, I want to walk into a hotel room and find you just like this. Will you do that for me?"

"Yes."

"You like being under my control, darlin'?"

"*Yes.*"

"I wonder how long I could keep you this way. Maybe we should find out?"

Greta parted her legs wider. "Next time. Today . . . *please*? Don't make me wait until the next visit."

Kaelee stared at her and asked, "Will you do something for me?"

"Yes."

"No touching until I'm with you again," Kaelee asked, voice tremulous. "I'll do the same. Can we . . . can you . . . starting right now."

"Yes." Greta bit her lip. "Now . . . *please*, Kaelee?"

Without another word, Kaelee lowered herself onto the foot of the bed and lifted Greta, canting her hips so she was held fast in Kaelee's hands. She didn't start slow and languidly this time; she dove in like a woman possessed, feasting on Greta as if she were trying to chase away any possibility of being forgotten or replaced now or ever. She licked and suckled; her tongue moved like she was writing sonnets on Greta's skin. Her grip on Greta's hips would undoubtedly leave fingerprints, marking her as Kaelee's.

When she paused at the edge of Greta's orgasm, Kaelee ordered, "Oh your knees. I want you to ride my face, darlin'."

"Will you let me touch you?"

Instead of answering, Kaelee shucked her jeans. She pivoted so she could put her head on a pillow between Greta's thighs.

As Greta parted her legs wider, she fell forward. Her face was inches from Kaelee's pussy. "Hands or mouth?"

"Fingers in me," Kaelee said, her voice again unsteady. "Unless I say other . . . just that. Maybe . . . I could. I *want* to let you."

"Your rules," Greta moaned as Kaelee pulled her hips down, and her tongue darted out. Within moments she was back at the edge of orgasm, hips moving in a combination of her own movement and Kaelee's firm direction.

The closer Greta came to orgasm, the more Kaelee's hips bucked under Greta's hand.

Finally, as Greta tumbled over, Kaelee gasped, "Tongue."

Greta lowered her mouth and licked. She only had a few seconds before Kaelee orgasmed and pulled away. In the next instant, Kaelee had flipped Greta around and pulled her close. Her body was trembling in aftershocks, and tears spilled from her eyes.

"Thank you," Greta whispered, kissing a tear away.

Kaelee laughed. "Pretty phenomenal for me, too. I'll get there. With you, I'll get to the point of letting you go down on me for real."

"I'll be here, but Kaelee, if you aren't ready? I'll still be here." Greta snuggled in. "Even if that's all it ever is, a few seconds, or if that's the only time, I still want to be here with you. You get that, right?"

"I do." Kaelee's embrace tightened. "I want that, but I want to get past my hangup there, too, and I want that with *you*."

Greta made a purring noise. "Happy to be of service eventually then."

# 31

## Greta

**MID-DECEMBER**

By Thursday, Greta was back in New York and alone. Being with Kaelee and socializing with Toni and Addie had her thinking about the changes she wanted in her life. She sat down with Ian and Emily in her office. They had Kaelee's blessing to get the ball rolling on the potential legal situation.

Luckily, Emily had sent a message yesterday that her biopsy was negative. Greta would've had a hell of a time asking Emily to be there to manage the legal drama if Emily were sick, too.

"Thank you for meeting with me." Greta smiled at both Ian and Emily.

"Of course." Emily gave her a curious look.

On Greta's desk was a copy of Kaelee's book, which she handed to Emily. "First and most exciting order of business. Look at this."

The page edges were a dark burgundy on the top and bottom, and the front edges were printed with flames licking up them. The cover itself was hidden under the dust jacket, but like the dust jacket, it had a beautiful, stylized image of a flaming phoenix. The bird's eyes were red foil, as were the title and Kaelee's name.

"The book looks great." Emily flipped it over and looked under the cover, taking note of the details. "It's so different from Toni's art style."

"Different genres," Greta reminded her mildly. "Toni's book is supposed to say 'literary' and 'historical' whereas Kaelee's book is trendy fantasy."

"True." Emily rested the book on her lap. "Do you realize that Kaelee *called* me? Do you know how hard it is to get her to communicate about anything that isn't in writing? She sends 'memo of conversation' emails after every call."

"She did that to Charlie in PR, too," Ian offered lightly. "She's a record keeper, organized, early. I am lucky I'll get to edit her next book. I will run anything I am unsure about by Greta, Emily, but I hope you know that I'll be a thorough, diligent editor."

"Obviously." Emily smiled at him.

"Ian will be her editor going forward," Greta stressed. "However, she has asked me to start the preliminary details on the legal front . . . as her . . . *person*." Her voice didn't waver, despite the anxiety this decision, this public admission of emotion, caused her.

"It's really not like you to let your private life become public." Emily gave her an assessing look.

At that Greta relaxed a little bit. "Oh, trust me, I know. I've lived and breathed this job and nothing else for the last two years. I'm still going to do that above and beyond expectations, but that's not enough. It's not living."

Ian shot her an approving smile.

"I *care* about Kaelee, Emily," Greta said. "I don't know what, if anything, will come of it in the long run, but I'm grateful for right now. Kaelee is . . . a *remarkable* person. I want to be sure she is protected, beyond what the publisher's legal team handles. We don't want another Toni and Addie media storm."

Emily scowled. "Toni and Addie are well behaved in public these days."

"Or better at not getting caught," Ian amended.

After a moment, Emily sighed. "Fine. They are about to be married, though, so I can't say they'll avoid public drama. I can hope they will. This thing with Kaelee, though . . . it's different."

"It is." Greta nodded to Ian, who left to summon the rest of the team. Then she handed Emily the packet that legal had already received and that marketing and publicity received in a less detailed form. The top page was a notarized sheet from Kaelee that allowed Greta to discuss these things. "I told her I'd manage this without her having to sit here while we discuss her."

Emily skimmed the pages. "Kaelee is the missing Alden kid? I read about this."

"A lot of people did." Greta knew now why the name had sounded familiar. "She wasn't kidnapped or murdered. She ran away because her father is a vile man."

"She could have told me." Emily flipped through the pages. "She *should* have told me. Does Toni know?"

"I don't know how *much* detail Toni has; that's not my business. The Aldens are not a thing Kaelee wants to bring up," Greta stressed. "But they reached out after a decade of silence and want her to cancel the book."

"I know you said that her family had reached out, but I didn't know they were . . ." Emily looked like she had accidentally tasted something foul. "It doesn't matter ultimately. Well, I assume we aren't doing that, so we need a plan for her safety and how to counter their next steps."

"Agreed. And *Kaelee* agrees now." Greta relaxed more now that Emily had read enough to want to plan. "There's one more thing. Her 'engagement'"—Greta made air quotes—"was not her choice. *Nothing* that happened with him was her choice. She gave me permission to talk to you and the attorneys for this part." Greta stared at Emily, hoping she didn't need to be explicit. Talking about that man hurting Kaelee made Greta want to ignore laws and seek him out.

*Destroy him.*

Greta gripped the edge of her desk as she said, "Kaelee came out, and to control her, her father made a choice that included his protégé, who agreed to marry Kaelee."

"Am I understanding you correctly?" Emily whispered. "He . . . they . . . *hurt* her."

"Yes. Her father gave her away in marriage, and his proxy assaulted her." Greta swallowed back the rage she felt simmering. "As a result, Kaelee ran. She changed her name, built a life, became the amazing woman she now is."

"Fuck them if they think they can steal the life and career she built." Emily pinched the bridge of her nose as if to stop a building headache. "Step one, where are we on legal? Are her rights protected that way?"

"I have a consultant coming in, as well as house legal." Greta looked at her list. "Marketing will be making sure there is security at the events. Since Toni is with her at the first four stops, we can cover that cost in-house."

"And the consultant?"

"Kaelee has already paid her retainer. I've been getting all the ducks in a row."

Greta looked up as the door opened.

Ian shot her an apologetic look. Behind him were two attorneys; one was the woman Greta had spoken to on the phone and the other was Tasha. She eyed Greta in that possessive, assessing way of hers that had once felt flattering, but now it simply felt like she was being appraised for her worth.

"Ms. Connolly . . . and Ms. Everette. I hadn't expected *both* of you." Greta felt like a wall of fire was sliding over her. Her skin felt clammy and hot all at once, and she hoped she wasn't going to lose her temper. She'd expected only Marissa—Risa—Connolly. Seeing Tasha was not on the list of things she'd braced for today. Since they'd stopped their one-night fuck sessions, Greta had not seen her in person. A part of her worried that she'd feel something, temptation or regret.

Tasha was still stunning. Tall, bespoke suit, and eyes like ice chips. No one could look at her and think she was anything other than commanding and beautiful, but Greta felt no longing, no hunger, nothing but trepidation that this would upset Kaelee.

"I'm Natasha Everette," Tash said, offering her hand to Emily, who had come to her feet. Then Tasha looked at Greta and nodded. "Greta. Marissa said you had called, so I thought I could help. Two attorneys for the price of one. It's an 'old friends' special rate."

"That's very generous, but Risa is—"

"The Aldens keep an entire team of attorneys on retainer," Tasha said. "I wouldn't be here if I didn't think you could use the backup. Marissa is an exceptional litigator, but she'll be buried in paperwork. That's what they do."

Risa met Greta's eyes. "She's right."

Greta nodded. "Assuming the client agrees, so be it. If not, I trust Risa completely."

Tasha gave her a wry look, hearing plainly what was left unsaid. The jab might have been unnecessary. Tasha was a shark when it came to her job, and on that front, she was exactly the right attorney for this job. They locked gazes far longer than was considered polite.

Then Tasha smiled.

"Shall we?" Marissa said in what Greta was sure was the patented efficient attorney voice.

*How am I to tell Kaelee? I hate to suggest that this is the right path, but Tash is amazing at her job.* For Kaelee, Greta was fairly certain there were very few things she wouldn't do. Finding a way to push past her own bitterness to work with Tasha suddenly seemed perfectly easy.

*Anything to keep Kaelee safe.*

## 32

# *Kaelee*

**CHRISTMAS WEEK**

Kaelee had been impressed when she learned that Toni and Addie's wedding would be hosted at the National Museum of American History. Walking into the museum tonight amped that feeling up several notches. The wedding would be in the Flag Hall, where the flag that inspired "The Star-Spangled Banner" was on display. As Kaelee marveled at the idea of getting married in a room celebrating freedom, she wondered if that seeming dichotomy was intentional.

The Smithsonian as a whole rented out various venues for special events, and Kaelee had attended one event—a book festival—that used the Library of Congress for a cocktail party. That had seemed incredibly well chosen, but it felt mild in comparison to this venue choice. A professor of history and writer of American historical novels and the vivacious actor who had starred in a film adaptation of one of said novels were being married in a building that housed Dorothy's ruby red slippers from *The Wizard of Oz*—an innovative film that transitioned from black and white to color—as well as the first car, and other innumerable artifacts from history. It was ideal.

Of course the brides were dressed in modified late 1800s attire. Toni wore a white tuxedo, complete with tails, and a top hat. In her hand was an opalescent mother-of-pearl-topped cane. She stomped around the venue like an angry polar bear.

"Addie wanted white flowers. Are those white enough? That looks yellow." Toni glared at the offending flowers.

"Sweetie?" Emily, best woman, stepped between Toni and the table arrangement. Like Kaelee, Emily was wearing a more modern take on Toni's ensemble. Her ivory tuxedo-style dress flared into a skirt that came to her calves; Kaelee wore the same ivory top, but it had a pantsuit bottom.

Emily took Toni's face in her hands and made her pause for eye contact. "Addie already approved each detail. It's perfect."

"I want this to make her happy. That awful woman wouldn't let us have it at Dove House. I even offered her triple her rental fees." Toni darted her gaze around the room like she was hunting danger or maybe a target.

"Addie loves you. I think as long as you are there to receive her when she walks down the aisle, everything will be magical," Kaelee offered as she joined them.

Toni looked back at her and then again at Emily. "I might be panicking."

"Seems like." Kaelee stood, checking again that the tape holding her jacket in place was secure. The deep vee cut of a jacket with no blouse or shirt underneath it made her slightly self-conscious, but this was the wedding party attire that Toni—or possibly Addie—had selected.

"Where are your escorts?"

"My date is wandering the museum," Kaelee offered.

"Single." Emily shrugged. "I thought you might need me more than usual, and I thought Lil could use company."

"The Memory Care staff said they'd have someone extra for my mother if needed." Toni scowled.

"That's me. I'm someone extra. There is a nurse, too." Emily laced her fingers with Toni's. "Between me and the nurse, Lil will be fine."

"Greta and I are here, too." Kaelee knew she didn't need to ask Greta if it was okay to volunteer to help as they'd already discussed it. Her cheeks flushed slightly as she added, "We only need time for one dance."

"Your cheeks match the bridal party when you say her name," Toni said, not unkindly. "Light pink. How did that happen? I'm marrying a woman who loves light *pink*."

"And you," Kaelee added. "She loves you."

"She does, doesn't she?" Toni murmured, sounding somehow stunned by the thought. A few moments later, she looked at both of them, cleared her throat, and said, "Em, you've had my back and been at my side forever. Kae, you're becoming the little sibling or cousin I wish I could've had . . . although I'm glad you weren't around to steal all the women over the years. I'm really grateful to you both for being here."

"Are we doing the toasts here privately?" Emily teased.

"No. I just don't do feelings as well in public." Toni scowled at her. "I don't like all that emotional stuff, but I feel emotional right now. I never thought I'd be here, getting married. You know, it wasn't even legal to do this when I came out, so I didn't really think about marriage. Now, I can't imagine her *not* being my wife. I want that for both of you, you know. Happiness like this, and no, I won't be saying anything like that in public. Just . . . you should know that this is the most terrifying, amazing feeling in the world."

Emily's expression remained unchanged other than the pinch around her lips, as if she were holding words back.

Kaelee nodded. "Never been on my to-do list, but I'm happier this year. Good friend. Good agent. Sold a book. Met a woman. Most of that is because of you two. I'm glad to be here for your day." She paused, decided it was getting too heavy, and added, "Plus Emily and I get to admire your bride. That makes any day better, right?"

"She's pretty amazing," Emily said in a voice that was bordering on laughter. "Have you seen her dress? It's so—"

"I haven't seen it," Toni interrupted in a stern voice. "Not even a glimpse. So don't you two say another word."

She stalked off to check on more details. Kaelee and Emily trailed after her after exchanging a smile. "Let's hope the pink ribbons are the right pink," Emily whispered. "If not, you and I will need to run to a store."

"I can hear you." Toni looked back at them. "Wait, are you saying they aren't pink? Are they that orange-pink hue? She doesn't like that."

Kaelee laughed as they had to walk faster to keep up with Toni.

When the guests started to arrive, all four attendants seated them. Addie's man of honor was her cousin Eric, who was strikingly handsome in his pink tuxedo. Her other attendant, a woman named Maren who would walk with Kaelee, wore the dress version of the tuxedo. Addie had decided to have the guests seated at their tables for both the ceremony and reception, so each guest had to be taken to the correct location. It complicated things slightly, but guests' invitations had their table numbers, and the guest list was small.

The pair of photographers on site were snapping pictures of some guests and all four members of the wedding party. Because of the television show, there were more than a few Hollywood people here, along with members of the college. Kaelee walked up to Harold, the head of the history department, who was there with his husband.

"Miss Carpenter." Harold nodded at her, seeming more serious than he was around the department.

"Right this way." She offered an arm to him, and he took it with a little chuff of laughter. She offered the other to his husband who lightly put his hand on her elbow as they walked to a still empty table.

One of the last guests to be seated was Greta.

Kaelee's heart tightened at the feeling of having Greta's hand curl around her arm. Here. At a wedding. Despite everything, it was impossible not to feel a flutter of *what if* as she walked her toward the front of the crowd where she was seated.

"Thank you," was all Greta said. She glanced over then, and in a low voice added, "I am ever so glad to be petite right now. The view from here . . ."

"Darlin'," Kaelee managed as Greta's gaze fixed on the opening of Kaelee's tuxedo jacket.

The pretty smile that came over Greta made Kaelee's cheeks warm again. They hadn't been able to talk as much the last week, other than flirtatious notes.

"Save me my dance later," Greta reminded her before turning away to take her seat. "I'm beyond ready to be in your arms again."

The thought of their agreement not to touch themselves while they were apart flooded Kaelee's mind, and she knew from the intense look on Greta's face that she wasn't the only one thinking about it.

"Be good," Kaelee muttered.

"I have," Greta whispered. "But tonight . . . that ends."

Kaelee walked away before she was unable to leave Greta's side.

Once every seat was filled and each guest had their wine or water, the music started. A string quartet switched to playing a Victorian piece, Mendelssohn from the sounds of it. A wedding officiant walked to the front of the room and waited as a hush fell over the room.

Toni began her walk. On one side was her mother, Lil, who had an arm wrapped around Toni's. On the other was a woman who could only be Addie's mother. Behind them was Addie's father. At the front, all three parents took seats at a table where one guest—the presumed nurse for Toni's mom—waited.

Once Toni took her position, Kaelee and Maren began their walk, separating at the front. Next up were the best woman and the man of honor, and then walking alone with every eye in the place fixed on her was Addie.

The bride's dress was a Victorian dream, and the back of her veil trailed behind her almost long enough to match her dress's train. The train stretched along half the length of the aisle in a glittering puddle of silk and sparkles.

Toni stared at her as if she were a magical creature, not a mere mortal. There was no doubt of their affection. The usually surly professor and writer looked like she couldn't see anyone but her bride, and Addie stared directly at Toni as she walked.

Kaelee glanced at Greta, only to find her staring at Kaelee rather than at the brides. With effort, Kaelee looked away from Greta just in time to watch Toni greet her bride. Toni lifted the sheer veil over Addie's face, leaned in, and kissed her softly.

"A bit ahead of schedule, Toni," said the officiant.

The guests laughed, but Addie just looked thoroughly delighted by the gesture. She rested a hand on Toni's cheek and there in front of everyone the two stared at each other as if the words promising forever were completely unnecessary for them to pronounce aloud. Everything was conveyed between them without a word spoken.

For all Kaelee's doubts about marriage and even relationships, there was no way to see this couple and think that true love was a myth. *Could I have that one day?* Her gaze went back to Greta's.

Again, Kaelee forced her attention back to her friends' vows, but a whisper in her mind suggested that yes, that sort of love could be possible. She could have that, a marriage of equals, a future of joy.

The thought of such a possibility was terrifying—both because it had never been a future Kaelee had considered and because she fundamentally craved it in that moment. The weight of that epiphany had Kaelee staring at the couple fixedly. By the time they were through with vows, the officiant said, "I pronounce you *legally* wed this time."

Kaelee watched as Toni held on to Addie as if she were the most precious creature in the entirety of time.

*I actually* want *that,* Kaelee confessed in the privacy of her mind. Her gaze shot to Greta, and she saw a glimmer of tears in Greta's eyes.

The newlyweds pivoted to face the assembled group, and Toni

said, "We're going to take a moment to mingle before dinner is served."

Then she swept Addie to the balcony where a photographer was waiting. The bridal party pictures followed, and then dinner was served. Kaelee kept watching Greta so often that Addie's mother patted her hand and whispered, "I've learned a lot about planning these things, so if you need help when your time comes, you call me."

Kaelee opened her mouth, but no words came.

"Toni said you were without family. Did I misstep?" Addie's mother, whose name Kaelee still didn't know, widened her eyes. "Oh no! I'm sorry. Do you want to go to the balcony and talk?"

"She means get high," Addie said as she overheard them. Then she looked at her mother. "I thought we agreed. No pot until after the dance."

"Fine. After the mother-daughter dance." Addie's mom dabbed her eyes and whispered, "You'd think my only child would appreciate my willingness to support another woman falling prey to the patriarchal—"

"Lesbian." Kaelee pointed at herself.

"She's definitely never fallen to patriarchal lies, Marlene," Toni added. "Our Kaelee is a staunch advocate for equality."

"Oh, well, that's good!" Marlene smiled at them each in turn. "Do you see, Lenny? Girl power all around!"

"Shall we take a walk?" Addie's father, Lenny, asked. "See the view?"

The two walked away, and Addie laughed. "She'll be high in a minute, but I didn't expect her to last through the whole ceremony, to be fair. I expected objections and a lecture on The Man midway through."

"I bribed her," Toni said lightly.

Addie giggled. "I do love you, wife of mine."

"I know," Toni preened. "Want to escape and show me how much while dinner is served?"

"I'll cover for you," Kaelee offered, marveling at how odd and lovely this was. The families here were the precise opposite of the uptight mess that Kaelee had once thought was normal.

After the meal and the cake and the bridal toasts and the bridal dance, Kaelee walked over to Greta's table and extended a hand to her date. "My official duties are done."

"Oh? Are we leaving, then?" Greta accepted her hand and allowed Kaelee to pull her into her arms.

"No. I want to dance with you."

"Just me?"

Kaelee kissed her temple. "Only you. I mean, the brides may order their wedding party to dance but . . ." The image of trying to dance with Toni, when they would both undoubtedly try to lead, or Addie, which would irritate Toni, made Kaelee laugh. "I somehow doubt that Toni will want to dance with anyone else, and I doubly doubt that she wants Addie doing that either."

"So you're stuck with me," Greta teased.

"Oh, the horror! The most beautiful woman in the room in my arms? However shall I cope?" Kaelee looked back at the table where Greta had been seated with several familiar faces, including Kaelee's publicist, Charlie. "I'm stealing her now."

A giggling Greta clung to Kaelee's arm. "I shouldn't have had the champagne."

"Tipsy?"

"No. Just really relaxed." Greta looked up at Kaelee. "Rumba?"

Kaelee led her to the floor and briefly wondered if she'd recall all the steps from their lesson. "I can lead you in a waltz if that's easier."

"Both. Rumba then waltz." Greta took her position, and Kaelee forgot to be nervous about everyone who could be watching them. None of it mattered. All she could think about was the beautiful woman in her arms.

*I want this. Always.*

Even after Greta was no longer in her arms to dance, as they walked around seeming very obviously a couple, Kaelee realized that no one *cared* they were here together, not the people in the department, not the people from Hollywood, or from New York. They were just another couple at a wedding.

*This feels more natural than I thought possible,* Kaelee mused as they chatted and danced and eventually said their goodbyes.

Afterward, when they grabbed their bags and caught the train to New York, Kaelee thought about the possible future, about *having* a future. It wasn't a thought she'd allowed herself to have often over the years, somehow always expecting her past to catch up with her. Now that it had, she felt like she had stood up and said, *No. I'm not running. I'm not giving up or changing.*

And that reality meant for the first time, Kaelee was thinking about her dreams beyond degrees and publishing.

*What else do I want?*

The answer filled her mind instantly. *I want love. I want someone who has my back, who is at my side.* That was what Toni had said about her friends, but Kaelee wanted that plus the sizzling sex she had with Greta. *I want it all.*

*And I think I want it with Greta.*

# 33

## *Kaelee*

**CHRISTMAS**

Two days later, Kaelee was still at Greta's apartment. An oversized, potted tree that would be picked up and planted somewhere after the holiday filled the room with the scent of Christmas, and the entire apartment looked like a Christmas movie had popped into it. Delicate ornaments and candles, fresh boughs of pine and several poinsettia plants, the scents of whatever deliciousness Greta had cooked while Kaelee had been reading or napping. Everything was holiday-movie perfection.

And instead of panicking, Kaelee felt settled in and warm. She didn't remember the last time she had felt so at home. Tonight, she'd had one glass of wine with dinner, and then Greta brought out a fruit tart and a bowl of whipped cream. "I know you said no more baked goods, but I swear I made this one for myself. Sometimes when I'm anxious I bake."

"Why were you anxious?" Kaelee sat in the chair beside Greta, not across the table, but beside her. Maybe it was a cop-out, but she couldn't sit across from her and delve into the way that made her feel. "And it's not that the baking is in any way unappealing, but I need to find a local gym if I'm going to eat so much sugar. I feel sluggish if I eat these and don't work out."

Still silent, Greta was in the chair on the opposite end of the table from the seat Kaelee had sat in when she'd had Greta spread out like a dessert on this same table. She was uncommonly quiet tonight.

"Is this about the lawyer meeting?"

"No . . . but you know my ex is one of the lawyers consulting on the case, right?" Greta said. "You heard when I said that the first two times? She's part of the team—"

"Are you fucking her?"

"No!"

"Have you since we met?"

"No. Not at all, not even tempted!"

"Then I don't care," Kaelee said bluntly.

"Oh."

"Greta. Look at me."

"What?" Greta looked up from the tart she had neatly sliced, took a deep breath, and started rambling: "This is triple berry. They aren't in season right now, but—"

"Why were you anxious?"

Greta dropped the pie spatula on the table with a clatter. "I need to confess. I have *feelings* for you."

"Yeah?" Kaelee wasn't sure she could say it yet, but she shared those feelings. "Were you not sure about telling me?"

*Some people are just too fucked up to love. Just because* I *love*—Kaelee ran her finger across the bowl of whipped cream and raised it to her lips. Greta stared at her the whole time.

"I feel it, too," Kaelee admitted.

"You don't need to say it," Greta said quickly.

"I know. I'm not. Not right now."

Greta looked sad at that. For a moment, Kaelee felt like the world had paused, like she'd broken something.

"I've never said that to anyone," Kaelee admitted. "Or had a lover say it to me, and since you're the first woman I've *dated* . . ."

"I won't say it. I feel it, though." Greta looked away.

"Hey?" Kaelee waited until Greta looked back at her. Then she slid her finger into her mouth and made an exaggerated noise of approval. "This is good, but it needs something more."

"Oh?"

"Taste." Kaelee swiped up another glob of the admittedly perfect homemade whipped cream and held her finger out toward Greta. "Unless you don't want . . ."

Greta let out a breathy laugh. "I definitely want. I always *want* when you're near."

"What is it you want? A taste?" Kaelee teased.

Greta smiled at her. "Are you offering?" She caught Kaelee's wrist and held on to it as she sucked Kaelee's finger into her mouth, swirling her tongue around it. When she licked all the whipped cream off, Greta teased, "Anywhere you want my mouth, just dab a little of that. I can follow a trail."

Kaelee paused, expecting the same panic she usually felt at the thought of being open and vulnerable. It wasn't there. Not with Greta. "Yes. I think . . . yes."

Greta stared at her in a mix of longing and awe. "Is that what you're offering? You can still be in control, Kaelee. I'll stay only where you lead me."

Greta waited, watching her as if there was something of a negotiation happening, and Kaelee loved her just a little more for understanding her hangups. She took a swipe of the whipped cream and put it on her lips.

The smile Greta gave her was joyous. She pushed her chair back and murmured, "Happily go there."

Kaelee felt like her heart was going too fast as she watched Greta approach her. Almost without thinking, Kaelee's hands fell on the curves of Greta's hips. She wanted her near, and she wanted to let go of her control for a minute.

Then Greta bent down and licked the whipped cream from Kaelee's lips, nibbling and sucking and caressing her mouth so thoroughly that Kaelee wasn't sure she'd ever been so properly kissed in her life.

When Greta straightened, she stood waiting, gaze locked on Kaelee. "Anywhere else?"

Kaelee peeled her shirt and bra off. Without saying a word, she smeared the whipped cream along her throat where it met her collarbone and then she stared at Greta and dabbed it over her nipples. Her voice sounded softer than normal as she said, "A few other places."

Greta didn't comment as she flicked her tongue over Kaelee's nipples, one and then the other. She suckled and nipped. Her breaths were hot against Kaelee's throat as she moved upward to nibble along the edge of her throat. Then she chased the trickle of whipped cream that was now trailing down Kaelee's chest.

"I like this dessert," Greta murmured before she leaned back to watch the very slightest trail of cream drip down the curve of Kaelee's breast and onto her stomach.

"You missed a bit," Kaelee managed to say.

"Gravity is my friend here," Greta said before she mouthed the swell of Kaelee's left breast and bit her nipple again gently.

"I wasn't planning on this," Kaelee confessed as she arched into Greta's mouth. "Not being seduced. I do that. Seduce you."

Greta chuckled. "If you don't think *I'm* seduced right now, too, you aren't paying attention."

"Maybe I'm not as observant as you." Kaelee clutched the back of Greta's hair, tangling her fingers in the mass of loose curls there and pulling her back so she could see her face.

"Let me have you." Greta held her gaze.

A part of Kaelee's heart wanted to yell *yes* and offer Greta everything, forever. She paused, waiting for the anxiety she always felt when considering allowing anyone to top her. The panic was silent. Completely absent.

"Where do you want me?" Kaelee said.

A smile bloomed on Greta's face. "You're still in charge, Kaelee. Just tell me where you want my mouth."

"I don't need that. Not the whipped cream or the control." Kaelee shivered as she said the next words, "Make love to me, Greta. Take me to your bed, and *take me.*"

Greta stepped back and took Kaelee's hand in hers. She led her to the bedroom and turned on the bedside light. "You'll tell me if that changes? At any point. You can stop me, say no, whatever you need."

"Yes."

"I mean it. If that changes or if you want me to stop or pause—"

"I want you. I *trust* you more than I have ever trusted another person. I feel those same feelings, you know?" Kaelee hated how shaky she sounded, but she needed to get the words out. She couldn't imagine ever trusting anyone else this way. In a raspy voice, she confessed, "I've only let one person . . . a friend . . . and I was drunk. I had to be in order to try to . . ."

"If you don't want me to go down on you, I won't." Greta cupped her face in both hands. "I am one hundred percent okay with whatever you want here."

And maybe because that was true, Kaelee wanted this. "I want your mouth on me tonight."

"Best Christmas gift ever." Greta took her hand and led her to the bed where they'd been sleeping. Silently, she used her free hand to pull back the duvet and top sheet.

They both paused. Kaelee released the hand Greta was holding. Neither of them spoke, and it felt as if there was a weight to the silence. The only sound was breathing—and the thunder of Kaelee's heart.

*I love her. I love her, and that's why I trust her.*

A part of Kaelee wanted to confess that truth, wanted to hear Greta say it, too.

"I can't promise that I can do this again," Kaelee admitted.

"You don't have to even promise to do it right now," Greta quickly countered. She waited, not hurrying her as Kaelee unfastened and shoved down her trousers and shorts. She held her gaze and asked, "May I kiss you everywhere? Can we start with that?"

"Yes."

The smile on Greta's lips was only visible for a moment before she leaned in and captured Kaelee's mouth. Kissing Greta was always wonderful, but tonight felt different, more, and Kaelee hoped that her insecurity and anxiety would stay dormant.

Greta pulled backed. "Head on the pillow, please."

She watched as Kaelee reclined, and there was no way that Kaelee could see anything but acceptance and affection in Greta's gaze. She watched her in a way that would've eased any worries she had—if she had them.

"Touch me," Kaelee ask-ordered.

"Gladly." Greta's hands and lips skimmed the lines of Kaelee's body, not missing the sharp cuts of her biceps or the small rise of her breasts.

Despite the muscles that she worked hard to maintain, Kaelee still felt self-conscious. There was no airbrushed perfection in real life. Her ribs felt too visible, her tattoos too dark, her scar from a childhood fall too stark. Then she looked at Greta's expression.

*Awe. Joy. Love.* Everything in her gaze was positive.

Greta's fingertips brushed over a ticklish spot and Kaelee jumped slightly. Her lips curled into a smile. "I forgot how ticklish I could be."

"Good thing? Bad thing?" Greta met her eyes.

"Neutral."

As Greta worked her way lower, she lavished affection on Kaelee's hip bone, belly button, the flat firmness of her stomach.

And still Kaelee was at ease. She parted her legs wider, cradling Greta there, and said, "Keep going, please." Her voice was steady, even though she had to hold on to the headboard of Greta's bed to force herself not to reach out.

*I am surrendering control.*

*I want this.*

*I want her to feel the way I do when I get her off.*

That was the part that Kaelee had never experienced. Sure, she enjoyed pleasure, but an orgasm was an orgasm. She didn't need much to get there, so why trust anyone to put their face near her most tender place? The difference was that with Greta, Kaelee felt safe. She cared that Greta had everything she could want in bed—not just orgasm after orgasm—and Greta was blunt about wanting to satisfy Kaelee in every way.

Kaelee watched as Greta slid her fingertips along Kaelee's damp flesh and looked up, seeking permission yet again. There was something beautifully erotic about seeing the woman she loved staring up at her in that hopeful way, and Kaelee understood Greta's earlier words that she was still in control, even on her back.

*In control of my body.*

*In control of my pleasure.*

"Yes," Kaelee reiterated.

And Greta lowered her mouth to Kaelee's flesh. Her tongue was firm and sure, and her attention was slow and seductive. Within moments, Kaelee's hips were lifting, offering herself up, wanting more.

She could feel the answering smile against her skin.

"Please," Kaelee whispered. "Faster."

The light, slow, flirtatious licks sped, and Greta's hands, rather than holding Kaelee down, scooped under her to steady and lift. Greta was not holding Kaelee down at all.

"Don't stop," Kaelee begged.

Greta's touches grew faster until Kaelee had to reach down and hold on to her. The only part of Greta she could reach was her mane of curls. Her hands slipped into Greta's hair and held on as Greta licked, kissed, and suckled until Kaelee felt herself hurtling toward satisfaction and falling over the edge.

*I love her,* Kaelee thought as she pulled Greta into her embrace and held her tightly.

"You're amazing," Greta murmured against Kaelee's damp skin.

Kaelee lifted her head to stare at her for a moment. "Says the woman who did the impossible. Never once have I done that sober until you."

Greta smiled and snuggled closer.

"Say it," Kaelee whispered.

Propping herself up to stare into Kaelee's eyes, Greta said, "I love you, Kaelee Carpenter. I'm not trying to trap you or ask for anything you don't want to give, but I love you."

Kaelee nodded. "I feel that same way for you, too," she managed to say.

"I thought so," Greta said lightly, but her expression had dimmed slightly when Kaelee hadn't said the words.

<h1 style="text-align:center">34</h1>

<h1 style="text-align:center">Kaelee</h1>

## NEW YEAR'S EVE

"I know it's early," Greta started as she tinkered with the candles lining a low shelf. The entire place was warm and festive, but Greta was forever adjusting this or that. Kaelee was fairly sure that entire tree had been rearranged over the past week. The cute little bear ornament that was near the top had definitely been in the middle yesterday.

*I ought to take pictures next year,* Kaelee thought with a fond smile. That thought, however, was quickly followed by the realization that she thought they'd still be doing whatever dating thing they were currently trying out an *entire year* from then.

*Will I be that lucky?*

Kaelee watched Greta eye one of her various branches of pine or whatever sort of evergreen it was.

"Can we really just get this meeting out of the way before we start the New Year?" Greta asked, eyes wide and hands on her hips. Her entire body was tense. "Are you sure? Risa called and—"

"Of course. Tell the attorney that it's fine. First . . ." Kaelee walked over to her and wrapped her arms around Greta, tugging her into a loose embrace. She stared down at her. "I want to say that I really like you."

"Oh?" Greta's tension visibly relaxed.

"I do. I was just thinking about next year," Kaelee admitted. "I think we need to chart the little polar bear on the tree next Christmas. I can count at least five places you've moved it this year."

Greta's cheeks pinked. "I want everything to be perfect. I may be a little nervous about not messing up."

"Everything *is* perfect. *You* are perfect. I like being in your home. I like the meals and the wine and the snuggling on your sofa. I like the days you walk around naked. I like touching you and discovering all the ways you sigh or moan. I like when you put your hands or mouth on me. I like when you tell me random things." Kaelee brushed Greta's hair back, partly because she liked touching her and partly because Greta leaned into every caress like it was the most wonderful thing ever. Her eyelids fluttered closed as Kaelee kissed her temple before continuing, "And I like when you curl up and read next to me. You're like a book review in motion. I know when a book is good or okay or startling or exciting simply by watching your face."

"Kaelee . . ."

"You have made this the single best holiday in my life," Kaelee whispered against her ear. "And I hope you still want me here next year. I know what I can give you might not be enough for—"

"It is. Anything with you is enough," Greta countered. "Honestly. Being with you is everything."

Kaelee pulled her closer. "So let's get the meeting sorted out. Then I want to dance with you and toast to the new year with you."

"Yes, please."

"How much time do we have? You say yes like that, darlin', and I'm not going to want to meet anyone or go anywhere." Kaelee kissed along Greta's throat as Greta tilted her head in invitation. "So, tell me, darlin'. Are you going to be a good girl so we can make it until midnight?"

"If I have to." Greta pressed closer.

Kaelee caressed her shoulders and arms. "If you wait until after the meeting with the lawyer, we can break out that remote control of yours and take a walk. . . ."

Greta's pupils dilated in hunger. "I'll be *very* good, then."

"If we started earlier, I'm not sure you would make it to midnight, darlin'." Kaelee trailed her hand over Greta's spine and rested it on the small of her back. "Because once we start, you're going to have to wait until I say you're allowed to get off."

With a deep sigh, Greta rested her head against Kaelee's chest. "Yes, please."

Roughly an hour later, two attorneys came to Greta's apartment, which, to be fair, Kaelee thought was a little odd, but she wasn't interested in spending the last day of the year in a legal office, so it was perfectly fine. Maybe Greta had paid for the unexpected house call on a holiday.

The first woman, who introduced herself as Marissa Connolly, was a polished-looking woman of average height in her mid- to late thirties. Her hair was a vibrant red that was pulled back in a tight, simple French braid, and her suit was a subdued charcoal number. She wore flats, sensible and black. The second woman, Ms. Everette, hadn't offered a first name. She was taller, standing roughly eye to eye with Kaelee. Her suit was tailored, trousers and jacket in a cornflower blue and a darker blue blouse. Shoulder-length, honey-toned hair, the color of which could only come from regular salon trips, was pinned in a short tail at the back. She moved with the ease of a person who either practiced yoga or barre, the posture that hinted at ballet or equestrian lessons, and the general arrogance that said she was born to wealth.

*Like recognizes like.*

Kaelee wondered briefly if Ms. Everette had personal reasons to want to strike out at the Aldens or if it was merely the awareness that defeating Tripp's team would be an ego boost. Either way, Kaelee was glad that the chilly woman was on her side. Tripp would never hire a woman, so there was only one side open to her when legal matters included her father.

Women were not seen as his equals.

The two attorneys made themselves at home at Greta's table, pulling out forms to sign that would, ideally, protect Kaelee from harassment and safeguard her privacy. There was also an affidavit from several therapists, employers at the university, professors, and Greta herself expressing that Kaelee was of sound mind and was not a danger to herself or others.

"His best play is to manage to declare you in need of a conservatorship. He has suggested that you are mentally unwell." Ms. Everette tapped the signed papers on the table to straighten them. "If he controls your money, he controls your freedom. That would enable him to force you into compliance."

"I'll change my identity and live off the grid before I allow that." Kaelee folded her arms to hide the shudder that rippled through her at the thought of such an infantilizing state. "And his version of mental illness is simply that I'm a lesbian. That's *not* an illness."

"That's why we're here," Marissa, the calmer of the two lawyers, spoke in a comforting voice.

"If we can prove he knew you were alive, we can also use the pressure of embarrassing him for holding a memorial," Ms. Everette said in an almost gleeful tone.

"I don't care about embarrassing him or getting revenge. I just want them to stay out of my life," Kaelee stressed.

"His attorneys agreed to no contact with the stipulation that the book is canceled. Mr. Alden has offered to pay the kill fee, replace the advance the publisher has paid to date, and pay damages. That offer is on the table, and as your representation, we need to present it to you. His attorneys are submitting a similar offer to the publisher, as well as to you, to compensate them for the time and money spent and recoup the portion of the advance they have already paid to you."

Greta looked at Kaelee. "If it would make your life easier . . ."

"I sold two novels. I am not canceling them." Kaelee folded her hands tightly together. "These aren't tell-all biographies or memoirs. They are *fictional.*"

"His attorneys *also* made the offer to pay you the sum that the books were advanced, as well as an additional seventy-five thousand dollars *if you would agree* to cancel them." Ms. Everette stared at Kaelee. "As your attorney, I am obligated to share this generous offer. Book projection from his research"—she slid a sheet toward Kaelee and a copy of it to Greta—"shows this as the likely high end of royalties earned after recouping the advance."

"Fuck him. I'd give the publisher another book *for free* before I accepted anything from Tripp."

Greta smiled. "Well, if this research is correct, we'll definitely not be expecting a *free* book, and Emily certainly will expect an increase in your next advance." To the attorneys, she said, "Her agent. You met her at my office."

The meeting went far to ease a lot of Kaelee's worries. In essence, Tripp was trying to throw money around to get his way, but she had no realistic legal issues he could exploit.

"What about a protection order?" Greta asked after the team finished going over everything to date. "Risa? You mentioned—"

"Sorry." Marissa shook her head. "A father making one phone call and an envelope of news clippings with a letter from a mother were not considered grounds for an order of no contact. Those are for domestic violence, stalking, or harassment. Nothing here meets that criteria. His legal actions mean that until the matter is resolved, we might be able to present it as an attempt at manipulating you, but when we started this, the legal matters weren't yet in play."

"He knew you were hired, and that was enough to make him initiate this nonsense." Kaelee stood and paced away from the table. "What about Kyle?"

"Your former fiancé? He's reached out?" Ms. Everette leaned forward. "Was there a reason to argue no contact there?"

"He assaulted me. Sexually. No, I didn't file charges or report anything. I left. Changed my name." Kaelee shrugged like it was no big deal, and although she had included that in the information

Greta had disclosed previously, it stung to have to tell anyone what had been done to her.

"We'll generate the paperwork. You'll need to sign an affidavit indicating that his sexual contact with you was nonconsensual." Ms. Everette was very matter-of-fact, no pity, no softening. It made Kaelee like her just a little more.

"Nonconsensual sounds so mild," Kaelee mused. "Fine. *In my opinion and recollection,* I rejected his advances. I was not aware of the engagement and had not dated Kyle. Following his *assault,* I left Durham, moved, and changed my name. I discontinued contact with the Aldens as a result of their compliance in the acts that led to unwelcome congress with Kyle, a protégé and employee of my father's, who was significantly older than me."

Marissa wrote down every word, and Kaelee paused and read the sheet.

"Make sure to send a copy to Julia, too. Tripp doesn't communicate well with women," Kaelee said mildly. The hope that her mother hadn't known was a thin one, but it existed despite time and countless evidence that she was his puppet.

Kaelee walked away while Greta and the attorneys finished whatever business was needed. She was reasonably in control of her emotions, but in this case, she still needed a moment to collect herself. She strayed into the living room where she looked out a window at the sea of towering buildings.

A few moments later, Marissa came to stand beside her. "You're handling this all so very well. Be proud of yourself."

Kaelee nodded.

Marissa continued, "Would you want to split a cab? I don't think I'd feel right sending you into the wild alone just this moment."

Kaelee didn't want to say she was staying right here, so she just said, "Thank you, but no. That was kind of you to offer, though."

"I am heading out, then," Marissa called.

"Thank you, Risa," Greta said, walking into the room. She glanced at Ms. Everette. "Are you going with her?"

"Not just yet. If you want to walk out with her, Kaelee, please do. We'll be in touch." Then she stepped over to Greta. "I like the décor changes," she said, hand brushing the back of the sofa.

Greta frowned at her.

"Were there other matters?" Kaelee prompted.

"No. You can head out for whatever festivities you have planned." Ms. Everette smiled, and Kaelee felt an unfamiliar rush of possessiveness toward Greta.

"Actually, my plans are with Greta." Kaelee walked over to Greta's sofa and sat.

"Oh." The attorney looked between them. "So that's why you're so protective, Greta!"

"Tash."

Kaelee looked between them. "*This* is Tasha?"

"She talked to you about me?" Tasha asked, sounding stunned. "She's usually very discrete."

"We're close," Greta countered, lips tight and entire expression tense. "Kaelee is my guest."

"And here I was going to apologize for my mistaken theories about your late nights." Tasha's tone became catty.

Greta shook her head. "Until I met Kaelee, I had never, not once, slept with anyone in the industry."

"And we didn't meet in the industry," Kaelee felt compelled to add. "We met online."

"Ah. The *app*." Tasha nodded. "I meet most of my fuck friends there, too. Simplifies matters." She smiled again in her very intimidating way, but this time, Kaelee didn't find it appealing. "I matched with Greta a year ago. I'm sorry, *Marie*."

"Is this going to be an issue?" Kaelee asked.

"No. Is it for you? Knowing that I was . . ."

"She told me," Kaelee said bluntly. "I knew you were consulting."

"Oh." Tasha's entire demeanor shifted. She glanced at Greta. "Honestly, I stayed to ask if you wanted to grab a drink some night, Greta. Maybe start the new year together. I made a mistake in giving up on us. I thought that every time I saw you after the breakup, but then you stopped answering my calls."

"I'm seeing someone, Tash. What did you think would happen? You *cheated* on me."

"I panicked, okay? I wanted to be . . . where I am now, and I felt lost trying to do that and be yours and . . ." Tasha threw her hand upward in frustration. "I was still trying to figure me out, and you were just so sure of everything."

"I *wasn't*." Greta stared at her, mouth agape. "I had a career that was slow to build, and you were climbing the ladder like it was flat ground. Polished, poised, so sure of yourself."

"I just wanted you to think I knew what I was doing." Tasha's voice was soft. "Law and winning arguments are pretty much *all* I knew then. Now? I've spent a lot of hours in therapy. I should've said something when we . . ." She glanced at Kaelee. "When I called you all those nights."

"Okay, I don't need to hear all this. Can you or can you not represent me without bias?" Kaelee said in the tense silence. "Because it sounds like there are some big issues here."

"I can. I *will*," Tasha spoke so unwaveringly that Kaelee felt certain it was true.

Kaelee nodded. "I'll leave you to talk, then."

She didn't look back as she walked toward the bedroom where she had been sleeping with Greta. Walking out and leaving the two women alone took a lot of self-control, more than Kaelee typically felt like she had—and she wasn't a weak-willed woman. Even so, she felt panic rise at leaving them.

*They were engaged.*

*They loved each other enough to plan for forever.*

*Tasha is poised and powerful. Greta likes that.*

*I love her, but until I came along they were still hooking up and . . . they were engaged.*

With visions of needing to leave filling her mind, Kaelee pulled her suitcase out of the corner of the room where it had been sitting since they arrived here after Toni and Addie's wedding. She opened the drawer she'd been using and gathered up her clothes.

*There's no way she'll want me if Tasha wants to get back together. And she shouldn't. They both live in New York. They deserve time to . . .*

"What are you doing?" Greta asked, closing the door quietly behind her with a soft *snick.*

"Packing."

"I should've told you that was Tasha when she walked in." Greta took the shirt out of Kaelee's hand and dropped it on the bed.

"I should've guessed when she didn't offer her name," Kaelee said. "I swear my mind is muddled when I think about Tripp and Kyle."

Greta scooped all of Kaelee's clothes up and carried them back to the drawer. She dropped them in a now unfolded heap. "Don't leave me."

"You and Tasha would look good together. She seems nice." Kaelee half choked on the word. "Nice" wasn't what Tasha seemed. Deadly. Fierce. Sexy. There were a lot of words, but "nice" wasn't one of them.

"Tasha's a bitch. A smart, cutthroat bitch. It's one of the many traits that meant that when she offered to help Risa with your legal needs *for free,* I didn't refuse."

"And you didn't think that was a suspicious offer?" Kaelee pressed, staring at Greta.

"Oh, I suspected it was an apology of sort." Greta widened her eyes in what Kaelee suspected was to be an innocent look.

"You *knew* she was trying to make amends and you . . . took advantage of it?"

Greta shrugged. "She owes me an apology. Why not let her apologize with her offer of free legal services?"

Kaelee laughed unexpectedly. "Damn, woman. Remind me not to underestimate your temper."

"I wasn't trying to make today awkward. I specifically told Risa that we only needed her for the meeting." Greta pushed Kaelee backward onto the bed.

"So her apology didn't sway you to go back to her arms?" Kaelee stared up at her as Greta straddled Kaelee's lap. "We can stop this and—"

"I have no feelings for *her*. I thought I might when we were . . . when she started calling after the breakup. I thought we could fix it, but she only wanted to see me in her bed or a couple times in some club."

"Did she get you off on a dance floor, darlin'?"

"She wouldn't. Just the bathroom," Greta said. "Even in her drunken calls for sex, she still only wanted what she wanted. Not my interests. Not my needs."

"You were engaged, though," Kaelee countered. "If you still love—"

"I don't. I love *you*."

Kaelee swallowed back the words.

"I don't think my heart even has room to hold on to anger or disappointment in her. What I feel for *you* has taken up all the space," Greta said boldly. "You. You fill my thoughts; my heart is yours, Kaelee. And I want you. Just you. As much as you'll give me, even if that's just texts and weekends and some holidays."

"Greta . . ."

"No. No arguing right now," Greta said. "I keep telling you that I don't expect you to say it back, but I love you. Only you. I still have my work and my life here, and you have yours. Two independent women who meet, have beautiful experiences, and then go back to our regular lives."

Kaelee rested her face against Greta's shoulder. "Can we stay in and just . . . have a quiet night?"

"Rain check on the rest?" Greta asked.

"I'm sorry." Kaelee looked away, feeling uncharacteristically exposed by the day's events. "Talking about my past and . . . meeting your ex . . . I feel a little overwhelmed."

"Popcorn and television with you? Sounds like a perfect night to me." Greta kissed her cheek. "I am here with you, Kaelee. No matter what. No matter how. I cannot imagine my life going back to a Kaelee-free one. And as much as I like being adventurous in our sex life, I *also* like snuggling up with you."

"I'm here, too. In this," Kaelee said, her voice rough and scratchy. "I *want* to be here. I want both of those things you said, too. All of them. I feel the same as you. You know that, right?"

"I know," Greta said before giving her a sweet kiss.

And Kaelee let herself be held as she tried not to let all the feelings of today drown her in a flight of panic. This thing with Greta was the best thing to ever happen to Kaelee, and she had to be willing to say those feelings aloud.

*Saying it won't make Greta leave me.*

Kaelee felt like she'd been starving for something her whole life, only to find it unexpectedly. The thought of saying those words made her panic and choke.

**35**

# *Kaelee*

When Kaelee left New York—and Greta—a day later, she still felt like her heart had been ground up, both by talking about all her old trauma and by trying to let herself love Greta without panic. Everything between them had happened so quickly—although "quickly" was somehow already four months now. Every time they decided to face where they were, Kaelee felt like they immediately leaped forward.

Kaelee let herself spiral for almost two weeks, and Greta simply sent texts and messages as if nothing was wrong. She sent cute memes and silly videos. She allowed Kaelee to be who she was, process her feelings at her own pace, and ultimately that was why they worked. They both accepted the other person for who she was.

*I don't deserve a woman like her,* Kaelee's insecurities taunted over and over in a voice that sounded like Tripp's. *I'll ruin it.*

When release week came along, Toni and Kaelee were supposed to launch Kaelee's book in Houston, at a store that managed to sell both fantasy and mystery.

"You look constipated," Toni said as they walked through Dulles toward their gate.

Kaelee exhaled. "Not sure why I'm doing this."

"Because it's in your contract?" Toni nodded. "That's why tours exist, according to Emily." When Kaelee said nothing in response,

Toni added, "Fine. To support sales, meet readers, and also because the booksellers at Murder By The Book are amazing."

"That's why you're going," Kaelee stressed. "No one is going to read my book, and if they buy it it's just because of your endorsement quote and—"

"You are starting to make me look cheerful in comparison." Toni led her to a pair of seats that were not actually at their gate, but at an adjacent one with no flight currently scheduled. "Better here. It's empty."

Walking through the airport with Toni made Kaelee feel like a huge imposter.

"Kae? They cannot like it until they buy and read it," Toni pointed out for the third time in the last week.

Kaelee nodded. "I know. I do."

They lapsed into silence until boarding, and Kaelee popped in earbuds to drown out the doubts in her head. It was done. The book was out, in libraries, in stores, in packages shipping to houses from online stores, in hands carrying it home, in audio or ebook formats that had automatically downloaded at midnight last night.

When they grabbed their bags and went to the hotel, Kaelee had finally managed to quell her panic. That was further simplified when they walked into the lobby and a beautiful woman in a wrap dress stood up and said, "Hi."

"*Greta?*"

"I wanted to surprise you." Greta held out a bouquet of flowers. "Happy release day."

When Toni cleared her throat awkwardly, they looked at her.

"You're making a scene." Toni nodded at a man with a camera. "Never a good thing when the vultures are near."

Greta handed them both a key card. "The car will be here at six. Meet in the lobby. Charlie will be on site, too." Toni walked away. Then Greta took Kaelee's hand and tugged her to the elevators. "Come on. We can grab room service unless you'd rather go out."

In answer, Kaelee leaned in for a quick kiss. "Cancel the event. Cancel everything ever after. I just want to be in your arms."

Greta's laugh trilled out. "You are the most romantic woman I've met—or really anxious about the signing. Either way, I'm glad you don't mind me showing up."

"I was sad not to launch in DC or New York where I could see you on release day." Kaelee jabbed the elevator button. "What if everyone hates it?"

"You got a starred review already."

"But that other review—"

"They hate everyone." Greta rolled her eyes. "Preorders look good; reviews overall are good. Let's celebrate release."

The elevator doors slid open, and they stepped in.

Before the door closed, an arm reached in and stopped it. "Sabrina."

Kaelee felt like her stomach rose up and caught in her throat. Standing there was Tripp Alden, and behind him was a small army of people. Tripp was older, which Kaelee had known intellectually, but *seeing* him in person shocked her so badly that all she said was, "You got old."

He raised his brow. "Excuse me?"

"I knew time passed, but you were taller in my memories. Younger. More intimidating." Kaelee stabbed the button to close the elevator doors before she stepped in front of Greta. She looked back at Greta and whispered, "Sorry."

And then she stepped out.

She stayed beside Tripp so the only way for Greta to get out, too, was to shove one of them. Hopefully, Greta would stay upstairs. The thought of her having to face Tripp—even this older version of him—made Kaelee's fears boil away.

*Why is it easier to protect someone else than to protect ourselves?*

*Why did no one protect me?*

Kaelee took in her father. He was a shade over six feet, wide shouldered, and his suit screamed "money" to anyone who looked his way. His wedding band glinted on one hand. A thick ring adorned the opposite hand, and a diamond-decorated watch glinted on his wrist. Despite what the media wanted to project, not all villains were ugly. In fact, Kaelee believed the most successful ones were probably innocuous or at the least moderately attractive. They blended into the fabric of society better that way.

"Came for the book signing?" Kaelee asked as she strolled past him. "If I'd known writing a book would make you crawl out of your tower of self-righteousness, I wouldn't have done it, but now that I have, it's not going away. Thousands of copies sit on shelves already today."

"You embarrass the family name." His hand tightened in a fist, but Tripp cared about his reputation too much to hit her in public.

"I don't share a name with you, so no, I don't. Although, honestly, I used to bank on your fear of embarrassment, you know?" Kaelee walked over to a chair and sat, thrilled that he followed her. She was leading.

*I am not afraid. I am not a child to cower in front of him. Not now. Not ever again.*

"Sit like a lady, Sabrina." Tripp scowled at her.

So Kaelee threw a leg over the arm of the chair. "Nah."

His lips tightened; his jaw clenched.

She waved at the four attorneys trailing behind him like a bad smell. She had no doubt that they were competent at their job, probably among the best that money could buy. "How's things?"

"My offer was generous. The kill fee to you and to the publisher. I'll double it right now." Tripp held out a hand, a check already in it. "Written out to that ridiculous name you chose."

"You know, I don't feel like a Sabrina. I don't think I ever did." She looked at the check in his hand. She couldn't see all of it, but she had no doubt that it was an obscene amount. If not for the money her grandparents had left her, if not for the book deal, the number of zeros on that check would be impossible to refuse. "Was I the only problem your money couldn't fix?"

"If not for your mother's parents' money—"

"Ah. Nice ploy trying to have me declared dead or incompetent," Kaelee said, voice still not wavering. "Now you want to lie about my mental state to take away the money that allowed me to be who I am. Clever. Deceitful. Cruel. It's a very *you* thing to do."

The elevator chimed, and Kaelee didn't have to look up to know that Greta was here. Her steps stabbed the floor in a quick, aggressive march.

"Did you give Kyle permission for what he did to me? He said you did. Is it true?" Kaelee asked. "That's the only question I have before I leave. Did you?"

"Women need a firm hand. Discipline. Some more than others." He didn't even have the grace to look ashamed. "Yes. I suggested he encourage you to see the right order of things. Your rebellious claim that you were a . . ."

"*Lesbian*," Kaelee filled in, dragging the word out exaggeratedly. "I am a lesbian, Tripp."

Needing to look anywhere else to keep her minimal in-flight lunch from rising, Kaelee jerked her gaze away from him. Greta was staring at her, not looking angry but worried. She had reached Kaelee's side and stood like a sentinel. Her hand closed on Kaelee's shoulder. "Okay?"

Kaelee nodded once.

"Thank you for coming. Ms. Carpenter and I were hoping this wasn't necessary. . . ." Greta wasn't looking at Tripp, though. The attorneys, Marissa and Tasha, flowed across the lobby like avenging angels. "Do you have this?"

"We do." Marissa looked at Kaelee. "This will be what we need to argue for a no-contact order."

"I do appreciate you doing the work for us, Mr. Alden. Your actions today will be enough to convince the judge that you are, in fact, threatening our client." Tasha had the sort of vicious glee in her eyes that would be more suited for someone holding a sword or a gun. Instead, she had a sheaf of papers.

"Sabrina." Tripp stood and extended the check. "Don't be unreasonable."

Kaelee took the check. She stood there and calmly shredded it into tiny pieces.

Then she met his eyes again. "Unreasonable was giving Kyle permission to rape me. Unreasonable is hitting my mother. Unreasonable is donating your money to hate-mongers." She dropped the pieces of the check on the floor. "My name, incidentally, is Kaelee. Kae for my grandmother. Lee for my grandfather. And Carpenter . . . you'd think you would have caught that reference since you *claim* to follow Christianity, despite your hate, your adultery, your lies and greed and gluttony and pride."

"You talk to *me* that way? Surrounding yourself with harlots and jezebels." His face was red with rage.

Kaelee laughed briefly and whispered, "Fuck you."

And then she took Greta's hand in hers and walked away. Someone had already pressed the elevator button, so they strode from the lobby into the elevator car without pause.

As the doors closed, Kaelee let out the breath she'd been holding. Telling Tripp off felt validating, and she wished she could tell the teen version of herself who had cowered before him that one day, they would finally get their say. She wished she could tell young Kaelee that everything she could dream would be hers one day—freedom, safety, courage, security, love. All of it.

*Instead, I will write my sapphic books, and tell other kids that we can be heroes, that we can find love, that we can be happy.*

The adrenaline crash from facing Tripp was real, though. She shivered. Once they were in the elevator, Kaelee felt as if the strings that held her upright had loosened.

She tugged Greta into her arms. "You know, I was trying to keep you out of his path while I confronted him. That's why I sent you away. I wanted to protect you."

"And I was trying to be sure you knew you weren't alone. You don't have to face every monster alone." Greta stroked Kaelee's back in small soothing circles as Kaelee clutched her. Greta added, "Risa and Tash will take care of things."

"He's smaller." Kaelee flushed, feeling foolish saying it, but it was the truth. "As a kid, he seemed huge and terrifying. Today . . . I don't know. He was an old man in a nice suit, but he didn't scare me the same way."

"It's easier to terrorize children, to try to intimidate those who are physically smaller than you." Greta led her out of the elevator and into the hallway.

Kaelee twined her fingers with Greta's. "Honestly, men like him are part of why I go to the gym. I hated feeling weaker, afraid of him, flinching when he moved like he was going to hit me."

Greta opened a hotel room door, and Kaelee realized that her bags were already here. Greta shrugged. "They were in the elevator with me."

"Would you hate me if I said I need a few minutes to get my head in order?"

Greta kissed her tenderly. "Shower. Nap if you need. I can order food."

After a shower, sex, food, and a nap, Greta calmly led Kaelee to the lobby where Toni and Charlie were waiting.

"Your father was here?" Toni said as they approached.

"Waving around checks and spouting hate." Kaelee shrugged, trying to blow it off.

Toni, in a completely uncharacteristic move, pulled her into a hug. "I'm proud of you for standing up. Charlie filled me in, as did your dynamic duo here." She lowered her voice to a whisper, "If you need to talk to someone, my therapist is really good."

When Toni released her, Marissa was waiting. "So, Mr. Alden and his legal team have left. We explained that any further contact in any way—call, letter, email, package, in person by him or his representatives—would be considered harassment. It was a productive conversation."

"So we're all okay? My book event? My career? All of it?" Kaelee stared at her attorneys. "For real?"

"For real." Marissa smiled, her face looking softer in the moment. "If he missteps, you have our information."

She stepped away to talk to Greta, leaving Kaelee alone with Tasha who added, "We'll be entering the paperwork for an order of protection." After Kaelee nodded, Tasha paused. "She loves you, you know? Greta."

"I do know." Kaelee's gaze drifted over to Greta and Marissa.

"I asked Risa to distract her for a minute."

"Oh. Why w—"

"Consider today's fees for the entire firm deeply discounted," Tasha spoke over her. "The joy of seeing Tripp Alden sputter was a bonus payment."

"So pro bono?"

Tasha laughed. "Oh, honey, no. Just discounted as thanks for my joy. I'm not the sort of woman whose services are ever *fully* free—even though I was going to just add my hours to Risa's."

Kaelee laughed in grudging respect. "If you weren't Greta's ex, I think I'd like you."

"Treat her well, or I'll see what I can do to amend the *ex* part of that." Tasha pivoted and left with a sort of feline grace that Kaelee could admire.

36

# Greta

Toni insisted that she could take her own car, and she'd gathered Charlie into it with her. That left Greta and Kaelee alone in the back seat of a black car headed to the book event. Houston being its complicated self in weather had managed to offer up more humidity than Greta's hair ever needed. Her waves seemed to be functioning as a sponge, soaking up the humidity in the air and slowly growing. Even though Kaelee had seen her in morning-afters and with middle-of-the-night after-sex hair, Greta kept trying to contain her hair.

"Are you braiding it again?" Kaelee stared at her in what looked a lot like fondness.

"I don't want to reflect poorly on you and—"

Kaelee caught her hand. "You're gorgeous. Always." She kissed the palm of Greta's hand. "Why are you freaking out here? I'm supposed to be the nervous author, remember?"

"I wanted everything to be perfect for you." Greta kept her voice pitched low, although the driver undoubtedly heard them.

"You're here. The lawyers stepped in because you had planned for crisis intervention. Toni is here, and whether she likes it or not, she's a huge influence. I would've liked Emily and Ian here, but we'll see them in New York tomorrow, right? Barnes and Noble?"

"Yes."

"So, honestly, this week is a dream come true. Even if I don't sign a single book, or get on any lists or any of those other things that Toni makes look easy, today is the culmination of a lifetime of dreams. Getting to tell my father to fuck off and getting to have a beautiful woman next to me is turning my dreams into the sort of perfection that makes me wonder if this is all just a coma dream. My life doesn't go this well, you know? Where's the other shoe drop? The failure? The panic?"

"Are you so used to disappointment that it's so hard to believe things can go right?" Greta stroked Kaelee's wrist with her thumb absently when Kaelee didn't answer. The urge to make her world run smoothly, to protect and shelter her, was almost overwhelming. *There are few things I wouldn't do for her.*

Greta marveled at the fact that the big difference in Kaelee was that she'd never ask anything of Greta. Even when faced with the monster from her past, she had tried to handle it herself, to shield Greta. "Things can and *are* going right. In your career, finances, and family baggage. I hope you think they're going right in your dating life, too."

Kaelee squeezed her hand. "I'm terrified of trying to move forward and failing. I don't want to hurt you. Ever."

"I know," Greta whispered back. "And if right now—what we are in this minute—is all there ever is, I want you to know that this is still worth it for me."

A few minutes later they were stepping out of the car and going inside the bookstore. Murder By The Book wasn't a huge store, although Greta could have easily spent hours in it. What made indie bookstores so remarkable was that the books on the shelves were *curated*. They weren't simply a collection of whatever publishers pushed that season. The store made judicious choices, often based on the shop's clientele, but sometimes also on what the booksellers or owners liked.

Inside, Kaelee was swept away to join Toni in stock signing. The shop did a solid business in selling signed copies, and Greta was relieved to see how many Kaelee had to sign. She considered introducing herself. She had edited both the books that Toni had written, as well as Kaelee's book. However, there was something nice about just being a *reader* tonight. She wasn't in Texas as an editor. She was here as the woman who loved Kaelee. The business stuff was Charlie's domain, and Greta knew Charlie had the two authors well in hand.

Unfortunately, that meant she was decidedly in the way of the process of signing, rebundling, and stacking the preorders for the event, so Greta went to browse the collections of books and the occasional snarky T-shirt that the store sold.

By the time the Q and A part of the evening started, Greta had tucked herself into the back row to enjoy the presentation. John, the bookseller who was running the event and seemed to be everywhere at once handling all the details, had introduced them. His husband, a history teacher or professor from the sounds of a few of his remarks to Toni earlier, had the charm to lure out the surly writer's more charismatic side.

Charlie and Greta locked eyes and shared a sigh of relief.

*Maybe we can start hiding history buffs in the audience at each of Toni's events. . . .*

The whole thing lasted maybe thirty minutes before the sizable crowd started lining up in orderly groups for signing.

"If all book events were this well organized, it would be easier to get Toni on the road," Charlie muttered. "That went *really* well. I think it bodes well for the other stops."

"Your lips to God's ears." Greta watched Kaelee charm readers in the line and periodically make remarks to Toni. "They play off each other really naturally."

"They do." Charlie glanced at her. "Are you two serious, Greta? You know that foul man will be out for vengeance. Let me get in front of it."

"Only if Kaelee is okay with it. Her right to privacy super-sedes—"

"He'll expose both of you. It won't be directly tied to him, but you know his type." Charlie scowled. "He'll make your relationship look like you took advantage of her or . . . 'converted' "—she made air quotes—"her into a lesbian."

"I should've stayed away today." Greta looked up as Kaelee laughed at something a reader or Toni said. "She wanted me here at launch, though, and she sounded so sad that I wasn't going to be here. But I should've talked to you and—"

" 'Should've' isn't a helpful word." Charlie caught her gaze. "Either they control the narrative, or we do, and I know which spin would be better for you and for her book *and* for the overall image of the publisher."

"If Kaelee okays it, I'm fine with whatever."

"Then let me ride back with her, and you can meet up with her at the hotel." Charlie gave her a tight smile. "Let me plot with her. I know that nothing inappropriate happened because I know *you*. That doesn't mean we can simply let the story land where it does without a bit of judicious intervention. Strangers will have questions unless we take control of the narrative."

Greta nodded. Then she walked up to the signing line and behind the authors. "You both were fabulous. I need to head out while you finish up."

Kaelee, ignoring any sort of etiquette and propriety, asked, "Are you okay?"

"Just a small headache, love. I am heading back to the hotel to grab an aspirin and some water. Too much humidity and perfume and not enough rest." She squeezed Kaelee's shoulder because she wasn't going to kiss her in front of her readers. "I'll see you after!"

The look on Kaelee's face made clear she still had questions, but she let it go.

Then Greta slipped out of the store and into one of the two waiting cars.

## 37

# *Kaelee and Greta*

### KAELEE

Kaelee was distracted as soon as Greta left. Her gaze darted toward the door, and she had to force her smile to stay steady. Several minutes passed before Charlie walked up beside her and leaned down to quietly say, "She's fine. I just wanted to talk to you."

"Everything's okay?"

"With Greta? Yes." Charlie smiled. "I want to be sure we have a plan in place before Alden goes to the press with some sort of vitriolic nonsense."

"Oh. Can he? I thought after the restraining—"

"Can he *legally*? No. Can he go through back channels to the court of public opinion with plausible deniability? Of course."

"Plan?"

"Sign. We'll talk in the car," Charlie said before retreating several feet.

The rest of the book signing went smoothly, and afterward, Toni asked, "Do you want me to leave separately? I don't want to get in your business."

"No. It's fine."

After saying their goodbyes to the booksellers, they all ended up buying several books, and Kaelee also bought a shirt. Bags in hand, Kaelee and Toni followed Charlie to the waiting car.

"I'm thinking we set up an article or three. I can pitch a feature on the former Alden heiress striking out on her own, carving out a place in the world, and moving forward. You aren't disparaging anyone by saying you chose to pursue academia and a career without using family connections." Charlie nodded at the idea. "It's not untrue."

"So leave out the homophobia and rape I was fleeing?"

"Exactly. Simply focus on being a self-defined woman. You chose a new identity, an homage to your grandparents whose trust fund you had as a cushion," Charlie continued. "Then you lived frugally and earned scholarships and assistantships, so that trust fund is still intact?"

"Correct."

"That's inspiring. You chased your dreams, and along the way, you sold a phenomenal, well-reviewed book and found love." Charlie had a definite cat-who-ate-the-canary look. "This will spin well."

"You can quote me," Toni offered. "She queried agents without me introducing her, too. No strings pulled. Em will offer a quote, too."

"Risa and Greta will, too." Charlie paused, looking thoughtful. "Follow-up piece on strong role models . . . I'll run everything by you."

Kaelee shook her head. "I trust you. That's what you do with a great publicist. Trust them to do the job."

Charlie preened. "Thank you, Kaelee. We'll manage this, and they'll come out looking like villains without us having to outright say it. I'll run it all past legal, too."

"My *wife* will be happy to offer a quote, too, since poor Kae was wrongly photographed as the 'other woman' last year." Toni looked intimidating then. "I'd be upset if that nonsense surfaced again, so . . . while we're at it."

"Of course! A quote from Addie would carry sizzle, too." Charlie leaned back in her seat, looking gleeful. "Tripp Alden won't know what hit him with so many influential women speaking up."

Kaelee couldn't stop the wide smile on her lips. She really had found everything she needed. She had the friends, the career, the security, and the woman. *Dreams can come true sometimes.*

The car pulled up at the hotel, and they all got out and headed into the lobby.

"I'll see you tomorrow," she told them both as she headed to the elevator.

## GRETA

By the time Kaelee returned to the hotel room an hour or so later, Greta was a wreck. She'd changed into a hotel robe and ordered a bottle of wine and light snacks. Kaelee hadn't eaten much before the event, so she was likely to be hungry—unless the talk with Charlie was too upsetting.

Greta was under the duvet, reading a book, when the hotel room door opened, and Kaelee's gaze found her unerringly. Kaelee dropped her stuff on the desk and sat in the office chair beside it.

"I'm sorry. I wasn't trying to complicate your life." Greta folded her hands together and waited. "I'll handle the fallout myself. You don't have to expose your—"

"*What?*" Kaelee leaned forward in the chair.

"I know you're a private person," Greta started.

"So are you." Kaelee stood up, moved closer, and crawled up the bed toward Greta. "You're fucking ridiculous. I want to protect you from the bullshit in my past that seems to have crept into my now."

"And I want to protect you from anything that ever could upset you," Greta whispered as Kaelee put a hand on either side of her, pinning her in place. "Once I stopped trying to resist falling for you, nothing else mattered. I know my career is safe, so that leaves one priority in my entire life. *You.*"

Kaelee's arms framed Greta against the pillow, holding her pinned by the duvet. One leg slotted between Greta's eagerly parting thighs.

"Sexy and considerate. You're pretty amazing." Kaelee kissed

Greta's throat and worked her way along her jaw. She covered Greta's mouth with her own, leaning against her from chest to hip, pressing one leg firmly against Greta's center and rocking forward. "Did you know you were amazing, darlin'?"

"I'm so glad you think so." Greta arched upward. When Kaelee brushed kisses along her throat, Greta tilted her head so Kaelee could continue along her path. "Mmm. If you want, I can remove this robe."

"Well, I *did* just have a book release, and I wanted to celebrate that with something fun." Kaelee put her whole body weight on one arm so she could peel back the duvet. "Greta?"

"Yes?"

Kaelee swallowed visibly. "I want to do something different tonight."

Greta felt like her heart sped as Kaelee stared down at her. "Yes."

"You don't want to know what first?"

"Will you or I be naked?" Greta asked.

"Yes."

"Then I'm in." Greta removed her robe.

"I love you, darlin'." Kaelee froze, seeming to realize what she'd said.

Greta pulled her closer. "I love you, too."

# 38

# *Kaelee*


After returning from her tour dates, Kaelee filled out the university paperwork to take a term off. There were two other classes she would need to take for an MFA, or she'd have to write her dissertation for the literature PhD. She'd taken extra classes while she was thinking, so the question of what degree she had rightly earned was the one to figure out. Was it better to call an end and have an MFA? Was it more useful to be ABD (all but dissertation)? Or should she finish the dissertation? Was there any use in that if she wasn't going to teach?

*Knowledge for knowledge's sake still matters!*

"Dr. Darbyshire entered the paperwork last month to be your advisor," Suzanne, the woman at the English department main office, told her. She was a sweet older woman, the sort that would make a great grandmother in media portrayals, but Kaelee had talked to her often enough to know that Suze did not suffer fools. She was a transplant from somewhere deeper south than Kaelee's home state of North Carolina.

"Wait. Toni did *what*?"

"Her department head allowed it," the woman continued. "Dr. Darbyshire has the credentials to be your thesis advisor if you are doing the Master of Fine Arts. Do you not want her as your thesis advisor?"

"No. I mean, *yes*. Yes, I want Darbyshire, but she's so busy."

Kaelee's eyes widened in surprise that Toni just declared herself Kaelee's advisor. "And she's in the history department."

"Dr. Harrison signed off on it. She's really persuasive, and of course, she's a successful commercial author as well as historian." Suze paused and smiled wide enough that she looked a bit frightening. "Close your mouth, girl. You don't want flies to get in or your remaining manners to get out."

"Yes, ma'am."

Suze nodded approvingly. "You were her TA last term, so it's not surprising. She might as well get credit for mentoring you, since she obviously already is!" Then her stern demeanor faded into something sweet. "We're all just so pleased by your successes, Ms. Carpenter. I will say, though, that the scene in the forest with those girlies in your book. Wow wee." She fanned herself. "That kind of spice will make an old woman consider dating."

"Right. Err, thank you." Kaelee stared at the papers clutched in her hand. "I'm only taking the fall term off to think. I'm not deciding to withdraw from the program."

"You've completed your classes and written not one but two novels," the woman tutted. "If you wanted to finish your dissertation instead of the MFA . . ."

"Honestly, I can't even think about what's next."

Suze reached out and patted her hand. "You're young and have time to figure it out and then go ahead and change your plan several times. Life is long, Ms. Carpenter. Don't rush through the exciting parts."

Kaelee sighed. "I feel at home here. I think that's the real issue. I have a master's in history already, and in all practical ways, I now have everything I need for the MFA . . . but what I want is the feeling of fitting in here."

"There's no place in the world quite as comfortable as academia for some of us." Suze smiled and then stood up. She stepped around the side of her desk. "You're a good egg. If you want a hug, I often find that helps me."

Kaelee bent to hug her. "You're proving my point about the people here."

There was a lightness to Kaelee's mood when she returned to her apartment. She'd taken control of her life, and everything was working out. Her debut novel had hit the far end of both the *New York Times* and the *USA Today* bestseller lists. Everything had turned out better than her dreams.

. . . Which was why seeing her mother standing primly at the door of her apartment was unexpected.

"Kaelee." Julia stared at her, not in disgust but in the way she once had when Kaelee came in from softball practice or riding lessons, as if seeking any injuries.

"Hi." Kaelee stared at her. Age had added lines to her mother's face, but she still looked wonderful. She was too thin to be genuinely healthy, but there was a lightness to her that Kaelee didn't recall ever seeing. Her hair was tastefully dyed, and her clothes were impeccable designer fare. Light makeup—eyes, foundation, and natural lip color—countered some of the years she'd added. Small but expensive jewelry adorned her ears, throat, and fingers. Surprisingly, she wore a smartwatch.

"Could we speak?" Julia asked.

"Go ahead." Kaelee folded her arms.

"Perhaps inside? Over tea?" Julia nodded toward the door. "I would appreciate sitting down. I've been here waiting for over an hour. Your schedule had you home—"

"My schedule?"

Julia had the grace to look abashed. "I had the PI get me a copy." She offered a tight smile. "I bought the building, and that helped."

"You bought . . . my apartment building?" Kaelee stared.

"Last month. My parents left me a discretionary fund, too, and I wanted to be sure your home was safe and in good repair."

Mutely, Kaelee unlocked her door. She gestured her mother inside. "You're my landlord?"

"Technically." Julia walked over, rinsed and filled the teakettle, before looking at her. "Tea?"

"Sure." Kaelee pulled out a few options.

They were silent as the teakettle heated.

Julia busied herself adding tea leaves and sugar to the cups. She added enough sugar that Kaylee winced.

Her mother gave her a sad smile as she poured water into the cups. "That's changed, too? You used to like it this way."

Kaelee sighed and accepted the overly sweet cup of steeping tea. She walked over to the table and pulled out a chair. "No, I didn't. I accepted it. I accepted a lot of things that I won't ever again."

"Fair enough." Julia joined her at the table. "I didn't want you to be unhappy. I tried to do what mothers are to do, for you and your sister. It worked for Betsey."

"Are you sure?"

Julia smiled. "I asked Betsey, after I found out about what happened to you . . . with Kyle . . . and the things he did."

Kaelee swallowed. Talking to her mother about her trauma wasn't on her list of things she ever wanted to do. So she redirected the conversation. "I'm glad Bets is okay. Does Tripp know you're here?"

"He wasn't always like this, you know?" Julia stared down at her tea. "I think the man I married, the one my parents liked, would be appalled to see who he's become. At first, it was his affairs that hurt, then when I tried to stand up, he hit me and . . . until now, I never thought about what message that gave my daughters."

"That doesn't erase everything," Kaelee said roughly. "You realizing it."

"I am well aware, but I'm filing for divorce, and if he doesn't drop his nonsense about you or your book or . . . well, he'll have bigger problems than embarrassment over a book."

"And Kyle?"

"I think it's too late to press charges, but"—Julia met her gaze now—"I wasn't born an Alden, but I've learned from him. I have enough dirt on Kyle and your daddy to—"

"I would rather you don't call Tripp that," Kaelee interjected.

"Fine. I have my PI, and he has files on both of them that I can use if I need to encourage their better angels to be front and center." Julia sat there, ankles primly crossed, sipping her sugar-saturated tea and making threats.

For a moment, Kaelee admired her, truly admired her. "Are you safe? I have lawyers that are handling things on my side. They're good."

"I do, too. I'm filing for divorce, dear, and I want to take *everything*." Julia laughed. "No mercy. That's the Alden way, and as I'm still an Alden . . ." She shrugged. "His missteps with you will be useful to my divorce attorneys. I was going to use it to encourage him to improve his actions, but he authorized the assault of *my child*."

"Oh."

"I wasn't the mother you deserved, but I want to try again." Julia reached out to take Kaelee's hand in hers.

"I don't know," Kaelee whispered. "I need to think."

Julia nodded. "In the meantime, I'm going to join the leagues of middle-aged women who start over. You gave me the motivation to learn to be happy, and I hope you'll allow me to find a place in your life. I want to get to know you, be the mom I should've been, if you'll allow it."

"*I need time*," Kaelee stressed.

At that Julia stood, dumped her tea out, and washed her cup. After drying her hands, she pulled a card out of her pocket and dropped it on the table. "I hope I hear from you. I know I was a failure in many ways, and I don't understand your choice to be with women but I'll try to understand if you let me."

Kaelee stood and stared at her.

"I hope we can at least talk occasionally, but even if not, I'm going to put a stop to Tripp's and Kyle's behavior." Then she walked to the door and let herself out.

39

# *Kaelee*

After Julia left, Kaelee looked around her tiny studio and thought about what *she* wanted. She'd let her fears of her father rising up like a boogeyman cage her, and she'd let the image of marriage that she had from her mother limit her vision. Kaelee thought about the last few weeks; she deserved love as much as anyone.

Kaelee opened the app and selected her dormant conversation with Marie.

**Lee:** I wanted to let you know I met someone. Her name is Greta.

**Marie:** Oh?

**Lee:** You were the first step in figuring out what I wanted.

**Marie:** What's that?

**Lee:** Great sex, which you provided, but also love.

**Marie:** Love?

**Lee:** The sort that can evolve into forever.

**Marie:** So what does that mean?

**Lee:** I can't do casual sex or dating without a future, Marie. I love Greta and want to build a future with her.

**Marie:** . . .

**Marie:** Greta is a lucky woman. Good luck to you both.

Kaelee waited for a moment, and her phone rang. She knew without looking that it was her. Smiling, she answered the phone.

"Do you mean it?" Greta asked.

"Mean what?" Kaelee asked.

"That you're . . . that you . . ."

"Want a future with the woman I'm in love with? Yes. I *do* mean that." Kaelee grabbed a few odds and ends and tossed them in her bag. She could go anywhere. Writers weren't locked to a location, and her degree plan meant she was taking this term and the next off. So she had no obligations tying her to DC other than a rent payment that was low and on auto-draft.

"What does that mean? How am I to reply to *that*?"

"You have a little under four hours to figure it out." Kaelee laughed, feeling freer than she had in a lot of years. "Honestly, I have no fucking idea what we do now, but I'm going to Union Station and heading to New York to tell my person I love her and ask if we can figure out a future *together*."

"We can. We will." Greta sounded stunned. "Let me know when to pick you up at the train station . . . ?"

"In about four hours if my train schedule is right," Kaelee said. She paused then. "Is this okay? Just showing up?"

"It would be better if you didn't leave." Greta sighed. "I've missed you so much, and I wasn't sure if pressuring you for a visit was too soon or—"

"Not too soon."

"I can spend weekends in DC if you want to spend weekdays in Manhattan," Greta offered.

"Or I can put my stuff in storage and spend the semester up there," Kaelee countered, heart racing too fast at the thought of staying in New York, staying with Greta, trying this relationship every day. "My lease ends in two months anyhow, and I didn't renew because of the whole business with Tripp. I thought I might have to . . . run away from here."

"Move in with me for real, not just the semester," Greta blurted out.

Kaelee's voice felt raspy in her throat as she said, "Are you sure? I don't want to pressure you, and I can afford—"

"Move in with me," Greta repeated. "Come here. Tell me you love me, and stay with me."

"How long?" Kaelee asked.

"How's forever?"

"I'd like to try that, Greta. I really, really think I would," Kaelee said. "Let me grab a bigger suitcase, and then we can come back here to deal with storage and—"

"Kaelee," Greta interrupted with a laugh. "Pack faster. I want to hear you tell me you love me and want to stay with me when you are here in front of me. *Pack*. Get on the train. *Come to me now*."

Kaelee laughed. "On the way."

There were a million details to sort out, but the real issue—the fear that had caged her—was gone. She'd do her best to build a life with Greta, to treat her like the treasure she was, and to build a future where they were both happy and together. That was everything. Her rules to avoid a relationship had failed miserably, and now? Now she was right in the middle of one.

With a huge smile on her face, Kaelee closed her bag and walked out the door to head toward her future with the woman she loved.

# Acknowledgments

Thank you first to Amber. I started writing these books for you when you grumbled over wanting to read more athletic women in fiction. (Disclaimer: These books are *not* inspired by her, and some of y'all have confused me when you've asked me that. I've never been possessive until Amber, but old dogs apparently can learn new things.)

Thank you to Sophie for talking to me on my panic days, especially when I called for the twenty-third time to say, "Is this too graphic?"

Thank you to my eldest child, Dr. Asia Alsgaard, who reads this but *skips the naked parts*. No offense to any of the talented editors I've worked with the last two decades, but twenty years in, you're still the best editor I've had, Asia.

Thank you to Monique Patterson and to Mal Frazier for the enthusiastic response to this series. You are both incredible editors. (Even though my kid is so good at it, you still more than hold your own!)

Thank you to the team at Bramble. You are many and fabulous. I know that books succeed in large part because of the team. Also, thank you to all the phenomenal art, marketing, and publicity folks over these many years at various publishers. Charlie and Ian in this book exist because of all of you collectively.

Thank you a million times to Leni Kauffman. Your art for *Toni and Addie Go Viral,* as well as *Greta Gets the Girl,* is perfection. I knew it would be, of course, because of the tower of books I have bought because of your art on the covers. I can skim a table and pick out your covers, and I am thrilled by the ones you made for my characters.

Thank you to John and Matt McDougall. You made me believe in the possibility of a happy marriage when I'd seen so many bad examples. You are my family by choice, and I love you dearly.

And to all the many fabulous bookstores, booksellers, reviewers, and influencers I've met these last two decades. You put my books in front of readers even as I hop between genres and demographics. Sorry I fail to stay in a lane, and thank you for still supporting me.

And a weird thank-you to those who had no idea you were part of my process—

> the many amazing WNBA players who played the games that were "cookies" I used to bribe myself to work just a few more hours. (In particular, thank you to the Phoenix Mercury. I'm proud to be a season ticket holder.)
> the San Diego Wave, you were worth the drive to California.

Maybe cookies isn't the most logical plan, but I've finished a lot of books this way. I set goals, and I earn rewards.

And, of course, thank you to all the readers who have been with me for two decades of books in so many different genres. Your support lets me take care of my family and health. Thank you for the love, emails, and book events.

# About the Author

Melissa Marr writes fiction for adults, teens, and children. Her books have been translated into twenty-eight languages and been bestsellers in the US (*New York Times, Los Angeles Times, USA Today, Wall Street Journal*) as well as overseas. *Wicked Lovely*, her debut novel, was an instant *New York Times* bestseller and evolved into an internationally bestselling multi-book series that was just re-issued for its twentieth anniversary. From fantasy to picture books, including her bestselling *Bunny Roo, I Love You* and *Wild Horses* (a book of her photography), Marr has reached far more readers than she ever dreamed possible. If she's not writing, you can find her in a kayak or on a trail with her wife.